Praise for Louise Phillips

'Phillips has been compared to US crime writers James Patterson and Patricia Cornwell and with this book, she certainly lives up to that accolade' *Sunday Independent*

'A most intriguing and compelling story of grief, loss, memory and the quest for the truth ... this story will enthral you to the end' Liz Nugent

'A first-class crime writer' *Irish Independent*

'A riveting thriller with dark secrets and murky lies ... which Phillips has pulled off not only with authenticity, but aplomb' Catherine Ryan Howard

'Subtle, clever and thought-provoking ... is one of the best books I've read this year' *Woman's Way*

'Full of twists and turns. A cracking good read' Karen Perry

'Top drawer crime writing by Ireland's finest crime writer' *San Diego Book Review*

'Riveting, thought-provoking and compulsive' Arlene Hunt

'A thrilling page-turner' *Sunday Business Post*

'What's particularly great about Phillips' writing is her fearlessness' *The Irish Post*

Dublin-born crime author Louise Phillips won the Crime Fiction Book of the Year prize at the Irish Book Awards for *The Doll's House*, her second novel. Each of her other bestselling novels, *Red Ribbons*, *Last Kiss*, *The Game Changer* and *The Hiding Game*, were shortlisted for this award. Along with other literary awards, in 2016 she was longlisted for the CWA Dagger in the Library Award in the UK. Her first two novels have been published in the US and her fifth novel *The Hiding Game* is currently in development with a major film company. *They All Lied* is her sixth novel.

www.louise-phillips.com
@LouiseMPhillips

ALSO BY LOUISE PHILLIPS

The Hiding Game
The Game Changer
Last Kiss
The Doll's House
Red Ribbons

LOUISE PHILLIPS

THEY ALL LIED

HACHETTE
BOOKS
IRELAND

First published in Ireland in 2022 by
HACHETTE BOOKS IRELAND

1

Cataloguing in Publication Data is available from the British Library

ISBN 9781529304558

Typeset in Constantia and Century Gothic by Paula Elmore

Printed and bound in Great Britain by
Clays Ltd, Elcograf S.p.A.

Hachette Books Ireland policy is to use papers that are natural, renewable and
recyclable products and made from wood grown in sustainable forests. The logging
and manufacturing processes are expected to conform to the environmental
regulations of the country of origin.

Hachette Books Ireland
8 Castlecourt Centre
Castleknock
Dublin 15, Ireland

A division of Hachette UK Ltd
Carmelite House, 50 Victoria Embankment, London EC4Y 0DZ

www.hachettebooksireland.ie

For James

1

NADINE

MY MOBILE PHONE RINGS. I note the time on the wall clock, 10.55 a.m. The call is from an unidentified number. I pick up. 'Hello.'

The next voice I hear is my eighteen-year-old daughter Becca's.

'Mum, it's me,' she says, her words high-pitched.

An instant panic takes hold. 'What's wrong?'

The prolonged silence at the end of the line worries me. I repeat her name, softening my tone, conscious I need to keep her onside – aware we haven't spoken in weeks. 'What is it? Please, honey, tell me.'

'I ...' She stalls.

'It's okay,' I say, reassuring her, even though I can't know this for sure.

'I did something terrible.'

I hear her suck in air. The clock reads 10.57 a.m. I'm so scared about what's coming next. I think of the nights Becca didn't come home, the terrible people she's been hanging out with, and how much she's changed over the last six months, shutting me out. The last time we fought, we said such awful things to one another, and that dark, sinking feeling, the one that's been there for weeks, unravels snakelike inside me.

'Mum ...' she says, her voice sounding far younger than her years – vulnerable, lost.

'Whatever it is, Becca, you can tell me.'

'I can't.'

She is sobbing now, large breathless sobs. 'Please, Becca,' I beg, my voice shaky, no longer able to hide my fear, 'what have you done?'

'I ...' She stalls again.

'What is it?'

'I ... killed someone.'

I grip the kitchen counter. She's not talking sense. I try to say something, but the words won't come out. I think about that guy she's been with – he's capable of leading a young girl astray, but surely not this.

'Becca, you can't have. You're wrong. You're making a mistake.'

'Mum,' she cries, even more desperate than before. 'I didn't mean to.'

Another silence follows.

I fear she's going to cut me off.

'Becca, don't hang up.' The mobile phone feels sweaty in my hand. A neighbour's lawn mower goes quiet. The odd car turning the corner can no longer be heard. All outside sounds dissipate, but inside, the noise from the refrigerator grows louder, the ticking of the wall clock becomes deafening, and the internal buzzing in my eardrums fights hard to send her words away, for them not to have been said, for them not to be true.

My mind goes into lockdown, but finally, I ask, 'Who did you kill?'

The words hang in the air, strangely distant, as if they belong to someone else, to a person I'm unfamiliar with, a woman with a daughter who did something terrible.

'I can't tell you.' She is crying louder now.

'Please, Becca, I want to help. You need to believe me.' My voice is sharp, affirmative, parental.

'I'm too scared.'

'You have to go to the police.'

'I can't. We can't.'

I stare out the window. I see the leaves rise off the ground, carried by a soft autumn breeze. I've an almighty pain in my chest. This is my worst fear, every parent's nightmare.

'Mum, listen to me.' She sounds now like she's the mother, and

I'm the daughter, not the other way around. 'Are you listening?'

'Yes.'

'Then do exactly as I say, or we could both end up dead.'

The last sentence hovers, my brain refusing to accept it. I tell myself she's panicking. I hear her muttering to herself, fast, hysterical, terrified words that I can't make out.

'*Becca!*' I roar into the phone, fearing she might still hang up. 'Tell me where you are. I will come and get you. I will make you safe.'

She doesn't answer. I hear her crying again, deep, gut-wrenching sobs, the same way she used to cry as a child, so loud and hard it would take her hours to stop.

'Mum, do you love me?'

'Of course I do, but—'

'There's a man here. He's locked me in a room. I can't escape. There's no way out.'

'I'm going to the police. They'll be able to trace the call. They'll help me find you. I'll bring you home where you belong.'

'You can't go to the police.' Fresh panic enters her voice.

'But—'

'Didn't you hear me, Mum? I killed someone, and if you don't do as this man asks, he will kill us both.'

'Becca—'

'Mum, I need you to write something down. Get a pen and paper *now.*'

'Okay.'

I search the countertop, frantically looking for the notebook I use to write down grocery lists.

'Do you have the pen and paper?'

'Yes.' Inside, my inner voice is screaming: *Don't let any of this be happening. Maybe she's taken some sort of hallucinating drug and is coming down from a bad trip. That can happen to people. Oh, God, please let that be what's happening. But Becca said she killed someone. No one makes up something like that.*

'Mum, are you still there?'

3

I need to pay attention. I need to do as she asks. 'Yes.'

'There can't be any mistakes.' Her voice is lower than before, as if she doesn't want anyone else to hear.

'What do you want me to write down?'

'A man's name and address.'

'Who?'

'John Simons.' She's speaking so low now I can barely hear her. I can't be sure I've got the name right. I repeat it back to her.

'Yes, that's it,' she says. I hear the shuffle of paper as if she's reading from a note. 'He lives at thirty-two Serpent Parade, Harold's Cross.'

A blob of water drops onto the name and address, smudging it. It's a teardrop, even though right up to this second I didn't even know I was crying.

'Becca,' I beg, 'please tell me what's going on. I promise I'll fix it.'

'You can't, Mum, not unless you do exactly as they want.'

She is so scared. My daughter is scared.

'What do they need me to do?'

'Go to the address. You will find a large brown envelope in a plastic bag under a bush in the front garden. If for whatever reason the envelope isn't there, you need to wait for John Simons. He will give it to you.'

'And then?'

'On the envelope there will be more instructions. You have to follow them exactly. There can be no mistakes.'

'But—'

'I'll ring you tomorrow.'

'I'm going to tell Gavin. He'll help. I know he will.'

'Don't tell Uncle Gavin. Don't tell anyone anything. Mum, I have to go. I can hear them coming back.'

The phone goes dead. I stare at the name and address on the notebook. My hands are shaking.

I look at the wall clock: 10.59 a.m.

It has been only four minutes since the phone rang. I try to send back time to the moment before any of this happened, when

4

everything was okay, when Becca wasn't in danger, but deep in my gut, from the second I picked up the phone, I knew something was wrong, as if I was expecting it all along.

I stare once more at the name and address, asking aloud, 'Who are you, John Simons, and what the hell do you want?'

2
WREN

THE MUSIC CENTRE IN THE CORNER OF the living room, a retro pine unit, bellows out David Gray's 'Dead in the Water'. The sound system, complete with record deck, was given to me by my dad before he became ill, mainly because he knew I liked old and quirky things. I'm in no rush this morning. I've earned the break after yesterday's early-morning raids – four homes, all located in south Dublin, each targeted for a dawn hit.

They were brought down simultaneously by the squad, along with teams from the Armed Response Unit. Mine was the only one requiring the front door to be kicked in. We couldn't take the chance that someone inside wanted to get rid of evidence.

Instead, it turned out to be a grandmother with bad hearing, and a nineteen-year-old grandson, who looked terrified. A teenage baby with a burner phone, his means of taking orders for his punter's drug of choice, confiscated along with the rest of the shit we found.

I flick on the kettle. The music shifts to Adele's 'Daydreamer', slow and pensive, and suddenly I'm back to the last call from yesterday: a suicide attempt, and another sledgehammer job at the front door.

They usually start with a phone call, and this time it was no different. Friends of the young girl couldn't reach her, and they were worried because earlier they'd seen fresh cuts on her arm.

Speeding through traffic, I felt sick.

'Gardaí, open up!' I bellowed, as we banged on the flat door. I called again, and when there was no answer, the sledgehammer came into play, bludgeoning the lock.

Suddenly my apartment is filled with the sights and sounds from the night before. Our fast movement entering the girl's small flat, the air charged with danger, all of us hoping she's alive, and not another desperate statistic.

'Gardaí entering the premises,' I shouted, but still we got no response. Soon, we concentrated on the closed bathroom door, knocking at it hard.

This time we didn't wait for a reply, kicking it in. Within seconds I saw her, keeled over by the bath, the room in darkness with pools of blood beneath her on the floor and splatters on the walls.

'Put down the knife,' I said, edging closer.

We made eye contact.

'Good girl,' I whispered. 'Now drop the knife.' I knelt beside her. 'Show me your hands and arms.'

She uncurled her tightened fists. Even in the dark, the fresh lacerations were clearly visible. I turned to my partner, Mike. 'Let's lift her.'

As we guided her from the floor, I kept telling her she was doing well, reassuring her, telling her she was a good girl. I wanted to pull her back from the edge. 'It's going to be all right,' I said. 'We're here to help.'

Afterwards, I stared at the knife, redundant on the bathroom floor, as tiny red rivers streamed down the side of the bath. I swore aloud. No kid deserved this.

Not so long ago, she was probably thinking about how exciting it would be to be all grown-up, until some smart guy on the street told her it might be fun to try something and loosen up a little. I've little sympathy for the likes of the pushers, the dealers, the ones who decide to play the targets, instead of being one. I see them every day, with their plush designer runners and Canada Goose jackets worth far more than my last mortgage payment.

In some ways, they deserve what they get, but not her. Victim versus dealer: on the sympathy stakes, for me victim always wins out.

Later in the night, when the girl's condition stabilised, we held her under the Mental Health Act, which empowers us to detain anyone at risk of harming themselves or others.

Soon after that, a female doctor arrived. It was her role, after examining the girl, to play God, deciding whether she would be involuntarily admitted to a psychiatric unit, or sent off with a letter to return to the hospital voluntarily the next day. Luckily, the doctor decided on the former, the latter not always working out so well.

I turn off the music in the living room, switching over to RTÉ Radio 1. In the kitchen, I drop a teabag into a chipped Disney mug, *circa* twenty years young, with an image of Ariel from *The Little Mermaid*. I pour in hot water, realising my mind is simply doing the usual debrief that mostly happens at two in the morning when I can't sleep.

The news is playing on the radio.

'A man in his early twenties is in a critical condition in hospital after he was shot and seriously injured in west Dublin last night. He was hit three times in the chest, and once in the back of the head. The current focus of the investigation, according to garda sources, is to establish a motive for the attack, and to find out who is responsible.'

I switch the radio off. It's not my district and, for now, not my concern.

I catch a glimpse of myself in the living-room mirror. My dark hair, now shoulder-length, curls at the ends. At work, I usually tie it back, making it harder for idiots to grab. As I'm fixing the top of my shirt, a recent find in the local vintage shop, my mobile phone rings. It's Mike.

Mike is fifteen years my senior, but junior in ranking. It doesn't bother him. He told me once, ambition sucks away too much real life.

'Someone's decided to do a DIY job on the ATM in Rathfarnham shopping centre,' he says, 'so you and I have the gig.'

'Why us?'

'Luck,' he replies, sounding a bit too cheery for my mood.

Mike likes to play the fatherly role with me, and at times, I wonder if he views me in the same light as he does his teenage children. Right now, I'm tempted to replace the *l* in luck, with an *f*, but instead I say, 'I'll see you there in ten.'

3
NADINE

ACCORDING TO GOOGLE MAPS, it's 6.25 kilometres from my house to the address on the piece of paper, but other than Becca's sparse instructions, I've no idea why I'm going there.

For about five seconds, I consider phoning my brother. He'd drop everything in a heartbeat to help Becca. But I know Gavin. He'd want to take over, to be the one in charge, control things. I can't let him do that, not yet, not until I know more.

I tell myself, Becca isn't a killer. It had to have been self-defence, but then a doubting voice takes hold, questioning everything, remembering our last argument when I totally lost it with her. I shake my head, pushing away all the negative thoughts, forcing myself to believe that if Becca did kill someone, it wasn't intentional, not unless she was pushed. I understand that. I recognise the point when survival dictates everything.

I'm now 3.5 kilometres from the address. The radio is playing my favourite Sunday midday show, talking about the week's newspapers. The main topics are house prices, gender quotas, and monetary overruns in the health budget. I can't listen to it, so I switch it off.

Driving over Templeogue bridge, I pass the spot where Becca was knocked off her bike at eight years of age. She had been hit by a truck, which gained in size the closer I got to it. I still remember turning the corner after that phone call, the one telling me she'd been in an accident. The caller had said everything was okay. I didn't know he was lying, believing it best not to panic me, not until I'd got there safely.

Becca had been visiting a school friend. They were supposed to use their bikes only in the back garden. She shouldn't have been on a main road, but she was. She had dashed out without looking moments before her body flew through the air. When my car drove around the corner, I saw the ambulance and fire brigade, the crowds of people gathered around, the truck that had hit her, and there, in the middle of everything, on the cold concrete ground, I saw Becca lying like a tiny rag doll. I abandoned my car on the footpath. I told myself to be strong, to hold back tears, as in the ambulance the emergency crew did what they could, and later, the rush of nurses and doctors at the hospital, the frightened look on Becca's face when they cut off her clothes, covering her with aluminium foil to keep her temperature steady as machines bleeped. They did one scan after another, taking X-rays, hooking her up with oxygen, all with one focus in mind, saving her. Thankfully, somehow, she survived.

And now, I'm one kilometre to my destination.

My satellite navigation tells me to turn right in 200 metres. I will reach my destination in less than four minutes. I slow the car as I turn the bend, the same way I did all those years before when my little girl lay broken in the midst of strangers, and I take in everything I can.

The houses on Serpent Parade are small, red-brick and terraced, with tiny front gardens. They look as if they were built in the sixties, which most likely means there are large gardens out back. My car cruises to the top of the cul-de-sac, passing number thirty-two on my right. I glance towards it. I take in the panelled front door, painted black. At the top of the road, I turn the car in the opposite direction and park. I have a full view of the row of houses. I can clearly see number thirty-two from here. I note the small camera positioned above the front door and the others beneath the gutters. CCTV. Shit, Becca, what have you got involved with?

I watch an elderly gentleman pull a large black bin inside his gate, placing it in the small front garden. I swallow hard, searching the road again. What if I see this John Simons? What do I do then? My heart races. I don't even know what he looks like. What if I end up doing something that puts Becca's life in even more danger?

I reach for my handbag, taking out my phone, realising for the first time that I'm shaking. I attempt to key in my PIN code, getting it wrong at first, but finally opening a Google search with the name John Simons. There are 1,677 hits. The first is a politician in the UK, the second a gardener in Cork, the third a Facebook link. I double click it. The profile picture is a character from PlayStation, Kratos, the god of war. I know it, because one of the junior clerks at work used to play it at lunchtime.

On the Facebook page, the individual posts are images of hunted animals, deer, rabbits, and pheasants with their legs tied together. Is this the John Simons I'm looking for? A hunter? I go to his 'About' section, but it's blank.

I try a few more links, seeing other John Simons from outside Ireland. Three live in Australia, and a few more in different parts of Europe. I desperately want to phone someone, to ask advice, to seek help, only Becca was very clear on that front. I can't tell anyone.

I heard once that most people can't keep a secret for more than two days. After that, they have to share it with someone – a friend, a partner, a stranger – but what if they can't? What if the worst thing in the world would happen if they did? That changes everything.

The windows in the car fog up. What am I waiting for? Go to the house, get that damn envelope, then do as Becca asked.

I roll the driver's window halfway down, hoping to clear the fog and get a better view of the street as I lock the car doors for extra safety. Then I see him, the man opening the black panelled door of number thirty-two. He looks in his mid to late thirties, my age. He's wearing a dark peaked baseball cap hiding his face but, still, there's something familiar about him. It's the way he walks and holds himself, as if he's attempting to make himself look taller, stronger.

When he steps out, he stares up and down the street. I try to see more of his face, but it's still half covered with the cap. He appears super careful, double-checking everything. If he notices me, or the car, he doesn't appear to pay me any heed. I keep my eyes fixed on him, taking in his clothing, a grey sweat top and dark jeans. He's wearing runners that are brilliant white, squeaky clean, as if they're straight out of the box. I wonder again why he seems so familiar. I think of the question I've been afraid to ask ever since I answered that phone call from Becca, only now it won't stay silent. Is this nightmare connected to *my* past?

The man turns back towards the opened door, calling out. I consider taking a photograph of him with my phone, the way they do in movies, but stop myself.

A little girl, aged about five, with a ponytail and a My Little Pony backpack comes out, as the man tries to light a cigarette with his lighter. His first attempt fails in the breeze. He repeats the action, successful this time, before he takes the child's hand. My eyes watch the two of them step out from the garden. Is the envelope already there, hidden, waiting?

The little girl is dressed in a pink jumpsuit. I think about Becca at that age, and wince. I wait until the man and the child are completely out of sight before I get out of the car.

Nearer the house, I'm aware I'm being picked up by the CCTV cameras. Will someone watch the footage later and study me? I walk right past number thirty-two, trying not to arouse suspicion. I slip into the small supermarket at the top of the street, and pick up a takeaway coffee, as if this small task is my real errand.

Outside the supermarket is a good vantage point to study the rear of the houses on Serpent Parade. I was right. They have large gardens. Sixty to seventy feet at least. My eyes count ten houses until they reach the rear of number thirty-two.

There are cameras there too. After a couple of sips of coffee, I walk towards it. The only thing I care about is Becca. I'll pick up that envelope, do as I was instructed, but not before I try to find out what I'm dealing with. Everything I do matters now, especially if I want to get Becca home safe.

With each step I take, my daughter's words repeat in my mind: *Mum, I killed someone – I killed someone – I killed.* The enormity of it hits home hard now, as if my mind hadn't quite caught up with this horrible new reality. It feels too big, too scary.

I keep walking, slowing as I near the house, not wanting to get too close, or be picked up by the cameras again. I take in the mature trees in the garden, and the barbed wire along the garden wall. The blinds on each of the windows are pulled down. I listen hard, hearing cooing and the fluttering of wings, as if a bird is caught within a small space. It's a pigeon loft. My uncle kept pigeons. I'd recognise that sound anywhere. As kids, he'd let Gavin and me hold them to stroke their feathered backs. Sometimes, Gavin would raise a bird up high, caught tight in his grasp, pretending it was an eagle. When he released it, I would think how beautiful it looked flying free, and how small a space the loft was, when all the birds were trapped inside.

I lean against the wall, hidden in the shadows, as my mind jerks back again to the phone call. Becca said a man had locked her in a room. She also used the word 'they', meaning he wasn't operating alone.

I consider stepping out onto the road, but if I do, the cameras will pick me up, so instead, I keep in tight until I'm at the garage gate of number thirty-two. The sounds of the pigeons are louder now, the cooing and flapping, and without knowing why, I stare up at the sky, imagining the birds the way I used to as a child, magnificent and free, before settling down to the task in hand, examining the rear of the house.

There are tiny slits either side of the garage gate. I peek inside, seeing three cars parked, all this year's models, top of the range, a BMW, a Lexus, and a Mercedes. They alone would buy a decent-sized house. I consider the CCTV cameras again, the expensive cars, the way the man, whoever he is, looked up and down the street, nervous, making sure it was safe. Everything points in one direction – gangland, organised crime, people prepared to do whatever it takes to get what they want.

I step away from number thirty-two. I tell myself I need to keep focused on the only thing that matters, the phone call from Becca, telling me she killed someone, and if I didn't follow her instructions, both of us could end up dead.

As I walk back towards the front gate, it starts to rain. Lightly at first, then larger, heavier drops. Within seconds, the sky is a blackened grey, as a torrent falls, unexpected, beating down, bouncing off the concrete.

I speed up, cursing myself for leaving my coat in the car, and immediately wonder why I'm thinking about stupid things like this when my daughter's life is in danger. A young man turns the corner at the end of the road and runs towards the shelter of the trees. I run too, but not because of the rain: I need to do this next thing fast. I have to get that envelope.

At the gate of number thirty-two, I pause for a millisecond before opening it, searching below the bushes for the envelope. I see it wrapped in what looks like a clear refuse bag. I grab it. The thick laurel bushes have kept it dry. It's about the size of a telephone directory. I don't stop to think about anything other than getting the envelope into the car, aware I'm being recorded on the CCTV cameras, a soaked, desperate woman grabbing what looks like a piece of rubbish instead of an envelope that could save her daughter's life.

In the car, I flip the windscreen wipers on at full speed, firing the package onto the passenger seat. I'm not going to check it here. I'll find some place where I won't be noticed. I wipe the water off my face and put the car into first gear, not bothering to indicate as I pull out. I can't help but look at number thirty-two again. The man is back. He's alone now, standing inside the gate, studying me. Is he John Simons? His baseball cap is still low on his face, but it doesn't hide his snigger, unmissable even in the pouring rain, as if he's enjoying making me, Nadine Fitzmaurice, his victim, afraid all over again. I already hate him for it.

I keep driving until I reach the shopping centre in Rathfarnham, only ten minutes from my old family home. I haven't been there since shortly after my mother died six months ago. The place constantly reminds me of sadness and anger, along with the brick wall my mother placed between us, unwilling, until near the end, to accept help from anyone, least of all me.

When I arrive at the shopping centre car park, the place is jammed. The package on the front seat feels like a ticking time bomb despite its innocuous appearance. I pull into a spot near the recycling area. I watch people drop bottles and unwanted clothes in the bins, easing my breathing as I check the car doors are still locked. My fingernails rip open the plastic and there, just as Becca had said, I see the instructions on the envelope. I tell myself I don't want to know what's inside. I just need to do as they've asked, and hopefully, soon, speak to my daughter. But then I pick up the package, fingering its shape. It could be a gun. It's bulky enough.

I memorise the instructions, putting the envelope back on the passenger seat with the instructions turned down.

I key the location into Google Maps. I'm only twenty minutes away from the next address. Soon, the nightmare that began this morning will be over – but Google Maps takes me out a different exit from the shopping centre car park, and as I approach the local Bank of Ireland, I see the police squad car with its flashing blue lights double-parked at the front. The wall of the bank is badly damaged. An ATM hangs out, like a broken jack-in-the-box, and two plain-clothes detectives, a man and a woman, are stopping random cars.

What if they stop me? I've never liked police cars. They put me on edge, even if Gavin used to be a cop. I wish now I'd put the envelope in the boot, instead of leaving it in plain sight.

Sooner than expected, I'm nearing the squad car. My car's engine splutters, but thankfully keeps going. I put my foot on the accelerator, then brake. It splutters again before cutting out. When I re-start it, applying more pressure, I jerk forward. One of the police officers, the woman, turns and stares at me. I try to avoid eye contact, but I can tell she's viewing me suspiciously. She stops the car two ahead, leaning in to talk to the male driver.

Minutes tick by. I wait.

I tell myself again that soon all of this will be over, but then another thought takes hold. What if I'm wrong? What if I'm fooling myself?

With people like this, you can't be sure of anything. It might not be over until someone is dead.

4
WREN

THE LINE OF CARS IN THE SHOPPING CENTRE stretches out, but still Mike and I go through the motions. We wave a couple of cars on, trying to speed things up.

'Some crooks are awfully stupid,' Mike says, looking back at the damaged wall with the ATM hanging out.

I'm only half listening to him, because I'm staring at a woman whose car has cut out a couple of vehicles back. She's giving that engine some whammy. She looks agitated, too, as if she needs to be somewhere in a hurry.

'What do you think, Wren?'

'About what?'

'The level of intelligence crooks are displaying these days.'

'I imagine, for some, being out of their heads on coke has quite a debilitating effect.'

I wave the next car on, before I spot Dwayne Moran in a silver Golf. I put up my hand, indicating he should stop. He rolls down the driver's window.

'Doing a bit of shopping, are you, Dwayne?'

'No law against it.'

I lean in, giving the inside of the car a quick visual. 'Any chance you might have done a bit of DIY on that ATM last night?' Dwayne's MO is mainly breaking and entering, petty stuff. He isn't part of the drug scene, but that doesn't mean he survives on his communion money.

'I was in my bed all night,' he smirks, 'sleeping like a baby.'

I doubt Dwayne was ever a baby. 'You packing a firearm?'

'Nah, totally clean.'

'So, you don't mind if Mike here has a look in your boot.'

'What for?'

'Just doing our job, that's all.'

'Police harassment, that's what this is.'

'I'll take that as a yes. Pop it open there, Dwayne, like a good man.'

He releases the boot from inside the car. I don't take my eyes off him. If you stop a car driven by a known criminal, chances are you'll find a firearm. There's no point in being stupid.

Mike beckons me over. I eye the contents of the boot, before picking up with Dwayne where I left off. 'Any reason you've a mallet back there?'

Some cars further back, those who can't see the squad car, beep their horns, annoyed at the delay.

'I was doing some work for me ma, you know, helping her out, like.'

'You weren't involved in any tit-for-tat stuff, were you, Dwayne? Attempting to put some manners on people?'

'Nah, nothing like that, just helping me ma.'

'And that ATM over there. It looks the worse for wear, doesn't it?'

'I know nothing about that.'

The woman's engine cuts out again. I glance back at her. There's something else about her that's bothering me, only right now I can't put my finger on it.

I lean in closer to Dwayne. 'Here's a bit of free advice. Get rid of the mallet, because next time I stop you, I'll be charging you with possession of offensive weapons.'

'You're fecking joking me.'

'Couldn't be more serious. Now get out of here before I change my mind.'

I wave the next car on, and stop the one with the nervous female driver. Have I seen her somewhere before?

She rolls down her window. 'Doing some shopping?' I ask, keeping my tone soft, professional.

'No, no, I was dropping things off at the recycling area.' She sounds as nervous as she looks.

I note the bulky envelope on the front seat.

She catches my glance. 'I'm delivering a parcel to a friend,' she says, a little too fast and defensive.

Normally I'd send her on her way, a well-dressed woman from suburbia, where probably the worst crime she ever committed was not paying her TV licence, but instead I ask, 'Do you mind if I see your driver's licence?'

She reaches for the glove compartment. 'Is something wrong?' she asks, still anxious.

'No, just routine.' I smile to reassure her.

I take in the details, her address, the date of birth, and her full name, Nadine Fitzmaurice. Then it hits me, a flash of memory coming back. I was out with Gavin, my ex, and he'd made a brief stop to give something to his sister. At the time, she'd been some distance away, and Gavin had no intention of introducing us, but now, as I study Nadine Fitzmaurice more closely, I see the family resemblance.

I return her driver's licence. 'There was an attempted ATM robbery last night,' I say, 'and we're just canvassing the area.'

'Oh?'

'You didn't happen to see anything, did you?'

'I'm afraid not.'

'Okay, then. Thanks for your time.'

She drives forward.

I look at the enormous tailback of cars in the car park. 'Let's leave this, Mike,' I say. 'I doubt any of these people were here in the dead of night.'

'That last woman seemed a bit tetchy.'

'Yeah, she did, didn't she?'

Aborting the car-to-car interviews, we go back to the scene of the crime.

'They could have organised a bigger digger to get that damn thing out,' I say to Mike.

'No argument there.' He takes a step closer to the ATM. 'Do you ever watch those true-crime documentaries?'

'Sometimes,' I say, my eyes still studying Nadine Fitzmaurice, her car stopped at the lights at Butterfield Avenue.

'I hate the way they make it so easy for the cops, leaving clues in the trash bin, and not cleaning up the bloodstains properly.'

Nadine is moving her head from side to side, as if checking each pedestrian as they cross the road. Why is she so anxious?

Mike is still talking. 'If it weren't for all those ad breaks, they could have the whole thing wrapped up in less than a quarter of an hour.'

'It wouldn't be very entertaining then, would it?' I reply, as Nadine pulls away at the lights.

'I guess not.'

'Do we have the CCTV footage from the bank?' I ask.

'We've a week of it, in case those bright sparks did some early reconnaissance.'

'Get the fingerprint team to do a full job on the machine too, although even if our guys weren't wearing gloves, most of Rathfarnham would have touched it by now. That keyboard will be a complete waste of time.'

'Needle in a haystack, Wren, but you know what they say. We've three hundred and sixty-five days of the year to do our job. We only need one to get lucky. The bad boys, they need all of them.'

'Or girls,' I add, as Nadine Fitzmaurice's car goes completely out of view.

5
NADINE

THE FEMALE DETECTIVE KEEPS HER EYES on me right up until I turn off Butterfield Avenue. I hold my breath until I'm out of her line of vision, but I'm still angry at myself for not putting the envelope in the boot. She could have asked me to turn it over, and then she'd have seen the details of the next pick-up point. That would have alerted her to something dodgy going down. I could have blown everything. It was a narrow escape. I need to be more careful.

On the N81, Google Maps reroutes the destination path, warning me there's a crash further up. 'Shit,' I say aloud, as the car moves forward at a snail's pace, then comes to a complete stop. Right now, I feel as if I'm in some kind of bubble, trapped, as the car edges forward once more, and my mind drifts to another time when I did something I couldn't share with anyone. For so long I've tried to convince myself it was in the past. But that's the thing about secrets and lies: they never go away, not fully.

I repeat the mantra I've been saying for the last fifteen minutes. Follow the instructions, await Becca's phone call, then somehow get her home safe.

The detour brings me to Killininny Road. I see mothers with buggies pushing children, and neighbours chatting over garden walls. There's a couple of joggers out too, and an elderly woman with a stooped back walking her small black dog. The dog looks energetic, unlike its owner. I think about my mother again, and how sick she was before she died. I shut that thought down and instead, keep driving until I reach the Old Mill pub, and take a left turn.

All the way towards the mountain road, my mind is in planning mode. Becca said she would contact me tomorrow, which means I can't go to work, not considering the emotional state I'm in. Others are bound to suspect something isn't right, plus I'll most likely find it hard to concentrate. I might not be able to take in the information from Becca's phone call or ask questions. No, it's best to ring in sick. A bug, something contagious, a way of giving the impression I still care about work, not wanting to make anyone else unwell by spreading germs. Hell, why am I worrying about what other people think of me? My daughter is in danger and I'm micro-managing my bloody career.

No, as soon as I get home, I'll ring my boss. She'll wonder why I'm phoning in over the weekend, but she'll be understanding. I never go out sick – I didn't even after my mother died. Every day I turn up on time. I get the work done, often staying late when others have long gone home. You have to do that kind of thing if you want to maintain a position at the top, constantly looking for fresh avenues to increase profit, or more intricate ways of protecting data from hackers, especially after that recent attack. False insurance claims are big business these days, and criminals know it. There are lots of ex-cops working for the firm. I think about approaching one after I've done what's been asked of me, but immediately I push that idea away. I can't risk it, not if I want Becca home.

My mind is racing so fast I wonder if I should take a sedative – I've plenty in my bag. I decide against it. Recently Gavin warned me that if I keep going at the same hectic pace, I'll burn myself out. He wanted to know what I was trying to prove. Becca used to ask me the same thing. Even as a child, she could see right through me.

'Why can't you be more like other mums,' she'd ask, 'those who don't stress about everything?'

But I have to. It's the only way I've been able to cope thus far. How did Becca think I managed to keep a roof over our heads all these years as a single mother? I've had to work harder and smarter than anyone else, moving up the ranks because up was the only direction I could go to earn enough money. Sure, money doesn't buy you happiness, but it pays the darn bills.

There was a time I thought Gavin might join the company too. Fraud prevention is such a lucrative number for ex-cops, but he preferred the corporate security side of things, safe, undemanding.

Neither of them understands what I've been through. There are things they don't know, especially Becca. All her life I've tried to protect her, and as I'm thinking this, I'm also wondering if my desire to keep her safe is partly why I've driven a wedge between us, weeks going by without any contact from her.

I moved away from home at her age, but that was for a whole different set of reasons. I remember how furious I was when Becca decided against going to college, accusing me of trying to live my life through her. And when she got that part-time job in the deli, saying she didn't want to turn out like me, overly stressed, anxious, unable to see the wood for the trees, it hurt.

I take the turn onto the mountain road. Driving upwards, I revise the instructions on the envelope in my mind. The next parcel I've to pick up will contain money. The pickup area is a few kilometres short of Military Road. The marker will be a pair of grubby runners tied to the entrance of Fettercairn forest. I'll find the parcel beside a rusty container. I've to walk in ten steps and then, on my left, I'll see a miniature conifer, a tiny Christmas tree. Beside it will be the container, and behind that, nestled in the undergrowth, there'll be a large granite rock holding the package in place. I repeat the instructions to myself again, because I can't afford to make any mistakes.

The further up the road I go, a mist is forming. Soon it's hard to see where it ends and the clouds begin. I've barely passed another car on the road, and the last house I saw was about two kilometres down the mountain. There are various markings on the road, instructing me to drive DEAD SLOW, signs for hill walkers, and graffiti-style notices erected by farmers, warning that dogs bothering sheep will be shot on the spot.

I park and get out of the car, then pause for a few seconds. I hear birdsong, the swaying of branches and the rustling of leaves. I see and hear sheep grazing on land nearby, and in the distance, there's the trickling of water from a mountain stream. On another day, I might feel good about all of this. I might reflect on the wonder of nature, and how there's so much beauty in this place, barely a twenty-minute drive from the Dublin suburbs. But today, I can't waste time on reflection: the sooner I get this over with, the better.

It doesn't take me long to find the parcel. Again, it's covered with plastic, protecting it from the weather. I clutch it to my chest as if I'm holding a child. I stare briefly at the miniature Christmas tree. It looks sad and abandoned. I think about my daughter, and again, the dividing wall she put up between us, while I stood on the other side, waiting.

As I head back to the car, the wind gains pace, savage now I'm beyond the protection of the city. Spits of rain wash across my face. I find myself sprinting, and feel better for it, as if I'm telling myself I can still do this, and reach a prize that might not even exist, aware that neither Becca nor I may survive this.

I place the parcel on top of the envelope I collected earlier, the one I'm sure contains a gun. I think about putting them in the boot, but I don't want to get out of the car again, my desire to keep moving being a form of assurance that I'm doing the right thing. I put the car into gear, casting my eyes on the packages once more. The second is so bulky – it must contain a massive amount of money. I think about the people holding Becca: why do they need someone like me to do their dirty work? Surely they have a queue of people willing to do their bidding. There's only one answer that makes sense. They want to implicate me, because if they do, they'll have more power over me, which also means this nightmare is unlikely to end here.

I check the clock on the car dashboard. The drop-off isn't due for another hour, but the traffic into the city can be a gamble in the afternoons, and the destination, a public house on the quays, means I risk getting stuck in tailbacks along the Liffey. Returning down the mountain road, I decide to go straight to the destination point. I'll park the car near Christ Church and walk the rest of the way. I've a large shoulder bag in the boot that I can use for the packages, ensuring they don't draw any unwanted attention.

Nearing Tallaght village, my ears pop with the change in altitude. I feel as if I'm physically and mentally spiralling downwards, fast. I slow the car on the bends: most of the mountain road is barely wide enough for one car, let alone two. More questions jump into my mind. When will Becca call tomorrow? And what if she doesn't? How can I be sure she's still alive? For all I know, she could have done something else to anger them. She has a temper. She might not realise, when it comes to certain people, you have to play along to survive, at least until you find another means of escape.

I switch on the radio, hoping it might calm me down, but then I start to think about the man in Harold's Cross, the one with the little girl, and the My Little Pony backpack. Was he John Simons? And why did he look so familiar?

I jam on the brakes having taken a bend too fast: I almost hit an oncoming car, a red Fiesta, driven by a boy with a tight haircut. He doesn't look old enough to drive a car. I reverse backwards into the ditch, letting the red car drive by, all the time telling myself to stop panicking. If I don't get it together, I'll make mistakes. I stare at my face in the rear-view mirror. My eyes reflect what I'm feeling inside, pure terror, and it's not just because of what's happening right now, it's because of the past. That's the thing about guilty secrets: you can never be sure who else knows about them, or the lies you told, because, irrespective of the intervening years, or the safety net you've placed between you and them, the things you wanted to stay hidden could rise up at any moment and slap you in the face.

6
NADINE

REACHING THE CITY CENTRE, I pull the car into the underground car park near Christ Church Cathedral. I place the packages inside the shoulder bag from the boot and use crumpled tissue from the back seat to conceal the opening at the top.

Out on the street, I walk like a woman in a hurry, and in the immediate distance, I see the high steeples of the cathedral.

There are lots of people on the footpaths. I have to navigate past them, and at times the way through is tight. A male tourist knocks against my shoulder bag. My heart beats a little faster. I say, 'Sorry,' to the man, even though it wasn't my fault. I walk on, gripping the handle of the bag ever tighter.

At Burdocks chipper, a popular attraction, tourists are waiting for their takeaways. Some smile at the prospect of their salt-and-vinegar treat. Under normal circumstances, I might smile too, but not today.

I start counting in my head to shut out other thoughts because my mind keeps going back to the possibility that Becca might already be dead. I shake my head, the idea too horrible to hold onto for long. For the rest of the walk, my brain functions on autopilot, and by the time I finally reach the public house on the quays, I've already counted to a hundred twenty times.

The pub door squeaks as I open it. Faces, mainly men's, turn. I see a woman in the corner seated at a table, checking messages on her mobile phone. It's dark inside too, as if I've entered some kind of cave. The worn floral carpet in the bar has the smell of stale booze oozing out of it. Cardboard beer mats, with Guinness harps, are scattered across each of the small round wooden tables, held up by ornate black iron legs. All the beer mats look used and dirty, like the rest of the place.

There's a television above the bar with a group of men sitting on stools underneath it. The barman is staring at me. He knows why I'm here. I can see it in his lined and roughened face.

I walk towards him.

'Wait there,' he instructs, as he points to a free stool a couple of feet from the crowd of men beneath the television. A breaking news story comes on the TV. A male reporter is talking about another gangland shooting in Dublin, and how the police are asking people who may have been in the area at the time to come forward, especially if they saw a car fleeing the scene. I feel relief when I hear the victim is male. It's not Becca. A photograph of a young man appears on the screen. He is smiling. I see a Happy Birthday banner in the background. The victim most likely had a mother, and now that woman may no longer have a son.

I recall Becca's phone call.

Mum, I killed someone.

I'm so distracted that at first I don't notice the barman walking towards me, until he is standing right beside me. He seems taller and broader close up. He looks angry, as if I'm some kind of hideous inconvenience. He tells me to go to the Ladies and place the packages behind the cistern in the cubicle with the upside-down brass woman on the door. I nod and slip off the bar stool.

Nervous, I grip the shoulder bag tight again, walking towards the Ladies as instructed. Inside, I see the upside-down brass woman almost immediately. The place smells of urine, potent, strong. Through the music system, Judy Garland is singing the chorus of 'The Trolley Song', filled with clanging and dinging and falling in love.

I head for the cubicle and lock myself inside. The smell isn't as bad in here. I force myself to breathe deeply in an effort to be calm, staring at the graffiti on the cubicle door, still clutching the shoulder bag. What am I waiting for?

Leave the packages where you were instructed and get the hell out of here.

Only I can't, because now I'm staring even more closely at the graffiti. Near the bottom of the door there's a heart shape with Becca's name inside. Of course, it could be another Becca, except that there's a second name in the heart. Henrietta, or Henri, as Becca used to call her best friend. The girl died last year after taking some dodgy tablet at a music festival. Becca had sworn she hadn't been doing drugs and that it was Henri's first time too. The death hit Becca badly, and immediately afterwards, she cried in my arms, only, the following day, she refused to talk about it again.

Henri's death gave her another reason to shut me out, even if I told myself all she needed was time. I was wrong about that too. She needed a mother. I should have been able to find a way through.

I hear footsteps entering the Ladies. Seconds later someone bangs lightly on the door. Sweat runs down my neck. I drop the packages behind the cistern and brace myself to open the cubicle door. I expect to see the barman looking annoyed because he's been kept waiting, but instead I see an Asian girl. She's slight in stature, and I'm drawn to her beautiful blemish-free skin. She turns her eyes downwards, avoiding mine, shyly. She's holding a bucket and a mop – she's there to clean the cubicle. She steps out of my way, putting down the bucket and mop, before taking out a damp cloth. She walks towards the washbasins and starts to wipe one. I go to another basin to wash my hands. I stare at my reflection in the mirror, shocked to see myself in this place, as if somehow I'd convinced myself this was a bad dream, something I imagined.

The Asian girl walks towards the cubicle with the upside-down brass woman on the front. She sticks an 'Out of Order' sign on the door, before pulling it closed. I don't bother drying my hands. I need to get out of there.

In the bar everything looks exactly as before, except the woman on her mobile phone is gone. I want to be her. I want to be able to walk out without a care in the world.

The barman is no longer behind the bar. I visualise him in the cubicle picking up the packages, and as I'm thinking about this, heading towards the exit, I freeze. To my right, I see someone I haven't seen in years. He has his back to me, but I'm sure it's him. I tell myself it's not possible. I must be mistaken.

Perhaps the strain of worrying about Becca is jumbling things in my head. For a second, I consider walking over to him. A part of me wants to, but my feet are stuck to the floor. They're warning me to keep my distance, to stay away, to remain safe. The voices in the bar grow louder. In the corner, the television is showing a shampoo advertisement: an actress with dark wavy hair flicks curls off her shoulders. I need to leave. He could turn around at any second and recognise me. Time stops, but somehow I recompose myself. I tell myself the only thing that matters is getting away from him.

I reach the front door. Again, it squeaks loudly as I open it. Will he turn? Will he see me? Will he call out my name? The thought of hearing his voice fills me with so much dread that I almost fling myself through the opened door onto the street. Outside I gasp for air, unaware, until now, that I've been holding my breath.

I take a step away from the doorway, checking my mobile phone for any new messages from Becca, but then I lose my balance on the cobblestones. The phone falls to the ground, and when I pick it up, the top of the screen is smashed into tiny pieces. Narrow spider lines move outwards, like a complicated web, and instead of seeing the phone, I see a cracked mirror. In it, blood is streaming from my forehead, like tiny red tears.

I move further down the footpath, putting one foot in front of the other, slow and careful, concentrating on keeping my balance. I pass a beggar in a doorway with a green tartan blanket wrapped around him. His face is lined and puffy, with a mix of purple blotches and protruding veins. His skin seems hardened by the elements, unshaven, dishevelled, beaten down. He has a tiny terrier in his arms. He shakes an empty plastic cup in front of me. I want to help him, but right now I have to keep on moving.

'I don't have any change,' I lie, but even after he is well out of sight, I'm thinking about him, how he wasn't born that way. Once he was a boy with his whole life ahead of him, unknowing. A child cannot see their future. I certainly didn't. How could I have known that one day, someone would beat me to within an inch of my life.

Finally, I'm on the road heading towards the car park. My breathing is more settled now, but then my mobile phone vibrates in my bag. I stop and take it out. Another unidentified number. I desperately hope it's Becca again.

I look behind me, checking for the umpteenth time that no one has followed me from the bar.

'Hello,' I say.

'I hear you delivered the package,' the male voice says, the sound muffled as if something's covering the mouthpiece, disguising his voice.

'I want to talk to my daughter.'

'You can't. She's switching location.'

'Where?'

A silence follows.

'Where is she?' I ask again, the anger that has been building inside me since that first phone call bubbling to the surface.

He lets out a snort.

'I'm going to the police,' I insist, sounding more adamant than I feel. 'I swear,' I repeat, 'I will go to the cops.'

'You're not going to do that, Nadine.' His words are slow and emphatic.

'What makes you so sure?' There's a false bravado in my voice.

'Apart from the bullets that will end up in your head?'

I hear another snort.

My right hand, the one holding the phone, starts to tremble.

'Nadine,' the voice taunts, 'are you still there?'

I can't afford to show this man any weakness. 'Yes,' I say. 'I'm still here.'

I slip down a side-lane, wanting to get as far away from the people walking up and down the street as I can. The lane is empty, apart from garbage bins. The closer I get to them, the more vile the smell of rubbish becomes. I spot used syringes littering the gutter. I look up and down once more, making sure no one is close enough to hear me, then say, steady and determined, '*I want my daughter back.*'

The man doesn't answer me. I wonder if he has hung up.

'I want her back,' I repeat. 'I've done everything you've asked of me. I don't care how many bullets you put inside my head. If I don't get to talk to Becca, I will go to the police.'

'*No – you – won't – Nadine.*' His tone is colder now, harsher too, as if I've really pissed him off.

'I just want to talk to her.' I hear the tremor in my voice. He must hear it too.

'Truth – or – Dare, Nadine,' he says.

I can't breathe.

'*Truth or Dare,*' he repeats.

My head is whirling. I think I'm going to throw up. And then, the line goes dead.

I stare at the spider-web phone screen, the enormity of his words hitting home. How can he know about the Truth or Dare game? How can this stranger know?

The fear that has gripped me since this morning takes hold all over again. What if he isn't a stranger?

I step out of the laneway. The road to the car park seems busier now, filled with far too many people and cars. There must have been a heavy downpour while I was in the bar, because now, with a break in the clouds and the sunshine shooting through, rainwater sweats from the ground. More tourists clutch street maps. Others talk on mobile phones. Everyone is moving fast, with lots of people walking in the opposite direction to me. I clamber my way through, and somehow I reach the car park.

Walking towards the car, I remember my reflection in the mirror from years before, blood streaming down my face and it's as if his hands are on me again. They're wrapped tight around my throat. He's pinning me against the wall, my body aching from the kicks he's given me. I feel trapped. A victim. Unable to get away.

'Stupid bitch,' he's roaring, pulling me further back in time. He tightens his fist, the knuckles white. They grow larger the closer they get to my face. He stinks of alcohol too. I'd thought it was him earlier in the bar, my ex-husband, Cian. I'd thought he'd come back into my life to make it hell all over again. But I must have been mistaken. This nightmare can't have anything to do with him. I think about the last phone call – Truth or Dare – as I play out all possible scenarios in my mind, not wanting to believe any of them.

Finally, I see my car. I press the buzzer to turn off the alarm even though it's still some distance away. It makes me feel better that some things are still within my control.

When I reach it, the words from the last phone call replay in my mind. Opening the driver's door, I struggle to get inside, as if the need to be safe makes my movements awkward. I turn the key and put the car in gear. It moves forward. This can't be happening. The past is in the past. I don't live that life any more. I can't and won't be a victim again.

I keep driving towards the exit, unwilling to accept, even now, that my past is in any way connected to Becca being in danger. I won't allow it to be true.

The sunlight, as I drive out of the car park, is blinding. I can barely see in front of me, but still I push forward. A horn honks as I cut across a car, ignoring the yield sign, but I don't care. I need to keep going. I need to put as much distance as I can between me and the sinking feeling inside, telling me the past is never over. That it will always exist, in the same way that the body in the garden still exists, and that all the terrible things I've done will never go away.

7
WREN

I'M EXPECTING MEG, MY BEST FRIEND, to call over this evening, so I've made fresh ice for the pink gin, it being her current favourite. She was due to arrive twenty minutes ago, but she's never on time. To some, we're an unlikely pairing, the ultimate yin and yang, me wanting to save the world, while Meg would prefer to view it from a sunny, exotic beach. Mostly our friendship has little to do with our differences. We look out for each other. We've done so ever since school, when I lost my mother and Meg's parents separated, badly.

The doorbell rings. I already know it's her because she does her signature ring of three rapid dings, followed by a knock. Physically, she's quite different from me too, looking like a cross between Lady Gaga and Scarlett Johansson, with blonder than blonde hair, green eyes, and deep red lips. When we're out together, guys always notice her first. Tonight, her hair is tied up. There are loose strands that look as if they've fallen out by accident but, most likely, she's spent an hour perfecting them. An hour, in Meg's opinion, that is a completely reasonable excuse for being late. I don't mention the time. There's no point.

'Christ, I'm gasping,' she says.

I give her a hug.

'Never mind the loving.' She smiles. 'Get me that drink.'

Minutes later, we're in position, me curled up in an armchair, her sitting on the couch opposite.

'What's the latest with you?' she asks, between her initial gulps of pink gin to get her into the mood.

'Same shit, same mountains to climb.'

'I hear that poor sod didn't make it in west Dublin.'

'Nope, he didn't. Full-scale murder inquiry.'

'But you're not involved, are you? It's not on your turf.'

'Getaway car was found burnt out near the Dodder this evening. A witness thought they saw someone fling something in the river.'

'The gun?'

'Maybe. Either way, that will be my morning tomorrow, meeting the charming DI Declan O'Keeffe from Lucan.'

Meg tilts her head to one side. 'So, no hangover, then?'

'No,' I reply, as I take the first sip from my glass.

'You look as if there's something else on your mind.'

'You can read me like a book.'

'Maybe I should be the detective, not you.'

'You're wasted in tourism,' I joke.

'Go on, spit it out.'

'I saw someone today.'

'Who?'

'Gavin's sister.'

'Oh, God, not this Gavin crap again.'

'We were checking cars, and I saw her,' I continue, ignoring Meg's rebuff. 'I knew there was something familiar about her, and when I checked her driver's licence, I made the connection.'

'So?'

'So, it was odd. She was odd, acting all nervous.'

'Maybe she recognised you too and wanted to be a million miles away.'

I let out a low laugh. 'Maybe you're right.'

She leans forward on the couch. 'Look, Wren, you need to let it go.'

'I have let it go.'

'Nope, you haven't. You're still looking for answers that you're not going to find.'

'I might.'

'Your relationship is over. He was a shit. He cheated on you. He messed with your head, and all because you thought you could change him, make him better, less angry with the world.'

'A lot of cops have issues, especially anger issues when the work gets tough.'

'Ex-cop,' she corrects me.

'Okay, ex-cop.'

'Ex-boyfriend.'

'That too.' I stand up and take her glass to get a refill.

'Anything else happen today?' she asks, changing the subject. I pour a double measure of gin.

'An aborted ATM theft, a twelve-year-old entering the Juvenile Diversion Programme, and a scrambler bike out of control.'

'I hate those things.'

'You know the score, Meg. We're not supposed to chase them, despite them being nothing but trouble, even when the driver is shouting abuse at you, and giving you the fingers, or whatever.'

'The bloody things should be banned.'

'Couldn't agree more,' I say, taking my second sip, and handing her back her glass, 'but if we put them under pressure, and they drive more erratically, they can do reckless things and lose it. If they come off the bike and end up dead, it would be seen as our fault. Thankfully, today's scrambler ended up in the ditch of his own accord with nothing more than a few cuts and bruises. He'll be back on the streets within the week, although the bike is a write-off.'

I get up and drain the pasta bubbling on the stove, then add a jar of Bolognese sauce. I used to cook for Gavin, looking up recipes, my domesticity being a kind of unofficial nod to the possibility of happy ever after. Who was I fooling? If Meg could read my thoughts right now, she'd tell me I'd watched too many princess movies as a kid.

She flicks on the TV, zooming through the channels. 'What about watching *The Others* again?' she asks.

'Thanks, but no thanks.'

I put the two bowls of pasta in front of us.

Meg gets up and fills two large glasses with water, but she stops halfway back, outside the spare bedroom, the door ajar. 'What are you up to?'

Sometimes I use it as a temporary office and, Meg being Meg, she doesn't bother asking if she can go inside, just pushes the door wider and walks in.

There are newspaper cuttings on the bed, along with a couple of black-and-white images. She picks up the top one, a group of teenage kids sitting on a wall in Rathmines. 'Is this Gavin as a teenager?'

'Him and others.'

She gives me a disapproving look that screams, *Why*?

'I printed off some stuff earlier on, after seeing Gavin's sister. I've always been curious about that missing girl from years ago.'

'Gavin's teenage love?'

'Yep.' I move closer to Meg, taking the image from her. 'Look, there she is.'

'She's gorgeous.'

'Thanks,' I say, annoyed.

'What are you trying to do, Wren? Reopen an investigation or something?'

'There wasn't really an investigation. It was more a case of an eighteen-year-old girl who wanted to disappear so she did.'

She gives me the dagger eyes again. I know it's because she wants to stop me doing this kind of stuff, in case it hurts me even more. 'Don't judge me,' I say.

'I'm not.'

She follows me out of the room.

I pick up my gin, ignoring the pasta. 'It's hard, Meg, not being able to understand.'

'Understand what?'

'If our relationship meant anything to him.'

'He's a fucker, end of.'

'But why did I fall for it?' I put down my drink.

She takes my hands. 'You wanted him to be a good person. He

37

wasn't. You thought you could help his moods. You couldn't. He cheated on you. He did something you would never do to him, and all the investigations in the world into some girl who disappeared –'

'Evie Hunt. Her name was Evie Hunt.'

'– aren't going to change a damn thing. Nothing's going to give you answers.'

'He only ever spoke about her after copious amounts of alcohol, and whenever I approached him when he was sober, he'd brush it off, and put up that brick wall of his. You know what he was like. If he wanted to, he could convince you night was day.'

'All the more reason not to trust a word out of his mouth.'

'I'm beginning to think,' I say, ignoring her last comment, 'that Evie Hunt's disappearance was the reason he went into the police force in the first place. I mean, it must have had a huge effect on him. Most guards have a reason for joining. I certainly did.'

We both know mine was my mother's death, even if the stolen car killed her when I was only a child.

With the conversation shifting emphasis to my mother, Meg's approach softens. 'Hey,' she says, 'let's enjoy the night, and forget about him who must not be named.'

'Okay,' I say, happy to let it go.

Two hours later, after she leaves, I pour myself another pink gin, although I shouldn't. Meg's right, of course. My relationship with Gavin was a mistake, but that doesn't mean it's easy to stop looking for answers. I need to make sure I don't make the same mistake again.

In the spare bedroom, I pick up one of the newspaper clippings, flopping back on the single bed, forgetting about the pink gin. Evie Hunt never did turn up – at least, not in Ireland. That didn't mean she came to a bad end. Back then, lots of girls took off somewhere else, many cutting ties with their family and friends, often because of an unwanted pregnancy or something else that meant they needed sanctuary in another jurisdiction. Either way, she was eighteen, so legally she was an adult, and apart from these articles in a few local newspapers, she was regarded as another statistic. I pick up another printout, this one describing Evie as a model student, having recently completed her Leaving Certificate. The last paragraph has brief statements from some of her school friends, including a direct quote from Gavin: 'Evie would never have left of her own accord.' He was described as 'very close' to the missing girl, which meant they were an item, but I already knew that.

Most of the friends, it seems, had gone to the same secondary school, one viewed as pioneering at the time, having a cross-section of students from different socioeconomic groups. I stare at the image that initially tweaked Meg's interest. Underneath it, there's a list of the friends' names, but the digital copy isn't of great quality so it's hard to make them out with any certainty. I'd recognise Gavin's face anywhere, but I'm also drawn to another male member of the group, Cian Campbell. I know he's Nadine's ex-husband, because Gavin talked about him once, saying he just upped and left, walking out on Nadine, never to return. One disappearance, Evie Hunt's, is odd, but a second?

Meg was wrong. My new-found interest in Evie Hunt, and the others in the group, doesn't stem from an inclination to dig up old cold cases. It's something more than that. I'm curious because it involves Gavin, and therefore, indirectly, involves me. I know we're over. I know finding out what happened to a girl from years before won't change that, but it forms part of who we were together. She was important to him, extremely important. He didn't have to talk about her constantly for me to grasp that. There was anger and hurt in his silences, more than any words could convey. I think that's partly why I was so drawn to him: I understood hurt and anger. Either way, he got close, and at times, when we were together, it was almost as if he'd known me long before we ever met.

I take a sip of my gin, as my focus shifts back to Nadine, Gavin's sister. It's easy to recognise her in the image, too, although she looks more shy and sheepish than the woman in the car park of Rathfarnham shopping centre: the woman who seemed awfully keen to get a million miles away from me, and fast.

8
NADINE

A TEXT BLEEPS IN MY PHONE. It's from my boss. The message tells me to look after myself, and not to worry about work.

In the living room, I pick up a faded photograph of Becca as a baby. The last eighteen years speed before my eyes, my infant daughter becoming a toddler, playing with dolls, climbing trees, cutting her knees, crying, reaching out for me. I glance around the room at all the images documenting her milestones: her first steps, winning a race, singing in a school musical. I had laughed, and loved, and when things got hard for her, when she didn't have a father any more, and became angry with him for walking out on us, and never making contact, I'd cried, feeling I was the one to blame. The lost sensation I'd experienced then is creeping up on me now, but I can't afford to crack, not when Becca needs me most.

My mobile phone rings. Please, let it be Becca. I look at the caller ID – unknown again.

It rings another couple of times before I press the answer button.

'Nadine,' the male voice says, slow and menacing.

'Yes,' I reply, my voice croaky.

I hear a noise coming from outside. It's a motorbike turning the corner at speed. Gripping the phone, I look out the living-room window in time to see the biker slowing down. He pulls in at the top of the road.

'Hello,' I say, hearing crackling on the line. 'Are you still there?' I sound nervous.

I keep staring at the biker. Perhaps I shouldn't be standing so close to the window. I move back further into the room. The man climbs off his motorbike. He's dressed in black and is still wearing his helmet. He walks towards the house.

'You'd better stay alert, Nadine,' instructs the muffled voice on the phone.

'What do you mean?'

'Don't do anything stupid. Don't even think about talking to the cops. We're watching you. Our eyes are on you all the time. You, your house and, of course, Becca.'

My heart thumps with the mention of my daughter's name. 'I did what you asked of me,' I plead. 'I want Becca back. Do you hear me?' The panic in my voice confirms for both of us who's really in charge.

'It doesn't work that way, Nadine.'

'But I delivered the packages.'

'We need you to do another favour for us, an important one.'

'What?'

'You'll get the details soon.'

'I don't understand.' I look towards the window again. The biker is standing opposite the house, staring right at me.

'All you need to know, Nadine, is that if you fuck up at any point along the way, you're dead. A large debt needs to be paid. You get nothing for nothing in this life. You know that, don't you?'

Across the road, the biker pulls down the zipper of his jacket. He puts his right hand inside. He removes something, then stretches out his arms, holding the object, pointing it in the direction of the house, and at me. It's only then I realise it's a gun.

I scream. I pull further back, pinning my body against the wall, still clutching the phone in my hand.

'Shut it,' the man's voice says. 'You don't want to disturb the neighbours, do you?'

There's a thwarting tone in what he says. He's playing with me, wanting to scare me, to be in control. I understand control, so I'll play his game for now.

'I'll do whatever it takes,' I say, breathing in deep.

'Then take this as a warning, Nadine. Mess with me and, I promise you, you will end up dead. No one will hear you scream, because next time, if you don't do exactly as I tell you, there will be no warning. You'll get six bullets in the head, and you won't get a chance to open your mouth because you won't see it coming. I'll find you, and I'll kill you. Do you hear me?'

'Yes.' I visualise the biker across the street standing in my bedroom, perhaps in the dark as I sleep, then the bang, bang, bang of his firearm, and all of it, my life, the love I have for my daughter, everything, gone.

I close my eyes before I beg. 'Please, can I talk to Becca?' My voice sounds as it used to when I first understood fear, the kind of fear that traps you, that warps your mind until only the remnants of the person you used to be are left.

'Not yet,' he says. 'You've a long way to go before the score is even close to settled. Those parcels you delivered were just a test.'

'A test of what?'

'Of you playing ball.'

I swallow hard, the reality hitting home.

'You'll have to pay big-time, Nadine.' He laughs.

'I want my daughter back.'

'We both know you're not in a position to negotiate.' His words, chilled and angry, before the scary voice, the one from the past, enters my head.

You control nothing.

You are nothing.

Fuck with me and I'll kill you.

I stare at the biker across the street, his arms still outstretched, the gun, even now, pointing right at me.

'I hear you,' I say.

'Good girl, Nadine,' the voice says, as if I'm little more than a child. 'Do you see that guy across the street, the one with the gun and the trigger he's itching to pull?'

'Yes.'

'When you hang up, he can do one of two things. He can walk

away, or if you're not prepared to keep doing as instructed, Nadine, he can blow your bloody brains out.'

His repetition of my name feels like some kind of horrible intimacy, a closeness demanded but not earned.

'Okay,' I reply. 'I'll do whatever you ask.'

After I hang up, I stare at the biker, a man who could kill me without a care. What use would I be to Becca then?

For a time, it's as if this stranger and I are caught in some nightmarish pact, where the outside world is of little consequence, until finally he lowers his arms, ready to return the firearm to the inside of his jacket. I breathe, deep, heavy breaths, before he stalls once more, almost as if he's considering whether he might still do it, but, at long last, he puts the firearm away. He turns and walks back towards his motorbike, but there's reluctance in his movements, as if he's been deprived of something: the joy of killing me.

I walk to the back of the house, into the kitchen, and away from any further view of the street outside. It seems safer here, out of sight. Only I'm not safe. I'm not safe anywhere.

I replay the phone calls from the male caller in my head. He said there was a big score to be settled, and that is exactly what I'm going to do. I'm going to pay whatever debt exists, and when I do, they won't need Becca any more. I tell myself she'll phone soon. I'll get to talk to her, even if she isn't the one calling the shots.

I wonder about John Simons again. Have our paths crossed before? The man on the phone had mentioned the Truth or Dare game. Only a few people knew about that.

I imagine the biker across the road, and the young man shot dead in Dublin. People like his killer, and the man on the phone, would kill me in a heartbeat. They wouldn't think twice about it. If it were only me, maybe I'd let them do it, but I can't let anything happen to Becca.

I look out the kitchen window above the sink and study the back garden. I stare at the pebbled area beyond the washing line, behind the raised flower bed, and think of the day the men came to fill in that large hole, levelling the top with those tiny gold pebbles. I know what lies beneath those stones. I'm well aware of the decisions I've made, especially the darkest ones, which means I also know what I'm capable of.

9
WREN

EN ROUTE TO THE DODDER, Mike is rabbiting on about a new gardening programme on TV, but I'm barely listening to him. I'm not exactly hung-over, although my head is a delicate mix of three pink gins and sleep deprivation. I need him to change the subject.

'Why do you think, Mike, the guys who carried out the assassination in west Dublin came over to our patch? There's any number of places they could have burned out that car, and they could easily have disposed of the weapon there too.'

'Maybe they're local to Rathfarnham,' he jokes, 'and they wanted to get in some exercise jogging home.'

'More likely, another stolen car picked them up.'

I'm already thinking about CCTV footage from the neighbouring houses. It's an affluent area, and affluence requires additional security.

'Did you ever wonder,' Mike continues, 'if folks have built up a tolerance to people getting shot?'

'You know the attitude as well as I do. Most think, "Let the bad guys kill themselves off", but it doesn't work that way, does it? Innocent people get caught up in it too, and if we don't take them on, who the hell will?'

'It's a bit like that gardening programme I watched,' he says, 'when they were talking about dealing with weeds.'

'Yeah?' I say, only half listening again.

'You do what you can, but you're never going to beat them.'

I don't disagree with him, but out of the blue, I say, 'My mother loved dandelions.' I don't usually talk about her, so it takes Mike by surprise. 'Most people hate them, preferring a neat green lawn, but she saw their invasion of the grass as an opportunity.'

'Oh?'

'Yeah, she painted them,' I say, remembering how, as a child, I used to love the way the bright yellow would bounce into the room, vibrant, unapologetic.

'Are you all right, Wren?'

'Sure,' I reply. 'I'm fine.' Then, changing the subject, 'Is O'Keeffe positive the west Dublin hit was drug-related?'

'Yep. Isn't the bloody city awash with cocaine?'

A well-dressed man with a briefcase dashes across the street, hurrying to catch a bus.

'At times, Mike, it pisses me off how everyone, especially those directly removed from the problem, wants to wash their hands of it, unwilling to admit that taking the odd recreational line of coke makes them responsible too.'

'They wouldn't see it that way.'

'Maybe not, but it gets to me how so many of these so-called well-educated folk don't give a damn about *how* the stuff they're taking got here, or the shit that goes into their favourite poison. They're probably the same people who won't eat a burger, insisting on buying organic, needing to know every last detail about what's at the end of their fork, including which farm the food came from, yet they put coke up their noses, and don't ask any questions about the misery or murder it causes.'

'Let's pick our battles, Wren, okay?'

'Okay,' I reply. Ranting isn't going to change anything.

He pulls the car in close to the low Dodder wall. An early-morning mist has formed, and stepping out of the car, I shiver with the damp still lingering in the air. I spot O'Keeffe in the distance. He's standing a few yards from the riverbank, his collar up around his neck, keeping an eye on the divers ducking in and out of the freezing water. A few forensics guys are in situ, wearing white suits and booties, waiting patiently in case they get lucky. The uniformed guards hang back too, their only duty to ensure the area is cordoned off to prevent the public doing any more damage.

As I walk down the bank, my feet crunch on the frozen leaves, the soil soggy after the last few days of rain. The sound of traffic above us fades as Mike and I descend. The natural beauty spot, with its mature trees and habitat, seems totally at odds with what's happening within it, the quiet filled with the sound of the divers plunging and emerging from the water. The branches on the trees, some devoid of leaves, collide against one another in the breeze.

O'Keeffe turns to greet us when we're a couple of feet away. 'Hello, Wren,' he says, nodding to Mike beside me.

'Anything yet?' I ask.

'A supermarket trolley or two, but nothing of value.'

'I'll organise some of the crew to canvass the area as soon as your guys are done here. We'll check for CCTV from private houses too.'

Mike takes a step closer to the divers and the tech team.

'Did the victim have any immediate family?' I ask O'Keeffe.

'A sister, and both parents.'

'Who did the house call?'

'Me,' he says, putting his hands further down into his pockets. Declan O'Keeffe wouldn't be my favourite person, as he's often overly zealous in pushing other people around, but he's in the force, which carries an unspoken respect.

'Tough,' I reply.

'You know the way it is, Wren,' shrugging it off, 'we never call to a door to tell someone good news.'

'He was very young, though, wasn't he, even for that line of work?'

'Yep.'

'Life over, and for what?'

It's a rhetorical question, so I'm not expecting an answer. 'He ran to escape them,' O'Keeffe continues, 'but they still gunned him down. By the time I got there, the girlfriend had to be held back by a couple of our uniform guys. She was screaming her head off.'

'Christ.' There isn't much else to say.

We stand side by side in silence. Moments later, we watch a white bin bag with a pull string being hauled to the surface. Neither of us gets excited: it could be nothing. But one of the forensics team raises his hand.

'What is it?' O'Keeffe asks. 'Is it the firearm?'

All three techies in their white suits shake their heads.

Mike, who's been overseeing things from closer, takes a few steps towards us.

'What is it?' I ask. 'Could you see in the bag?'

'Yep,' he says, 'there's a rock and what looks very much like a body part.'

'What kind of body part?' O'Keeffe is irked to be put on the back foot.

'An arm.'

'So, it's definitely human?' O'Keeffe quizzes, frown lines appearing on his brow.

'Not much doubt about it.'

O'Keeffe walks towards the tech guys, keen to get a full view for himself.

'From what you could see, Mike,' I ask, 'was the hand still on it?'

'No, it was severed.'

'A clean cut?'

'Yep.'

'So, it was man-made?'

'I'd say so.'

'Anything else?'

'It was covered in plastic, the way you'd wrap a piece of meat for the freezer.'

O'Keeffe walks back towards us.

'Listen,' I say, 'I don't want to be a party spoiler here, but that piece of treasure has been found on our turf, and an investigation always follows the body or, in this case, part of it.'

'I've no intention of arguing with you, Wren, but for now, I want the divers to keep going. It may well have been that plastic bag that the witness saw being fired in the river, but we can't be sure. The gun related to the Lucan hit could still be down there.'

'Okay, but let's get more of this stretch of river cordoned off.' I turn to Mike.

'I'm on it,' he says.

O'Keeffe keeps a watchful eye on the diving crew. 'It'll be tricky determining cause of death, Wren.'

'No argument there.'

'On the positive side, though,' he smiles, 'if we hadn't been looking for the murder weapon for the killing in Lucan that arm might never have been found.'

10
NADINE

THERE'S STILL NO WORD FROM BECCA, and the more time passes, the more anxious I'm becoming.

I hear the doorbell. Opening the front door, I see my next-door neighbour, Aria. It feels weird, with my world being turned upside-down, how some things remain ordinary, normal.

'Nadine,' she says, a sympathetic look on her face, 'is everything all right?'

Aria is the same age as me, mid-thirties, and attractive, with long, wild auburn hair, adding to her bohemian look. She has never married, claiming matrimony is nothing more than a shackle of religious dictates and societal conformity. Aria knows everything there is to know about the neighbourhood. Her abundance of knowledge is because she works from home, offering a combination of homeopathic treatments, yoga classes and the odd mindfulness session. She has encouraged me to join in, but our proximity as neighbours is enough closeness for me.

I should be glad of a nosy neighbour, but right now I don't want to talk to anyone, least of all someone who will share everything I tell her to anyone prepared to listen.

'I'm great, Aria.'

'Only,' she says, 'I thought I heard something yesterday evening.'

'Oh?'

'I was in the back bedroom upstairs, meditating, and I could have sworn I heard female screams coming from your house.'

I can tell she's looking for a reaction. 'No,' I say. 'You must be mistaken.'

I need her to go away.

'I got to wondering if *he* might be back.'

I know she's referring to my ex-husband, Cian.

'No,' I say, giving her a reassuring smile, 'he isn't.' I attempt to hide the edge of contempt in my voice. Every now and then, Aria likes to mention Cian as confirmation that her views on matrimony are still intact.

'You're better off without the likes of him,' she says.

I nod.

'Only I've been very worried about you, Nadine, especially since the break-in.'

'No need to worry. Nothing was taken.'

'Odd, though, wasn't it, that they went to all that trouble to break in and didn't take a single thing?'

'Perhaps they were disturbed,' I suggest, my fingers tensing, keener than ever for her to leave.

'Hmm,' she says, contemplating my last sentence, but still looking sceptical. She takes a step closer, the way a lazy cat might glide. I hold her stare.

'I haven't seen Becca for a while either. How is she?'

I freeze at my daughter's name, the nightmare of the last couple of days crashing in.

'She's fine,' I say, keeping my answer brief and to the point.

'Teenagers,' she laughs, 'there's no accounting for them, is there? They're far too strong-willed at that age if you ask me.'

'Thank you, Aria, but if you don't mind ...' I let my words trail off.

'I think procreation is overrated. This tiny planet has enough humans sucking it for all it's worth, although once the offspring arrive, it doesn't do to turn a blind eye, does it?'

'What do you mean?'

'The world is full of so much temptation, especially for younger people.'

'I guess you're right.' It's easier to agree with her, if I want her to go away. 'Thanks again,' I say, wanting more than ever to end the conversation. I shut the door, and lean my back against it, wondering if she's still standing there, waiting for another snippet of information.

I stare down the hallway to the kitchen. I think about the break-in again, the opened drawers in my bedroom, the contents scattered across the floor. The place was ransacked from top to bottom, as if whoever did it was desperately searching for something. It had happened in broad daylight while I was at work and, from the awful mess that greeted me when I got home, they must have been here for hours. The police thought it odd too. Normally, they said, if there was a break-in like that, the culprits would either be staking the place out to return later, or would have grabbed what they wanted the first time. There were plenty of valuables they could have taken. My first concern, even though I didn't want to admit it, was that it could have been Becca, but when I realised my surplus cash was still hidden in the freezer, I knew it wasn't her. She would have known my hiding place. I've been putting spare cash in there for years, especially when Cian was still in our lives. I used to call it my escape money, adding to it whenever I could.

I hear Aria walk away. I visualise her light, delicate steps, as if whatever mission she's on in life gives her nothing but pleasure.

It seems so alien to how I feel right now. Alone in the hallway, suddenly, I see the younger me, the woman I used to be, being dragged across the floor, my black tights ripped, my dress up around my waist, while my high heels, the ones he insisted I wear, are flung aside, safe in the shadows, unlike me. I dare not speak. He only ever got worse when I did. I imagine his fist grabbing my hair, pulling me across the room once more, like an animal getting ready for slaughter. I never screamed, or fought back, because I knew he loved that too.

I hear Aria opening her front door. I tell myself again that all of this happened a long time ago. My anxiety over Becca is causing me to dwell on stuff I haven't thought about in years. It couldn't have been Cian I saw in town. That would have been impossible. Besides, I didn't see his face, so realistically, it could have been anyone.

In the kitchen, I repeat those awful words: Truth or Dare. The male caller was trying to taunt me, but it was more than that. It was his way of telling me he knows things about me, things I don't want other people to find out.

I look out the kitchen window. The windowpanes are fogged up. I wipe my palms across them leaving behind wet streaks, like a child's early drawing. I see the signs of autumn settling in, the days getting shorter. I see the shadows too. They always start in the same place, at the end of the garden above the gold pebbles. Soon, they'll creep around the trees. I study the leaves on the branches: crisp and dry, as if they're desperately trying to hang on. They remind me of myself.

The moon is already visible. It brightens as I stare at it, creating a narrow beam of light illuminating the damp, tightly trimmed grass. Cutting it had felt so important a few days ago, giving it the final trim before the colder months took hold. Lots of things had felt important before that phone call from Becca.

Truth or Dare. The words repeat over and over in my mind.

The faces of the barman in the pub and the Asian girl swirl as if this is some horrible nightmare I might soon wake up from. The voice of the man on the phone gets louder. *Truth or Dare, Truth or Dare.*

Soon, my breathing becomes deeper and faster until, finally, I collapse onto the kitchen floor. I hit my head on the way down. The room darkens. I recognise the signs of a panic attack. I'll be no use to Becca if I have a meltdown. But I can't help myself. As I lose consciousness, it's a relief to give in to the darkness, almost as if, inside it, I might find safety.

When I finally come around, I'm not sure how long I've been out for, but I imagine a couple of hours at least. My head is sore, but it will recover.

I make my way towards the staircase, and more images of my ex-husband come back. A hard slap across my face.

'You think you're better than me, bitch, don't you?'

'You're nothing more than an ugly, whingeing cow.'

The skin on my face tingles, but not in a good way.

Somehow I make it upstairs. I edge towards my bedroom, passing the door of the room I used to share with him. I think about the body in the garden again. I see him flinging me down the stairs, the ones I just walked up, his boot thumping on my back, hearing the crack, which tells me I'll be bent over for months.

He wanted to steal every bit of me for himself. He wanted to make me weak. But in the end, it was I who made the horror go away.

I switch on the bedside light. The yellow glow feels warm, familiar. At the window, I glance down at the garden once more, at the now darkened lawn, the shadows still creeping around the trees. I pull the curtains closed, blocking it all out.

In the bathroom, I brush my teeth, as if I'm still living a regular life. I use a cleansing wipe on my face. I'm too exhausted for a shower, even though I know sleep will elude me. The same words keep going around in my head.

Truth or Dare.

They have Becca.

They have my little girl.

I am her mother.

I need to save her.

The man on the phone had said she was being sent to a new location. Without them having my daughter, I would probably have gone straight to the police.

I place my mobile phone on the bedside locker, staring at the smashed screen, more aware than ever that I need to find a way to fix things.

I have to believe Becca is still alive. I wonder about the person she killed. I remember one guy in particular. He seemed important to her. Was he the one?

Right now, all the cards are stacked in someone else's hand. They're calling the shots, just as Cian used to when I thought the horror would never go away, and then, I made it disappear.

I imagine Becca, frightened and alone. When she told me she'd killed someone, I was shocked but I shouldn't have been. All of us are capable of killing given the right set of circumstances.

11
NADINE

DURING THE NIGHT, I WAKE with the covers kicked off. The bedside lamp, still lit, is on the floor, the shade hanging off, the light bulb dangerously close to the carpet. I stand the lamp upright.

I had a nightmare. The same one I've had many times before. It must have caused me to thrash out in my sleep. Fragments of the dream remain. I'm being chased. I run as fast as I can, but just as I think I'm free, he steps out in front of me, blocking my path, and I know what's going to happen next, only my mind can't allow it. Then, like all the other times, I wake up, terrified.

It takes me only a few seconds to come to my senses, and when I do, everything that has happened with Becca floods back.

I walk to the dressing-table, sitting down in front of the wood-framed mirror where Becca, as a child, played with my lipsticks and perfumes. I remember the joy I felt brushing her hair, and how sometimes I thought I loved her far too much.

'Becca,' I whisper, 'where are you? Oh, God, please be safe.'

I walk back to the bed, repositioning the lamp on the locker. The mobile phone is still there, having survived the worst of my nightmare. I scroll down my contact list, easily finding Gavin's number. It's 5 a.m. He won't be awake now. If I ring him at this hour, he'll know something's wrong. I hesitate, but I can't afford to be thinking about irrelevant details. If I don't start putting the pieces together, I risk running out of time. I won't mention Becca to him, but I will ask him about John Simons. That's the only name I have, my only lead, so I have to start there.

I wait as the ringing tone at the other end vibrates in my ear, remembering the two of us, Gavin and I, playing as kids. 'Ready, steady, go,' he would say, and I would run, and it felt like fun, like happier times.

'Nadine,' he says, his voice sleepy and annoyed, 'what the heck? Do you know what time it is?'

'Yes.'

'Are you having another nightmare?'

'Something like that.'

'Take one of those pills the doctor gave you for stress. They'll help you sleep.'

'It's not like that.'

'No? What is it, then?'

'I need to ask you something.'

'Okay. Hang on.'

I hear him get out of bed. He moves quietly, like a burglar creeping about. There was a time he'd shared that bedroom with his wife, but she is long gone, unable to deal with his dark moods.

I hear a door creak open. 'What is it?' he asks, the impatience still in his voice.

'Do you know a John Simons?'

The eerie quiet at the end of the line feels like the silence of an ex-police officer trying to work out how much he wants to reveal.

'What do you want to know about him?' he asks.

I can tell he recognises the name. 'I saw him the other day,' I say. 'I stopped at a corner shop in Harold's Cross to pick up a takeaway coffee. Someone called after him and he looked familiar, only I don't know a John Simons.'

Now, I'm the one being tight with the information. 'You know him, Gavin, don't you?'

'He's done some prison time for sure.'

'And?'

'Last I heard, he and another guy hit a building site in town looking for protection money. The builder paid out thousands in cash to keep

57

them off his back so he could get the houses built, only it turned out the pressure wasn't coming from the criminals alone.'

'What do you mean?'

'Nadine, it's the middle of the night.'

I'm not going to let him off the hook, not with Becca in trouble. 'It's nearly morning,' I say.

'Jesus, if you must drag the whole story out of me ...' He gives a long sigh. 'The council put pressure on the builder to take the guys on as security officers. *Someone* got to a pen-pusher, and you know how that goes.'

'Who was the second guy?'

'A thug called Joe Regan with a rap sheet as long as your arm. Twelve years, to be precise. He started his luxurious career by being done for cruelty to animals. The idiot kept an African wild cat in the garage of his parents' house. Pity the thing didn't eat him alive and do the world a favour.'

'Tell me about John Simons.'

There's another pause.

I look towards the bedroom window. I think about the shadows creeping around the lawn, but there isn't a sound from outside, almost as if the place has no secrets at all and the only thing that exists is a suburban garden awaiting a new day.

'What are you holding back, Gavin?' I ask, my voice more determined, fortified, as if my senses are warning me that whatever my brother is about to tell me, it isn't something I want to hear.

'That's not his real name.'

'I don't understand.'

'He likes to use aliases.'

'Why?'

'A scam, but every now and then the guy tries that particular name on for size, especially when a criminal record gets in the way.'

'What's his proper name?'

'Nadine, go back to sleep. You know what you're like when you get agitated.'

'Please, I need to know.' Seconds tick by. What if he doesn't tell me? I have to push him. 'Gavin, his name, tell me.'

There's a sharp intake of breath before he says, 'Ben. His name is Ben Donnelly.'

I drop the phone, cutting off the call.

I visualise the man at the gate, sniggering, and again I'm drawn back in time, to me as a young teenager, at first thin and lanky, with a flat chest barely developed. Ben was in our old gang, as was Gavin, but of all the boys he was the one who made me feel the most uncomfortable.

As an adolescent, I wasn't as pretty as the other girls in the group. There were times I wanted to be invisible. Things changed as I grew into the shape of a woman. That was when I developed a crush on a guy I didn't think would be interested in me in a million years, while Gavin fell ever more deeply in love with the beautiful, popular, ever so perfect Evie.

I never mention her name now, not to Gavin, not to anyone.

Truth or Dare.

Truth Number One: Evie went missing.

Truth Number Two: she never came home.

12
WREN

THE STATE PATHOLOGY DEPARTMENT IN Dublin City morgue isn't a place anyone enjoys visiting, including the poor unfortunates who've lost their lives, often by unnatural means. I've been here several times, and the old adage that things get easier over time does not apply.

Lauren Bennet, the assistant state pathologist, is younger than her predecessor, but equally sharp. The first time I met her, I was taken aback by how slight she was, as if the white gown she wore was far too large for her. With short dark hair, and red-framed glasses, she's a no-nonsense, let-the-science-talk, fact-based voice of the dead.

As I stride towards a room equipped with mortuary tools, scales, buckets and stainless-steel sinks, my focus is simple. Find out as much as I can about the unidentified limb removed from the Dodder.

'Morning, Wren,' Lauren bellows, washing her hands at one of the sinks.

I take in the room, bracing myself. 'How come you always sound so cheerful?'

'I have a job that constantly reminds me how lucky I am.'

'That would do it,' I say, spotting the small shape hidden beneath a white sheet.

'Is that our victim?' I ask, walking towards the steel slab at the far end of the room.

'That's him all right.'

'So, it's definitely male.'

'No doubt about it.'

Lauren pulls back the sheet. I fight revulsion, breathing in the sterile smell of pathology – once inhaled, always familiar.

'The flesh on the bones,' she continues, 'tells me this young man hasn't been dead for long. Two to three days at most.'

'Young man?'

'I've based the age profile on the growth period of skin.'

'Which is?'

'Early twenties.'

'How did you determine the gender?'

'Muscle tone, and some other factors, all point to it being male, but the DNA analysis will confirm it.'

'The cut was clean, wasn't it?'

'Yes.'

'Any guesses as to the implement used?'

'I don't guess, Wren. I study and determine a range of probabilities.'

'Point taken,' I reply, but duly put in my place. 'What are the range of probabilities?'

'Large implement, sharp blade, something like a cleaver.'

'The kind used by a butcher?'

'Not necessarily, but similar in size and sharpness.'

'What else do you have?'

'The limb was severed post-mortem.'

'Why do you say that?'

'After death, the blood congeals in the body, pooling into the interstitial tissues, but always downwards. In layman terms, it drops to the lowest point. If someone is lying on their back, it will be found on the reverse of the corpse. If they're lying on their stomach, it'll be on the frontal area.'

'Go on.'

'In this case, the limb was severed after the body had already gone through this process.'

'What about rigor mortis?'

'What about it?'

'Had that already happened? Even with a sharp instrument, it must have been difficult to crop rigid body parts.'

'Yes, and yes. Generally, the entire body will become rigid within a few hours of death, but it wears off over time, making it more limp and pliable. This body part had already progressed to that point before the incisions were made, which is why the plastic found on the limb is important.'

'Okay?'

'Forensics have the plastics now, but even without knowledge of its existence, tiny remnants of them remained on the skin, two different types in fact, but quite clearly there.'

'And your thoughts?'

'Basically, the body was wrapped in plastic almost immediately after death. The plastic was then removed, and a second layer applied after the limb was severed.'

'Covering it initially in plastic would make it easier to move the victim from the crime scene.'

'That's your area of expertise, not mine, but based on the pathology, it seems reasonable to assume the body was wrapped and held somewhere until rigor mortis passed.'

'When the body was limp again?'

'Yes, and the task of severing individual parts became easier, which is where the second layer of plastic comes in.'

'How can you be so sure the body was wrapped immediately after death?'

'A body is rich pickings for flies and other insects, but in this case the tissue was perfectly intact.'

'So, someone moved extremely fast.'

'Yes.'

'Which also means they wanted to get the body away from the crime scene as quickly as possible.'

'Again, your area, not mine.'

'What about substances taken before death?'

'I can't be much help there, unless another body part turns up, ideally with the contents of the stomach and the intestines.'

Leaving the pathology department, several questions are uppermost in my mind. Who is our John Doe? Why did he end up dead? And who killed him?

13
NADINE

I PACE THE FLOOR IN THE BEDROOM. It's hours since I spoke to Gavin, when he revealed the true identity of the man who sniggered at me in Harold's Cross. Now that I know it was Ben Donnelly, it makes complete sense, especially since he knows about the Truth or Dare game.

Downstairs, I make myself a strong coffee, hoping the caffeine will kick in fast. I need to work out what this fresh information about Ben really means. He's obviously involved with the criminal underworld, and his career choice doesn't surprise me. Even as a teenager, he wasn't afraid to break the rules, and do things the rest of us would never have done.

I write Ben's name in the notebook I use for grocery lists, the one I used that first day during Becca's phone call.

My daughter's life is at stake.

I take two gulps of coffee, positive now that all of this has to be connected to my past, and with that, I've no choice but to think about something I've avoided since the scorching summer when Evie disappeared.

Almost immediately, I see her smiling face. She seems happy, as if she doesn't have a care in the world, her long blonde hair caught in a light summer breeze. I remember my desire to be her, to be that beautiful.

That year we had each completed our Leaving Certificate. Gavin and I were in the same class. He'd done transition year, and I didn't. Free from school, it felt like every day was the same, filled with endless blue skies and no need to do anything other than await our exam results. I never awoke expecting rain. It felt as if nothing bad could happen. I was wrong about that too.

Sometimes a few of us would take the bus to the beach at Sandymount, sitting upstairs at the back, loud and powerful in our small group, pretending the other passengers didn't matter. We saw ourselves as important, that tiny gang – it had formed a couple of years before, when Gavin was first dating Evie. I didn't know then that the group was a camouflage for him to be with her. I didn't know how strict her father was, and how she had to lie about seeing Gavin. I was simply happy to tag along, part of something because of my brother. He was considered cool, and I was considered harmless. The Truth or Dare game had started as a means to eat away at the hours of idleness, but it was Gavin who suggested we create our own Truth or Dare cards. I do remember that.

My mobile phone rings. I grab it, hoping more than anything it's Becca. Instead, I see Gavin's phone number. I don't want to talk to him. It isn't the early hours of the morning any more, which means he'll be more alert, more inquisitive. I can't risk telling him anything. I can't risk Becca's life. I let it ring out unanswered.

He was irritated earlier on, but beneath his annoyance, there was concern for me. A big brother is always a big brother, but I also know that after Evie disappeared he became a different Gavin. He learned not to trust anyone or anything, at least, not fully. He was unable to accept that sometimes things happen without an explanation, and when they do, the only way to survive is to move on.

Truth Number One: one day Evie was there and the next she was gone.

Truth Number Two: one day Becca was there and now she is gone too.

Is history repeating itself?

The muffled voice on the phone said he knew my secret: *Truth or Dare*. I imagine Ben laughing at me, as if I'm still the awkward teenager whom others put up with because of my brother, someone to be pitied, pushed around, someone they could scare.

The last game before Evie disappeared we'd made a makeshift picnic near the ruins of the Hell Fire Club after a hike in the mountains. Like everyone else, I was surprised when Evie said she was going to pick a Dare card. It wasn't like her. She always took Truth. When you're confident, you're never afraid of telling the truth.

The rules of the game were simple. If you picked a Truth card, you had to answer any question the group decided upon, both immediately and truthfully, but if you chose a Dare card, you had forty-eight hours to carry out the dare, which was determined by the wording on the card.

Evie's card read, *Do something you will always be remembered for.*

Afterwards, the others teased her about what she was going to do. She didn't share her plans with them, or with Gavin. I noticed something else about her that day. She wasn't her normal, upbeat, self-assured self. She was a quieter Evie, more like me, withdrawn and unsure. I thought about approaching her. I even imagined her taking me into her confidence, choosing me as the special one, someone she could trust, a close and true friend.

I used to observe the other girls in the group too. Studying them gave me clues as to how I should behave, dress, wear my hair, or how to say things. If I behaved like them, I might be accepted. I might be popular. I might be more like Evie.

When Evie disappeared, none of us spoke about the Truth or Dare game, not to our parents, our ex-teachers, the police or anyone else. Most thought Evie would return. Gavin clung to the belief that she would, but when it became obvious Evie was gone for good, the Truth or Dare game became a secret that bound us. Later that year, our parents didn't object when Gavin and I decided to defer our college places for a year. Looking back, I think they believed it would be good for us. Gavin escaped to Europe, but I escaped elsewhere.

I repeat the words in my head aloud: 'One day Evie was there and the next she was gone. One day Becca was there and now she is gone too.'

I bite my bottom lip. If it weren't for that muffled voice on the phone mentioning the Truth or Dare game, I might dismiss seeing Ben at that pickup point as a coincidence, but whoever has my daughter, I sense they're taking pleasure from scaring me, as if they already know my weaknesses, and despite the intervening years, forging a successful career, raising a daughter, they equally know that, deep down, I'm still a scared, awkward young girl.

I replay all the events since Becca's first phone call. The man with the muffled voice knows things about me, and his message is simple. There's nowhere for me to hide, because now they have the most precious part of my life, my daughter, and if I really love her, I will continue to do everything they ask.

14
WREN

Twelve officers, including myself, are gathered in the incident room. There's a heightened buzz of adrenalin, each of us aware that the first twenty-four hours of any investigation are critical, and in this case, based on the pathology findings, we've already lost time.

I stand at the top of the room, heading up the briefing. 'Okay, this is what we know.' I point to the first slide, an image of the severed limb.

'The arm removed from the water was cut using a large sharp implement, similar in size to a cleaver, or butcher's knife. It was severed at two points, below the shoulder blade and above the wrist. It's reasonable to assume the removal of the hand, and therefore, lack of fingerprints, may have been a tactic to ensure identification of the deceased is made more difficult. We know the victim is male, most likely in his early to mid-twenties. We believe the corpse was wrapped in plastic prior to the onset of rigor mortis, the arm severed when the body had passed that point. The body part was later wrapped for a second time, put into a bin bag with a large stone, and fired into the Dodder. At this stage we can neither rule out nor rule in a connection to the shooting in west Dublin. However, once a full DNA analysis is available, we'll be able look for a match on our PULSE database. We may get lucky, but equally, we may not. Fingerprints would have been invaluable to us because, as you know, even if our victim had a criminal record, DNA samples aren't taken from everyone. Also, our DNA database is relatively new, so we'll be in contact with Europol, our colleagues across the pond, and in the North.'

I flick to another slide, this time of the Dodder area. 'Canvassing is ongoing at the location and, if necessary, house-to-house will be extended. As mentioned, if this is connected to the gangland shooting in west Dublin, each of us knows the potential for tit-for-tat killings. Bottom line, involvement in the drug trade or organised crime means that if one of your lads gets hit you have to be seen to retaliate.'

'Are we looking at this as a professional hit?' Mike asks.

'The disposal of the body would have required a level of professionalism so, for now, it's a strong possibility. Hired killers are getting cheaper by the day. Five grand would get you a hitman in Dublin these days, maybe less. You might even get the job done for free if some of these guys apply the right pressure.'

I continue: 'Although the limb was severed post-mortem, we can't yet determine if the death was accidental or premeditated, but someone went to a lot of trouble to hide the identity of the victim, and has most likely placed body parts in multiple locations. Nor can we rule out the possibility that multiple suspects are involved. The dismembering of the body may have been done by someone with anatomical knowledge, but it's equally possible it was done by someone with a strong stomach and a large knife.'

The next slide is that of the plastic removed from the limb.

'Forensic examination of the plastic confirms its components are of a shedding variety, which fits with the pathology findings from the flesh. A second plastic residue was also found, but both plastics are commonplace and, therefore, impossible to pin down.'

I flick off the overhead projector.

'However, we know the Dodder is not the original crime scene. Someone removed the corpse to a place where they had seclusion, space and safety on their side. The amputated limb isn't telling us anything as yet about the cause of death, but with potentially multiple crime scenes, a huge number of man hours will be going into this one, dredging other parts of the Dodder, canvassing further up the riverbank, examining any potential crime scenes that may turn up, CCTV from private homes and public areas, and a bloody partridge in a pear tree.'

I sit down at the table.

'This investigation is as much about what we don't know, as what we do. We don't know who the victim is. We don't know how he died. We don't know where the original crime scene is, or who was involved in cutting up the body. It could be gangland related, but equally, it may not. Most unlawful deaths, as you know, are impulsive, happening after a situation has escalated out of control. For all we know this could have been a domestic situation gone wrong, and an otherwise law-abiding citizen turned killer. We don't have much, but my hunch is, once we know who the victim is, we can start building a clearer picture. The motive at this point is unknown too, but the severing of the body indicates a level of control and planning, so keep an open mind. It's our job to find out why this young man ended up dead.'

Mike raises his hand. 'Any word on the firearm from that hit in west Dublin?'

'The Lucan guys got lucky after a few more dips in the Dodder, but that side of things is being pursued by O'Keeffe. If there's a link to our John Doe, the telephone analysis of the Lucan victim's mobile phone may be critical. The data is being downloaded as we speak. For now, until we hear otherwise, I want you to assume we could be dealing with two unrelated killings. If that proves to be the case, then at least it reduces the risk of reprisals.'

'What about the media?' Mike asks.

'We're going to keep this low-key for now. You know what some of those guys on the street are like – they read newspapers the same way regular people read *Hello!* magazine. Let's not massage anyone's inflated ego until we know what we're dealing with.'

'If this turns out to be about turf,' Mike continues, 'what then?'

'Then, we could be in for a hell of a shit-storm, because it will certainly escalate, and if it does, others will get caught up in it.

There are no prizes for knowing what we're potentially dealing with here – violent people who will order a killing in the same breath as they order pizza. They've no respect for the law, for life, and certainly no respect for us, but this is the job we signed up to, so let's get on with it.'

15
NADINE

FOR THE REST OF THE DAY, I WAIT. I walk. I sit. I count. I empty cupboards, and when I'm weak with hunger, I eat, but still I hear nothing from Becca. The lack of contact is nearly worse than following their awful instructions, because the nothingness is filled with a whole host of fresh fears. Fear that I'm not handling this right, that I'm already too late, that right now, as I wait, terrible things are happening to my daughter. My biggest fear is not seeing Becca again. That alone is enough to push me to the edge.

Night descends, and finally I go to bed. I keep checking my phone, but there are no new calls or messages. I hear a car horn blare in the distance, the sound a relief from the silence. Afterwards, I lie awake for hours. I feel helpless. I was like this once before, and it nearly killed me.

I get out of bed, wrapping my arms tight around myself, angry that I haven't come up with a proper plan. I pick up my mobile phone. It's my only link to Becca and, as if on cue, it beeps, and the screen lights up.

I have a Facebook message.

My hopes lift.

It's from my daughter.

With fumbling fingers, I click it open.

Await further instructions – Truth or Dare.

The temporary euphoria disappears. I start to question myself again. What if I'd gone straight to the authorities? What if I hadn't done all the awful things asked of me, turning me into a criminal? The police might have been able to trace that message, identify a location and find Becca. It would have been an opportunity, a potential lead, a means of ending this nightmare, but as I'm thinking this, I'm also asking myself if the real reason I didn't go to the police wasn't to protect my daughter but, instead, to protect myself.

By morning, sharp rays of sunlight flood the bedroom. I tell myself there has to be a solution, and finally, somewhere in the deep crevices of my mind an outline takes shape.

I had considered going to the address in Harold's Cross again, where I first saw Ben Donnelly, but that would be too risky. If the voice on the phone is his, he wouldn't be happy with me taking matters into my own hands, and Becca might suffer because of it. I need to shift my attention to someone else from the group. Apart from Gavin, Ben, Evie and me, there were several others. I visualise that heart shape with Becca's name on the cubicle door in the pub in town, the one with her friend Henri's name engraved beside it. Henri's mother, Sophie, is now my fresh focus. She doesn't live far from here, and until Evie's disappearance she, more than any of the girls, was closest to her.

I pick up the mobile phone, feeling awkward contacting her after all this time. I haven't spoken to her since her daughter's death, but I can't allow awkwardness to get in the way. I tell myself *my* daughter is still alive. I have to cling to that belief.

∞

Sophie agrees to meet at Mount Jerome cemetery, the graveyard in Harold's Cross where Henri is buried. Straight away, the location feels far too personal, too close to her loss, but while I'm waiting for her to arrive, I can't help but wonder if it's her way of reminding me that I still have a daughter and she doesn't. Even as a teenager she was like that, initiating pity while scheming to get whatever she wanted. Like Evie and Ben, Sophie came from a far less affluent background than Gavin and me, but each of them had a form of hidden power, a kind of badge of honour. With Ben, it was his willingness to take risks, to do whatever it took, legal or otherwise. For Evie, it was her attractiveness, with a certain aloofness, as if only the lucky few ever got close to her. Sophie was the weakest, seeking sympathy but never admitting it. They all had a slight chip on their shoulder, especially Ben and Sophie, but Evie tried to pretend the difference in our social status didn't matter. Gavin never brought her home, though, and she must have wondered why.

Standing at the graveyard entrance, I feel a sharp chill. A breeze whips around the corner near the front gates. I pull up the collar of my coat in an effort to keep warm. I think about the rows of gravestones, the names engraved on them, the wide-open spaces, and the horrible finality of it all. I don't want to visit Becca here. A mother isn't supposed to bury a child.

In an attempt to distract myself, I stare at the women selling flowers, huddled together over to my right. I examine each of the made-up bouquets, some with sunflowers, bright and bold. Others have chrysanthemums of white and cerise pink. There are roses too, deep blood reds with canary yellows, and sprays of gypsophila interspersed. I've always liked gypsophila, its tiny white buds on fragile stems, so delicate, and capable of being crushed.

The women had looked at me when I first arrived, taking me for a potential punter, someone in need of flowers to cheer up a grave. When I didn't pay them any heed, they ignored me. I was no use to them, and I want to keep it that way.

I check my phone again. There hasn't been a message since the one from Becca's Facebook account. I worry Sophie mightn't turn up. The flower women with the gloved hands eagerly chat to one another, as I stare further up the road to the main Catholic church, St Paul of the Cross, where at eighteen I married Cian in a rush because of Becca. The wedding took place outside our local parish in Rathfarnham to avoid scandal. I visualise myself walking up the aisle, remembering every inch of that place, the wooden pews, the stained-glass windows with the stations of the cross, those large white pillars near the altar, and the dark confessional boxes. Three Hail Marys and four Our Fathers aren't going to cut it any more. The outside of the church looks like a miniature version of Notre Dame, purposely built to tell a community it was the seat of all power, extravagant, regal and controlling. I remember wishing I could run away, disappear, but I was too much of a coward for that.

Gavin tried to control things back then too. After Becca was born, it was because of him that everyone ganged up on me, including my father and mother, believing marrying Cian was the right thing to do. It was a tidy solution to a messy problem. It may not have been the seventies or eighties, but that didn't mean having a child outside wedlock, especially for our older parents, was okay. The only saving grace to them was that Cian was middle-class, and therefore deemed acceptable and suitable under the circumstances. Nothing was ever directly said, but everyone knew what was going down, including my brother, and I think Cian, for his part, liked the idea of a baby, the embodiment of himself.

I look up and down the street again. Two elderly women pass by. One nods in acknowledgement, blessing herself in the sign of the cross as they approach the graveyard entrance. I watch them grow smaller, walking into the distance, until I feel a hand on my shoulder.

I turn around.

'Hello, Nadine.'

I recognise her straight away, as the past slaps me in the face. She indicates I should follow her. We walk silently through the tall wrought-iron gates. I take in everything about her, the spidery lines around her eyes, her frame stick thin. She isn't as tall as I remember, and her hair is different too, cut into a dark, neat bob now, but other things remain the same. The way she holds herself, the familiar energy in her step, as if she is always in a hurry, and that tiny lift of hers, indicating confidence as she strives forward. I warn myself to be careful.

Soon, we reach the oldest section of the graveyard. There are tombstones in the shape of Celtic crosses and ornate heavenly angels.

Some sink sideways into the earth, no longer cared for by anyone. Further in, a funeral is taking place. I spot the two old ladies from earlier as a coffin is lowered into the ground. The breath of the mourners rises, like smoke signals, into what is now a dusky pink sky. Four men dressed in muddy boots and dark clothes grip the two thick straps suspending the coffin as it disappears. One moment you can see it, and the next, it's gone.

Nearing Henri's grave, my feet crunch on the gravelled path. I feel for Sophie's loss, but I can't afford to trust her. For all I know she might be connected to the man on the phone. And she knows about the Truth or Dare game.

'I lit a candle for your daughter,' I say.

'We lit candles for Evie too.' Her words are cold and unflinching. 'It didn't change a thing.'

I visualise the flickering flames in the tiny brass cups, wax dripping down the sides.

Sophie's bony fingers grip my arm. 'It's Becca, isn't it? She's in trouble.'

'Yes,' I say, desperate to trust someone. 'She got involved with the wrong kind.'

'Drugs?'

I nod.

'People in that game are capable of anything. They'll destroy her and take pleasure in it.'

I close my eyes tight.

'You're scared,' she says.

'Yes.'

'We were scared when Evie went missing too.'

Suddenly, I don't feel safe with her.

'After she disappeared,' Sophie's tone accusatory, 'everyone thought you knew far more than you let on.'

'I don't know what you're talking about.' I take a few steps backwards. I want her to go away. This was a mistake. Worrying so much about Becca has caused me to make a wrong move. She isn't going to help me. She never helped me in the past.

I turn my back on her, and walk away, slowly at first, then faster. The nursery rhyme 'Three Blind Mice' plays in my head. *Three blind mice. See how they run. They all run after the farmer's wife, who cut off their tails with a carving knife ...*

I put my hands over my ears, as if I can stop the sound. Soon I see the graveyard gates. Within minutes, I tell myself, I'll be out of here, and Sophie won't be able to scare me any more.

Passing the women with the flowers, I sprint in the direction of the car. I hear a shrilling noise, it's my mobile phone.

The shattered screen tells me it's another unidentified number.

I answer, still moving forward.

'Mum,' my little girl says, 'it's me, Becca.'

'Becca!' I screech down the line, fighting back tears, no longer caring about Sophie. 'Thank God you're alive. I was so worried.' I keep walking towards the car. I need privacy. I want to be able to talk to my daughter without others listening in. I can't trust strangers. I can't trust anyone.

My breathing is heavy, but my little girl is still alive, and the immediate surge of relief is overwhelming. 'I love you,' I say, suddenly desperate for her to hear it.

'I know,' she whispers.

I hear whimpering. Is she crying? God, she must be so scared, the same way she used to be as a child, especially if Cian lost his temper. That was when she needed her mother most, not her father, or Gavin, or her friends, but me.

'Becca, where are you?' I'm almost at the car. If she tells me where she is, I'll go straight there and take her home, no matter how dangerous it is.

'I don't know, Mum.'

I sense her fear again. I need to think. 'Tell me anything you can.' My voice is solid, firm, forceful. I bleep the car doors open. I get in, the phone still tight to my ear.

'I'm locked in a room,' she says. 'There are no windows. I get my food on a tray. They weren't going to let me call you, but then they changed their minds.'

'I'll try to trace the call. Maybe one of the ex-cops at work will help me.'

'You can't. It's a temporary phone and card. They'll destroy it as soon as I hang up.'

'Who will?'

'I don't know who they are.'

'How many, Becca? How many of them are there?'

'I can't be sure, two at least.'

'Have they hurt you?'

'No, but I need to tell you something.'

'What?' I ask, clenching the phone so tight to my ear that the tiny cracks on the screen tear my skin.

'I overheard them talking. They're going to send you a package.'

'What kind of package?'

'I don't know,' she cries, as if in fear of her life. 'I heard the woman say you'll understand what it means.'

'What woman?'

'I already told you, I don't know.'

I can't bear to hear how scared she is. I need to reassure her. 'I'll work something out. I promise you.'

'I have to go.'

'Stay talking.'

'I can't.'

The line goes dead.

I want to scream, loud crazy screams, but instead I wipe away my tears. I should pull myself together. Becca is alive. I have to hold on to that thought.

She said they're going to send me a package. The package might have some clues. It also means they still need me, and while I'm useful to them, Becca may also be safe. This could buy me time to work out what to do next.

In the car my mind goes into overdrive. Becca said there were two people. She's locked in a room. She doesn't know who they are, or where she is. I think about the break-in again, the one from weeks before. If it's connected, what were they looking for?

My phone bleeps a reminder of an appointment for the following day, but appointments don't matter any more. I can't think about anything other than Becca.

Arriving home, I see the note jutting from the letterbox. I pull it out even before I open the front door, hoping it might be some form of explanation for all of this. I'm irritated when I see Gavin's handwriting. He wants me to call him. I can't have him interfering. The last thing I need is an over-inquisitive ex-detective, especially one who won't take no for an answer. He could ruin everything.

I slam the front door. I crunch Gavin's note in my hand, ready to fire it into the wastepaper bin – but if I don't get in touch with him, he'll be even more suspicious that something isn't right. After all, I phoned him in the early hours of the morning asking questions about Ben. I ignored his earlier phone call, and now he's put a note in my door. He won't stop until I contact him. *Damn him.*

I dial his number, clearing my throat, attempting to sound as calm as possible if he answers.

The dial tone rings out. I wait, counting to ten. The call goes to voicemail. I hang up, relieved. He'll see I've called him. He'll know I've received the note, but now I've a reprieve, more time to pull my thoughts together.

I empty the mailbox, looking for the package Becca told me to expect – but there's nothing other than household bills and marketing flyers. Gavin's crunched note is still in my hand. Becca said there was a woman. I reopen it, studying his handwriting. It hasn't changed since school, tiny letters crammed close together on the page.

Is he concerned about me? Or is his keenness to get in touch because of Ben?

Ben was always part of those unanswered questions about Evie. Questions that still haunt Gavin. He was traumatised after she went missing, but he was also unwilling to share his pain with anyone, including me. I had felt left out, as if he didn't love me any more.

Because of that, days after Evie disappeared I began to study my brother. I kept wondering what, if anything, he knew, and if there were secrets about Evie that he was keeping from me. His moods became darker too, obsessed with this new and important puzzle, one he desperately needed to solve. That was probably why he became such a good detective, learning to ask questions most people didn't think of, directing their interest away from him, thereby avoiding any unnecessary attention on himself.

I pick up the phone, re-examining earlier messages from Becca, searching for clues. Some are from months before, but there isn't anything of significance. All I can do now is wait. When that package arrives, I'll understand more. I may even be able to figure out the motive behind all of this.

A fresh image of my daughter locked in a room forms in my mind. I try to shut it out, staring into the garden instead. The blades of grass seem taller now. I hear laughter, the loud happy shrieks of a teenage girl. The sun is shining too, almost blinding, and once more I'm transported back in time, to the summer Evie went missing. I remember how tanned she was from early July. There was a glow about her too, adding to her beauty.

Now, standing in a house I've lived in for years, it's as if the past collides with the present. I can't take my gaze from the window. The tall grass is becoming more unkempt, like uncombed hair swirling in the breeze, the tips of the blades a white grey, scorched by the sun, and then I smell the sea, because now I'm at Magheramore beach in Wicklow, and Evie is there too, like a ghost from another time. She's waving at me, wanting me to come close so she can tell me her secret.

I close my eyes to block out the image. I can't go back there. I won't.

Sophie said everyone thought I knew more than I was letting on. She was right about that. Others kept asking the same questions. Where did Evie go? How could someone be part of your life one minute and gone the next? Answers are often far easier to work out than most people might think. Disappearing isn't that difficult. I had to make someone disappear, and now no one can see them.

16
WREN

I SIT AT MY DESK SMOKING a pretend cigarette of rolled-up paper. I kicked the habit a few years back, but in moments of stress I try to trick my brain into believing this small comfort still exists. With the DNA results in on the severed limb, we've found zero on the PULSE database, and zero elsewhere too. The sample has been fed through missing-persons, but whoever our John Doe is, nobody is ringing alarm bells for his welfare, raising another question: why not?

If this were part of a turf war, chances are something would have bubbled over by now. There's no heat on the street, and the rumour mill is so quiet it's deafening.

I flick again through the report on dredging the river, another dead end, still hoping to find something, but it feels like we're still at square one. I've received the telephone data from the killing in west Dublin, but along with the silence on the streets, and the no-show on the PULSE database, there's nothing to link the two deaths. I exhale a pretend waft of smoke, as my attention is drawn to a commotion outside the office door.

Stepping into the corridor, I see Suzanne, a young, uniformed officer, struggling with a male teenager in a Canada Goose jacket. She has him in handcuffs, and he isn't happy.

'Settle down,' she tells him, 'there's a good lad,' trying to defuse his anger as she leads him down to the holding cells below. There isn't a pick on him, so he's no match for her.

Another uniformed officer, Larry, is taking stock of the merchandise next door. With pale skin and red hair, he always reminds me of a

Viking who accidentally travelled forward in time. Larry is the overly enthusiastic and talkative kind.

I scan the items on the table in the centre of the room. 'Where did all this come from?'

'His parents' house,' Larry replies, his tone dismissive and annoyed. I can tell something's bothering him.

I step further into the room. Amy, another uniformed officer, is writing down a full inventory of the goods, while Larry does the recitals.

'Louis Vuitton watch, worth two thousand euros, Louis Vuitton belt, worth another eight hundred and twenty-five, Gucci hat, no idea of value. Black Alexander McQueen runners, again no idea of value. Studded gold and silver Louis Vuitton runners, no precise valuation.'

He picks up one of four Rolexes. 'This little guy,' he says, 'is worth thirty big ones.'

'A lot of stuff there,' I interrupt.

'Honestly, boss,' Larry says, 'if we worked all the overtime going, we wouldn't be able to afford any of this.' This last comment reveals the real reason for his annoyance.

'You wouldn't want that guy's life expectancy, though, would you?'

'Still.'

'Still nothing, Larry.' I keep eye contact with him, aware how easy it is for a young cop to become cynical. 'Chances are, he won't even make it to his mid-twenties. Bloody life over – and, besides, how many damn pairs of expensive runners can you wear?'

'I know, but—'

'Stay human, Larry. No one's doubting the guy's doing some bad shit, but remember, on the street they groom them young. The dealers recognise easy targets. They see the kids out for hours on end, no one caring where they've been or what trouble they've been up to, not even the parents. Anyone caught up in the sorry mess of the Dublin drug scene seldom sees a happy-ever-after ending.'

As I'm walking away, my mind flips back to Evie Hunt. Eighteen years ago, at the time she went AWOL, it was a different Dublin.

There were fewer drugs, fewer firearms, and less intimidation. The odd murder investigation got national coverage, but that didn't mean ordinary people didn't get caught up things.

Back in my office, I open the file with the pathology photographs of the severed arm. Even if this guy's death is a standalone killing, death often follows death, and therefore, anyone, gang-related or otherwise, could be the next victim.

17
NADINE

THE FOLLOWING DAY I DON'T LEAVE the house in case the package arrives. They say the first twenty-four hours of an investigation are vital. I've already lost that time with my daughter, and now, more than ever, I know I can't go to the police. I'm in far too deep.

After Evie went missing, the police told us thousands of people disappear every year, but most, except for a tiny few, turn up. They told her parents not to worry, that teenagers were known to disappear for days on end, only later to be discovered staying with a friend. But we were her friends, and none of us knew where she'd gone.

Perhaps if we had mentioned the Truth or Dare game, things would have been different, but as time passed, we became more terrified we would get into trouble. If the police had known about it, they would probably have dismissed Evie's vanishing act as a teenage prank. Then later, when she didn't return, they would have turned their attention on us, examining everything in much greater detail.

I already know the package isn't going to arrive by mail today. The postman never comes after three o'clock. Instead someone, a stranger, could just walk up to the front door right now. Which is why I'm watching, hawk-like, as cars drive past the living-room window, especially the ones I don't recognise, including an ice-cream van that doesn't bother to stop.

What would I do if someone walked up to the front door? Would I open it and demand they tell me where my daughter is, or would I continue to play it safe, behaving as they want me to behave? My gut tells me the latter, but still I cling to the notion that I might soon be able to come up with another plan. I'm edgy, I know that. I could take a couple of Xanax, but they would only make me less alert.

I hear a car door slam outside. I move closer to the living-room window in time to catch a glimpse of someone, a man, heading towards the front door. I dart into the hall, still wondering what I'll do if it's someone delivering the package. The temptation to open the front door and face him down grows. Then I hear the loud knocks.

I freeze. What if he has a gun?

He calls out my name.

I can't move.

'Nadine,' he repeats, 'it's me, Gavin. Let me in.'

Why is he here? He could wreck everything.

'What do you want?' I shout.

There are more loud knocks, faster now, like heavy hammering. He's annoyed, but I don't want to open the door. 'Go away,' I say. 'I'm tired. I've taken a tablet.'

'Please, Nadine, open up. I'm worried about you.'

'Go away,' I say again.

'Nadine, open the damn door.' His voice is louder now. He's behaving like Cian, my ex-husband, bullying me. I won't have it. I won't allow it.

I hear his heavy breathing, but the knocking finally stops. Then he says, his voice softer, 'Are you all right? You're scaring me.'

'You don't need to worry. I'm fine.' My words sound assured, adamant. I can't have him asking me about Becca. I have to wait for that package. Once it arrives, I'll know more. I'll be able to work this out by myself.

'Nadine, please let me in.'

My mind darts from one decision to the next. If I let him in, he might go away again, especially if I tell him a load of lies. I know my brother. He's stubborn. Which also means if I don't open the door, if he doesn't have his spare key, he'll probably kick it in.

'All right,' I say. 'Wait a second.' I steady myself. I have to appear normal.

I open the door.

He pushes past me, so fast I don't have time to change my mind. 'I meant what I said, Nadine. I'm worried about you.'

'I told you, I'm fine.'

'What were you thinking of the other night, ringing me at five in the morning?'

'It's not important.'

'Something isn't right, Nadine. I know it. I've been calling Becca too. She isn't answering her phone.'

My mind goes straight into panic mode, but somehow I say, 'You know Becca. She falls off the radar whenever she chooses.'

'But she usually ...'

He wants to say she usually contacts him, the fabulous Uncle Gavin. Right from the beginning he's spoiled her rotten. In part, I liked it. It felt like family, but at other times, especially when Becca and I had had an argument, I hated the way she would run to him, twisting things, turning Gavin against me. Only this time she hadn't phoned him for help: she'd phoned me, her mother.

If Gavin discovers Becca's life's in danger, he'll do anything and everything to protect her, which also means he could mess things up, and that can't happen.

'Nadine,' he says, his tone overly caring, patronising, 'you've been acting very strange lately, especially since the break-in.'

'Nothing was taken, remember?' Why is he talking about that? It's not important. 'I told you, I'm fine. How many times do I have to say it?'

'Look,' he says, wrapping his hands around each of my arms. 'I feel responsible for you. Ever since Mum died, all I want to do is make sure you're okay.'

'You mean you need to fret about me. You need to keep an eye on anxious Nadine. You think I can't handle things. That's it, isn't it? But, you see, I do handle things. I handle my job, my life, myself, and I don't need you to be constantly bringing me down.'

'It's not like that. I'm concerned about you. That's all.'

'You always want to control things.'

He loosens his grip. My last comment hit a nerve. My brother doesn't like criticism. He never has, not even as a child. He takes it as a call to battle, to fight back, to make a stand. He learned this from all the punishments our father dished out to him. You either collapse under the strain of criticism or you increase your resolve.

In the silence that follows, my mind jumps back to the days following Evie's disappearance. *Do something you will always be remembered for*. It was because of Gavin that the group stopped meeting up. He decided we shouldn't do it any more, and no one argued with him.

Now, he's giving me one of his questioning glares. I know he's trying to work out what to do next. I want to tell him that after Evie went missing it was me, not him, who worked out the answers to all those difficult questions. I turned the Dare question upside down, asking why Evie didn't choose the Truth card: realising for her, it was far more terrifying than any dare.

Gavin has his hands on his hips now. Intermittently, he looks in my direction. I do the same thing, as if we're sword fighters about to take each other on. The silence remains. I won't fill the vacuum for him. I didn't ask him to come here. I didn't ask him to be concerned. If he wants to play big brother, that's his problem, not mine.

'I keep thinking about that phone call,' he says, 'when you asked about Ben Donnelly.'

'What about it?'

'Your version of events didn't add up. It felt like too much of a coincidence.'

'I told you. I accidentally crossed paths with him. I heard someone call out to him, and it was because he looked familiar that I became curious, nothing more.'

'Perhaps you read something about him in the newspapers, or online, and you began to imagine things.'

'Why would I do that?'

I look down at his hands. They're curled tight into fists. Something is bothering him. Is it Ben's old connection to Evie?

'Ben was part of our past,' I say, 'yours and mine.'

His expression tells me I've hit another sore point. I try to visualise Evie standing beside us. If she were here now, what would she think? And then, like before, I see her. She's whispering in Gavin's ear, the way she used to when the two of them were close, so close, it was as if they were one person, not two. I want her to look at me, to turn away from him, and when she does, her stare surprises me because she seems so content, happy. I envy her that, but soon her expression changes again. Now she's smirking, mocking me, and although the windows and doors of the house are closed, a breeze enters the hallway, and her long hair takes flight, the strands dancing in front of me, like tangled seaweed beneath the surface of the water.

Gavin moves forward, his body casting a shadow over mine. 'Nadine, I need you to tell me the truth.'

I don't want to answer him. I'm afraid I might say something I shouldn't. I feel his breath on my face. I ask, 'About what?'

'You supposedly seeing Ben by accident.'

'It's true. Why would I lie?'

'I don't know. You tell me.'

'There's nothing to tell.'

'You'll feel better, Nadine, if you come clean.'

'You can't know that. You can't see inside my head.'

'No, but I know you.'

He's trying to undermine me. He wants me to crumble, to tell him everything, but I won't.

He clenches his fists once more. 'Nadine, I know what's good for you.'

'You're not my husband or my father. You're my brother. You can't tell me what to do. It's not like before, when I was ...'

'Unwell? Is that what you're trying to say?'

'I'm different now.'

'I was afraid this would happen, especially after Mum's death – that you'd crack up again.'

I wish he'd stop meddling. 'How many times do I have to tell you? I'm perfectly fine.'

'I'm trying to help.'

My phone bleeps another reminder of that appointment. I delete it fast, hoping Gavin doesn't notice, but my brother never stops being the detective. He takes the phone from me. I panic, terrified he might find the Facebook message from Becca's account.

'What did you delete?' he asks, holding my phone high above his head, beyond my reach. It's his way of telling me he won't give it back until I tell him.

'A reminder of an appointment.'

'Was it a doctor's appointment?'

'That's none of your business.'

'I'm making it my business.'

I have to get him to leave. I need to work things out. I have to find a way to save my Becca.

'Nadine, listen to me.'

I put my hands over my ears, but he keeps on talking.

'The last time you stopped seeing the doctor, you got really sick.'

I press my hands closer to my ears, but still I can't shut him out.

'We don't want that happening again, do we?' He places the phone on the hall table.

'I'm a grown woman,' I say, 'I can do whatever I want. Besides, it's only a reminder, nothing more.'

'When are you due to see Dr Ward?'

'Tomorrow.'

'I'll go with you.'

'No, you won't. I'm going alone.'

'Do you plan on talking to her about Ben?'

'Why would I talk to a psychiatrist about him?'

'Because you may have imagined him.'

'Don't say that.' More than ever, I want him to stop talking, but

89

then I wonder if he knows more about Ben than he's saying. Perhaps he knows about the phone calls, the threats, even the gunman outside my house. Or maybe he's worried I'll find out something about Evie. She could be the woman Becca talked about on the phone. If she were, Ben being the caller would make sense.

'It's not good for you,' he says, 'bringing up all that old stuff.'

Is he threatening me?

I pull away from him.

'Nadine, I'm not the enemy.'

'No?' I look all around me wondering if Evie is still here, but I can't see her. 'I want you to leave,' I say. 'Now.'

I don't expect him to agree, but suddenly it's as if he's exhausted with me, as if he's spent far too much time arguing with his crazy sister.

At the front door, he stalls. 'Promise me you'll go to that appointment.'

'I promise,' I say, watching him close the door behind him. I think about everything he said to me. I think about the past too, and how, ever since that first phone call from Becca, I've known all of it, the threats, the break-in, even the man with the gun pointed at the house, is connected to Evie, to the things that happened years before, including the lies that were told, and the terrible secrets people couldn't bear to share.

Which was why, in the end, Evie had to disappear for good.

18
WREN

'DON'T OVERDO IT,' MIKE SAYS. 'You look wrecked.'

'I know, but this case is driving me nuts. No fresh leads, no ID, no original crime scene, no clear motive.'

'And no more body parts.'

'That too.'

'We could run through things again if you want.'

'Yeah,' I say, 'let's do that. I'm getting enough pressure from above to keep me here till tomorrow morning.'

Mike sits down on the opposite side of the desk. 'Right, what do we have?'

'We have gender, age and DNA profile, but his identity is still a mystery. Also, the latest pathology findings have identified traces of cocaine.'

'Which means the death must have occurred no more than a day or two before the limb turned up in the Dodder.'

'Correct.'

'What about alcohol?'

'It doesn't last any longer than ten to twelve hours in the blood.'

'Assuming, Wren, he'd had a cocktail of drugs and alcohol, the killing could be narrowed down to a thirty-six-hour window.'

'Meaning whoever cut up the body did so within a very short time-frame and, considering no other body parts have turned up, they did a good job of hiding them.'

'It was a fluke we found the arm in the first place. It would still be at the bottom of the Dodder had it not been for O'Keeffe's investigation.'

'The bin bag is a non-starter too. It could have been purchased at any store in the Republic.'

'With zero forensics found on it.'

'Giving us two possible scenarios: whoever dumped it wore gloves, or whatever evidence might have existed got eroded by the length of time in the water.'

'And the stone used to hold it down, Wren, was likely picked up at the scene. Again, nothing conclusive.'

'Which means the only gem we have, within all of this, is the CCTV footage, right?'

'Yeah. One concrete sighting, and the timing broadly fits with the pathology findings on time of death.'

'Let's look at it again.'

I wait as Mike loads the video on the monitor in the corner of the room. He presses the play button. The whole sequence is only five seconds long. We rewind it a few times, before finally freezing the screen on the dark figure by the riverbank.

'You can clearly see, Mike, they're carrying a heavy object.'

'It could be the bin bag with the limb.'

'What's your guess, male or female?'

'The footage isn't long enough to be sure.'

'I've looked at this so many times my head is dizzy. I keep willing that dark figure to turn around and face us.'

'Do you want to put it out in the public domain? See if it rings any bells? Even if the face isn't visible, someone might recognise how our perp is moving, their height or build. The timeline could be important too.'

'When's the next TV airing of *Crimecall*?'

'Late next week.'

'Okay, let's go with that.'

After he leaves, I rewind the tape a few more times, but still come up empty-handed. Technically, I'm done for the day, but I'm still not ready to go home. The sound of my mobile phone ringing distracts me. I pick it up, only half interested, before I recognise Gavin's phone number. We haven't spoken since we split up, after I found out he was fucking someone else.

'It's me,' he says.

I want to tell him he has some nerve, that the last person I want to talk to is him, but instead I say, 'To what do I owe the pleasure?'

'Don't be sarcastic. It doesn't suit you.'

'I was only asking a question.'

He doesn't say anything for a couple of seconds, but then he says, 'Look, Wren, something's happened.'

The tension in his voice knocks my bravado back a notch. 'What?'

'My niece, Becca,' his words tumbling into one another, 'I haven't been able to contact her.'

'Okay, Gavin, slow down.'

'I'm really worried.'

The cop in me goes straight into information mode. 'What age is she?'

'Eighteen.'

'Maybe she's staying with friends.'

'She isn't. I know she isn't.'

'When was your last contact?'

'About a week ago.'

'Gavin, you know the score when it comes to these things. A teenager going missing is par for the course. She'll probably turn up in a couple of days and you'll want to kill her for getting you so upset.'

'I don't need the official line.'

I hear the anger in his voice.

'I know my niece, Wren, and I'm concerned. I want to file a missing-person report.'

'You could have filed it with the desk sergeant.'

'I want to file it with you.'

This is exactly where I should transfer the call. If Meg were here, she'd be screaming at me to do just that, but the concern in his voice sways me.

'All right,' I say. 'Let me get a blank report on the screen.'

Two seconds later, I have one in front of me. 'You said her name was Becca. Is that short for Rebecca?'

'Yeah, but she goes by Becca.'

'Surname?'

'Campbell, Becca Campbell.'

'Next of kin?'

'That's my sister, Nadine Fitzmaurice, her mother. She kept her maiden name.'

I think about the anxious woman in the car park of Rathfarnham shopping centre. 'You say the last time you had contact with Becca was about a week ago?'

'Yeah, we spoke on the phone.'

'A week is ...'

'I know what you're going to say. A week is nothing.'

'Your words, Gavin, not mine.'

I wonder if he's being overly concerned because of what happened to Evie Hunt. She disappeared at eighteen too, and things like that never leave you. The latest online newspaper clipping I found has her parents telling reporters she might have gone to the UK, and that she'd probably contact them when she was ready. It seemed odd to me, their lack of concern, but then again, I see it every day in this job, parents abandoning their responsibilities. Still, it's weird they didn't keep up the pressure.

'When I try to call Becca,' Gavin says, 'it's like her phone is dead or out of coverage. It's not like her to be out of touch.'

'Sometimes people need time to themselves. They slip off the radar for a while.'

'I know all about slipping off the radar, and it's not that.'

'Why isn't her mother, the next of kin, filing the report?'

'My sister sees things slightly differently from me.'

'I see,' I say, even though I don't. I think again about Nadine. Was she anxious in the car park because of Becca? I scroll down the missing-person report. 'Is there any other reason, other than lack of contact, for your concern?'

'She's been hanging around with the wrong people.'

'Be more specific.'

'This is hard, Wren.'

'Take your time.'

'I guess she's no different from most kids her age, dabbling.'

'Dabbling?'

'Coke is king these days.'

'Is she an addict?'

'No, nothing like that. A user, yeah, but only recreational.'

'There's no such thing in my book.'

'Well, Wren, we can't all be as pure as you, can we?'

And there it is again, his rage, another reason we were doomed from the beginning.

'You said she was hanging out with the wrong people. Who, exactly?'

'I don't have names, but Becca didn't have much money, so my guess is someone was supplying her for free, and there's nothing free in this life.'

'A boyfriend?'

'I think so, but she was secretive about it, so I was naturally suspicious.'

'Sometimes it pays to be suspicious,' I say. It's a backward dig at him, but I don't care.

I move down the on-screen form again, thinking about all those months we were together, the intimacy, the many conversations long into the night, the secrets we shared – or, rather, I shared.

'What about medication?' I ask. 'Does Becca require any essential drugs or treatment?'

'No.'

'Does she have any physical illnesses, disability or mental-health problems?'

'Other than her mother, no.' He lets out a low laugh, slipping into the dark humour most of us in the force survive on.

'So, your sister isn't worried about Becca, but you are?'

'Something like that.'

'Do you have any reason to believe Becca might self-harm?'

'No.'

I think about the young girl we found in the flat last week. 'Potential suicide victims hide a lot, and if drugs are in the mix, people change.'

'It's not like that.'

'What makes you so sure?'

'I'm not, but my gut tells me it isn't that.'

'Has Becca ever done anything like this before?'

He pauses. 'Once or twice, but that was different.'

'How?'

'She always contacted me.'

'Not her mother?'

'No.'

'Why not?' I make a mental note to dig deeper into Nadine.

'Things were tricky for Becca at home. It's partly why she moved out a while back.'

'So, she lives elsewhere?'

'Yes.'

'Have you checked her place? Looked for any signs that she had plans to leave? Packed clothes, that kind of thing?'

'I'm not sure where she's living.'

'I thought she kept in contact?'

'She does – did – but I don't think she wanted me to know where she was hanging out.'

'Was she hiding something?'

I wait for an answer, but it doesn't come.

I move to the next segment of the form. 'In relation to her mother, Nadine, or any other family members for that matter, is there any history of conflict or abuse?'

'Becca and Nadine have their moments.'

'Moments?'

'Arguments, that kind of thing. My sister can be over-protective.'

'And Becca? Is she still at school, college?'

'She was an A student, but she didn't go to college.'

I hear the disappointment in his voice. It softens my resolve. 'It takes some kids time to work out what they want.'

'I'm telling you, Wren, something isn't right.'

'I'm not saying you're wrong. I'm just saying, keep an open mind. You know how these things can turn.'

'Okay,' he says, calmer now.

'Was Becca employed?'

'Nothing solid.'

'What was her last place of work?'

'The Tasty Deli in Crumlin shopping centre.'

'Did you contact them?'

'Yeah, but it was only casual work. Becca would call in every now and then to check on available hours.'

'When was the last time she was there?'

'Three weeks ago.'

'And you said you spoke to her after that?'

'Yes.'

'How did she sound? Was she chatty, evasive?'

'At times, she could bend the ear off you, but other times, it was like getting blood from a stone.'

'And the last time?'

'She told me she couldn't talk for long, that she was meeting someone. We only spoke for a couple of minutes, but she promised she'd ring me back.'

'I'm assuming she didn't.'

'No.'

'And that was unusual for her?'

'Yes.'

'Look, Gavin, other than the possible drug connection, there's nothing here setting off major alarm bells. You're an ex-cop. You know people fall off the radar all the time, especially if they need head space, and when it comes to—'

'Wren, I told you,' his voice agitated again, 'things weren't good for her at home. Becca and Nadine argued a lot.'

97

'That's all the more reason why she might need space.'

'Nadine can be highly strung.'

'Okay?' I say, wondering where this is heading.

'You heard about my mother's death?'

'Yeah. I'm sorry, Gavin. I probably should have called, but—'

'It doesn't matter,' he says, cutting me off, but I can tell it does. 'It affected my sister badly.'

'In what way?'

'This is hard,' he says, for the second time.

A few more seconds go by. I wait.

'My mother's death brought back some old emotional scars for Nadine,' he finally says.

'Bereavement can be difficult,' I reply, mindful that, despite all the years since my mother's death, I still grieve.

'You know what it's like, Wren, to lose a mother.'

'Yes, but for me it was a long time ago.'

'It doesn't change it, though, does it?'

'No, it doesn't.'

Suddenly, it feels as if we're being intimate again. I can't let him get inside my head. I need to keep my guard up. I return to the sanctuary of the missing-person report.

'Is there anything else you can tell me about Becca that might be useful?'

There's another silence.

'Not about Becca,' he finally says, 'but Nadine.'

'What?'

'She's been acting erratic lately.'

'How?'

'On edge. Highly strung.'

'Are you saying she might be involved in her daughter's disappearance?'

'I don't know what to think but, yes, perhaps.'

'Do you have anything solid to link Nadine to Becca being missing?'

'No.'

'Did you ask Nadine about it?'

'I told her I was worried.'

'And what did she say?'

'She said Becca falls off the radar whenever she chooses.'

'Look, Gavin, try to stop worrying. Becca will probably call you soon, and all of this will make sense.'

'I don't think so.'

'Do you have a recent photograph of her?'

'I can get that.'

'Great.'

I add the date and time to the end of the report. I should finish the call now.

'Wren,' he says, 'it's good talking to you again, even if the circumstances are—'

'It's my job.'

'But you didn't have to take the call.'

'No, I didn't.'

'I still like hearing your voice. It reminds me of old times.'

I need to end this – *now*.

'We'll keep you posted of any developments.' The use of 'we' pulls the conversation back to a professional level.

I hear a grunt at the end of the line. He's pissed off, his mood turning on a bloody pinhead.

I'm about to say something when the line goes dead. I know I shouldn't be bothered that he didn't say goodbye, but I am.

The cursor at the end of the missing-person report is flashing at risk assessment. I start typing.

- Missing person has a previous history of disappearing.
- There is little or no evidence of any crime having taken place.
- Possible drug dependency could be an influencing factor.
- Domestic issues at home may also play a role.
- Although Becca Campbell is not a minor, and appears to be in good health, her age, at 18, is nevertheless a consideration.

RISK: LOW TO MEDIUM

I close off the report, and five minutes later, it feels good to be outside. Although it's a long walk from the station in Rathfarnham to my apartment in Rathmines, the distance helps me to pull my thoughts together. I think about Gavin again, and how the timing of our relationship should have been a red-light warning, kicking off soon after he left the force. I should have known better than to hook up with a guy in the middle of a big life change. You risk becoming collateral damage, a form of temporary hold-up arrangement necessary for them to get through some bad shit.

Forty minutes later, I turn onto Rathmines Road. I see the copper dome of Mary Immaculate Church. It brings me back in time to when my mother was still alive. I think about my father too, and how, because of work, I haven't seen him in days, a thought that fills my heart with joy and trepidation in equal measure.

19
NADINE

THE NEXT MORNING THE PACKAGE is in the post-box. Whoever placed it there must have arrived in the middle of the night. It's wrapped in brown paper and held together with white string and a bow tied at the centre. I pull the bow open, and the paper falls back, exposing the contents. There are several items, but it's the photograph I'm drawn to first. It's proof my suspicions are well-founded, and that whoever has Becca could be trying to enact some form of revenge for the past.

I study the image carefully, one of our old gang, taken by a passer-by not long after school finished that year. Everyone is sitting on a low wall on the Leinster Road in Rathmines, smiling. Ben Donnelly is in the image, as are Gavin, Sophie and Evie, plus my ex-husband, Cian. I press my index finger over his face, covering it. I shiver. I don't want to think about him. I don't want to see myself as a victim any more but, no matter how hard I try, I can't silence his voice, and then I'm back there, reliving it again.

'Bitch,' he roared, as if I was some form of pariah.

I know why he hated me. It's because when he looked at me, battered, bloodied and bruised, I reminded him of the kind of man he was, and he detested himself for it nearly as much as he detested me.

I watched him step forward. I was too terrified to move. I stared at the wall lights either side of the fireplace. They appeared blurry after the last blow to my head. I could barely see, the swelling around my eyelids making it difficult to open them, but then, as I looked away, and my narrow line of vision was drawn to the fire. I spotted the hot poker in the flames, realising, too late, it was another weapon. If he wanted to, he could use it on me. I was already praying he wasn't thinking the same thing, but then I saw his hand reach down for it, sliding it out of the fire, as he caressed the brass handle furthest from the flames, turning it in his palm, like it was an extension of his arm. He was probably imagining how much pain he could inflict with it. He stared straight at me, and I already knew what he was going to do next. Grabbing me by the hair, he yelled, 'You want me to hurt you, don't you?'

He was doing what he always did, putting the blame on me.

'You like to feel pain, admit it.'

I saw the hot tip of the poker, red, bright, flaming, capable of burning deep. I closed my eyes tight, bracing myself, praying that if I tried hard enough, I could survive the surging pain one more time. One day I would get my chance to be free of him and be myself again.

The memory feels so real, it takes me a few seconds to remember, he isn't here. That I'm alone and he can't hurt me.

I stare down at the image again. My hands are trembling. I bring the photograph upstairs. On the bed, I stare at the group of teenagers trapped in time, still unaware of how life will turn out, especially me. When I can't bear to look at it any more, I turn it face down on the bedside locker. My fingertips touch my upper left arm, the mark of a burn, dulled now, but permanent, where once there was clear skin.

I don't expect to fall asleep, but somehow, exhaustion takes hold, and I do.

Much later, I awake to the sound of the electric timer switching on the heating system. I hear water gurgling in the pipes too. I sit up, startled. It's bright outside. How long have I slept? I remember the photograph on the locker, and the package downstairs. I check the time on my phone. It's already 10 a.m. If I'm not ready soon, I'll be late for my appointment with Dr Ward, and if I miss it, Gavin will be on my case again, asking all his awkward questions.

I shower and change, but just as I'm about to leave the house, I check the mobile phone once more. The disappointment of not seeing any new message is hard to bear. It felt better when they were giving me instructions, telling me what to do. At least then things were moving forward, edging towards the end game of Becca coming home.

I keep thinking how afraid she must be. I understand fear. The mark of the poker on my arm throbs as a reminder. I touch it, trying to smooth away the horror, but it never goes, not fully.

Outside the house, I look up and down the street, almost as if I expect someone to be watching me. In the car, I double-check, before turning on the engine, telling myself to play it cool, at least until I know exactly what's going on.

I drive on autopilot to the address. I've already decided I'm not going to share any of the information about Becca with Dr Ward. I can't take that chance. Even if she helped me to recover after Cian, I've only ever known her in a professional capacity. It's because of Gavin's nagging that I'm seeing her again, but he's wrong about my grief. A part of me is glad our mother is dead, not just because of the cancer and how much she suffered, but because sometimes, I wonder if she ever really loved me, or if perhaps she had only enough love for Gavin.

Nearing the city, I concentrate on my prospective meeting with Dr Ward. In the past she's been understanding about the mental and physical abuse I've gone through, but she can be tricky. She's caught me out before, especially when she manages to get information from me that I don't want to share. Today, for Becca's sake, I'll be extra careful.

I park the car on a side-lane near Baggot Street. I walk along the canal wall and cross the bridge, stopping halfway over. I stare down at the dark, murky water. I think of all the things hidden beneath the surface: discarded city rubbish, dead rodents, old car tyres, all invisible to the naked eye, much like the many lies we tell. None of us are completely honest with others. There's always a part of us we hide.

I begin walking again as hungry seagulls swoop above me. They want to feast on the leftover food of the office workers. Like the pigeons from our uncle's loft, I'm drawn to their flight, their freedom, their ability to weave in and out, flapping their wings so fast. Their speed protects them. I need to move fast too. Somehow, I must unravel this puzzle, because until I do, there's no hope for my daughter.

Nearing my destination, I see roadworks halfway down the street. I step out to avoid them, walking on the wooden planks that form a temporary footpath. They move with the weight of the people on them. I think about the canal water again, and how, during that last summer when Evie disappeared, I was changing too, and with those changes, I didn't understand how I should behave, being expected to be interested in boys, kissing and all that other stuff. Gavin joked at my innocence, but it was my innocence that got me into trouble.

Finally, I buzz the intercom to the side of the heavy front door, which is blue and shiny. I hear a voice from the intercom. I introduce myself. Then I hear the long buzzing sound. This is my cue to push the door open.

Inside, I walk towards the lift. I press the button to go up. The steel doors open and soon I'm inside. When the doors are closed, I push the first-floor button. There's a slight jolt. I hold my breath to the count of five, releasing the air slowly through my mouth in an effort to relax. When the doors open again, I check my phone for the last time. There are no messages from Becca. I turn it to silent.

I don't have to wait long. Soon Dr Ward is opening her office door and smiling in my direction. She turns her back to me, but the door is left open. This is my signal to follow her. I close the door behind me. I sit down. This is all routine. This is the easy bit.

'Hello, Nadine,' she says, pressing down the button on the top of her pen, ready to take notes. 'How are you?' She places emphasis on these last three words, her eyes oozing with sympathy.

'Good,' I say, a delaying tactic. My feet twitch, uneasy. If I weren't here, I could be in the car driving around Dublin, looking for Becca. It would be a long shot, but I might get lucky. You don't get lucky by doing nothing. In the true-crime series I watched on television last week, the pharmacist whose son was murdered didn't stop looking when the police gave up on finding the killer. He kept digging, ringing random numbers from the telephone directory late at night, searching for witnesses. He took on forces far more powerful than himself, initially because he lost his son but later because other teenagers were at risk. I wish I were more like him.

'Have you had any more flashbacks?' Dr Ward asks.

She isn't wasting any time. 'Some,' I say, my voice low.

'Are they like before, about your ex-husband?'

'Yes,' I reply, 'only ...'

'Only what?'

'They seem more real now.'

'In what way?'

'As if he's actually back.'

'Why do you think that is?'

She's doing it again. She's getting me to open up. Ask a direct question, and you get a direct answer. 'I thought I saw him in town the other day.' I'm already telling her too much.

'You thought?'

'He had his back to me.'

'So, you can't be sure it was him.'

'I was terrified. I ran as far away from him as I could.'

'But you didn't see his face?'

'No, but still. There are things about people you never forget.'

She makes a short note on the piece of paper in front of her. 'Has anything else frightened you lately?'

'Yes, other things have scared me.' I fix my hair behind my ears and straighten my back. My body feels stiff, as if I'm trying to appear strong, unbending.

'What things?'

'Things about Becca.' The words are out before I can stop myself. This is all wrong. Stop talking. 'I'm probably being overprotective,' I say, attempting a U-turn.

Frown lines appear on her forehead. 'Nadine, you look stressed, agitated.'

'Do I?'

'Have you been using the calming techniques we talked about, the deep breathing when you sense a panic attack coming on?'

'Yes.'

'What about regular exercise?'

I nod, lying.

She leans forward. 'I take it you're still keeping a record of any episodes of stress, writing things down as we agreed?'

'Things have been a bit difficult lately.'

'Is it pressure at work?'

'I've taken some time out.'

'Oh,' she says. 'Why is that?'

'You've told me before I should be careful not to become overwhelmed.'

'I see,' she says, folding her fingers into one another.

I look at the clock in the corner. We still have lots of time to fill. I could try to cut our meeting short, but if she's communicating with Gavin he'll get concerned again and interfere even more. I can't have that. My phone vibrates in my bag. I have to check it. 'Sorry,' I say, 'I need to look at my phone.'

She frowns again, disapproving. I can't afford to care. I key in my pin number, immediately seeing the Facebook message from Becca's account. It says: *Did you get the package?*

I want to answer straight away. I lift my head and stare at Dr Ward, before looking down again and typing *Yes*.

'Nadine,' she says, 'please put your phone away. It's not helping.'

I do as she asks, but I'm still on alert for another message.

'What about blackouts?'

'I lost a couple of hours the other day. I collapsed onto the kitchen floor, and when I came to, I didn't know how long I was out for.'

'Have you heard that rhyme again, the one about the three blind mice?'

I shake my head, lying, again.

'You often hear it when you're under stress.'

'Why are you bringing that up?'

'Because it ties in with your blackouts.'

'It just happened the once,' I protest, 'it may not even have been for long.'

'Only,' she says, 'you've a history of blackouts since your teenage years.'

I don't answer her.

She makes another note on the sheet of paper in front of her. 'And your medication, Nadine?'

'What about it?'

'Are you taking it?'

'Yes.' I lie for the third time, like Peter denying Christ. I look at the clock again. Another ten minutes have passed. This is a waste of time. Dr Ward isn't going to help me. I'm in this mess on my own.

She's studying me intensely now, as if I'm a creature requiring additional observation. I want to tell her about Evie, about how over the last few days there were times I thought about her too, but I can't. Nor can I tell her, or anyone else, what it was like all those years before, when I found her, and knew, more than anything, I needed to keep her secret safe, that we both needed to lie. At first, I was happy being her only friend, thinking I was special to her. I loved our long walks along Magheramore beach. I promised her that one day she would be able to leave. I would take care of everything. After all, I was the one who found her when the police couldn't.

Dr Ward is moving around the room. I remain silent.

'I'm concerned, Nadine, that you're not taking your medication correctly. You do understand that if you don't take the allocated amount, as prescribed, your stress levels will increase.'

I need her to believe I'm playing along. 'I understand,' I say. 'I promise I'll keep taking the medication.' I check the clock again. There is another twenty-five minutes to go.

She sits down opposite. 'Good,' she says, but I sense she doesn't trust me.

My phone vibrates again. It's another message. She holds my gaze. Again, I know she doesn't want me to answer it, but I have to.

'Sorry,' I say, grabbing the phone from my bag. I click open the message: *I sent you a few presents.* I think about the other items in the package, and heavy beads of sweat appear on my brow. It feels as if there's no air in the room. I stand up to leave. 'I have to go,' I say, insistent, anxious.

Dr Ward stands up too. She looks even more concerned. I have to convince her everything is okay. 'I promise you,' I repeat, 'I'll take the medication.'

'Perhaps, considering everything, Nadine, that is enough for today.'

I nod, relieved.

'Remember, if you take your prescription, it will help.'

I nod again.

'Let's set another appointment for next week.'

I key the allotted date and time into the phone, the one with the latest message from the people who've taken Becca. I don't put it back into my bag. Instead, I hold it tight.

Outside Dr Ward's office, I walk as fast as I can. I'm terrified she might call me back. When I reach the lift, I count again, letting out more long breaths through my mouth. Finally, I pull the front door closed. I walk out onto the stone steps and then, with relief, I'm heading back towards the car. I follow my earlier path in reverse, over the wooden planks, the canal bridge, again looking down at the water. The car isn't far away.

I press the button at the pedestrian lights. I wait to cross to the other side. I stare into the faces of strangers. They don't know my secrets. I can pass them by, and they'll simply see me as ordinary, mundane. They won't see a woman capable of doing terrible things.

It won't be long before I'm home. Once there, I can examine the items in the package again, including that photograph. There has to be some clues there.

The lights turn green. I cross the road, and it's only then I see her, the woman standing at the corner on the opposite side. She's wearing a cream raincoat, closed tight with a belt around her narrow waist. She has the same blonde hair. It's slightly shorter now, but as I stare at her, the wind catches the strands, sending them wild and free. Her green eyes hold my gaze – all-knowing. I think once more about our time together, how simple, precious and caring it was. Two young girls linked through tragedy, a dark secret, a lie, a truth no one could ever know.

The woman is further from me now. I tell myself this can't be happening. It's one thing imagining Evie in my kitchen, but this is different. This is the older Evie, real, alive, not imagined.

The seagulls flap above. *I sent you a few presents*, the message had said, as if the items were objects of affection, something between lovers, or from someone who cares.

A cyclist whizzes past. I almost lose my balance, and when I look back to where Evie was standing, she's already gone. For a second, I think I might actually be going mad, that Gavin is right, but I saw her with my own eyes. She was real. She was there. She was watching me.

I already know Evie's hairbrush is in the package. As I'm remembering this, I'm thinking about those tiny bristles smoothing her hair, just as I used to brush Becca's, and how, when I first found Evie, I became fascinated by how her body was growing larger by the day, with the new life forming inside her.

I also knew, once I discovered she was pregnant, that things would never be the same again.

20
WREN

MIKE AND I ARE ABOUT TO pull into a garage to grab some lunch when we pick up a call on the radio. An elderly man, living at 13 Lower Nutgrove Avenue in Rathfarnham, hasn't been seen in days.

'Let's take it,' I say.

'Are you sure? You don't work well on an empty stomach.'

'I'll be fine,' I reply, 'and, I promise you, we'll get lunch directly afterwards.'

With the siren blaring, we head towards the destination. The house is a few doors down from where Evie Hunt used to live. I hold back this piece of information from Mike. He doesn't need to know.

Ten minutes later we arrive at the rundown corporation house. From the moment we pull up outside, I don't have a good vibe. The outside of the house looks bleak, with the front garden overgrown. Our arrival immediately grabs the attention of some neighbours, coming out of their homes, curious.

We walk through the small gate at the front. The closer we get to the house, the more run-down the place appears, the paint peeling off the walls, the window frames rotten, all suffering years of neglect.

The postman had raised the alarm after days of mail built up in the letterbox. The old man, who lives in the house alone, didn't respond when the postman called out his name. At first, the postman put it down to the occupant being elderly, then wondered if he was asleep upstairs, but today he rang in his concerns.

We go through the usual motions, much like the postman probably did earlier on, including going around to the rear of the house to knock and peer through the windows. None of it results in a response. It's never good with an elderly person to kick a door in but sometimes you're left with no choice.

Mike obliges with three rapid kicks. The door opens easily, and as soon as we're in the hall, the waft of rot and damp hits us. Walking through, it feels as if we're intruding in someone's life, but still, we call out the old man's name.

'James, are you here?'

'James, it's the gardaí. Are you okay?'

The silence is eerie, and the bad feeling I had outside gains pace. My heart thumps in my chest as Mike and I work through the downstairs at speed. There's a small understairs toilet which is old and stained. The kitchen, to the front of the house, has stale bread opened on the counter. Finally, we reach the living room at the rear. We're aware every second wasted might be a second we can ill-afford to lose, but opening the living-room door, another stench blasts through. I see the old man lying beside the sofa. For a split second, Mike and I stop in our tracks. The odour of death is suffocating. We cover our nose and mouth. Once that smell gets into your nostrils, it takes days to leave. There's no point bending down and searching for a pulse, or any other indicator of life, because the flies are already attached to the body. The bluebottles usually arrive first, sometimes only minutes after death, eager to lay eggs in any orifice they can find.

'Fuck,' I say, angry, a million thoughts jumping around in my head. If only the postman had alerted us sooner. If only a neighbour, or a family member, had intervened. If only the old man wasn't living alone.

I hear Mike ringing the emergency services. The death doesn't look suspicious, as there are no visible signs of injury to the body, but nothing can be assumed. Looking around the room, I take in the dark green velvet sofa. It wouldn't look out of place on top of a skip, ripped, stained, and covered with cigarette burns. The heavy curtains in the room are pulled over. I imagine several days earlier, when the man possibly drew his last breath, how time might have stood still. Now, the echo of his life seems to be hovering in the room, and a part of me hopes he had some happiness in it.

Walking back into the kitchen, I study the remnants of the hardened bread covered with green mould. Beside it are an opened butter tub, and a jar of marmalade. On the floor, there's a knife covered with sweeps of butter. I think about him making his breakfast the day he died. Perhaps he got a horrendous pain in his chest and dropped the knife. He might have dragged himself into the living room to reach the telephone, but his heart gave up before he could call for help.

Suddenly I need fresh air.

Outside, more people are gathered around the house. I hear the siren of the ambulance in the distance, like us, already too late. A woman in her mid-fifties, in her dressing-gown, is smoking a cigarette. She catches my eye.

'Is he a goner?' she asks, without losing a beat.

'Yeah.'

'Terrible.' She shakes her head in dismay. 'He was a nice man. He never did no one any harm.'

'Terrible all right.'

'Second death on this road in weeks,' she says, unintentionally gaining my interest.

'Oh?'

She points to a house further up the street. 'Yeah, Nigel Hunt went the same way, alone.'

'What happened him?'

'He drank too much.'

'I see.'

'And he wasn't a good person.'

'No?'

'People around here thought that was why his daughter up and left.'

'Evie?'

'Yeah, that's her,' she replies, looking surprised I know the name.

'Tell me about her.'

'A gorgeous young thing she was, as pretty as a summer's day.' She glances back towards the old man's house. 'But it was a long time ago.'

'Eighteen years.'

She nods.

'And the mother?'

'She died of a broken heart.'

'Why do you say that?'

'Her daughter never came back.' She walks over to another neighbour, no doubt to share the news about the old man.

Seconds later, Mike and I cordon off the area, just in case the death isn't of natural causes. After the body is removed from the house, neither of us has any appetite.

Instead, we return to the station. In my head, I repeat the woman's words: *as pretty as a summer's day*. It felt weird someone else mentioning Evie Hunt's name. It was almost as if it were some form of encrypted message, one willing me to ask more questions.

Is it a coincidence that Evie went missing at eighteen, and now Becca is missing too?

I'd told Gavin to stop worrying, but I doubt he paid much attention to that. We both know the score. You can't work as a cop and not be aware of the dark choices some teenagers make. The suicide attempts, successful or otherwise, are testament to that. If someone is desperate enough, especially if they feel vulnerable, life can become awfully bleak far too quickly.

Was that what happened to Evie Hunt? Was her neighbour correct? Did she disappear to escape her father? Or were other forces at play?

The last question hangs in the air. That's the thing about the unknown. Sometimes, it can turn out to be something none of us expects.

21
NADINE

ONCE I REACH HOME, I MAKE sure all the doors and windows are securely locked. Seeing Evie has really spooked me. It confirms my worst fear that she may have taken Becca, and that the one thing I've dreaded for so long is happening.

I pull the curtains closed, ensuring the house is in darkness. I don't want anyone peering in. I need to be alone with the contents of the package. Any or all of it could be a means of finding Becca.

I grab the notebook. Dr Ward was right. I should be writing things down, keeping a record of everything that's happening. How else can I know what might be useful in the future? I record seeing Evie today, along with the words from the Facebook message, talking about the package. I also write down everything I remember about my last conversation with Becca. Then, I examine the hairbrush, turning it in my hand, the way Cian once turned that hot poker.

Evie wasn't supposed to return. She was supposed to disappear for good, just like Cian. Neither of them should be part of my life, but I'm absolutely sure, Evie wanted me to see her today. It was her way of sending me a message: that she can get as close as she wants.

I stare at the hairbrush, thinking again about the break-in. What if Evie is connected to that too? I reread some of the words in the notebook. Becca had said I wasn't to tell anyone. She said she was being held by at least two people, one a woman. Everything in the package is connected to Evie. I cannot deny it any longer. Evie has Becca. She has taken my little girl.

I underline Ben's name. He always liked Evie. It wouldn't have been difficult to convince him to help her. He wouldn't have been able to say no, possibly making Evie the ringmaster in all of this, with Ben doing her dirty work.

I hear loud thuds at the front door. I don't answer it. Whoever it is will soon go away. The thuds repeat themselves. I edge closer to the door. Could it be Evie? Could she have followed me home? Maybe she wants to explain herself. Maybe she wants to give Becca back to me.

The banging continues, relentless. What if Aria hears it and gets suspicious again? She might even call the police.

My hand clutches the door handle and I open the door, gasping.

'You took your time,' he says.

I try to push the door shut again. I don't want him here.

'I thought I'd pay you a visit in person, Nadine.'

Every single part of my body is trembling. 'Why?' I plead, my voice so low I can barely hear it.

'You know *why*.'

I shake my head.

He steps further into the hallway. I hate him being inside my house. He should be at a distance, the way I saw him in Harold's Cross, with the little girl and the My Little Pony backpack, but now he's closing the door behind him.

'Are you ...?' I ask, unable to finish my sentence.

'Am I what?'

'Are you the voice on the phone?'

'Maybe I am, Nadine,' he sneers. 'I can be whoever you want me to be.'

'Gavin knows all about you,' I say, accusing, 'all the things you've done, criminal things.'

'Good to hear your brother is taking such an interest.'

'You always hated him.'

'He didn't deserve her,' he says, as if that explains everything.

'Who?' I ask, even though I know the answer.

'Evie. Gavin never cared about her, not really, not the way I did.'

'Evie disappeared,' I say, 'and she never came back.'

'We both know that's not true.'

I shake my head again, but it's a waste of time. He knows everything, because Evie must have told him.

'You weren't at the funeral,' he says, accusing.

'What funeral? What are you talking about?'

He looks at me as if I'm stupid, the way people used to look at me before, thinking I didn't understand things, that I was odd, and unimportant, but I showed them. I proved them all wrong. As I'm thinking this, the fear and anger inside me suddenly erupts. I lunge at him and within seconds my hands are at his throat.

At first, he's taken aback. He didn't expect this, the fighter in me, but then he grabs my wrists, tight, pulling my hands away, relishing his ability to hurt me so easily. I'm no threat to him.

'Evie noticed you weren't there,' he says, as if judging me again, 'and that hurt her, you not going to her father's funeral.'

'I hardly knew the man,' I say, trying to pull back from him.

He lets go of my wrists.

I tell myself to calm down. I need to get any information I can out of him. I have to find out what Evie wants.

He picks up a silver carriage clock from the hall table, as if he might smash it, but instead, he places it back in its original place. He's wearing gloves. He's come prepared.

A flashback of Evie's father comes into view, standing in the doorway of their house, his face unshaven, wearing dark trousers and a white string vest. I still remember how his eyes would follow her as she walked away, as if she were one of his possessions, something he was unwilling to lose.

I stare at Ben. 'Why did you come here?'

'Because Evie sent me.'

'What does she want?'

'She asked me to give you a message.'

'What?'

'She says she wants everything you took from her, and for you to pay for the harm you've done.'

'I don't understand.'

'Don't play stupid, Nadine.'

Neither of us says anything for a few moments, but he's right. We both know what Evie means. She wants what's rightly hers, and she wants her revenge.

He walks towards the door, and, opening it, he adds, 'We'll be in touch with more instructions soon.'

'Please,' I beg him, 'tell me where Becca is.'

'Not yet.'

'When?'

'When we say so.'

I hate the control and power he has over me, but I can't risk angering him.

'Nadine.'

'Yes?'

'I want you to be clear about something.'

'Yes?'

'I will kill you, if I have to, and I'll make sure you never see your precious Becca again.'

'Wait!' He can't leave now. He has to tell me more, but he's already outside, his body getting smaller, the distance between us lengthening with each new stride he takes, and soon, like Evie, I can't see him any more.

Finally, I close the front door. I walk back towards the kitchen, towards the package, the one with all the answers.

I pick up the hairbrush and run it through my hair.

Ben will kill me, if he has to, and he'll make sure I never see my precious Becca again. I write his words in my notebook. I write down the fact that Evie's father is dead, and therefore, with him gone, she will soon come after me.

22
WREN

BY THE TIME MY SHIFT FINISHES, I'm wrecked. The old man's death is still on my mind. I decide to make a phone call to the nursing home where my father is staying.

'Hi, Wren,' says one of the night nurses, whose name is Chloë.

'How's he doing?'

'He's okay, but he was a little distressed earlier on.'

'Why?'

'He may need his medication adjusted. This afternoon he was convinced someone was trying to break into his room. It was nonsense, of course, but that doesn't mean it wasn't upsetting for him.'

'Why didn't someone call me?'

'He settled down quite quickly. There was no need to worry you.'

'Can I see him now?'

'I'm afraid not, he's resting. Why don't you ring in the morning? If there's any change during the night, I promise you I'll be in touch.'

'Okay,' I say, ending the call, feeling even more restless than before.

I phone Meg.

'Hiya,' she says, 'how are things?'

'My dad had another episode.'

'I'm sorry, Wren.'

'Me too, but he's sleeping now.'

'Do you want me to come over?'

'No, I've an early start tomorrow.'

'Look, don't worry, Wren. Like the other times, it will pass.'

'Another Groundhog Day.'

'It probably upsets you more than it upsets him.'

'Do you think?'

'You said yourself he's sleeping. In the morning he'll have forgotten all about it.'

'You're probably right.'

'I am.'

'What are you up to?'

'Nothing much, reading my horoscope online.'

'Anything good?'

'It seems the love of my life is getting ever closer.' She laughs.

'I thought that was me,' I joke back.

'You're no use for cuddling up in bed, or anything else for that matter.'

'Point taken. What does mine say?'

'Expect the unexpected.'

'Great. More drama. That's all I need.'

'If you want to save the world, Wren, there's always a price to pay.'

When I hang up, the strain of a long day finally catches up with me. Maybe Meg is right, maybe I do keep trying to save the world, but sometimes, like today, the world has other ideas, and when it does, it's damn exhausting. Tomorrow, I promise myself, no matter what else happens, I'll visit my dad. I imagine him asleep in his bed, oblivious to what happened earlier on, and for that, at least, I'm grateful.

23
NADINE

IT'S DARK BY THE TIME I BUILD UP the courage to take the rusty key out of the package. I'll need to scrape it clean. I already know Evie wants me to use it. This is part of her plan, but it may lead me to where Becca is being held, so I can't ignore it.

My mobile phone rings.

I grab it fast.

It's another unidentified number.

'Hello,' I say.

'Mum?' she replies.

The relief of hearing my daughter's voice is overwhelming, 'Oh, God, are you okay?' It's such a stupid question. How can she be okay? Nothing is okay any more. 'Becca, listen to me. You have to tell me everything you can about that woman.'

'She's saying terrible things about you.'

'Don't listen to her.'

'You know who she is, don't you?'

'Yes.'

'I want to come home,' she pleads.

I can't bear to hear her so distressed. 'I want you home too, sweetheart.'

'I'm scared, Mum. I don't understand what's going on.'

'We'll work this out,' I say, trying to sound reassuring.

'It's all my fault, isn't it? If I hadn't killed ...' Her voice breaks.

'You can't be thinking about that now.'

I hear more sobbing.

'Becca, please don't cry.'

'Mum, I don't have much time, a few seconds at most. I just wanted to tell you that I love you, no matter what that woman is saying.'

'Listen to me, she can't be trusted. Do you hear me?'

Before I can say another word, the line goes dead. I've lost her all over again.

I need to think fast. Right now, I tell myself, the most important thing is that my daughter is still alive. If Evie, or whoever else is involved, wanted her dead, they would have killed her by now.

I won't delay things any longer.

Upstairs, I walk into the en-suite bathroom and wash my face with cold water. I ignore the medication in the cabinet. I can't risk becoming drowsy. Downstairs, I put the key from the package into my handbag. Whatever doubts I have about going to the address, I push them aside. I need to do this. I have no other choice.

∞

Outside, on the footpath, I take in the quietness of the neighbour-hood, the ordinary life I once hoped for. With the moon clear in the sky, there's barely a sound in the street. This time, getting into the car, I don't bother to check if anyone is watching. Whatever stupid game Evie is playing, I know she isn't going to prevent me going to that address. She wants me to go there. She wants me to relive the past, our past.

In less than five minutes, I'm on the M50. The traffic is light at this hour, so I whizz past each of the exits, aiming for the N11, heading for Wicklow and then Magheramore beach. If I'm right about the key, and it belongs to the room we once shared, the last time I stepped inside that house I was younger than Becca is now.

My mobile phone rings again. In my anxiety to check the call, I sway between lanes. When I steady the car, I realise it's Gavin. He'll want to know about my appointment. He'll be wondering why I haven't been in touch. I let it ring out. It rings again, and again, but still I ignore it.

Within forty minutes, I'm off the motorway, driving down the R750 towards my destination, and the row of houses, tight together, by the beach. Instinctively, it feels strange being here again, as if the younger me is returning to her past, only she no longer exists.

If it weren't for Becca being held against her will, I could have kept this place safely locked away in memory. I can't do that any longer, no matter how much I want to avoid going back there.

Soon the road narrows even more. I think about my seventeen-year-old self, taking that bus from Dublin, and all the plans I made staring out the window, and how afterwards it was so easy to get my parents to believe the lies I told them. After Gavin decided to take a year out before going to college, and work abroad, it didn't take a lot to bring my parents onside about me getting a job in Wicklow for a few months, especially as I had already found somewhere to live. They thought it was a good move for me, seeking to be more independent. They didn't know Evie was part of my plan.

When, finally, I reach the street with the tight row of houses, the one I'm looking for is boarded up. I slow the car down the closer I get to it, nervous, unsure of what I'm about to find.

After parking the car, I walk with a false bravado towards my destination, trying to convince myself this isn't going to be as dangerous as it might turn out to be.

At the front gate, I hesitate for a second. The place looks dark, ominous, empty. Could Becca be here? Could this be the end of the nightmare?

I count the steps towards the front door, remembering the younger me, far braver than I feel right now. I look at the key I'm holding tight in my hand. What if I'm wrong about this? What if this is a trap?

I attempt to turn the key in the lock. At first, it seems not to fit. I panic, but then it moves clockwise. I hear the click of the lock releasing, and within seconds I'm inside.

The front door opens into a darkened hallway, barely lit by the moon outside. Everything smells old, damp and uncared for. I look at the floor, recognising the marbled tiles with their ornate pattern of red swirls. Their familiarity causes me to pause, conjuring up so many lost memories.

The stench of damp and decay becomes more potent the longer I stand in the hallway, my senses elevated. I check the door behind me. It's now closed tight. I'm still clutching the key. I use the torch from my mobile phone to beam light towards the staircase, a staircase that is willing me to climb upwards.

I pause on the first step. 'Becca, are you here?' My voice echoes back at me. I call out again, but there's no response.

The house is three storeys high, and the room I'm looking for is on the top floor. Once I reach the upper landing, I pause once more, recalling myself standing in the exact same spot years before, and how happy I felt being part of this secret life, becoming Evie's closest friend.

I look towards the door of her old room. I imagine knocking on it the way I used to, and how I would hear her voice asking who was there, sensing her relief when I told her it was me.

This time, at the door, I don't knock. Instead, I turn the handle, still desperately hoping I might find Becca inside, feeling the chill of the doorknob against my sweaty palm. I half expect it to be locked, but then it moves freely, and the door creaks open.

Something brushes past my feet. I jerk back, shining the torch down just in time to see a rat scurrying beneath a hole in the floorboards. The whole place is probably infested. I take another step forward. A rotten floorboard gives way beneath me. My foot is caught. I panic again, but somehow, I pull it free. I can't feel any pain, although there's blood oozing from my ankle.

I could still leave, get out of here and no one would ever know I came, but suddenly, it's as if there's a stronger person inside me, someone who isn't afraid, a person who will do whatever it takes to get her daughter back.

I step inside the room. I call out for Becca again, but all I hear is the sound of my breathing.

There's no furniture in the small flat any more, but still I imagine myself being here years before, the place that became Evie's world, where we shared our secrets, and her bump grew larger by the day, and how stupid I was, failing to understand that the life growing inside her would soon change my life too.

I stare at the small window looking out to the sea. The wooden frame is rotten, falling apart like the rest of the house, as fragments of the past linger, gently echoing old sounds, a teenage girl's chatter, Evie asleep in her bed with me by her side.

I shine the torch around the room, the light darting back and forth, as the happy sounds become something darker.

I hear those horrible screams, so high-pitched I have to put my hands over my ears, urging them to stop. There's blood everywhere. I'm more terrified than I've ever been in my whole life, and then I see the ghost of my old self, my hands covered with Evie's blood, as she screams out for help.

24
NADINE

DRIVING BACK TO DUBLIN, I FIND it hard to concentrate on the road, my mind constantly returning to that room. But other memories are flooding back too, things I haven't thought about in years, as if the time in between doesn't matter. All that matters are the terrible things I've done, and even though I've tried hard to put it all behind me, it will always be there. This is exactly what Evie wants. She sent me to that room to force me to revisit everything.

On the M50, nearing Exit 9, there are more roadworks. The coloured lights from the machinery are blinding. I hear diggers, loud, repetitive drilling into the earth, and soon I'm thinking about that body in the garden again, and how I imagined I saw Cian in town the other day. I might not have seen his face, but that doesn't mean it wasn't him, because, in truth, I can't be sure about anything any more, which is why, twenty minutes from home, I make the decision to bring this part of the nightmare to an end. I know what I have to do next.

Opening the front door of the house, my breathing is becoming increasingly difficult. The shortness of breath, which always happens just before a full-blown panic attack, is getting worse. I've learned this tell-tale sign and others over the years, including how sometimes, afterwards, my mind shuts down, and there's nothing but blankness. Only now I can't let a potential attack get in the way. I'm more resolute than ever to end these doubts about Cian.

I bring my mobile phone out to the garden, needing the torchlight to carry out my next task. I can't take the chance of switching on the security light because the bright light would leave me exposed, and even though it's late, it might alert Aria, or others.

I take in a wide view of the neighbouring houses, making sure each house is in darkness. There isn't a light anywhere.

I remove a shovel from the garden shed. At first, the top layer with the pebbles is difficult to shift, but gradually, the shovel seems to go into the ground easier, the clay softening below. It will take time, but all I need to do is create a deep enough hole to reach even part of the skeleton.

Soon, my clothes are blackened with soil. If anyone saw me, they would think I was mad, but I don't care. I have to keep going.

The hole is larger now, and I'm guessing I don't have to dig much further, so I abandon the shovel, and remove the soil with my fingers. The moist earth feels cool against my skin, and after all the terrible things that have happened, it feels good to be doing something that will give me answers.

Some of my fingernails break from the digging, each laden with compressed soil, but all I care about is confirming that the body exists, that I didn't imagine killing my ex-husband and that, unlike Evie, he can't harm me any more.

When my mobile phone rings, at first it's an annoyance, an unnecessary disturbance, but then I think about Becca, so I have to pick it up. I see Gavin's number. *Damn him.* I try to lower the volume and shut out the noise, but my fingers can't manage the controls. They're stiff and cold from being in the ground. What if it alerts the neighbours? I have to answer him.

'Nadine, what's going on?'

'Nothing,' I reply.

'Your neighbour, Aria, phoned me.' His voice is angry. 'She says you're in the back garden. Jesus, Nadine, it's the middle of the bloody night.'

I stare up at Aria's bedroom window. The lower part is open, the lace curtain flapping in the breeze. I can't see her, but that doesn't mean she isn't there. 'You don't need to worry, Gavin, everything is fine.'

'No, it isn't fucking fine. I'm coming over.'

'Don't.'

The phone goes dead. I don't want him finding me like this. My brother doesn't like unsolved mysteries. That was why he became a cop – he needs to solve things, get answers. He's been that way ever since Evie disappeared, making it his mission in life never to be fooled again.

I don't know what to do next, so for a few seconds, I do nothing, suddenly exhausted, as if the emotion and physical movement of the last few hours have finally hit home. Only I have to try to put the soil back. Maybe it's not too late. Maybe I can still make everything all right.

Gavin lives no more than fifteen minutes away. My hands move frantically, but they can't work fast enough. I grab the shovel instead, trying to heave as much of the soil back into the ground as I can. I'm more panicked with each passing second, and then I hear his car pulling up out front, followed by the alarm being switched on, bleep, bleep, bleep. I'm not going to be able to get all the soil back in time. I want to cry in frustration. If only I had another ten minutes. The pressure feels overwhelming. If Gavin sees the dug-up soil, he'll push me until he gets answers, and I risk losing my resolve over Becca, and possibly saying far too much, telling him about the threats, the sighting of Cian in town and, worst of all, that Evie has come back.

I think about shutting down completely. I could curl up into a ball and never say another word again. I mightn't have to think about the past then, or Becca, or the bones buried in the soil, because I could let Gavin control everything. He does these things far better than me. I might not even be blamed. People would say, *Poor Nadine, she isn't well. She was unwell before, and even though she tried very hard to get better, it all became too much for her.* I can't do that, though: if I crack now, and my daughter were to suffer because of me, I know there will be no coming back from the madness, not for a second time.

Gavin is ringing the doorbell. In the rush to get here, he must have forgotten his spare key. The sound feels relentless, as if it's happening in some terrible dream, one I can't wake up from. I try to pull myself up from the ground, but my body won't move. I hear him call out my name, over and over. He's going to wake the whole neighbourhood. I try to speak, but nothing will come out of my mouth. I'm already too late. The panic attack has taken hold.

Soon, the ringing sound is replaced by *thump, thump, thump* – Gavin is at the side entrance of the house. He's at the wooden gate, trying to break it down. I imagine his body thrusting against it, the pain giving him relief against fear of the unknown, unsure what he'll find once he gets to the other side. Fear can push you. Fear can make you do terrible things.

My once cold hands are sweating, my breathing increasingly difficult as the pain in my chest grows. I search for an object to concentrate on. I stare at my mobile phone, the only link to Becca, as I attempt to push away all the horrible thoughts. I need to pull myself back from the edge. If I don't, I may not be able to move or speak for hours.

I hear an almighty crash. Gavin has broken through the gate. Lights go on in the surrounding houses. I can barely see his shape running towards me, but I already know the bulky frame is his. I expect him to grab me, to recognise the signs of my panic attack, being familiar with how my body reacts, but he stops about a metre away, shining a large torch in my face. I try to bring up my arms to block out the sharpness of the light, but I can't. Instead, I study his face in shadow, the blinding rays of the torchlight blackening everything that isn't in its path. He's trying to work out what to do next. His head turns from side to side, taking in everything about the scene, including the soil. The remaining heaps of earth look like miniature sandcastles. He pulls the torchlight away, illuminating the shovel, now abandoned beside me. More lights go on in the neighbouring houses. I still can't move. He darts the torchlight back and forth from one spot to another, finally settling on my face. I can't work out if he's angry or sad, but then his hand reaches down to grab mine.

I see my blackened fists and broken nails being gripped by his larger, cleaner, big-brother hands, and I sense he isn't angry now.

His movements slow down, his words are soft, as if he's trying to appease me, encouraging me to trust him, because he'll make everything okay.

When I get to my feet, he puts a reassuring arm around me. With the other arm, he waves in the direction of Aria's bedroom window, telling her he's got everything under control, and she has no need to worry.

I don't say a word. I let him lead me into the house like an injured animal. He escorts me to the bathroom, where I wash my hands, scrubbing my nails clean, hoping I can wash all of it away. Soon, we're in the living room, where it's warmer, only now my body begins to rattle as if it's freezing. I can't stop shaking. He takes a blanket off the couch and wraps it around me, before sitting on one of the opposite armchairs.

'Stay there,' he instructs after a few minutes, standing up again and walking towards the kitchen. I hear him switch on the kettle. He's going to make tea. For some reason, my ability to work out this small detail feels like an achievement.

'A cup of tea solves everything,' I whisper to myself. 'I'll get Becca back. Gavin will figure something out, and soon this nightmare will be over.'

When he returns to the living room, he hands me the hot tea. He doesn't say a word as I sip it. It's laced with something strong, brandy or whiskey – I can't tell which. My brother is the one breathing heavily now. He's biding his time. When I put down the teacup, he pulls his chair closer to me.

'Nadine, I'm worried.'

I stare at him, but I say nothing.

He takes my hands, cupping them in his. 'I haven't been able to reach Becca.' His tone is tinged with a hint of terror.

I find my voice. 'Becca is fine.' My words don't sound right. They're high-pitched, strained, the voice of someone trying too hard to be believed. I shiver again. I take my hands from his, pulling the blanket tighter around me.

Gavin keeps talking. 'I still haven't been able to reach her.' He scans my face, looking for a reaction.

What if I told him everything? Would he believe me? I would be taking a huge risk. This is Gavin, after all. Once he gets his teeth into something, he doesn't stop until he's unearthed everything and knows the truth. But the truth is useless if something happens to Becca. Telling him will put her life in more danger.

'You know what she's like,' I say, 'disappearing for days at a time.'

He doesn't take his eyes off me.

I keep talking, rambling. 'And when you least expect it, she'll turn up as if nothing has happened.'

I know he doesn't believe me.

'I don't think so,' he says, 'not this time.' His words are emphatic, all-knowing. Does he know Becca was taken?

'Nadine, you know more than you're telling me.'

I shake my head.

'I've spoken to Aria. She made a report to the police this evening about the screams she heard coming from this house the other day.'

'That was nothing. She made a mistake.'

'And then tonight, when she saw you in the garden, she rang me.'

'I told you. Becca is fine.'

'So why can no one contact her? When she went AWOL in the past, she always let me know she was okay.'

I shake my head again.

'Did you have another argument with her?'

'Stop twisting things.'

'I'm not twisting anything.'

I stare at him. Seconds pass.

'Why were you in the garden, Nadine, digging up soil? Why did Aria hear screams?'

'I've already told you that was nothing. She was mistaken.'

He places his face in his hands, rubbing hard, as if struggling under the strain of it all, before locking eyes with me again.

'Listen to me,' he says, his words slow, but firm, assuming the voice of an ex-detective, of someone capable of getting answers out of others. 'I've tried to reach everyone who knows Becca. *No one* has seen her.'

I should tell him about the phone calls, only I can't. I promised my daughter I wouldn't risk her life again.

He stands up, agitated, pacing the living room. I count his steps, but all the while, my stomach is churning with the alcohol-fuelled tea.

'I had to take action, Nadine,' he says matter-of-factly.

What's he talking about?

'People don't go missing without an explanation.'

'Yes, they do,' I insist, terrified he's still going to interfere. 'People go missing all the time.'

He keeps pacing the floor. I've lost count of the number of steps he's taken.

'You have to admit, Nadine, you've been acting odd lately, dragging up the past, missing your appointments.'

'I went to my appointment,' I say. 'I saw Dr Ward. I can show you the entry in my phone.'

He breathes in deep, his chest expanding. 'So, explain that stunt outside. What were you doing out there?'

'I thought ...' I want to explain, but I can't.

'You didn't leave me any other choice,' he says.

'Choice about what?'

'I had to contact the police.'

Everything stops. Even Gavin stops moving, locked in position. I repeat his words inside my head, about him contacting the police. I feel an immediate sense of terror and betrayal. I think about Aria too. Why did she have to make that phone call? I told her it was nothing, but now there's no way I can deny being in the back garden, digging up soil. There's no reasonable explanation for that. Gavin probably knows I haven't been taking my medication. Dr Ward might have told him, but even if she didn't, he would have worked it out by now.

I hear police sirens. I imagine a squad car pulling up outside. Surely Gavin doesn't think I've harmed Becca. Surely he can't think that. He must know I love her. Becca is my world, my life, but as I stare at him, I see the truth in his eyes. He believes I'm capable of doing something that terrible, of harming her, and that his sister, when he puts all the pieces together, has quite possibly lost her mind, because anyone looking at the facts would think the same thing.

Somehow, I tell myself, I have to convince him he's wrong, that I'm not the enemy, but as I'm thinking this, I hear footsteps in the hallway, and no words will come out, no matter how hard I try. The silence between us scares me, reminding me again of when we were children and we had to stay quiet because we didn't want to upset our parents. I used to think Gavin was my protector, but now I'm not so sure.

I hear more movement in the hallway, and then a female voice. She sounds as if she's giving instructions. If the police are already in the house, then Gavin must have left the front door unlocked.

The living-room door opens. I see the female detective, the one who stopped my car in Rathfarnham shopping centre. The same male detective is beside her. He's older than she is. She gives me one of those looks, the kind that offers pity. Gavin looks at her too. Their eyes meet. I know my brother well, and I can tell immediately, there's history between the two of them, something intimate. But the exchange tells me something else too. They both believe I'm capable of doing something terrible, which might result in them finding Becca's body buried in the garden.

'I didn't harm her,' I say, finding my voice.

The female detective walks towards me. She touches my elbow. It feels delicate, caring. 'We just want to be sure Becca is okay.'

I want to believe her, so I listen intently as she tells me that it's best if I accompany her to the station.

I nod because, right now, I don't have any other option.

Gavin's eyes are fixed on me again. I see a mix of disappointment and fear, and something else: shame. I see it in how his eyes are bulging, and how he turns away when I return his stare. He lowers his voice, talking to that female detective. He's wondering how it all came to this. He wondered the same thing when Evie disappeared.

The female detective is now standing beside me. She reaches out her hand again, this time guiding me upwards, encouraging me to move forward. It's such an ordinary, simple act that, for the briefest moment, I wonder if all of them are right, if I have gone mad, and everything that's happened of late is nothing more than a lie.

25
NADINE

GAVIN SITS SILENTLY BESIDE ME in the rear seat of the squad car. As it pulls away, the male detective, Mike, and the female detective, Wren, are quiet too. I know their names because I've listened to their conversations. I stare back at the house. The exterior security light is now on, and out front, men and women are putting on white protective clothing. I want to tell Gavin it's all a big mistake, that it's ridiculous, and if they dig up that back garden, they won't find anything, but I already know that isn't true.

He stares out the window, trying to ignore me. He spoke to the female detective several times before we left, intimate, private conversations. I heard him apologising to her too, saying he was sorry for contacting her, as he knew her shift was over for the night. They could be old work colleagues, but I've an inkling their relationship is, or was, something more. Right now, their silence allows me to think. I replay all the facts in my mind.

They were able to get a search warrant, and I need to figure out why. I understand some of these things from Gavin. Becca being missing for a week isn't nearly enough, but when you consider her age, it has a bearing. Still, the icing on the cake is probably my previous psychiatric history, and that, coupled with a neighbour hearing screams from the house, is certainly damning. The likely clincher, though, was finding me in the garden in the middle of the night, digging. This tells them they're dealing with a person on the edge, a woman capable of anything, and very soon they'll have another reason to suspect me.

We turn the corner onto the next street. I can't see the house or garden. Strangely, I feel calmer now – as if out of sight is out of mind.

'You're wrong,' I say to Gavin. 'Even if myself and Becca argued, I would never harm her. Just because you *think* you know things doesn't mean you do.'

'I know what she told me,' he whispers in my ear, his secrecy an indirect warning to be quiet.

'What did she tell you?'

'This isn't the place,' he says, annoyed.

I can't let it go. 'What did Becca say?' I tug at his shirt, eyeballing him the way I used to when we were children, and we played that staring game, the first to blink being the loser. Yet another childhood game to keep out of our parents' way. Gavin to avoid another beating from our father, and me because I wanted love and attention from someone, even if it was only my brother.

He leans in closer, still not wanting others to hear. 'She said your behaviour was suffocating, constantly asking questions, and that your damn obsessiveness became unbearable. She couldn't put up with it any more.'

'I didn't harm her,' I say, defiant. 'I wouldn't.'

He goes into lockdown mode again. The only way I'll get through to him is if I tell him everything. There's no other way. If I don't, he'll keep jumping to conclusions, and one way or another that, too, could place Becca in danger. For all I know, Evie and Ben might already believe I'm the one who alerted the police, which could mess up everything.

I turn his face towards mine. His eyes dart to the two police officers in the front seat, as if in warning, then back to me.

'What?'

'You're right, Gavin. Becca was, and is, in danger. Someone has taken her.'

He shakes his head, his face contorting, enraged.

I have to make him believe me. 'I've been receiving phone calls,' I say, 'threats, bad people wanting me to do bad things. That's why I was asking you about Ben Donnelly. I saw him after I collected that first package.'

'What package?'

The female detective, Wren, turns towards us, then glances at her partner.

I can't stop now. I need Gavin to believe me. After all, I'm not under arrest. If I were, someone would have read me my Miranda rights, mentioning my right to silence, and that anything I say may be taken down in writing and used in evidence against me.

'I had to pick up two packages,' I say, my voice energised now. 'It was their way of testing me, to see if I was willing to do what they wanted, but it didn't stop there, because then Ben came to the house, threatening that if I didn't follow instructions I may never see Becca again.'

I can tell Gavin thinks I'm crazy. It all sounds so far-fetched, something a person could only make up, but I need to keep trying.

'There's other stuff too, Gavin.'

'Stop it, Nadine.'

'I realise now,' I say, almost pleading, 'I should have told you before. I should have been upfront with you from the beginning, after that first phone call from Becca, when I realised she was in such deep trouble, but Becca said I wasn't to tell anyone. Don't you see? I couldn't put her life in danger.'

The squad car pulls up outside the police station in Rathfarnham.

'Who are *they*, Nadine?' Gavin asks.

'Ben, and ...' I pause, unsure how he'll react if I tell him about Evie.

'Who else, Nadine?'

'Evie is back,' I blurt out. 'I know this is hard for you to believe, but she is. I saw her the other day. And I know she's behind all of this.'

He reaches for the car door, ready to open it. 'I'm not listening to any more of this crap.' Every muscle in his body is tight with rage. He thinks I'm lying. He thinks I'm crazy. 'You shouldn't have stopped taking your medication, Nadine. You're unwell, and as for Becca, I pray to God I'm not too late.'

'No, no. You don't understand.'

'Stop it. You're only making things worse.'

'It's all Evie's fault.'

'Evie left. She never came back, remember?'

I pull at his sleeve, desperate for him to stay in the squad car. 'She was here for her father's funeral,' I tell him, and it's only then I remember the hand-delivered package. 'I can prove it,' I say. 'Evie sent me a package with an old photograph of our group. She sent me a hairbrush too, and a key. They're all in the house. The police will find them. They can examine the package, can't they? They can pick up Evie's DNA from the hairbrush, and that would be proof, wouldn't it?'

Gavin pulls away, this time opening the car door and slamming it behind him.

'It's okay, Nadine,' Wren says. 'We'll look for the package.' She sounds reassuring, comforting, but I know she doesn't believe me either.

I step out of the squad car. The male detective, Mike, walks in front, with Wren close behind. Gavin is already inside the station, probably still furious. He's blaming me for everything, but when they find that hairbrush, he'll know I'm not lying, and if I'm telling him the truth about that, then maybe he'll believe I'm telling the truth about the other stuff too.

Right now, he's in denial. He doesn't want to acknowledge to himself, especially after all this time, that Evie is back, because if he does, he also has to face the biggest question of all: why Evie left the boy who loved her with all his heart.

26
WREN

'I'M SORRY FOR DRAGGING YOU into this, Mike,' I say, 'I know your shift was over too.'

'Don't worry, my latest true-crime series is set on record.'

'I've told Gavin to stay at the front desk. I don't think he's impressed.'

'It will do him good to stew for a while.'

'Maybe, but either way, I've a feeling we'll get more out of Nadine with him at a safe distance.'

'You're probably right.'

'What do you make of her?'

'I'm not sure, but His Highness at the front desk seems to think he's calling the shots. As soon as we arrived at the house, he wanted to negate anything his sister was saying. I don't trust him.'

Mike isn't a fan of Gavin, and it's not just because he did the dirt on me. It's because Mike always marked him as a *mé féiner*, an expression my grandmother used, talking about people who thought much more about themselves than others.

'She was in some state, though, Mike, wasn't she?'

'Yeah, but I still don't believe a word out of that guy's mouth.'

Mike's rebuttal isn't surprising, but he also has a point. It felt strange seeing Gavin in this new setting, his sister stooped over in the living room, and him awkwardly keeping his distance, as if he was ashamed of her. With that came a warning. There would be very little straightforward about any of this, especially considering the undeniable friction between the siblings. It was almost as if there were years of untold truths hanging in the air, and neither of them was capable of communicating with the other without excess baggage.

'Before we question her, Mike, let's go over a few things, beginning with that conversation in the car.'

'She seemed pretty absolute that something has happened to her daughter.'

'But it was Gavin who filed the missing-person report,' I say, thinking aloud, 'and now Nadine claims Becca's been taken against her will.'

'It could be just ramblings, Wren, especially if her mental state is in doubt. And then there's the screams heard from the house.'

'I'd like to talk with that neighbour, Aria Jackson. I want to get a full handle on her statement. I'd also like to talk to Nadine's shrink. This is uncharted territory, and anything Nadine says right now will have to be taken with a health warning.'

'Not to mention the domestic issues between her and Becca.'

'But no matter what way you look at it, Mike, a woman digging up the back garden with her bare hands in the middle of the night isn't normal.'

'What do you think about this panic-attack angle?'

'It fits with her mental health being under pressure.'

'Yeah, but up to now, she seems to have been doing fine.'

'People snap, Mike. It happens all the time. They think they're coping, until they're not. According to Gavin, she's had episodes of emotional stress throughout her life, including panic attacks, blackouts, as well as crippling depression. It's all been there since her teens, including societal withdrawal and delusional thoughts.'

'Making it difficult for her to separate fantasy from reality.'

'This will be a tricky one.'

'Are you still sure about the excavation, Wren? We could use geophysics and quantitative means to examine the soil before the guys dig down any further?'

'With the earth already disturbed, there's very little point. Besides, the sooner we know what's down there, the better.'

'Okay.'

'Mike, one last thing: I need you to phone through to the forensics team. I want to make sure they look at that package, the one Nadine spoke about in the car, with the hairbrush and the other stuff.'

'On it.'

'Okay, then. Let's do this.'

27
NADINE

THE FEMALE DETECTIVE, WREN, HAS A quizzical look on her face as she enters with the other detective. In the bright lights of the interview room, I see how attractive she is, but it isn't only that. I also realise she looks like Evie. There's something about her eyes. If she and Gavin were an item at some point, was that why Gavin was drawn to her? I think about the police back at my house, searching for clues, strangers pulling my life apart, and also that recently dug-up soil. A familiar terror takes hold because I know what they'll find.

Wren assures me again I'm not under arrest. 'All we want to do,' she says, 'is establish the facts.'

I nod.

'Would you prefer to have someone else with you, a doctor perhaps, someone who might help you through this?'

I shake my head. I don't want Dr Ward here. She could undermine me, casting doubt on everything I say.

Wren wants to record the interview. I've no objection to that. I want the police onside. When they find that hairbrush, all of this will make more sense.

I clear my throat, readying myself for questions. If it weren't for the body in the garden, the police intervention might be a good thing. After all, on my own, I wasn't getting any closer to finding Becca, or convincing Evie or Ben to let her go. But when they find Cian, which very soon they will, they'll know I'm capable of murder.

My eyes dart around the room. I see a small camera positioned high in the corner. It's probably there to record the interview, to record me. I also notice the red panic button on the wall, and briefly consider pressing it. I don't.

Wren gives me another comforting look, attempting to put me at ease. I remind myself that she doesn't really care about me. She has a job to do. She might say she cares about Becca's safety, but that's only in so far as she wants to solve a potential crime, not in the way a mother cares for a daughter.

Now she has a questioning expression, similar to the one Gavin sometimes wears, only different. It appears kinder, more open, but I can't afford to trust her. I may not be a detective, but I know enough from Gavin about police interviews to understand that, initially, it can be beneficial if they appear kind and supportive to potential suspects. That way, they trick the interviewee into saying something they might soon regret.

Wren and the second detective are facing me now.

'Do you want some water, Nadine?' Wren asks.

'Yes, thank you.'

It's the male detective who fetches it from the cooler in the corner. I take the paper cup into my hand and drink a little.

'Let me formally introduce myself,' she says. 'I'm Detective Sergeant Wren Moore, and my colleague here is Mike Windward.'

There's something in her appearance that reminds me of my mother too. Perhaps it's her facial features: the narrow nose, the perfectly positioned eyes, a form of classic beauty. After Evie's disappearance, I recall studying an old photograph of my mother, one taken in her early twenties. The physical similarities between her and Evie were uncanny. And I'd wondered if that was why Gavin fell for her. They say men fall for a version of their mother, don't they?

Suddenly I'm annoyed at myself for thinking about stupid stuff. This isn't the time for rambling.

'Nadine,' Wren says, attempting to get my attention.

I take another drop of water. It feels like a protection of sorts, a delaying tactic. I tell myself I can still walk out of here. Wren said I wasn't under arrest. You hear about it all the time, people who've done terrible crimes being released without charge.

She switches on the recorder, noting her name, the name of her fellow detective, and mine, along with the date, place and time. I wait for her first question.

'When was the last time you saw Becca?'

It's a simple one, but with everything that's happened of late, it's hard to grasp a proper timeline. 'I'm not sure, a couple of weeks ago, maybe more.'

'Take your time, Nadine. It's important we get this information right.'

I close my eyes to concentrate, but then I think about Becca being held against her will, and how she isn't able to contact me. My mobile phone is in a metal tray with my other personal possessions, way beyond my reach.

'Are you all right, Nadine?' Wren asks.

I open my eyes and stare at her. I want to scream, *Of course I'm not all right! My daughter's in danger. How can anything be all right?*

'I'm worried about Becca,' I say. 'I want her home, safe.'

'We understand. We want that too.'

'Do you? Do you have any idea what it's like to know the person you love most in the world is in danger?'

'I would probably feel the same as you do, Nadine. I would be frightened and anxious.'

'I'm anxious, yes, and afraid.'

Her face softens. I want to believe there's still a chance I can convince this detective someone has taken Becca, and that her disappearance has nothing to do with me. It would feel good to have another person onside, someone prepared to listen, but the self-protective voice inside my head reminds me again to be careful. I look away from her, and down at the floor instead. She may be trying to lead me on, pretending she cares, the same way Evie pretended, when all the time she was using me. She was never fond of me. She was never my friend, not in the real sense. All she cared about was herself.

'Nadine,' Wren interrupts, 'you were trying to work out when you last saw Becca.'

'I'm pretty sure it was three weeks ago.'

'And how did that go?'

'We had an argument.'

'About?'

I shrug my shoulders.

'It's important you give us as many details as you can. You want us to find Becca, don't you?'

'Yes.'

'Then help us.'

She's right. Even if it's a long shot, I have to talk to them.

'She said I was smothering her,' I say, my voice too loud, 'but I'm a mother, I worry. Any mother would do the same thing. I mean, when a child gets older, and you see them out in the world, it can be difficult. Everything is easier when you're able to put them safely in bed at night and you know they're okay. The world can be a scary place, especially for young girls. One wrong move and they could find themselves in big trouble.'

I think about what Cian did to me before we were married, when I was younger than Becca is now. That night, he filled me with so much alcohol that I thought he was being romantic, kissing me with such passion, putting his hands all over my body. I felt special, loved, but soon he wanted more, becoming rougher, and then I couldn't breathe. I thought I might black out. I tried to pull away but that enraged him. He told me to shut the hell up, and something that had felt loving became horrible. Afterwards he said he was sorry, that he hadn't known it was my first time. It would be better next time. He walked me home and kissed me on the forehead. I fooled myself into believing things would be okay. It took me years to name what he did to me, to understand it was rape.

'Was Becca in trouble?' Wren asks.

I don't want to answer her. I don't want to betray my daughter. I can't tell them she killed someone, so instead I say, 'She was hanging out with some people she shouldn't have been.'

'What kind of people?'

'The wrong kind.'

'How were they wrong?'

I hesitate. 'The kind who sell drugs.'

'Do you have names, contacts Becca might have developed?'

'No, but after my daughter lost her friend, Henri, Henrietta, I got suspicious Henri might have been a user, even though Becca said it was her first time. After Henri died, Becca changed. Her moods became difficult. We argued even more. I told her I wouldn't tolerate any form of drug use.'

'And what did she say?'

'She told me to mind my own business, but I was worried. I mean, a mother knows these things.'

Wren looks to the other detective, a non-verbal cue, and most likely they're thinking if drugs are definitely in the mix, perhaps that's why Becca went AWOL, and this whole thing could be a waste of time.

I think about what I said to Gavin, about people going missing all the time. I know it, and they know it too.

I feel an immediate need to defend my daughter, to say lots of young people try out all kind of substances. It was Henri's death that was the trigger. Becca, for all her bravado, could be emotional. I read about that once, how certain people have a thin emotional skin, meaning they need to put up barriers to protect themselves from being hurt.

'Did you ever give Becca money to support her habit?'

My mind flips back to the break-in at the house, and how, at first, I'd thought Becca was responsible, but then later, she called to see me, and asked me directly for money. I refused, trying to show tough love.

'No,' I say.

'When was the last time you saw Becca with these people? The people you thought were supplying her?'

'I can't remember,' I say, keeping it vague.

I see disbelief on their faces. Gavin has probably told them I'm an overbearing mother, and even though he hasn't said it directly to me, I know what he's thinking. That I did something awful to her. He's wrong. I love her too much.

'Nadine,' Wren continues, 'being completely honest with us is important, especially if, as you say, your daughter has been taken and is in danger.'

She's playing the emotional card, implying if I really cared about Becca, I would tell them everything.

'I understand what's at stake.'

'Then let's go back to your last meeting with Becca. You said it was three weeks ago?'

'Yes.'

'And you argued?'

'Yes.'

'About her drug use?'

'That and other things.'

'What kind of things?'

'As I said, she thought I was being overprotective.' I need to be careful not to reveal too much. I probably shouldn't tell them I followed Becca. That would only fuel their suspicions.

'And were you overprotective?'

'Obviously I wasn't protective enough,' I snap.

'You lost your mother several months ago, didn't you?'

'Yes.'

'That must have been difficult for you, and for Becca.'

'It was.'

'Did your arguments escalate after that?'

'I think my mother's death, and Henri's, caused Becca a lot of emotional pain.'

'Your mother's death must have caused you emotional pain too.'

'It did, even though she could be a difficult woman.'

'How?'

'She wasn't always capable of showing love, not the kind of love a mother *should* show a child.'

'Do you think you overcompensated with Becca?'

'Perhaps.'

'So, were you overprotective?'

'She's still a teenager, for Christ's sake. Even if she moved out, I was still her mother. I needed to watch out for her, which is why I—' I stop mid-sentence. I've already said too much.

'You what?'

'It doesn't matter.'

'It obviously does to you, Nadine. I can tell you're upset.'

'I am upset. I'm terrified.'

'Then tell us the truth.'

'I followed her once or twice,' I say, unwilling to admit it was several times.

She turns to the other detective again, with another look that says, *Take note of this.*

'Did Becca know you were following her?'

'No, but I think she was suspicious the second time.'

'And what did you find out?'

'Once I saw her heading into town in the early hours of the morning.'

'Was she alone?'

'No.'

'Who was she with?'

'A young guy.'

'Who?'

'I don't know.'

'Can you describe him?'

'I only saw him from behind.'

'Height?'

'Slightly taller than Becca, about five foot eight.'

'Age?'

'He was young. I mean, he dressed young, jeans, a dark hoodie, that kind of thing.'

'Anything else?'

'No.'

'Did Becca ever look to you for extra money?'

'Sometimes. She'd feed me loads of excuses, telling me her hours were cut, and other stuff, but I saw right through her. I told her she needed to take stock of her life, get herself together.'

'And what did she say?'

'She said she could do whatever she wanted, and that she could be with whoever she wanted too. That I was making a big deal out of nothing, exaggerating things, and how I didn't love her.'

'That must have hurt.'

'She didn't mean it. All teenagers argue with their parents. Only ...'

'Only what?'

'I could tell she was hurting inside. I can always tell when something gets to her, and the drugs didn't help.'

'I'm sure they didn't.'

'I was trying to be strong for her, you know, so she could be strong too.' Tears well in my eyes.

'Do you need a tissue?' Wren asks.

I don't answer her.

She stands up and takes one from a box in the corner, handing it to me.

'Thank you,' I say, trying to pull myself together. All this stuff with Becca is so scary, but it's not only that. Soon the police will find Cian's remains in the back garden. What will Becca think of me when she knows I'm the reason Cian went away and never came back?

'This kind of emotional rollercoaster,' Wren continues, 'worrying about your daughter, can put a person under a lot of pressure.'

'Yes,' I say, 'it can.'

'When you were concerned about Becca before, when you thought she was using drugs, did you ever get upset or angry, hit out at her?'

'No, of course not.' What's she talking about? Why aren't they doing something more? They have to realise Becca's been taken, that's she's in danger.

'You should be out looking for her,' I say.

She opens a file with some notes on the desk. 'I understand, Nadine, you're attending a psychiatrist.'

I stiffen my back. Gavin must have told her about Dr Ward, keen to fill in all the background details, hang his sister out to dry. 'Yes.'

'And several years ago, after your husband left you, you had a nervous breakdown?'

'I'm fine now.'

'So why are you currently attending a psychiatrist?'

'Gavin felt I should, after we lost our mother. He thought it prudent.'

'Do you always listen to your brother's advice?'

'Sometimes.'

'And your relationship with your ex-husband?'

'What about it?'

'What was that like?'

'He could be cruel.' My throat is dry. I put my fingers to my neck.

'Would you like some more water, Nadine?'

'No, I'm fine.'

'Did he ever hurt you, physically?'

'Yes.'

'Did you ever make an official complaint?'

'No, I was too scared.'

'And after he left, did he stay in touch?'

'No.'

'What about child support?'

'We didn't need his money. We were okay on our own.'

She writes something down in the file. 'You're currently on medication? Is that correct?'

'Yes. My doctor prescribed something to help me relax, but it's nothing permanent, more like a temporary safety net.'

'Your brother is worried you may have stopped taking your medication, the anti-depressants.'

'I wanted to be alert. I wanted to be able to help Becca.'

'So, you're not taking your medication?'

'I'm back on it now,' I lie.

'It can take a while for certain medications to kick in properly.'

'Why aren't you asking me about Ben or Evie? I know you heard me talking about them in the squad car.'

'Let's stick with the medication for now.'

'I told you, I'm fine.'

'Only you weren't fine in the back garden, were you?'

'I was having a panic attack.'

'Because you believed Becca was abducted, being held against her will?'

'She *was* abducted,' I say, even more irate than before, 'and you should be doing something to find her.'

'Your daughter must have been angry when she realised you were stalking her.'

'I wasn't stalking.'

'You were following her without permission.'

'What's wrong with you? Don't you understand? While you're sitting here asking all your stupid questions, my daughter's in danger.'

She stalls, weighing up my reaction. I can tell she doesn't believe me. My brother has made her question everything I say. It's his fault, but still, I'm going to have to calm down. I'm running out of time. When they find that body in the garden, all bets will be off, and I'll become the prime suspect in Becca's disappearance. They'll see me as a killer, and the police, like Gavin, will string all the information together and believe I did something terrible to my daughter, and that, to protect myself, I'm making up some crazy story about others being to blame.

'According to your brother,' she continues, 'your behaviour was causing Becca a huge amount of distress.'

'My brother doesn't know everything.'

'He's worried you imagined all this stuff about Becca, her being taken, being held against her will.'

'I'm telling you the truth.'

The detective pauses again, but then she asks, 'Tell me about Evie Hunt. She disappeared several years ago, didn't she?'

'Yes, when we were teenagers.'

'And you told your brother you've been threatened by another old acquaintance, Ben Donnelly. That you were forced to deliver suspect packages, do certain things you knew were unlawful.'

'I need you to look for my daughter.'

'You also said Evie came home for her father's funeral.'

'Yes, she did.'

'Only, we've already put out feelers, and it seems no one saw her at the funeral, or anywhere else for that matter.' She leans back in the chair.

I shrug my shoulders.

'If Evie returned home, Nadine, after all this time, I imagine it would have created quite a stir.'

'I guess.'

'Did you see her at the funeral?'

'No, I wasn't there. Ben told me when he called to my house.'

'Was that when he threatened you?'

'Yes, and other times too.'

'When?'

'There was this voice on the phone, the one giving me my instructions. It was disguised, muffled, but it could have been him.'

This is the moment I should come clean about the body in the garden, but I can't, not yet.

'Were you and Evie close?'

I want to tell her I was the one who found Evie when no one else could. 'I wouldn't say we were close,' I say, avoiding yet another minefield. Then I remember the hairbrush, and the other stuff in the package. 'When you find that hairbrush, the one Evie sent me, you could check for fingerprints, perhaps even DNA. I'm telling you, she's come back.'

'You seem very agitated, Nadine.'

'My daughter is missing. How do you expect me to feel?'

She gives me another of her sympathetic looks. 'What was your friendship with Evie like?'

'We were in the same gang. Gavin was closest to her.'

'Really?'

'He loved her, and after she disappeared, he became angry for a very long time.'

'Did you like Evie?'

'She was popular.'

'You didn't answer my question.'

'She was the kind of person everyone centred around, but she could be selfish too.'

'Why do you say that?'

'A feeling I had.'

'Tell me a little more about back then.'

'Why?'

'If Evie is connected to your daughter's disappearance, it could be relevant.'

She's right. 'What do you want to know?'

'Before she disappeared, did anything unusual happen?'

'There was a Truth or Dare game.'

'Did the police know about that?'

'No, it was our secret.'

'Our?'

'The gang.'

'But surely you were all questioned about the circumstances leading up to Evie's disappearance.'

'Gavin didn't think we should mention it.'

'So you all lied.'

'Yes.'

'Okay, go on.'

'Before Evie vanished, she picked a Dare card.'

'What was the dare?'

'She was supposed to do something she would always be remembered for.'

'Do you think her disappearance was connected to the dare?'

'It might have been.'

'Anything else?'

'Her father wasn't a nice man.'

'How?'

'He could be violent and ...'

'And?'

'I can't tell you.'

'Why not?'

'Because Evie made me swear not to tell anyone.'

'But that all happened a long time ago, Nadine. Surely you can tell me now.'

This detective is more astute than I'd thought. Somehow she's brought me around to talking about something I don't want to talk about. Once you start revealing secrets, others are capable of rising to the surface. I hear myself say, 'He did terrible things to her.'

'What kind of things?'

'Sexual things,' I murmur, below my breath, but I know she heard me.

Again, she looks to her partner, but I can see I've hit a nerve.

'Did your brother know?' she asks.

'I don't think so.'

I look up at the camera in the corner of the room. I imagine Evie in my mind's eye, those wretched tears of hers after I gained her trust, after she told me how scared she was, especially because the child she was carrying was her father's. She begged me to keep her secret. I liked her sharing a secret with me, so I confided in her too. I told her what Cian did to me, how he raped me, even though at the time I didn't call it that. I had to tell her, because when someone shares a secret, you need to tell them one in return.

'What else did Evie tell you?'

'She said her father would visit her room at night, while her mother slept, doing things a man should only do with his wife.'

'What age was Evie when the abuse started?'

'I don't know.'

'She must have trusted you, to tell you all this.'

There's a tap on the door. Wren pauses the recording. The door opens.

'A word,' says a male uniformed officer.

Wren walks over to him. He whispers something in her ear. She nods back in reply, before turning to face me again.

'We're going to suspend this interview for now, Nadine.'

'Why? Is it Becca? Has something happened to her?'

'No,' she says, 'it's not Becca.'

'If it is, you would tell me.'

'Yes, Nadine, we would.'

When they leave, my mind goes into overdrive. They must have found something in the garden. I was stupid not to tell them about the body. Now, they won't believe anything I say to them. If they come back, I'll come clean. I'm only complicating matters by not telling them the truth, and that isn't helping Becca.

28
NADINE

THE DOOR opens again.

I jump.

Both detectives take up position as before. Wren switches on the recording equipment. She repeats the earlier information, noting the amended time and the other details, ready to recommence the interview.

'I have to tell you something,' I say.

'Okay,' she replies, 'what?'

'The reason I was in the back garden.'

There's another glance from one detective to the other.

'We're listening,' she says, but her tone is colder now.

'I needed to make sure of something.'

'What did you need to make sure of?'

'That the body was still down there.'

'Whose body?'

'Cian, my ex-husband's.'

She stares at me blankly.

'I killed him,' I say. 'I killed my husband, and afterwards I hid his body in the garden.' I look away, ashamed, knowing it was always going to come to this, and now that I've started, I need to keep on talking. 'A few days ago,' I say, 'I thought I saw him in a pub in town, only I was wrong, wasn't I? Because you found him, you found his body, didn't you?'

Neither of them replies. I can't read their expressions, but they're both staring at me. It's only then I realise I've seen that kind of look before, especially with Dr Ward, when I cross some invisible line, and she has to contemplate what to say next.

Wren clears her throat. 'Nadine, you do understand our officers have been searching your home and garden.'

'Yes.' I lower my head, bracing myself.

'That's why we had to step out of the room.'

I think, *My God, this thing I've feared for so long is actually happening.* And after all these years, there's some relief in that, knowing this part is finally over. Secrets can't stay buried for ever, and, no matter what happens next, there's consolation in that.

Seconds pass.

Both detectives remain silent.

I think about telling them it was self-defence, that he could be terribly cruel, that I had to do it, to protect myself, to protect Becca, but then I wonder the same thing I've wondered for years, how much I really wanted him dead. Did I wait for the right moment to retaliate, and in the waiting, perhaps, I'd always planned to kill him?

'We've concluded the excavation of the garden,' Wren says.

I raise my head. I see another emotion lingering in her eyes. Is it pity? Is that it? Perhaps she understands the horror I went through.

'Nadine, we didn't find anything in the garden.'

'I don't understand.'

'We've examined the entire rear of the property. All we found was the normal rubble one might expect.'

'You're wrong,' I say. 'He's down there.'

'No, Nadine, he isn't.'

'I buried him myself,' I insist. 'I put him into the earth. I covered his body with my bare hands, and then later, when the builders filled in the area for the patio, despite how awful I felt, I knew I didn't have to live with that man ever again.' I can't hold back the tears. I cry, loud, wrenching sobs, the relief of finally telling someone the truth overwhelming.

'Nadine,' Wren insists, 'you need to listen to me.' Her voice is sharp, clear, absolute. 'No one is buried in the garden.'

'No.' I refuse to believe her. 'You're wrong.' I look from one officer to the other. 'It was a long time ago, but there must be skeletal remains. You must have missed them.'

She shuffles in her chair, but her eyes remain fixed on me. 'Nadine, I know this is difficult for you.'

I see that sympathetic look again.

Neither of them believes me. They think I've made it all up, that I lied about Cian, and if his body isn't in the garden, why would anyone believe anything else I tell them? And all the things Gavin might have said, about me imagining stuff, that I could be doing the same thing again, is all true. Only they're wrong. This time it's different.

Wren hands me another tissue.

I wipe my tears away.

'Your brother will collect you shortly,' she says.

I nod because, right now, there's nothing else I can do.

'If there are any updates on Becca, we'll let you know.'

She switches off the recorder, ending the interview.

I'm not sure if I should stand up, or stay where I am.

There's another knock on the door.

The other detective opens it. It's Gavin.

'But what about the package?' I plead. 'You must have found it at the house, Evie's hairbrush, the old photograph, the key. They exist. I didn't make them up. You have to believe me. You must have found them.'

Wren hesitates, looking at Gavin, then back at me. 'Yes,' she says, 'we found a brown envelope without a postage mark, an old photograph, a hairbrush, and a key.'

'They're not mine,' I say, talking fast, 'they're Evie's. You can run tests on them, can't you? I know I've touched all of them, so I may have contaminated evidence, but there could be something.'

'We'll need to take a sample of your hair, Nadine, and fingerprints too, to check it out.'

'Anything.'

'Mike, can you organise that?'

'No problem.'

'We'll check it out,' she says, as if these are her final words.

'And what about Becca?'

'As I said, if we get any fresh leads, we'll be in touch.'

'You don't understand – someone has taken her. You need to help me find her.'

Wren opens the interview-room door. 'I trust, Gavin, once Mike has taken Nadine's prints and hair sample, you can take it from here.' Her words sound official, but there's more than a hint of annoyance in them too. 'I may need Becca's bank account details too, to follow up on access.'

'I can get them for you,' he says, taking charge again. 'Sometimes I send her money, just to keep her on a level keel.'

'Great,' Wren replies. 'You can leave the details with the desk sergeant.'

Everything is slipping from my grasp. I stare at all three of them, trying to work out what they're thinking.

Gavin looks like someone who's been dismissed, directed to the desk sergeant, when he thought he was being so helpful. Wren may be wondering if she rushed to judgement. Perhaps the decision to search the house and gardens will backfire on her as a waste of police time. She strikes me as a woman with ambition and, no doubt, questions will be asked of her further up the line, but as I'm thinking this, I'm also trying to work out something far bigger.

Why didn't they find Cian? Could it have been him in that pub in town? Is it possible he's still alive?

The police don't miss skeletal remains.

None of this is making any sense.

'Nadine,' Gavin says, 'we need to collect your things.'

How can this be happening? Why won't they believe me?

But I already know the answer.

They think I'm mad, and even though I want to roar from the high heavens, and convince them everything I've told them is true, instead, like an obedient lapdog, I follow Gavin quietly through the room.

At the front desk, I sign an official form, confirming the return of my possessions. I don't say a word to Gavin as he leads me through the police station, and soon we're outside. The street is deserted, most people still asleep in their beds, their lives carrying on as normal while my world is being torn apart.

There's already a taxicab waiting outside. I get into the back seat as my brother tells the driver where to go. He's sitting up front, having given the man my home address. I don't know what time it is. My mobile phone is dead, but as we near my house, I see the first rays of morning light. It's already another day.

I stand obediently on the footpath as Gavin pays the cab fare. I think about Aria, who may already be up, standing like a sentry by the window or, perhaps, listening to a guided morning meditation, wearing that cerise pink kantha dressing-gown with the large orange and black flowers. They always remind me of hedgehogs, scurrying in various directions. She would be happy to delay her breakfast of herbal tea and fresh fruit to catch yet another glimpse of the crazy woman who lives next door.

My brother doesn't say a word as he enters the house, this time with my key. I sit in the living room as he goes upstairs and packs an overnight bag for me. When he comes down, he tells me that hopefully I'll only have to stay with him for a short while, and that tomorrow, when I'm rested, and I've taken my medication, I'll see things in a fresh light. If I do, I may be able to return home. Everything feels conditional on my behaviour being considered *normal*.

I don't care. His words don't matter. The only thing that matters is the knowledge that I'm fighting this battle alone. I'm not going to waste any more time trying to convince Gavin. When people don't believe you, trust is broken, and it's best to keep important information to yourself. Otherwise you risk them turning it against you.

Moments later, I'm sitting in my brother's car, the one he abandoned when he found me in the back garden. On the way to his house, we stop at a twenty-four-hour pharmacy. I don't ask any questions. What's the point?

While he's gone, I wonder if I should try to make a run for it, but where would I go?

Soon, he returns, telling me with a degree of satisfaction that Dr Ward's office emailed the prescription over straight away. Again, I don't care.

When we arrive at his house, I don't protest getting out of the car. I don't argue when he tells me I need to go upstairs to rest.

Ten minutes later, when I'm in bed, he comes into the room. He tells me Dr Ward has recommended new medication to be taken in conjunction with my anti-depressants. He places a large glass of water on the locker beside the bed, dispensing the tablets from their foil container, and others from a small plastic pill box. I swallow them in one gulp. This seems to satisfy him, as if at long last the bold child is doing exactly as she's told.

Before he leaves the room, the tablets kick in, the tension in my body loosening, although my mind is still trying to remain focused. I'm finding it increasingly hard to concentrate. There's something important I have to remember about Becca. She needs me – but I can't remember what it is, and soon it's as if I'm already dreaming, entering a long, horrible nightmare, one that sucks me in deep, and within the depths, I see Evie. She's telling me I can never escape the sins of my past, that I lied to her, tricked her, but most of all, I broke my promise: after Becca was born, even though we agreed I would tell everyone Becca was mine, I was never supposed to keep her. I was supposed to give her up for adoption, because no one could ever know Evie's secret. They couldn't know that Becca, this small, innocent, beautiful infant, was created by the sins of Evie's father, because if they did, perhaps no one would ever love her.

But you were wrong, Evie. I loved Becca. I loved her far more than you ever could, which is why I told all those lies, even to Gavin when he came back from Europe, having sought me out months after you left. I told him Becca belonged to me and Cian, and afterwards, my brother did what he always does. He took charge. Less than three months later, I married Cian, keeping Gavin and my parents happy.

I fooled myself into thinking everything would be okay. I told myself I did the right thing, because when you love someone, especially the way I loved Becca, you don't have a choice. Only now nothing is okay, and it's not just because of Cian, but because I fear I've already lost Becca. I fear Evie has come back, and now, more than ever, she wants revenge.

29
WREN

AT AROUND 7 A.M., WITH THE SUN rising on another day, and zero sleep over the last twenty-four hours, Mike gets ready to leave. I imagine his wife and kids eagerly waiting for him at home, an uneaten supper on the kitchen table.

'You should finish up too,' he chides.

'I know, but my head's all over the place.'

'There are good days and bad days, Wren. Chalk it up.'

'The super isn't feeling quite so benevolent. What did he call it? A complete waste of fucking police resources.'

'Sometimes you've to take a punt with these things.'

'I told him that.'

'Even if nothing turned up in the back garden, there was plenty of due cause.'

'I said that too.'

'But something else is niggling you, isn't it?'

'Yep.'

'What?'

'Becca being the same age as Evie Hunt when she disappeared.'

'It's probably a coincidence.'

'Maybe, but both of them are linked to Nadine and Gavin.'

'Do you want my thoughts?'

'Sure.'

'For what it's worth, Nadine Fitzmaurice is unhinged so therefore anything's possible.'

'Do you think she was holding something back?'

'Maybe.'

'I'm sure of it.'

'Wren, wrap it up, that's an order.'

'Okay,' I say, 'I will.'

Alone in the office, I think about him arriving home, walking past his uneaten supper on the kitchen table, climbing into bed with his partner, feeling the warmth of someone who loves him, his kids still asleep in their beds, all wrapped in the simplicity of domesticity and a functional family, a million miles away from the life of Nadine Fitzmaurice, and a million miles away from me too.

Mike is right, I should go home, but an empty apartment, right now, isn't appealing. It's far too early to phone Meg, or my dad. He wouldn't even be up for breakfast yet, and an unexpected phone call could startle him.

I ease my tired body into the chair, deciding instead to write up my notes, another means of covering my arse should the proverbial shit hit the fan. The super will soon be on the rampage again.

I start writing ...

A search warrant was requested and issued based on several mitigating factors:

1. The age of the missing person.
2. Witness statement referring to screams and possible domestic argument/abuse.
3. Psychological concerns surrounding the mental state of Nadine Fitzmaurice.
4. Reports of soil disturbance at the rear of the property.

- On entering the premises, I found Nadine Fitzmaurice to be in a severely traumatised state following what she and her brother, Gavin Fitzmaurice, described as a panic attack.
- Initial intel confirmed Nadine had tried to dig up part of the

grounds to the rear of the property. This was witnessed by her neighbour, Aria Jackson, and later by her brother.

- As the soil was already disturbed, the use of geophysics and quantitative measures to examine the physical properties of the earth regarding recent disturbance was deemed unnecessary. A full excavation of the area was completed by officers, with no evidence of human remains, or partial remains, found.
- All items of interest identified both inside and outside the premises were photographed, recorded, and taken into evidence. Among these were items pertaining to the subsequent police interview with Nadine Fitzmaurice in which she cited a missing-person case from eighteen years earlier, that of Evie Hunt, and a possible connection to Nadine's daughter's disappearance.
- According to her brother, Nadine has had episodes of severe emotional stress throughout her life, often resulting in the onset of panic attacks, blackouts, crippling depression, societal withdrawal and, on occasions, delusional thoughts, all of which make it difficult for Nadine to separate fantasy from reality. Her brother believes Nadine's claim of her daughter, Becca, being abducted is nothing more than a fabrication created by her diminished mental condition.
- During our interview, I found Nadine to be at times evasive, with periods of agitated outbursts.
- Towards the end of the interview, Nadine became increasingly edgy, at which point she made several references to her ex-husband, Cian Campbell, including a claim that she was responsible for his death: that she killed him years before and buried him in the back garden of their home.
- As an excavation of the site had already been completed, with no human remains found, either that of her daughter, Becca Campbell, or of her ex-husband, Cian Campbell, the reliability of Nadine Fitzmaurice's version of events must be considered within the parameters of her mental history.
- Nadine also made accusations about known criminal Ben Donnelly, claiming he, too, alongside historical missing person Evie Hunt, are holding her daughter against her will.

- Anecdotal evidence of illegal drug use on Becca's part was noted by both her mother and uncle.
- Also noted was Becca's inclination to go AWOL in the past, especially during difficult periods at home.
- A package, which Nadine claims to have been sent to her by Evie Hunt after her daughter went missing, contained a hairbrush, an old photograph, and a key. Forensic analysis of the hair particles found on the brush was expedited through the lab, and these were identified as belonging to Nadine Fitzmaurice. Fingerprints on the range of items taken into evidence, including the key and the old photograph, were also linked to Nadine.
- I've requested access to the phone and bank records of Becca Campbell, but at this point, it has been denied by Superintendent Nash, based on the teenager's known drug association, domestic issues at home, and previous episodes of disappearance.
- An image of Becca Campbell is being circulated via Europol and Interpol as is standard in all missing-person cases.
- The missing-person file remains opens although, as noted above, previous historical episodes of disappearance, along with a suspected drug dependency and domestic issues at home, are all strong influencing factors.

Future Action:

- Contact Nadine Fitzmaurice's psychiatrist, Dr Ward, of 10a Lower Baggot Street.
- Do follow-up interview with Aria Jackson (neighbour) regarding screams heard coming from the family home.
- Establish the whereabouts of Cian Campbell, either within Ireland or the nearest alternative jurisdiction of the UK.
- Talk to known criminal Ben Donnelly, regarding possible links to the missing-person report.
- Pull old case notes on missing person Evie Hunt.

Future Action for consideration, requiring approval by Superintendent Nash:

- Examination of bank and phone records (currently denied), and based on results, collection of air, bus and rail bookings since the last sighting, together with examination of CCTV footage at the usual haunts – airports, rail stations, coach and bus depots.

I sign off my notes. I also intend quizzing Gavin about the Truth or Dare game, but for now I leave it out of the report. There was no mention of it in any of the old newspaper articles, and even if the super is convinced Nadine Fitzmaurice is a total nutjob, I'm not. What if other influences are at play? Is Gavin's version of events as clear-cut as it seems? Could Nadine be telling the truth or, at least, a version of it?

30
NADINE

WHEN I WAKE IN THE BEDROOM, someone has pulled over the curtains, placing the room in complete darkness. But it's not only that. I also sense I'm not alone.

'Nadine,' the male voice says, so low I barely recognise it.

'Who's there?'

No one answers.

I repeat the question, raising myself upwards in the bed.

'It's me, Gavin.'

'What are you doing here?'

'Don't you remember, Nadine? I brought you here to take care of you.'

I study the shape slumped in the chair in the far corner of the room. 'Why were you watching me?'

Again, he doesn't answer.

'Do you think I'm going to do something stupid, Gavin? Is that it?'

'Are you planning on doing something stupid?' He sounds angry.

'No,' I say, 'but you've hurt me.'

'How did I do that?'

'When you didn't believe me about Becca.'

He lets out a long sigh.

'Don't deny it.'

'I'm not denying anything, Nadine, but it's been difficult.'

'I didn't lie.'

'You've lied before – or, rather, you've been mistaken before.'

'I'm not listening to you.'

'It's like Dr Ward says. You jump to the wrong conclusions about things, especially when you're under emotional strain.'

'This time it's different.'

'Are we back to the missing body in the garden?' he asks, mocking me.

I don't answer him.

He stands and takes a few steps towards me. 'I want to look after you,' he says, 'until you feel well again.'

'I need some water.'

'There's a glass by the bed.'

I turn and see it on the locker. There are tablets too. I recognise some but not others. 'They're not mine.'

'Dr Ward prescribed extra medication. Don't you remember?'

I think about the drive back from the police station, how he stopped at the twenty-four-hour pharmacy.

'Here,' he says, cupping the tablets in one hand, and the glass of water in the other. 'Take them.'

I do as he instructs, and once more, the medication kicks in fast, zapping my energy. I have to lie down.

After a few seconds I hear his voice again. 'Nadine, there's something I need to ask you.'

He's standing close by the bed, his shadow hovering over me, like those dark shapes in the garden, ominous, scary.

'It's about Evie,' he whispers. His breath is so close to my ear that the words feel like an echo, repeating themselves in my mind. 'Why did you tell Wren Evie was involved?'

'Because she's come back.'

'You know that isn't true, Nadine. Evie disappeared. No one ever found her.'

I want to tell him he's wrong. I want to say I saw a side of Evie he never knew, including how easily she abandoned her child. She could have faced down her father. She could have made him pay for what he did to her, but instead she ran away, and now, with her father's body rotting in the ground, she's come back because she wants to take Becca from me.

'She went away, Nadine. She never came back.'

'You're wrong,' I plead, 'and now she has my Becca.'

'You imagined it, the same way you imagined things when you were younger.'

'Stop twisting things.'

He sits on the bed. 'I'm not twisting anything.'

'Then why are you saying I've made it up?'

'Because, unlike you, I remember everything. I remember how, as a child, you tried to pretend you were living a different life. How you would peep into the windows of other houses, happy homes, wanting to convince yourself you didn't have a son-of-a-bitch father, or a mother who couldn't show you love.'

'I don't want to listen to this. You're being cruel.'

'You're not well, Nadine. You haven't been well for a very long time.'

I want to tell him he's wrong, that I'm not some crazy person, someone to be ignored, but instead I say, 'There are things you don't know. Things Evie kept from you.'

'And what things are they?'

I don't answer him. I can't. My mind is already shutting down, drifting into sleep, to a place where dreams become reality, and all the dark fears that can haunt you bear fruit, no matter how much you try to shut them out.

All of a sudden, I'm no longer in the room. Gavin doesn't exist any more, because now I hear the waves at Magheramore beach swishing against the shore. In my nostrils there's the potent smell of sand and seaweed. I see my teenage self getting off the bus from the city and looking all around her.

I wish I could go back in time and warn that young girl. I wish I could tell her that life is already far more complicated than she knows, and the decisions she will soon make will shape her life for good and bad. That girl is ill-equipped to deal with her future, but still, I can't take my eyes off her, as if I'm watching an old film reel, following the silly girl I used to be, walking from the beach road to the house where Evie is hidden. Very soon she's climbing the staircase to that small bedsit, the one that, for a short time, became Evie's world and mine.

I see her pause outside the bedsit door before going inside. She turns and looks straight at me, as if considering the older me, the way you might study a painting in an art gallery, searching for meaning, but something else is hidden behind her stare. It's as if she's waiting for me, this strange onlooker, to work out her thoughts, and then I see it, the fear inside her. With that comes the knowledge that, all those years ago, she was scared too, as if a part of her already knew she was getting in too deep.

Finally, she opens the door to the bedsit, creating a window into the past, and all I can see is Evie, six months pregnant with Becca, standing by the small window. She doesn't say a word.

My eyes dart around the room, first to the soft chair that doubles as a pull-out bed. I see the old rusty cooker covered with so much grime it's impossible to remove. Beside it, the small fridge, a stainless-steel sink and, on the counter, an array of groceries, breakfast cereal, bread, opened packets of pasta, and tins of everything from soup to tuna, wedged together in the tiny space.

The younger me hangs her coat on a nail hammered into the wall, and underneath it is Evie's backpack, the one she took with her when she first disappeared. In it, there's a hairbrush, given to her by an aunt, a bottle of perfume, which smells sickly sweet, and money in her 'I love Britney' wallet. The cash is important. It was given to her by Ben after she begged him for help. There's a photograph of the gang too, which she kept, I assumed, to remind her of Gavin.

I watch her stretch out her arms, as if she's suddenly aware of my younger self's existence. Evie seems pleased to see me. Both girls appear intimate, comfortable together, with the kind of friendship in which secrets are shared, and in which, for a time, my younger self felt important, because the only thing that mattered was the time she spent with Evie, as the life inside Evie grew, and between them, the girls conjured a plan, one that would be best for everyone. All of that changed when Becca was born, because when she came into the world, I already knew that even if Evie could walk away, I never could.

31
WREN

AFTER LESS THAN THREE HOURS' SLEEP, alongside my growing irritation that I'm not going to see my father for another while yet, I wait for Dr Ward, Nadine Fitzmaurice's psychiatrist. Her PA is busying herself tapping at her keyboard, answering phone calls, while intermittently pulling notes out of files. She glances in my direction only when absolutely necessary. The lack of sleep has made me tetchy. Not ringing my father has made me tetchy too. I could do with some caffeine. I could do with getting this interview over with.

I wonder if Dr Ward came into her profession as a sort of calling, the same way many cops enter the force. It can take a person time to work out why they do things, but it's always there, the underlying motivation. I never linked becoming a cop with my mother's death until the day a colleague assumed it was. They'd had a family member killed too, so they joined the dots and came up with the same answer for me: the hit-and-run that had killed my mother. When it happened, I'd just turned eleven, and both boys in the stolen car were juveniles, which meant their names were protected. I was too young for their identity to make any difference to me, because all I knew was that my mother was dead. That was the critical bit.

The PA, whose name is Sandy, glances in my direction. She has a kind of bird face, long and pointed with beady eyes and a complexion so white it's at odd with her raven hair. I need sleep. I check the time on my watch again as my mind goes back to Dr Ward. Normally the psychotherapists I've met in the past slot into two categories: those who treat their work as a vocation, and those who lean more towards an investigative process.

The sound of Dr Ward's office door opening jolts me from my thoughts. She's tall, exceptionally so, six feet at least. Her skin colouring gives her a northern European appearance, and her curled blonde hair feels somewhat unexpected. I hadn't pictured her this way, although I'm not sure why. She looks feminine, attractive, and her build tells me she works out, probably a lot. She doesn't turn in my direction. Instead she guides her client to Sandy at Reception.

The man in his mid-fifties is dressed formally in a dark suit, white shirt and red tie. Dr Ward leaves him with Sandy and closes her office door behind her. The name Sandy reminds me of a doll I played with as a child. Maybe the PA will grow on me.

As the man pays with his credit card, I look downwards, not wanting to intrude on his personal space. He wouldn't realise I'm a detective but, still, it's best to keep my presence low-key.

Once he leaves, Dr Ward reappears.

'Would you like to come in, DS Moore?' The question is rhetorical. I note a strong upper-class accent.

I follow her into the office, and once inside, I take in everything about the room. It's decorated in a minimalistic fashion, like something from an IKEA catalogue, brilliant white sprinkled with aged ash brown. She has taste – the two pieces of art on the wall tell me that. Both are abstract, but one is akin to a colourful version of those dark butterfly drawings psychologists use to interpret a patient's inner thoughts. Behind her desk, framed qualifications hang in a line. They tell the world she's important.

Once we're seated, she doesn't waste any time. 'So, you're here to talk about Nadine Fitzmaurice.'

'Yes.'

'You're aware I won't be able to discuss certain aspects of Nadine's care with you.'

'Yes, but I understand her brother, Gavin, has been in touch.'

'That may well be, but I'll be putting my patient's care and confidentiality at the forefront of our conversation.'

'I wouldn't expect anything less.' I take out my notebook. 'Do you mind?'

'Of course not.' She leans back in her chair as if preparing for a television interview. Perhaps she's enjoying this far more than I originally envisaged.

'I'd like to know more about the kind of delusional thoughts someone like Nadine suffers from. I'm not asking you to go into specifics. A more general outline is fine.'

'I see,' she says, as if clarifying in her own mind that she isn't about to break any patient–doctor confidentiality. 'Generally,' she says, 'delusional thoughts are extremely resistant to change, even when there's hard evidence to conflict with them.'

'They hold firm when others don't believe them?'

'Indeed, and they can be irrational, fuelled by the obsessional nature of the contradictory information.'

'The truth according to the patient?'

'Yes, especially if emotional distress is involved. All of which makes them absolutely vital to the person purporting them to be true.'

'Is that why they fight against reality?'

'Yes, and the logic is simple. Their delusional beliefs are not only extremely important to them, but any denial of those beliefs would also challenge the individual's mental function.'

'What did you mean when you said the obsessional nature of the contradictory information?'

'Depending on the level of delusion, it may lead to irrational, obsessive behaviour.'

'Can you expand?'

'A person suffering in this way has a predisposition to do things others with a normal grasp of reality wouldn't.'

'Do you think Nadine is capable of obsessional behaviour?'

'We're all capable of it, DS Moore, but some of us are more capable than others, especially when a person's psychological well-being is under strain.'

'Call me Wren, please.'

She nods, accepting this new level of intimacy. She doesn't ask me to call her anything other than Dr Ward. I'm already thinking she's leaning more towards the analytical side of things, but I could be wrong.

'It's part of how human beings survive,' she continues, 'the need to gain an understanding of the world we live in. For example, someone might follow a particular political persuasion, or religious belief, or even decide something as mundane as walking under a ladder will bring them bad luck, and, partly, they require these beliefs so the world makes sense to them. It doesn't mean their view of the world is necessarily totally true or false. It's merely a reflection of individual perception, and for those suffering from extreme delusional thoughts, their perception of the world is no more than an exaggeration of the normal process, but it can cause a lot of stress for the individual involved.'

'Go on.'

'When our minds decide something is true, it's far easier to continue believing it, rather than contradicting it.'

'Why?'

'Mainly due to the huge mental effort involved in altering thoughts and behaviour, no matter what counter-arguments or evidence exist.'

'What about paranoia?'

'What about it?'

'Can delusional thoughts lead to paranoia?'

'Yes, if our perception of reality is suspect. Delusional beliefs, coupled with other underlying anxieties, can elevate a person's fears, which can ultimately cause paranoia.'

'Would they believe other people are out to get them, up to and including fearing for their life, and the lives of those they care about?'

'As I said, delusion and paranoia frequently go hand in hand. Delusions arise from a variety of irrational beliefs, and paranoia can drive them. Indeed, we're all sensitive to the idea that we're being watched, talked about, or even deceived by others. The vast majority of the population frequently experience paranoia, suspicion and mistrust. We have to. It's part of our innate survival mechanism.'

'A sort of protection?'

'Yes, and I've no doubt you've experienced it in your line of work.'

'I don't understand.'

'You're likely to be overly suspicious of everyone.'

'I guess so.'

She gives me a puzzled look before continuing.

'When it comes to paranoia, people suffering from delusional thoughts, especially those driven by huge emotional turmoil, are exactly the same as you and me. The only difference is their reality is even more *corrupted*, and the patient is often unable, or unprepared, to realise it.'

'How can you help someone suffering this way?'

'First, you have to establish what brought on the delusion in the first place.'

'And second?'

'Why the delusion isn't immediately rejected, even when evidence exists to contradict it.'

'Nadine Fitzmaurice believes her daughter is being held against her will.'

'I heard that from her brother.'

I flip over another page of my notebook. 'Could it be Nadine's way of denying the breakdown of her relationship with Becca? The denial fuelling the delusion?'

'It's difficult in *any* case to be absolutely sure, but by tracking backwards, answers can be found. The root causes of the delusion are always there, including an over- or under-reliance on data.'

'How do you mean?'

'Have you heard of the dual-process framework?'

'No.'

She stands up and walks around the room, as if instead of conducting an interview she's facilitating a lecture.

'The framework indicates two contrary systems of thought. Most of our normal thought process is intuitive, which in turn produces a quick, automatic response to decision-making challenges. We may decide we like or dislike a given individual based on instinct, which is often fuelled by previous life experience.'

My eyes follow her around the room. She looks as if she's gliding.

'In contrast,' she continues, 'an alternative process, which is not based on instinct, requires a more detailed approach, involving both analytical and emotional decision-making.'

'Go on.'

'Delusional reasoning occurs when there's an over-reliance on instinctive thinking, and an under-reliance on a more analytical application.'

'Causing us to jump to conclusions that may be wholly inaccurate.'

'Yes, and the emotional drivers, especially those fuelled by loss, guilt, or even low self-esteem, can result in people who suffer from delusional thinking being prone not only to snap judgements but also to pushing other rational thoughts away.'

'So, let's take it, Dr Ward, someone sees two people chatting on the street. They could decide that, instead of it being a normal conversation, the people are plotting against them.'

'Precisely. Paranoia based on instinct in the absence of fact.' She sits down. 'An over-dependence on instinct is destructive, especially when there are severe underlying psychological pressures.'

'Can you give me an example of something more closely aligned to someone like Nadine?'

'Okay. You could have a situation in which one person hears a crackle on a telephone line, and immediately assumes it's a bad connection, or a technical issue of some kind. They wouldn't give it a second thought. Another person, someone suffering from delusional influences and paranoia, like Nadine, will come to a completely different conclusion. That person may believe the phone is bugged, that someone is listening in on their conversation, and that in the future these recordings could be used against them.'

'It seems Nadine has had several delusional episodes of late.'

'Which doesn't surprise me.'

'Why not?'

'Her recent bereavement.'

'Her mother?'

'Yes.' She checks her wristwatch. 'Death has a habit of digging up old psychological wounds.'

I take this as a hint that my time may be running out, so I ask, 'In your opinion, Dr Ward, considering Nadine's mental state, what is she capable of?'

She stares at me blankly.

'Nadine recently spoke about her ex-husband, Cian Campbell, going as far as to claim she killed him.'

She clears her throat. For the first time I wonder if she's nervous.

'He's partly the reason Nadine came to me in the first place,' she says. 'His aggression, the emotional control he exerted over her, was quite debilitating.'

'Do you believe Nadine Fitzmaurice harmed her ex-husband?'

'What's important is that Nadine believes it, delusional or otherwise.'

'Is she clinically depressed?'

'Quite possibly, yes.'

'Would her depression, coupled with extreme paranoia and delusional thinking, make her a danger to others?'

'You want to know if she's capable of physically harming someone?'

'Yes.'

'I've learned over time, especially in this line of work, to be rarely surprised.'

It's a fudged answer. She checks her watch again. I'm expecting Sandy from the front desk to buzz in at any moment. I give it one last effort.

'But you've known Nadine for a long time. You must have formed an opinion.'

'For what it is worth,' her voice sounding more empathetic now, 'I think Nadine poses more of a danger to herself than to anyone else.'

I'm not sure I share her confidence, especially considering everything I've just heard. For all I know, Nadine Fitzmaurice could be a ticking time bomb. I need to get more out of Dr Ward.

'Would it be fair to assume she viewed her husband's departure as a form of rejection?'

'Perhaps.'

'And now, with Becca gone, her daughter's disappearance is another kind of rejection?'

She gives me a derisive glance, as if tiring of my amateur psychology. 'It's possible,' she says.

'Nadine's condition sounds pretty desperate.'

'I don't agree. Despite her current delusional state, with proper medication and support, it's my hope she will turn things around. She's made of stronger stuff than people realise.'

'How so?'

'She has resilience. Nadine may have come across as emotionally frail to you, which, at times, she certainly is, but she's also capable of dealing with far more than others give her credit for.'

'Like?'

'Her work, for example. I've found in the past that when Nadine integrates into the work environment, the solidity and routine, the normal everyday aspect of it, grounds her.'

Her desk phone rings. She picks up. 'Yes, Sandy, we're just finished.'

I guess my time is at an end. I stand up. 'You've been most helpful, Dr Ward.'

I'm about to leave when she says, 'You seemed familiar to me earlier on. Only, it took me a while to work out why.'

'Oh?'

'You look similar to a psychology professor I met during my studies at Trinity. You have the same intense stare. He has the same surname as you too, Moore – Christopher Moore. We were good friends for a time.'

'He's my father,' I say, stiffening my resolve, preparing for the potential sympathy. I can almost see the cogs in her brain turn.

She hesitates, then says, 'Your father had a brilliant mind.'

'Yes,' I reply, 'he had.'

I reach the doorway. 'One last thing, Dr Ward.'

'Yes?'

'That example you gave about the crackle on the phone line being a bad connection, or someone listening in.'

'What about it?'

'Hypothetically, both could be true?'

'Hypothetically, yes.'

She holds the door open for me to leave, and as I do, I'm even more unsure about Nadine Fitzmaurice than before, but either way, I realise, whatever's driving her, true or false, is probably utterly terrifying.

32
NADINE

I TURN IN THE BED. The sunlight from the window illuminates zillions of dust particles, all aimlessly caught in flight. I try to get my bearings, remembering I'm in Gavin's house. I hear people talking. The sound is coming from beyond the window. I pull myself out of bed and walk towards it.

The voices belong to Gavin and Aria. She's in her car with the driver's window rolled down. Why is she here? Maybe she's pretending to be concerned about me, keen to get even more information on her crazy neighbour. Or perhaps they're scheming against me, trying to work out the best way to keep the nutcase under wraps.

I have a minute sense of power watching Aria, instead of her watching me. People think she's so kind and laid-back, but there's a vindictive streak in her too. I know this from the way she likes to bring Cian up in conversation, the same way she asked about Becca the other day, as if she senses my weakness.

I move closer to the window. I need to work out what they're saying, but they're speaking so low I can't hear the words. I can't risk opening the window in case I alert them. My breath steams up the glass. With my fingertips on the panes, the coolness feels good against my skin. A part of me wants to scream, but I can't risk that either. They'll think I'm even crazier than they do already.

Aria starts up the car engine. Gavin watches her drive away. I get back into bed, knowing he'll soon return. I don't think either of them saw me, which is important, because I'm not sure who to trust any more.

'Nadine,' he calls out, climbing the stairs.

I stay silent, pretending to be asleep.

He's in the room now, walking towards the bed. He leans down and whispers in my ear, 'It's me, Gavin. You need to wake up.'

The remains of my steamed-up breath are still on the glass. I pray he doesn't notice it.

'I need water,' I say, trying to distract him.

He brings it to my lips. I take a couple of sips, and then he does as he did before. He hands me the tablets. 'Take these. They'll make you feel better.'

I wish I could tell him I don't want to feel better. I want to find Becca, but I do as I'm told, except this time I place them under my tongue.

He's sitting on a stool by the bed now, satisfied because he thinks I've swallowed the medication.

'I'm going away for a few days, Nadine. Something's come up, and I can't ignore it.'

I nod in acknowledgement.

'You're feeling more like yourself today, aren't you?'

He means I'm behaving more stable, more like the quiet Nadine who doesn't loudmouth about conspiracy theories, and killings, and abductions. Again, I nod back.

'Good.'

I move the tablets to the side of my mouth. They're sticky and taste of sulphur.

'It might be best if I bring you home. You'll feel more comfortable there.'

He says this as if I'm part of the decision-making process, even though I'm not. He doesn't mention Aria, his new spy. He's probably arranged for her to keep a keen eye on me.

'If I leave out your medication, promise you'll take it?'

I need to answer him. A simple nod will not suffice. I have to swallow the tablets. I reach for more water to gulp them down. 'I promise,' I say, with as much sincerity as any liar can muster.

He looks pleased with himself again.

'I'll need to talk to work,' I say, 'tell them I'll be out for another while.'

'Don't worry about that. I've already told them your doctor believes you need more time. The illness cert is already in the post.'

'You shouldn't have done that without asking me.'

'I didn't want you worrying.'

I hate when he takes charge of my life.

'Why don't I make you some breakfast, Nadine. We can have it downstairs if you feel up to it.'

When he leaves, I think about that dream again, the one I had about Evie's old bedsit, and all the things I wanted to forget. I know now that blocking things out isn't going to help anyone, and looking back, I also know we were all guilty of terrible things.

Evie running away, and not telling Gavin about the baby. Gavin taking his rage out on others, shutting them out. Cian, with his twisted mind, being both mentally and physically cruel to me, and myself, stealing another person's child, claiming her as my own.

The Dare, like the Truth, card, has come full circle. It's been biding its time before the ultimate price is paid for the sins of the past, and the person paying the price right now is me. Only I can't be sure if it's Evie, Cian or even Gavin who's holding the Dare card, because when it comes to lies and betrayal, each of us is guilty.

Gavin calls me from downstairs. He says breakfast will be ready shortly. I shower and dress as fast as I can, and afterwards, despite the medication, my muscles and limbs feel more agile. I'm eager to go through the motions so I can soon be home. I feel more grounded there, and once I have Gavin out of the way, I can plan my next move.

In the kitchen, my brother keeps a close eye on me, watching carefully as I swallow every last bite of toast and poached egg. I feel like an animal in a cage, with people peering in, fascinated by my tiniest movement, and as I'm thinking this, I'm also thinking about Becca, and the horror she must be going through right now.

After breakfast Gavin drives me home. He remains silent all the way from his house to mine, as if his mind needs to retreat to a place more peaceful, one without a crazy sister to deal with. I don't mind. I'm used to long silences between us, a habit we perfected as children when our father was on the prowl and our mother was too concerned about herself to offer us the comfort and protection we needed. You develop skills fast as a child to protect yourself, and glancing at Gavin, I can't help but feel sorry for both of us, for the damaged goods we are, for the children and adults we were never allowed to be.

When we pull up outside my house, I'm suddenly hesitant, almost as if the physical change of location needs to be reconsidered, re-examined. The medication is starting to kick, so I'm slow getting out of the car, but somehow, my feet touch the pavement. The ground is solid, familiar. We walk together to the front door. Again, I allow him to unlock it.

Gavin puts away shopping in the kitchen. He tells me he's stocked up on everything. There's no reason for me to go outside. He wants me to be a prisoner, even if he doesn't call it that.

I desperately need sleep. He walks me upstairs, but before he leaves, he places my medication in a see-through plastic box in the en-suite bathroom. The box has divisions for every day of the week, and individual sections for morning, lunchtime and evening, mapping out the next seven days of my life. He places a large jug of water on my bedside locker. If I get hungry, he tells me, there are microwave meals in the freezer. Again, I nod and agree.

The minutes crawl by, like some hellish eternity, until finally he leaves the room.

Soon, the front door is being closed. Outside, his footsteps move fast. I hear the bleep of the car alarm being turned off, then the driver's door opening and closing. Is Aria watching him from her upstairs window? Does he glance up at her, reassuring her that the prisoner is at home and doped-up with all the medication required?

Once I'm sure it's safe, I go downstairs and, like a ghost returning to my old life, I'm instantly drawn to the living room, only now, everything looks blurry. I wonder if the drugs are messing with my head, because I'm finding it hard to concentrate on the photographs of Becca hanging there. They seem contorted, abstract, impossible to make out. I desperately want to see her face because, right now, I'm scared she might not even exist, that she might not be real.

'God,' I say aloud, 'please tell me I haven't imagined her.'

It has to be the medication.

'Becca is real,' I say, aloud again, needing to hold onto that singular belief before spotting the notebook I used to write down her instructions.

When I open it, all I can see are grocery lists. I can't find the name and address of John Simons, or any of the other notes I made about seeing Evie in town, or my last conversation with Becca. Someone has removed the pages. Evie, Ben, or even Cian? If he's still alive, that's exactly the kind of thing he'd do.

I still don't understand why the police didn't find his skeletal remains. I killed him. I know I did. I put his body in that hole in the ground, covered it with clay, and waited for the following day, when the builder dragged the rest of the soil over it, placing more layers on top. I couldn't take my eyes off that huge yellow digger. I even watched as the builder flattened the surface, then poured the gold pebbles over my awful deed.

Could Gavin be right, and all the things I've said, the things I truly believe, are somehow lies, imagined?

I close that thought down. It's not going to help me or Becca.

I hear my mobile phone buzz. It's coming from the hall. I rush out to check it, staring at the shattered screen as it flashes a reminder of my appointment with Dr Ward for two days' time. A lifetime has passed since I agreed to see her. I immediately delete the message.

Upstairs, I seek more clues about Becca, starting with her old bedroom. It's empty. Then I remember her packing up her stuff, taking everything from her room, as if she were removing every trace of herself from this house, separating herself from me. Suddenly I feel bereft all over again.

On the landing, my eyes pause on that old image of my mother, the one from her early twenties. She looks so different from how she looked before she died, wrinkled and in pain. I always swore I'd be a better mother than she was, and realising this, I'm even more determined than ever to do whatever it takes to save my daughter.

It doesn't matter that Becca didn't grow inside me, or that biologically we're different: from the moment she came into this world, when Evie didn't want her, I was the one who showed her a mother's love.

33
WREN

As I drive back to the station, Dr Ward's words about my father linger. No matter what else happens today, including talking to Gavin, after my shift is done I'm going to call to the nursing home to see him.

At my desk, I find it hard to concentrate, my mind drifting back to the months before he was diagnosed with Alzheimer's disease, when parts of his memory had already begun to disappear. Now, less than a year after his diagnosis, it's only on very rare occasions that his true self returns.

I flip open the autopsy report on the old man found dead at Nutgrove Avenue, doing a final overview. There are no indicators of foul play. The man had chronic heart problems, and although we can't be sure why his heart failed when it did, it was most likely due to a build-up of stress. He died alone, and I only hope, for his sake, it happened fast.

Mike knocks on the office door. 'That CCTV footage is going out on *Crimecall* tonight.'

'Good,' I say, 'because we could do with a break.'

'And, by the way, Aria Jackson, Nadine Fitzmaurice's next-door neighbour, called. She's wondering when to expect you.'

'Tell her I'll be there tomorrow. There's no way I'm putting in extra hours today.'

When Mike leaves, I check my watch. Gavin is due at the station in less than ten minutes, and I'm not looking forward to it. Our old relationship will be the elephant in the room, and, if I'm not careful, it could stomp all over me.

As if on cue, I get a text message from him. He's running late as he needs to prepare for going out of town. Damn him, I think, but I'm already reviewing the questions I want to put to him. What can he tell me about the Truth or Dare game? Why did he tell the others not to mention it? Does he think it's a coincidence that his niece and Evie went missing at the same age? And what about Nadine? After my conversation with Dr Ward, I looked deeper into her work situation, especially her current role as a senior manager in an insurance company. That surprised me, especially as Gavin was so dismissive of her. I want to ask him about that old group too, including the disparity within it, Ben, Evie and others coming from lower socioeconomic groups than Nadine, Gavin and Cian. Did he feel he was better than Ben or Evie? Did he feel superior? Was school the only thing that bound them, or was there something more? And what about Cian Campbell? So far, like Evie, he seems to have disappeared into thin air. One person wanting to disappear is questionable, if not uncommon, but two is bloody odd.

I hear footsteps in the corridor. The office door opens. It's Gavin.

'Hi,' he says. 'Sorry for running late.'

'Take a seat.' I point to the chair on the opposite side of the desk.

'You look well,' he says, removing his overcoat, and loosening the top button of his shirt.

He used to do the same thing when he came to my apartment. I half expect him to kick off his shoes, and kiss me, and before I can shut that thought down, I'm visualising the two of us having sex, his breath so close to mine, it feels like some crazy heat on my skin. I remember too how, afterwards, we'd curl into each other, and he'd slide his arms around my waist, and I'd feel protected, loved.

'It's all the sleepless nights,' I say. 'It does wonders for your complexion.'

He laughs at my joke. 'I'm glad you phoned, Wren.'

'Oh?'

'I wanted to see you face to face to apologise for my sister.'

'There's no need.'

'Did you speak to Dr Ward?'

'Yes.'

'So, you understand things with Nadine can be ...'

'Complicated.'

'That's one way of putting it.'

I open my notebook.

'You've changed your hair,' he says, smiling with his eyes. 'It's longer. I like it.'

'Gavin, don't do this.'

'Do what?'

'We're not an item any more.'

'Are you seeing someone?'

'That's none of your business.'

'Wren, I know I fucked up. I should have told you the truth way earlier than I did.'

What he should be saying is that it was wrong of him to lie to me, that he shouldn't have been fucking around with someone else behind my back, because telling the truth way sooner than he did, especially when someone conveniently snitched on him, leaving him with no other choice, is so far down the list of fuck-ups, it's not even worth mentioning. Instead, I say, 'It's ancient history.'

'You never asked me, Wren, who it was.'

'It doesn't matter.'

'I cared for you. I cared a lot.'

'How's Nadine?' I ask, switching the conversation.

'Resting.'

'The super thinks she's a total nutjob.'

'And you?'

I shrug my shoulders. 'That's partly why I've some questions for you.'

'Fire away,' he says. I smell his aftershave. Again, I think about the two of us together, intimate, close. Under the bright lights of the office, I note again the physical similarities between him and Nadine, the same broad forehead, dark eyebrows, and the kind of eyes that draw you in, almost as if there's something about them you can't quite explain.

'Your sister was very insistent during the interview,' I say. 'At times she seemed terrified for herself and your niece.'

'Nadine believes many things that aren't true.'

'She was quite dogged about Becca being held against her will, not to mention the body in the back garden that doesn't exist.'

He tightens his fists, irritated. I can tell I've hit a nerve. Maybe he feels embarrassed about raising the alarm, thinking his sister harmed Becca. If this was the first time our paths had crossed, I might feel sorry for him, only I'm too familiar with the Gavin Show, and everything revolving around him, to offer sympathy. Besides, history tells me he'll soon turn the tables. I don't have to wait long.

'I'd have thought, Wren, you'd have shown more empathy, especially considering your father's illness.'

It's a low blow, but I take it as a reminder to keep this conversation focused on what's important. My facial expression tells him everything he needs to know.

He reaches out, touching my arm. 'I didn't mean to ...'

'I don't care what you meant.'

'I've missed you.'

'It's too late for that.'

'Is it?'

'Things didn't work out, Gavin – end of story.'

He gives me a sorrowful look.

'About Nadine,' I say.

'What about her?'

'When we were together, you rarely mentioned her, or anything else about your family.'

'There's lots of things about my family I don't talk about.'

'Why not?'

'Because talking about them puts me in a bad mood.'

I think about the first night we went out, and how initially the conversation flowed so freely. It was the only time he really opened up about his family, telling me how cruel his father could be. I spoke about my mother too. I remember him asking me so many questions about the accident. Strange thing, thinking about it now, how interested he was in every last detail. I guess it lulled me into the false belief that he was someone who cared, but now, looking back, part of me wonders if it was all an act, a form of love bombing so I'd buy into the notion that he was special. If he was special, if he did care, though, he would never have done what he did.

Out of nowhere, I say, 'Why did you ask me out?'

'What kind of question is that?'

'A straightforward one.'

'I was attracted to you. I still am.'

'You spoke about your father that first night. You talked about all the beatings he gave you. Do you remember?'

'We spoke about a lot of things.'

'I told you about my mother.'

'Where's this going, Wren?'

'I'm not sure, but I guess I'm curious as to why initially you were more open about your family, then clammed up.'

'As I said, there are things about my family that put me in a bad mood.'

I review the questions in my notebook. 'Okay. Tell me about the Truth or Dare game.'

'That was a long time ago.'

'Still, I'm interested.'

'It was stupid kids' stuff, nothing more.'

'Evie was dared, wasn't she, to do something she would always be remembered for?'

'Who told you that?'

'Nadine.'

'As I said, it's a lifetime ago.'

'You invented the game.'

'I've always been creative.' He laughs.

I don't. 'Why did you tell the others not to mention it to the police?'

He shrugs his shoulders.

'Why?' I insist.

'I thought it would complicate things, that they might dismiss Evie disappearing as a prank.'

'And later?'

'Later, there was no point.'

'Don't you think it's a coincidence, Evie and Becca going AWOL at the same age?'

'No.'

'You don't think there's a connection.'

'Listen, Wren, I know where this is leading, but I'm warning you, don't go down any dark rabbit holes created by my sister.'

'It seems your sister is far more capable than you give her credit for.'

'What do you mean?'

'Her job,' I say. 'It's highly pressurised, demanding. Not the kind of career a woman on the edge can easily hold down.'

'My sister has spent her whole life trying to prove she's good enough. It takes its toll.'

'And this old group you used to be part of, the one with you, Nadine, Evie, Ben and Cian.'

'What about it?'

'Evie and Ben wouldn't have been normal playmates for you. Rich kids, poor kids, they don't always get on.'

'We went to school together.'

'Anything else?'

'No.'

'Did you feel superior to Ben and Evie?'

He leans forward. 'You want to know about Evie, don't you?'

'She's part of the equation, yes.'

'You still care.'

'I care about getting answers.'

'Okay,' he replies. 'Let me keep this simple for you. No, I didn't feel superior. Evie disappeared. I don't know why. I don't know how. And, after all this time, I don't care.'

I want to tell him he's lying, but instead I change tack. 'So, what happened to Cian?'

'Him and Nadine didn't work out.'

'Why was that?'

'They shouldn't have got married in the first place, but circumstances dictated otherwise.'

'In what way?'

'She had a child outside wedlock.'

'Eighteen years ago wasn't exactly the dark ages.'

'Maybe not, but our parents were older, more old-fashioned, traditional. They had a very one-dimensional view of the world. Babies weren't supposed to exist outside the sanctuary of marriage. My father was strict. My mother worried about what other people thought.'

'And what did you think?'

'I wanted everyone to be happy.'

'Including Nadine?'

'Especially Nadine. Look, she was only seventeen, and she hadn't got a clue. She went away to have Becca, not even registering the baby's birth until after I found her.'

'Where was she?'

'Some grubby bedsit near Magheramore beach.'

'And the child was Cian's?'

'She hadn't been with anyone else.'

'Are you sure?'

'My sister isn't a slut.'

'I didn't say she was.'

I allow a few seconds to pass. 'How did Cian feature in all this?'

'Back then, I thought he cared about Nadine.'

'And now?'

'Now, I think he's a bloody narcissist.'

'I don't follow you.'

'He liked the idea of having a child, a kind of embodiment of himself. He thought he wanted marriage too, but men like that aren't cut out for it.'

I want to say, *Neither are you*, but I hold my tongue. 'Let's get back to Nadine for a second.'

'What do you want to know?'

'Your relationship with her seems stressed, almost as if you're ashamed of her.'

'I'm not ashamed of her.'

'So, what is it, then?'

'I guess, one way or another, I've always had to look out for her, and sometimes it's a total pain in the arse.'

'Do you resent it?'

'I wouldn't say that, but I guess someone had to step up to the plate. Someone had to watch out for her.'

'Because of your father's cruelty.'

'And my mother too.'

'Oh?'

'I guess you could say, in my mother's eyes, I was the favourite, and Nadine wasn't, even though they could be very alike.'

'How?'

'Sometimes it took them a while to work out what's important.'

'And you could?'

'Getting the shit beaten out of you on a regular basis tends to concentrate the mind.'

'So, what you're saying, Gavin, is that, even as a child, you were the only person Nadine could depend on?'

'I guess so.'

'And you didn't always like it.'

'There are times I still don't, but I don't have much choice.'

'And Becca?'

'What about her?'

'Did you have a good relationship with her?'

'I adored Becca from day one. There's always been something between us, a kind of connection.'

'And Cian?'

'As I said, he was a fuck-up. He messed with Becca's head too. To be honest, I was glad when he was out of the picture, but that didn't mean he hadn't already done his damage. I know all about damaged souls.' He laughs again, but I can tell he cares about his niece, and deeply.

'And this protection you feel towards your sister?'

'What about it?'

'You seemed awfully keen to point the finger at her over Becca.'

'I can forgive Nadine almost anything, but if she'd harmed Becca, that would have been the line in the sand.'

I'm not fully sure what to make of his various responses. In theory, he's answered all my questions, but I sense there's something he's not telling me, and if I know anything about him, it's unlikely I'll succeed in getting any more out of him today.

'Okay,' I say. 'I guess that's it for now.'

'Look, for what it's worth, I'm sorry I got you involved.'

'It's my job.'

'When I heard about Nadine digging up the back garden, I should have phoned someone else, or dialled 999.'

'Why didn't you?'

'My immediate instinct was to reach out to you. I still—'

'Gavin, don't go there.' I stand up, signalling our conversation is over, needing to move this on. 'It's late and we've both got places to be.'

He stands up too. 'Listen, no matter what the super thinks, getting the warrant for Nadine's place was the right thing to do.'

'Unfortunately, Gavin,' I reply, a little overzealously, 'you're not a detective any more, so your opinion doesn't carry any weight around here.'

He walks towards the door, his shoulders held back, angry now, but his need to have the last word gets the better of him. 'Thanks, Wren,' he sneers, 'for reminding me.'

I call after him.

He turns.

'Gavin, I'm sorry again about your mother.'

'At least I had her for longer than you had yours.'

Instantly, my mind flips back, remembering that last morning she dropped me off at school, and how, seconds later, getting out of the car to buy some milk, she was hit by that stolen car. I imagine the driver and passenger fleeing the scene, two young kids, not knowing they'd taken another person's life. My mother never did regain consciousness. I think about my father too: the decision to switch off her life support was the hardest he ever made.

'I had a father who loved me,' I reply, my resolve back on track.

'Then you were lucky, Wren, because mine was a useless bastard.'

34
NADINE

I'VE A LIMITED AMOUNT OF TIME with Gavin away, so I need to use it well. I still don't understand why the pages are missing from the notebook, other than someone is trying to mess with my head, and if they are, it means I have to be even more alert.

I heat a frozen dinner in the microwave, aware I need my strength. When it bleeps, I remove the packet, but I don't bother to put the contents on a plate. I've already charged my phone. It's on the kitchen counter, close by, in case I get another call from Becca. I've stopped taking my medication. Instead I flushed the tablets wrapped in tissue down the toilet, hiding any evidence.

If Evie is behind all this, then piecing together the relevant informa-tion is vital, and thinking about it now, I remember how easy it was for me to find her. When I was younger, I was inclined to say very little, which meant I was better than most at listening, storing up information other people discarded. Everyone had forgotten about Magheramore beach. Evie had gone there several times as a child, visiting her aunt. That last summer, before Evie realised she was pregnant, Ben suggested we go there. Someone he knew had a place near the beach, so if we wanted to we could stay overnight. Of course, none of us did, fearing our parents would have a fit. Instead, after a day at the beach, we took the last bus home. Only there was something about Magheramore that seemed to fit with Evie, as if she had a certain affinity with the place. After she went missing, I began to wonder if she might have gone back there. I took a chance, getting the bus from Dublin, but it paid off when I saw her coming out of the newsagent with her fix of cigarettes.

In the beginning, I wasn't aware of the pregnancy. She shouldn't have been smoking at all, but when she saw me, her eyes lit up, as if she were relieved that someone, even if it was only me, had found her. She was surviving with the money Ben gave her. He may have only been a teenager, but he was already capable of getting money and fast, especially from the kind of people whose stock-in-trade was illegal deals. The same kind of people who are probably holding Becca now.

Years before, I used to wonder if Gavin ever noticed how much Ben looked at Evie, admiring her, constantly trying to get her attention. I could see it, but I kept quiet about it. Perhaps Ben is still in love with her and willing to do anything she wants.

I fire the empty microwave container into the bin, but jump when my mobile phone rings. It's another withheld number. I pick up, fast.

'I hear you've spent some time with the cops.'

'Is this you, Ben?'

He doesn't answer. Instead, he asks, 'Have you been blabbering to the boys in blue?'

'They don't believe anything I tell them.'

He sniggers.

'I want to talk to Becca. I need to speak to my daughter.'

'We're moving to the next stage.'

'What do you mean?'

'The task we spoke about before.'

I don't understand, but I wait, knowing he'll soon fill in the blanks.

'This next item is very important because it involves a shitload of money. A quarter of a million to be exact, which is why you have to be back at work.'

'What has work got to do with it?'

'A small matter of an insurance claim.'

'But I'm on sick leave.'

'Not my problem,' he says. 'You see, there was a terrible crash, a four-car pile-up. You know, one of those motorway jobs with an overenthusiastic driver coming to a halt too fast and bringing lots of cars down with him.'

'What's that got to do with me or Becca?'

'We need you to destroy evidence, incident reports, video footage, things that might throw suspicion on the claim.'

'I told you, I'm on sick leave.'

'Again, not my problem. That debt Becca owes has to be paid big-time. Those people she's upset, killing one of their own, are pretty pissed off with your insurance company, and all the technical issues they're raising.'

Somehow I find the courage to ask, 'Who did Becca kill?'

'You don't need to know.'

'But what if the body turns up?'

'It won't. I've made sure of it.'

'How?'

'Let's just say my early training in a butcher's shop came in handy.'

'You mean, you ...'

'Again, Nadine, not your concern.'

'My doctor won't agree to me going back to work.'

'I don't give a shit. If you want to talk to Becca, this is how it's going down.'

'How much time do I have?'

'There'll be a case review very soon when those crappy underwriters decide if they're going to contest or settle the claim. If they decide to test it, the guys Becca pissed off will be even more annoyed, and I don't have to fill in the blanks for you, do I?'

'What do I need to do?'

'As I said, damage some video footage and records. You'll also need to alter reports, but I'm sure falsifying data and signatures isn't beyond you.'

'There will be back-up copies.'

'Then sort them out. A well-respected member of the managerial staff like you isn't going to be watched too closely.'

'And if I agree, how do I know the debt is paid?'

'You have my word.'

'Why should I believe you?'

'That's your call, Nadine, but Becca won't be pleased if she finds out you cared more about shitty bureaucracy than saving her skin.'

'Okay, I'll do it.'

'You have two days.'

'But—'

'No buts, Nadine, not if you want to see Becca alive again.'

'Let me talk to her.'

'No.'

'What about Evie then? She's involved, isn't she?'

He laughs again, this time so hard, it soon turns into a sickening cough, as if the stupidity of my question has sent his head into a tailspin.

'How can Evie do this to her own flesh and blood?' I roar.

He stops laughing. 'She didn't steal a child, though, did she?'

'I—'

'Listen to me. Becca fucked up. This is simple economics. Someone has to pay the price, and right now, that someone is you, so write down these fucking details.'

My hands are shaking, but somehow, I manage to write the words down.

'I'll be in touch in forty-eight hours. Don't mess up.'

The line goes dead. My mind jumps into overdrive. I need to get back to work. Gavin is away, which helps, but I'd have to convince Dr Ward to let me return, and that'll be tricky.

I stare at the mobile phone, unsure what to do next, until I remember the appointment, the one I've already set up. I dial Dr Ward's office.

Her personal assistant answers.

'I was supposed to see Dr Ward tomorrow,' I say, 'but something's come up, and I was wondering if I could bring the appointment forward.'

'Oh,' she replies, as if I've just asked something mammoth.

'I wouldn't ask, only it's important.'

'Hmm,' she says, but I can tell she's moved from an absolute no to possible consideration. 'Let me check her schedule.'

She places me on hold. I hear a blast of 'Tie A Yellow Ribbon Round The Old Oak Tree' before the music comes to an abrupt halt.

'Nadine, Dr Ward can fit you in at five.'

35
WREN

AFTER GAVIN LEAVES, I'M ANGRY at myself for letting him get to me, but I'm angry at him too. It's the same rage that's been locked inside me since I found out he was cheating. Then, and now, it makes me feel soiled, as if the thing I thought we had between us wasn't real at all. I also wonder if in his own way Gavin loved me as much as he could love anyone, and that it was me, not him, who made it out to be something it wasn't.

I consider phoning Meg, but I've bent her ear so many times about him, there's little point. She'll only say he's trying to make himself feel better about what he did, and any talk of caring for me is just another means of gaining sympathy. Even before his cheating, that brick wall he often erected between us was another reason our relationship failed so abysmally. Most cops hold back a piece of themselves, but with Gavin, sometimes, it was a closed book.

Suddenly the office feels too big for one person. I refresh my mobile phone, seeing the screensaver of my father's face. I think about Dr Ward's words again, about him having a great mind, and half an hour later, at the end of my shift, I finally drive to the nursing home.

In the early stages, when my father first stopped remembering the simplest of things, I tried to dismiss it, not wanting to face the truth. It was the names that went first, quickly followed by familiarity with places. Soon what had happened moments before disappeared, falling off some imaginary cliff and ending up in the Gulf of Nowhere. His episodes of delirium heightened too, especially when he picked up a head cold or an infection. Once he believed the doctors were trying to kill him, culminating in his refusal to eat, and again, I think about Nadine Fitzmaurice.

Arriving at the eighteenth-century Georgian structure, standing tall and elegant, nestled in its beautifully landscaped gardens, I open the large front door, replaying the first day I came here. Everything looked so shipshape and up to the mark, an orderly balance between calm and medical care, but even back then there was something surreal about the place, and it repeats itself every time I come, because once that heavy door closes behind me, it shuts out the rest of the world.

Inside, I take the stairs to the first floor, leaving the lift for others with reduced mobility. My father requires help dressing now and washing too. At first, he used to climb the stairs, but now he says he feels safer in the lift, even though he doesn't know why. These things are part of his condition, but when he has one of his bad days, I hate it: then he isn't my father any more. He's someone else.

On the staircase, I pass Leonard, another patient, working his way downstairs. He clutches a packet of Silk Cut Blue, and a pink glitter lighter that's probably stolen. Leonard likes shiny things, so he lifts them whenever he can.

'Enjoy your cigarette,' I say.

He taps an imaginary cap in response. I know exactly where he's heading. Downstairs, there's a special place for him to light up, a chair in the conservatory where he can open a window and flick out his ash. I watched him once, sucking in the nicotine, treasuring each breath as if it might be his last.

My father's room is the last on the left at the end of the first-floor corridor. It looks out onto the garden. It's south-facing, so it's unusually bright. My father repeatedly tells me the light is great for painting, even though he doesn't paint. My mother was the painter, but he doesn't mention her any more.

'How is he today?' I ask the young nurse dispensing medication halfway up the corridor. Her name is Jasmine.

'He slept well last night,' she says, as if this is the most important aspect of his life now.

I turn the handle and open the door, unsure, as I often am, how he'll be, or even if he'll recognise me.

'Hello,' he says, staring at me as if I'm something new, a fresh object of curiosity he's meeting for the first time.

'Hi,' I reply, sitting in the corner chair. I like to sit in the same place, because sometimes, if I do, he makes the connection.

'Faces,' he says, walking towards the window, 'they're everywhere.'

'Oh?' I reply, although I've no idea where this is going.

'Have you ever looked at the sky, and seen a cloud that looks remarkably like a face?'

'Maybe,' I say, disappointed, because I already know he doesn't recognise me.

'Seeing faces in inanimate objects is quite common.'

'Really?'

'Yes, it even has a name.'

'What's that?' I ask, happy, for now, to play along.

He struggles briefly, his eyes darting back and forth, concentrating. He's worried he mightn't remember the proper word for it, but then he says, 'Pareidolia,' and I see the relief on his face, as if saying it aloud is a great achievement.

'It's a psychological phenomenon,' he continues, knocking his knuckles against the glass for extra emphasis, 'causing the human brain to lend significance to random patterns.'

I like it when he sounds like his old self. It probably won't last long.

'Dad,' I say.

He turns and looks at me as if he's been caught off guard.

'It's me, Wren.'

We stare at one another. Today, he's wearing a navy jumper, smart navy slacks, and green tartan slippers, with a pair of random red socks underneath. The collar of his white shirt peeps out over his jumper.

'Wren?' he quizzes, unknowing.

I can't stand it.

'It's okay,' I say, wishing I hadn't mentioned my name. 'That information on pareidolia is fascinating.'

His eyes light up again. We're back on safer ground.

'I see faces everywhere,' he says. 'Look, I'll show you. Come over to the window.'

I do as he instructs and stand beside him. I want him to hug me, to hold me the way a father holds a daughter, to feel the old familiar bond, even briefly.

'Do you see that blue car out front?' he asks, his words gaining momentum as he speaks, pointing to an old Mini by the main entrance.

'Yes.'

'Look at that bumper. Doesn't it suggest a mouth? And that long silver embellishment,' he continues, 'the one coming down from the windscreen across the bonnet, is definitely a nose.' He's pointing now. 'The windscreen wipers, cocked at an angle,' he continues, 'they're exactly like eyes.'

'Hmm,' I reply.

'What do *you* see?' he asks, keen to get my view.

'When you put it like that, I guess it does look like a face.'

He seems pleased. 'Different people,' he continues, 'see the same things quite differently.'

Once more, I think about Nadine Fitzmaurice.

He moves towards the bed. Has he forgotten about the face in the car already?

'Why do we do it?' I ask. 'Imagine faces, I mean.'

'Oh, that's easy.'

I'm relieved he hasn't forgotten the conversation.

'The brain prefers faces over patterns.'

'Really?'

'Yes. They even tried it out with macaque monkeys once, and during each of the experiments, the monkeys repeatedly responded far better to faces than objects.'

'Do they know why?'

'It's connected to humanity's heightened sense of awareness.'

'Awareness?'

'Making us more alert to other creatures, whether they're human or animal. If you lived in the jungle,' he smiles, 'it would be most helpful to be sensitised to tigers.'

'I'll bear that in mind.'

Again, he stares at me. Something changes in his face. 'Wren,' he says, 'is that you?'

My heart leaps. 'Yes, it's me.'

'But you look older, all grown-up.'

'I *am* grown-up.'

'How did that happen?' There's fresh confusion in his expression, as he tries to connect a set of imaginary dots with the intervening years missing.

'I'll always be your little girl,' I say, putting him at his ease.

'Good,' he says, but I can tell he's still unsure.

I sit down. He sits on the bed, looking tired now, staring out the window. I lean forward, taking his narrow hands in mine. They are more wrinkled than they should be. He's only sixty, but he already appears far older.

He doesn't object to me holding his hands. We don't say anything to each other. For now it's enough, because I know, soon, he'll forget me again.

The young nurse, Jasmine, comes into the room with his medication. 'What are these for?' he asks, suspicious of the tablets.

'You need them, Christopher, for your heart, and other stuff.'

He doesn't argue. Maybe this routine has become primal – tablets, water, swallow.

'We'll be going for your bath soon,' she says, clear and instructive.

He nods, submissive.

'I won't be much longer,' I tell her, aware the nursing home likes its routine nearly as much as the patients do.

After she leaves, I open his wardrobe to get him a fresh bath towel. Everything is stacked so neatly it looks like a military operation, which is why my eyes are drawn to a brown cardboard folder sticking out of the bottom shelf, partially hidden by a pair of slippers. I lean down, pulling it out, and when I flip it open, I see a manilla envelope inside.

'What's this?' I ask, not really expecting an answer.

My father shrugs his shoulders.

Opening it, I immediately see the newspaper clippings as my eyes are drawn to the young girl's face. This doesn't make any sense. I pull the clippings out, still trying to grasp what they mean. I read and reread the articles, even though I've seen them several times before. Why does my father have newspaper clippings about Evie Hunt? There's no logical reason for it. I place the clippings to the side, my father still oblivious, as I examine an A4 page with notes in his handwriting. At the top is the date of my mother's accident. This is followed by a brief description of the weather conditions that day, wind and heavy rain. The exact time of the accident is there too. Below this, there are several names, one of which I recognise. My mind does a couple of somersaults as I try to piece it all together. I repeat the names in my head, Patrick Mescal, Martin Prendergast and, finally, Gavin Fitzmaurice. I guess my father could have taken Gavin's name from the news clipping, but again, why? Gavin never met my father. By the time we got together, my father was already diagnosed with Alzheimer's disease, so either Gavin's name is in my father's notes because of Evie's disappearance, or because of my mother's accident.

'Why do you have these?' I ask, holding up the clippings about Evie Hunt.

He shrugs again, giving me a blank stare.

I don't want to frighten him, but I need to know the truth. I sit beside him on the bed. 'Dad, did you know this girl?'

He looks at the face of Evie Hunt. 'Should I?'

Jasmine knocks on the door. 'Are you ready, Christopher?'

I help him up, handing him his bath towel. 'Do you mind if I stay a little while, Jasmine, to fix a few things?'

'No problem,' she says, taking my father by the arm.

Before he leaves, he turns back to me. 'That young girl is very pretty,' he says.

'Yes,' I say, 'she is.'

'And remember, Wren, the next time you see a face in an object, you're not crazy.'

'No?'

'Because sometimes when you look hard enough, what seems like one thing can become something else entirely.'

After the door closes behind him, I pull the contents of the wardrobe apart, but everything else appears normal. I compare the date on the news article about Evie to the date of my mother's accident. Evie went missing nearly a year after my mother was killed. Is there some kind of connection? Did my father know Evie Hunt? And why was Gavin's name in his notes? Each question hangs like forbidden fruit, pulling me further in, which is why I know exactly what I need to do next.

36
NADINE

I press the intercom for Dr Ward's office. I'm five minutes early. Sandy buzzes me through, and I repeat the same motions as before, pressing the lift button, then going up in it, all the while steadying my breathing.

I arrive with one minute to spare, but still I have to wait for Dr Ward. She rarely sees anyone on time, but it's frowned upon if you're late.

With Sandy concentrating on phone calls, I pull out my mobile phone, checking for any new messages.

There's a text from Gavin. *How's things?*

I message back. *Fine.*

Are you still at home?

I wonder if Aria told him I left the house. *No,* I reply, *I'm waiting for Dr Ward.*

I wait for another text, but instead the phone rings. It's Gavin, unwilling to leave well enough alone.

'I can't talk right now, Gavin. I'm waiting to be called in.'

'You shouldn't be driving on that medication.'

'Dr Ward didn't say that,' I reply, defiant.

'Maybe not, but I've seen how that new prescription affects you. You're exhausted with it. You should be getting rest as we agreed.'

Then I remember the missing pages from the notebook. 'The last time you were in the house, Gavin, did you take anything?'

'Of course not. Is this more—'

'Lies? Is that what you mean?'

'Yes.'

'You're not my keeper.'

'No, I'm your brother.'

'Did you meddle with my notebook?'

'What notebook?'

'The one I use for grocery lists.'

'I've no idea what you're talking about.'

'There are pages missing.'

'Nadine, I can't listen to any more of your crazy shit. You need to get a grip.'

Dr Ward's door opens. I shut off the call before he has a chance to say anything else.

'Nadine,' she says, smiling, 'I didn't expect you until tomorrow.'

'I was keen to see you.'

'Oh,' she says, instructing me to sit down.

Inside my head, I attempt calmness, hoping my voice will follow. 'I've been thinking about a few things.'

'What kind of things?'

'I'm feeling more like my old self.'

'Have you been taking your medication?'

'Yes,' I lie.

'I'm glad to hear it. Avoiding your medication will only bring additional problems.'

'I realise that.'

'The police called to see me yesterday.'

I don't expect this. 'Really?'

'A Detective Sergeant Moore.'

I reassess my thoughts with this fresh information.

'I understand you've been extremely concerned about Becca.'

'She hasn't been in touch for a while.'

'And you had another panic attack.'

'Yes.'

'Your brother is very concerned about you, as am I.'

'That's why I needed to see you today,' I say, talking fast. 'I was thinking it might be a good idea if I returned to work.'

'That would be a little premature.'

'It could be good for me.'

'I'd prefer, Nadine, to track your progress over a longer period.'

'I understand, but honestly, I always feel better when my mind is occupied. You said yourself work can be therapeutic for me.'

'Yes, I did say that. You're calmer when your thought processes are stimulated in a healthy manner. Only these things are delicate. Any undue pressure could tilt your emotional well-being in the wrong direction. There is the question of balancing the levels of stress you're exposed to.'

'Being alone all day isn't good for me either. I can talk to my employer, discuss reduced hours, taking it slowly.'

'What about your brother? What's his view on this?'

'I'm your patient.'

'We can review this again in a couple of weeks. I'm not saying *no* for ever.'

'But—'

'It's for your own good, Nadine. None of us are particularly skilled at sensing when we need time out, least of all the people who need it most.'

This is useless.

'Let's diary forward for a couple of weeks.'

Obediently, I key the new date into my phone. I have to think of another way.

Dr Ward is still talking, but I've already stopped listening. All I can hear are Ben's words circling in my head, false insurance claim, tampering with documents, damaging video files.

Finally, after listening to more advice from Dr Ward about taking things easy, I shake her hand as if I'm a regular person, instead of a desperate woman trying to do whatever it takes to save her daughter.

At the front desk, I smile at Sandy, then glance down at her desk.

It's neat and organised, but I spot a batch of headed paper about to be loaded into the photocopier.

'Sandy,' I say, 'Dr Ward asked if you could step in for a minute.'

'Did she?' She looks at me as if she's been asked to break out of jail, but still, she stands up. With her back to me, I grab a couple of sheets, putting them in my bag. Ben is right. Forgery isn't beyond me. I've done a lot worse.

I hear Sandy and Dr Ward talking inside her office. I could escape now, but it's best to brave it out, and avoid any more unnecessary suspicion.

Sandy doesn't take long. 'You must have been mistaken, Nadine,' she says, reassuming her position at the desk.

'I've been getting a lot of things mixed up lately,' I say, looking suitably chastised. None of it matters, because now I have the means of forging a note for work.

Outside, I check my bag again to make sure the blank headed paper is still there. I stare at the spot where, less than a week ago, I first saw Evie. I can't see her now, but that doesn't mean she isn't nearby.

Crossing at the traffic lights, I phone work. They agree to me returning tomorrow morning at eleven. I shouldn't be able to do any of this, but sometimes it's at the very moments when you're pushed the hardest, when you feel most vulnerable, that you gain the strength to do whatever it takes.

37
NADINE

WHEN I REACH HOME, I KNOW straight away someone's been in the house. The mail on the hall table has been disturbed. There are letters on the floor, spread out, like a fallen deck of cards. I look towards the kitchen, seeing more destruction there, jars knocked over, the various herbs and spices forming a potent mix.

Is it another break-in?

Could someone still be in the house?

My heart races, my breathing heavy, as a shiver darts through me. Should I call out? Alert them I'm home? Instead, I prise open the living-room door, half expecting the intruder to leap out at me, but all I see is more carnage, drawers emptied, chairs and other pieces of furniture knocked over, a photograph of my mother upside down on the floor. There's broken glass beside the frame. I kneel down. The shattered glass reminds me of the screen on my mobile phone, its spider lines creeping out in all directions.

I listen for any sounds. I hear the odd creaking of floorboards, then the trickling of water moving through the pipes. A droning noise comes from the refrigerator in the kitchen. I count backwards from twenty to zero, continuing to be alert. As I stand up, my eyes are drawn to the fireplace, seeing charred paper in the grate. It doesn't make sense. I haven't lit a fire in weeks.

Walking towards it, I notice there's a tiny corner of white paper curled up at the end. My fingertips pinch it, and immediately I recognise my handwriting. It's a page from my notebook, the one I use for grocery lists, the one in which I wrote down Becca's instructions that first day. I see a partial name, Jo – John Simons, Ben Donnelly's alias? Did someone try to destroy the proof of these pages' existence?

Despite being terrified, I check upstairs, finally convincing myself I'm alone. The whole house is a mess. In my bedroom, clothes are strewn on the floor, drawers emptied, as if someone was searching for something.

My eyes keep scanning the room, until finally they rest on the door to the en-suite bathroom. It's closed tight. I always leave it open.

I take a step closer, hesitating before I turn the handle, scared of what might be behind it, frightened that the intruder may still be here.

The door creaks open. I jerk back. I'm finding it hard to breathe, my palms turning instantly sweaty, the early signs of another panic attack. I try to take in everything I can, unwilling to accept, even now, that this could be happening.

I force myself further into the room, examining the writing on the mirror, and what looks like a bloodied message from a dead man. I see an open gold lipstick container in the sink. I recognise the shade, Pillowtalk. I pick it up, replacing the lid, as if I'm still in denial, wanting to refute the words right in front of me, then staring at the glass once more, each letter in red telling me what I already know, what I've known ever since the police dug up the back garden: the person I fear most in the world isn't dead. He's alive. And now he wants to push me further still, because nothing in life ever gave him more pleasure than seeing me suffer.

I read the words aloud.

'YOU

LEFT

ME

TO

DIE.'

I back away. 'I buried you,' I scream.

I feel sick, the enormity of it all suddenly hitting home fast. I should call the police, but then I remember that detective's face when she told me the police hadn't found Cian's remains, or anything else in the back garden. I knew then she thought I'd imagined it all, that I was a madwoman recovering from a panic attack, with her daughter gone AWOL, who came up with a crazy story about her daughter being held captive, and that more than anything, I should be pitied for losing my grip on reality. Now, as I stare at the words on the mirror, a part of me begins to wonder if she's right.

∞

I've had another blackout, only this time when I come to, I can't remember going downstairs. This has happened to me before. I lose consciousness, and when I wake, I'm somewhere else, with chunks of time missing. The house is in darkness, but more than anything right now, I've an immediate desire to put everything back to the way it was. I won't wipe that message off the mirror, even though I want to. When Gavin comes back, I'll show it to him, along with the piece of paper from the grate.

Again, I consider calling the police and telling them about the break-in. Only nothing about this is simple any more, and even if I called them, after my last episode in the police station I'm positive now they wouldn't believe me. They'd think I used my own lipstick to write those words on the mirror as another ploy to get attention. They might even believe I tossed the place myself.

I walk back upstairs, and stare at those horrible words again. Like Evie, Cian has waited to seek his revenge on me, and now there is no one I can turn to for help, not Becca or Gavin or the people at work, and certainly not the police. If Cian is alive, they'd be useless. They couldn't protect me before, so why would they be able to protect me now?

In the darkness of the bedroom, I curl up in a ball in the armchair, my mind switching back to childhood, to a time when I pretended

I had a different life, a different mother, one who openly showed affection, who'd tell me, if I was scared, that everything would be okay.

I worry now that I might be getting close to the edge. More than anything, I want to hear Becca's voice, but that's not possible. I think about Gavin too. He always thinks he knows what's good for me, telling me I shouldn't take on any more stress, saying he needs to keep an eye on me, as if I'm weak, dependent. Sometimes I wonder if he likes putting me down, always questioning my decisions, causing me to doubt myself. It was the same when we were kids: he always wanted the upper hand, the last word, the control.

Now, my mind feels exhausted, worn down, and yet somehow, tomorrow, I'll have to face work.

I need sleep. I make sure the en-suite door is closed tight. I can't bear to read those words again, but before getting into bed, I decide to look at Becca's early memory book. It's in a large black box hidden in a compartment at the back of the wardrobe, a space I used when I needed to hide things from Cian. The box has my mother's last will and testament in it too. Thank goodness Gavin is looking after the legal stuff. I wouldn't be able to deal with solicitors and probate, especially now.

Near the bottom of the box, I find what I'm looking for. At the front of the memory book, there are two old passport photographs. The first one is of Becca aged four, and in the second, she's nine. I look from one image to the other, recalling her first day of school, her sky-blue uniform, her hair tied back tight in a long ponytail. She was nervous but excited, like any regular four-year-old. I study the older image too, remembering Cian's abuse all over again, aware that, no matter how much I tried to shelter my daughter, it affected her, especially that horrible night when Cian got so angry, I had to lock him out of the house. I was sobbing so loudly I didn't hear him place the ladder up to Becca's bedroom window. At first, she refused to let him in, but then she opened it, and he told her she was a good girl. Seconds later, he came after me, and in the beating that followed, I heard her plead with him to stop. Soon I didn't hear anything. It was Becca who helped me get well, bringing me water and painkillers, gradually getting me to eat.

I cradle both passport photographs close to my chest, and then I do something I haven't done in years. I pray. I beg a higher power that Cian will leave us in peace, and that soon Ben and Evie will allow my beautiful daughter to come home.

38
WREN

After visiting my father yesterday, I returned to the station in Rathfarnham, pulling whatever details I could on Evie Hunt from the PULSE database. The historical missing-person report came up straight away although, as I'd suspected, the details were scant. That didn't matter. What I wanted was the case number, because with it I could pull the notes and statements from the central storage depot in Santry. When I included this on my to-do list after interviewing Nadine Fitzmaurice, it had had nothing to do with my father, but now it has.

Nearing Santry, a million questions are jumping through my mind, not least of which is how my father is involved. He had those news articles for a reason. There was a purpose to them, which begs the question, who was his focus: Gavin, Evie or even Cian Campbell?

Inside the depot, it doesn't take long to get clearance for the box, but as I wait for it to arrive, I write Evie Hunt's name in bold print on my notepad, circling it over and over. I think about what I was like as a teenager, and how at times, it was a mix of confusion and exhilaration, almost as if you were changing skin. You go from being perceived primarily as innocent, to attracting the eyes and attention of boys and men long before you've caught up with the magnitude of it all.

I've circled Evie's name so many times, there are holes in the page. I imagine what she was like back then. Like many other teenagers, she was probably bombarded with the same questions I was. What size chest are you? Have you done it yet? Do you have fake ID? Or, when attempting to buy booze, what age are you? Are you flirting with me? How far are you prepared to go? Do you use protection? What are you going to do at college? Are you a feminist? Are you gay? Do you want a smoke? Have you any vodka? The list was endless, almost as if everyone else was trying to get to know you when you were trying to get to know yourself.

Was Evie under pressure? Was that why she needed to get away? And worse, could my father have been involved with her disappearance?

I think again about first hooking up with Gavin. He was scheduled to leave the force with an early severance package. While others clapped him on the back the night of his leaving party, I initially kept my distance, as I hadn't been at the station that long. It was he who approached me. He was charming, older, interesting, and I admit, even now, there was a dangerous edge to him, a kind of irreverent side that should have put me off, but somehow it didn't. Is that why I willingly got so quickly involved, that underlying sense of danger? I wouldn't be the first cop accused of being an adrenaline junkie. And, if it's true, I also know, if I could turn back time, I would probably do it again.

Footsteps approach. I see the duty officer carrying the box containing whatever information exists on the missing person, Evie Hunt. I need to work out why this young girl disappeared, and to know if her disappearance was by choice or design.

I wait until the duty officer leaves before I open the box of evidence. Again, I'm not surprised there isn't a huge amount of data inside because, at eighteen, it was Evie's sole right to disappear if she wanted to.

The first photograph of Evie is the one used for the Interpol and Europol online records. I think about Nadine's words, later confirmed by Gavin, that Evie responded to a dare and possibly a whole lot more. She stares back at me, her long hair falling past her shoulders with hints of blonde and honey shades. In the image, she's wearing a bright yellow dress. She seems to be at a party. I note her slim tanned arms. She's pouting at the camera, provocative, as if taunting whoever is taking the image, daring them to think her anything but cool. I contemplate the accusations Nadine made about Evie's father, and if she's telling the truth, then there was a lot more complicated things going on in this young girl's mind. What do I feel about her? If I'm being honest, when I was with Gavin, she was like an unwanted memory from the past. Someone I might have to live up to. Only you can't live up to a ghost.

Staring at her now, a young girl with her whole life in front of her, I can't help but feel sad for whatever dark secrets she may have kept from the others, possibly even Gavin.

Using my phone, I photograph everything from the box. One name jumps out at me. It's the name I saw yesterday in my father's handwriting: Patrick Mescal.

Now I know who he is: the family liaison officer allocated to Evie Hunt's case. He could be retired at this stage, considering how far back the case goes, but that doesn't mean I can't track him down.

∞

Driving back to Rathfarnham, Mike phones. 'Good news, Wren.'

'Hit me, because right now, good news is exactly what I need.'

'We got a lot of calls on the *Crimecall* CCTV footage.'

'Anything concrete?'

'Still shifting through them, but there's something else.'

'What?'

'Lauren Bennet has a new theory on her pathology findings.'

'I'm listening.'

'She's done further analysis of the skin and found surface brushing and tears on the lower wrist area.'

'And?'

'She's positive there must have been a physical interaction of some kind.'

'So, our victim was in a fight?'

'Yeah, but she says the pattern of bruising and tears is interesting.'

'In what way?'

'She can't be one hundred per cent sure, but she thinks the tears were made by a female.'

'Why does she say that?'

'They were created by someone with long fingernails, the kind with rounded tips.'

'Any possibility of getting DNA from the skin?'

'Lauren says slim to non-existent, due to the plastic being applied and reapplied, but if she gets anything more, she'll be in touch straight away.'

'Okay. I shouldn't be long.'

'Oh, by the way, Aria Jackson, Nadine Fitzmaurice's next-door neighbour, has been on again, wondering when to expect you.'

'She's persistent, I'll give her that. I might as well get it over with now.'

'Want some company?'

'Nope. You keep shifting through that *Crimecall* stuff and buzz me if anything else raises its head.'

On the way to Aria's house, I pass the street where my mother was hit by that stolen car. It's directly across the road from my old school. For ages afterwards, I believed I could still see the skid marks, reimagining it in my mind. I could have been with her. Originally, we were going to stop at the shop for milk before she dropped me off at school, only we didn't. Who knows what difference that would have made? Maybe she would have survived, or perhaps both of us could have been killed. Surviving defines you. It tells you life is worth living, even on the crappy days, because other people aren't so lucky.

Soon I'm pulling up outside Aria's house. I can see Nadine's home from here too. There's only a low laurel bush separating the two. I'm wondering if Nadine is still in Gavin's place or, with him away, if she's returned home. If she's there, my visit will likely add to her anxiety.

When I step out of the car, the street is relatively quiet, other than a couple of young mothers chatting to one another, each with a buggy and baby in tow. I already know Aria works from home, so even without phoning forward, I'm not surprised when she opens the front door.

'There you are,' she says, as if she's been expecting me for days, and I've finally granted her an audience.

I show her my ID – standard procedure – but she barely glances at it.

'Come in,' she says. 'I'm about to make some herbal tea.'

'None for me, thanks.'

I follow her through to the kitchen at the rear of the house. The place is identical in design to Nadine's, other than everything being on the opposite side.

At the kitchen table, a fat grey and white cat curls around the legs opposite. Cats unnerve me, a likely throwback from watching too much Hitchcock as a child. I still remember the story of Toby the cat in the pram. I had recurring nightmares about it for years. I'm relieved when the overweight feline leaves the room.

'Have you lived here long?' I ask, breaking the ice.

'Nearly a decade, but doesn't time fly when you're having fun?'

She pours water through a metal tea strainer. The liquid in the cup turns a mint green.

I take out my notebook and place it on the wooden kitchen table. It's painted sky-blue with large white daisies. I googled Aria a couple of days ago, and sitting here, a picture of her forms in my mind: herbal tea, reclaimed flower-power furniture, holistic homeopathic treatments, yoga and mindfulness, creating a cocktail of new age, peace to the world, a living-in-the-moment bliss type, someone very different from Nadine Fitzmaurice, the highly strung woman next door.

'I wanted to ask you a few questions,' I say, as she takes her first sip of tea. 'You don't mind, do you?'

'Of course not.' She reaches out and touches my arm. 'I'm very fond of Nadine. All this nasty business must be most distressing for her.'

I flip open my notebook, dislodging her hand. 'I'm sure it must be.' I hope she takes the hint. I'm not keen on strangers touching me.

'So, Aria, after you heard the screams, did you call the police right away?'

'No, not immediately.'

'Why not?'

'I wasn't sure, you see.'

'About what?'

She takes another sip of tea, before placing the cup down and stretching out her fingers. 'Nadine hasn't had the easiest of lives.'

'In what way?'

'Well, her ex-husband for a start. He was particularly nasty.'

'You knew him?'

'Yes, but to be honest, I used to avoid him. It was a relief when he left and, no doubt, it was a relief for Nadine too. She and Becca were better off without him.'

'There were domestic issues?'

'I'd hear them arguing all the time.'

'And then he just upped and left?'

'That's right.'

'And you never saw him again?'

'One day he was there, and the next he was gone.'

I think about Evie Hunt. One day she was there, and then she was gone too. 'Getting back to the scream, or screams, Aria, and you not reporting them right away.'

'Initially, I thought that Cian, Nadine's ex-husband, had come back. I approached Nadine about it the next day, but she dismissed it as nothing.'

'You obviously believed she was in danger, whether it was Cian or someone else.'

'At first, yes, but then Becca came to mind.'

'Oh?'

'Lately, she and Nadine have argued a lot too. I suppose I wondered who the screams belonged to, Nadine or Becca.'

'And did you finally decide?'

She leans in closer as if afraid Nadine, who may be next door right now, might hear her. 'No,' she says, 'not completely.'

'An adult female scream and that of a teenager are quite different.'

'I know, but you see, I was upstairs, at the back of the house, and the screams came from the front living room below, so they were quite muted.'

'But you're still sure it was screams you heard?'

'Absolutely. And then after Nadine brushed me off the following day, I decided I should do my civic duty and notify the police. Then I saw her outside frantically digging up the back garden. I didn't know what to do, so I called Gavin.'

'You had his phone number?'

'He worries about Nadine. He gave it to me a while back, just in case.'

'Have you spoken to Nadine since that night?'

'No, but she's home.' Again, she stares at the connecting wall between the two houses, as if her neighbour's presence on the other side might be too close for comfort.

'Gavin has gone away for a few days with work,' she continues, 'so he brought Nadine back here.'

'I'm sure it's all been very difficult for you too.' I try to sound sympathetic. 'Is there anything else you can tell me?'

'There is one small thing.'

'Okay.'

'I might have seen someone hanging around outside, watching Nadine's house.'

'You might, or you did?'

'Well, it's difficult. With everything happening next door, I worry I may be letting my imagination get the better of me too.'

'Right, so the person you *might* have seen hanging around, did you notice them at night or during the day?'

'Night. I'm positive about that. Both times, it was dark.'

'So, it happened more than once.'

'Yes.'

'Male or female?'

'I can't be sure. They stood in the shadows below the tree on the far side of the road. I tried to make out their face, but it was too difficult.'

I consider my father imagining faces in car bonnets and wonder if Nadine isn't the only one on this street with an overactive imagination. 'Anything else?'

'They stayed there for an extremely long time.'

'How long?'

'Nearly an hour, both times. I waited for them to step forward, but when they did, they kept their head down, so I couldn't really make anything out. At first, I dismissed it, but when it happened a second time, it played on my mind. I mean, they certainly looked like a prowler, and with the break-in and all ...'

'What break-in?'

'The one at Nadine's place a few weeks back.'

'Was anything taken?'

'Strangely, no.'

'Why do you think the person hanging around outside looked like a prowler?'

'I don't know. Perhaps because they moved so fast in the dark.'

'There's a security light outside, the same as the one on Nadine's house. Why didn't it light up?'

'It only picks up movement from within the gardens.'

'Anything else?'

She considers this for a few seconds. 'They were agile too, like the way Cian, Nadine's ex, used to be.'

'Agile?'

'I mean extremely fit. Cian was always aware of his physicality. You could tell that by him. He liked to be admired.'

'Do you have any idea where Cian went, after he left Nadine?'

'Not a clue.'

'When did you last see this prowler?'

'The night before Nadine went crazy, when she dug up the back garden.'

'And before that?'

'I can't remember.' She settles her hands on the table, folding her fingers into one another.

I close my notebook. 'Okay. If you think of anything else, Aria, I'd be grateful if you'd let me know.'

The fat grey and white cat returns.

'I'll keep an extra special eye on events for you,' she says, reaching out to touch my arm again.

It's a relief to finally get away from her, alongside an additional level of sympathy for Nadine Fitzmaurice, having to live next door.

39
NADINE

THE SOUND OF THE DETECTIVE'S car parking outside drew me to the upstairs window. She's been in with Aria for nearly half an hour. I'm sure my wonderful neighbour has spun any number of lies about me, but I can't be thinking about that now. I keep my eyes peeled on the road, watching everything, hoping the detective will soon be gone, and I can then leave for work.

A teenage girl in a school uniform cycles into view. Her front wheel is wobbling because she's only holding the handlebars with one hand. The other has her mobile phone in it. I think about Evie again, as the smell of the beach rises in my nostrils. Smells hold such powerful memories. Freshly cut grass always reminds me of summer, and sea smells remind me of Magheramore. Old emotions come flooding back, the aromas potent, although I'm now miles away from the sea. Instantly, it's as if time falls away, and I'm back there, my feet feeling the sand between my toes, mingled with tangled seaweed. I hear the waves bash against the shore, angry, like some furious God in the heavens, warning me of danger, while the seagulls screech overhead.

Finally, I watch the detective drive away, and when I'm sure she's gone, I make my way out to the car. Immediately Aria opens her front door. She heads in my direction, waving me down. I pretend I don't see her, pulling away fast. As the car gains speed, her image in the rear-view mirror grows smaller until, finally, she's no longer in my view.

I've stopped taking my medication so my body and mind are working faster. Heading into work, I'm fully aware of what I have to do. And, just like my time in Magheramore, choosing a different path isn't an option.

I know as soon as I do what Ben has instructed I'll become a traitor to the people I work with, people who trust me. They've only ever seen a certain side of me. They don't know what I'm capable of. If any one of them were asked to describe me, the term 'upstanding citizen' might come to mind, along with 'a trusted colleague', someone who wouldn't break the law in a zillion years, someone with a good moral base, only morals go out the window when your daughter's life is in danger. If they were in my shoes, they would probably do the same thing I'm about to. Which is why, shortly before midday, I've pulled *all* the records on the Prendergast case.

Martin Prendergast is the main claimant. When he jammed on the brakes, the result was a four-car pile-up, with everyone rear-ending him. He's claiming extensive motor costs, alongside compensation for physical injuries, inclusive of spinal damage. This kind of case can easily reach a six-figure sum, but as I flick through the various witness statements, another thought takes hold. The name is familiar to me. As a teenager, my brother used to be friendly with a boy by that name. I remember them having a huge argument, and after that, Martin never came around to the house again. Could it be the same person? The age profile fits, but then again, there must be any number of Martin Prendergasts.

I open the reports from the in-house investigator attached to the surveillance footage. The first video shows Martin being aided, and struggling to walk into a gym, but I'm guessing the footage from inside will tell a different story. There are additional witness reports from the accident scene too, and my first thought is, with such a high number of statements, this whole thing stinks of a set-up right from the beginning.

I'm about to view the second load of footage when my line manager arrives. She's standing in front of me, so she can't see the computer screen. I close off the file just in case.

'Good to have you back, Nadine.'

'Great to be back,' I say, all cheery.

'Let's do some catch-up once you get your bearings.'

'Sounds great,' I say, aware of the list of criminal actions I'm about to commit, including in-house security breaches, tampering with evidence, aiding a felon, and much more. All sackable offences, but once my boss is no longer nearby, I don't waste another second, because soon, I know, I'll be getting that phone call from Ben, and if I haven't done what he's asked of me, losing my job or going to prison will be the least of my worries.

I click open the second piece of surveillance footage, the one of Martin Prendergast in the gym. I watch him walk unaided to the weights section. I see him mentally prepare his body, concentrating hard. Lifting weights would be a challenge for a healthy person, but impossible for someone with back injuries. I study his face closely. Could he be the same Martin Prendergast Gavin knew? Seconds later, he grips the weights at either end, his knees bending, the muscles on his upper body locking into position, quickly followed by several grunts as he applies full force to the task in hand, the bar rising upwards, until the final heave, as he strains to place the weights above his head, holding them for several seconds, before letting out a loud gasp, and returning them downwards. He's a big man, but there's no way anyone with the injuries he supposedly sustained would be able to lift that kind of weight.

I keep scanning the files, checking how many copies of the footage exist. There are two within the main database and a master copy held by security on the back-up system. You need a certain level of clearance to access the master files, which, thankfully, I have.

I divide the reports associated with the claim into two groups, those in support of the claim, and those disputing it, all the while making notes about how I will alter the negative data. Halfway through the witness statements, I see the name John Simons, the same name Becca used that first day. I didn't know back then it was an alias for Ben Donnelly, but I know it now, and seeing the name in the witness list is another way of telling me I'm merely a pawn in someone else's game of deceit.

40
WREN

BACK AT THE STATION, I TURN my attention to Cian Campbell even though, so far, I've come up with virtually nothing on his whereabouts. The last official record was for a short-term social welfare claim early in 2013. He also renewed his driving licence in 2013, but that had ten-year validity. The Revenue Commissioners didn't have a whole lot on him either, with no tax returns filed since 2010. The only information of value is his last known employer, Berkley Shipping, but again, it's from years before. Everything points to him being in another jurisdiction but, right now, I have to start somewhere.

I punch in the telephone number for Cian's last place of work. A female voice answers.

'Hi, my name is Detective Sergeant Moore. I'm hoping to talk to someone about an ex-employee of yours, a Cian Campbell.'

'When did he last work here?'

'Seven or eight years ago.'

'That's before my time, but I can connect you with Adam. He's the office manager.'

'Great,' I say, as I'm placed on hold.

She comes back about thirty seconds later. 'Detective Sergeant Moore, I'm afraid Adam isn't in his office at the moment, but if you'd like to leave your number, I'll ask him to call you.'

I give her my direct line and mobile phone number.

Mike opens the door. 'What are you working on?' he asks. 'I

recognise that expression of yours, and it usually spells trouble.'

'The Becca Campbell missing-person case.'

'I thought the super told you to wrap it up.'

'Yep, he did.'

'He also said he didn't want you to waste any more police resources on it.'

'He said that too.'

He shakes his head, disapproving, then asks, 'Would you like me to share the *Crimecall* info with you?'

'Only if we have something interesting.'

'You'll be interested all right, considering your current focus.'

'What do you mean?'

'We had an anonymous tip-off, someone claiming they recognised the person in the footage.'

'You've got my attention.'

'They claim our mystery person is male, and that they knew who it was because the guy moved in a particular way.'

'How so?'

'As if he was trying to make himself look taller, stronger.'

'A bit ambiguous, don't you think?'

'Maybe, except for one small detail.'

'What's that?'

'Our caller also gave us a name.'

'You're enjoying this, Mike, aren't you, stringing things out?'

'You have to take small pleasures where you get them.'

'Spit it out, for God's sake.'

'Ben.'

'Ben who?'

'Donnelly.'

'Are you serious?'

'Do I look like I'm joking?'

I stand up, pacing around the room. 'You don't think ...'

'What – that Nadine Fitzmaurice might be on to something about this whole abduction lark?'

'Yeah, but it's too crazy. I mean, how does it fit with a severed limb of a young male turning up in the Dodder?'

'The pathology findings said the marks on the skin were caused by a female.'

'Who are you thinking? Nadine? Becca? Someone else?'

He shrugs his shoulders.

'I think it's time, Mike, we paid Ben Donnelly a visit, rattle him, find out what he knows.'

'Okay, but I'll be doing the driving.'

∞

We take an unmarked police car to Serpent Parade, in Harold's Cross. The area is a mix of professionals who rent, affluent families, and people who might have recently come into money. Ben Donnelly falls into the final bracket, although how and where the money came from isn't clear. He isn't such a big player that CAB, the Criminal Assets Bureau, have their sights on him, but every dog on the street knows there's little about Ben's above-average lifestyle that doesn't stink to high heaven.

'Hang back a little,' I instruct Mike, as he turns the corner into the cul-de-sac.

'Are we stalking him now?'

'I'm not sure, but let's shoot the breeze for a minute.'

Ever since leaving the station, I've been wondering if I should tell Mike about my father's connection to Evie Hunt. It doesn't take me long to decide.

'I went to see my father yesterday.'

'How was it?'

'The usual mix of him knowing and not knowing me.'

'That must be hard.'

'Yeah, it is.'

Mike doesn't reply, but I know he cares.

'I found something in the nursing home.'

'Oh?'

'Newspaper clippings. My father had them in his wardrobe.'

'Okay ...'

'They were about Evie Hunt.'

He looks at me, confused.

'And notes too, referencing the day my mother was killed.'

'What's the connection?'

'I don't know, but he wrote down three names, Patrick Mescal, the family liaison officer attached to the Evie Hunt case, was one.'

A frown line appears on Mike's forehead. 'And the other two?'

'One was Gavin.'

'I see,' he says, another notch of disapproval lodged in his head against Gavin. 'And the last?'

'A Martin Prendergast.'

'Do you know who he is?'

'Not yet, but I will.'

'Where are you going with this, Wren?'

'I'm not sure, but then again, there's a lot about all of this I'm unsure of.'

'Patrick Mescal sounds like a good kick-off point to me.'

'I agree.'

'Want me to do some digging?'

'I thought you were on the super's side when it came to Nadine's conspiracy stories about Evie Hunt.'

'Maybe I was, but now it's got personal.' Mike stares at Ben Donnelly's house. 'The blinds are still down,' he says, 'even though it's the middle of the day.'

'It doesn't mean he's not home.'

'He's certainly got plenty of high-tech stuff guarding him.'

'I doubt Ben Donnelly ever walks out his front door feeling safe. It's a miracle he's made it this far.'

'He's old-school, Wren. They tend to be more careful.'

'You mean, not out of his head on coke.'

'Look,' Mike says, 'we've got movement.' He points to the front door of number thirty-two. 'It's Ben's younger sister, Natasha. What do you want to do?'

'Ask her about Becca Campbell. I've her photograph right here, just in case.'

Mike drives the car up on the kerb, partially obstructing Natasha's exit as she pulls the front door closed behind her.

'Hold up there,' I shout.

Natasha stops in her tracks, clutching the hand of a little girl, her daughter, I assume. 'What do you want?' she asks, her tone and body posture flipping immediately into defensive mode.

'Is your brother home?' I ask.

'Is this police harassment?'

'Nope, just a friendly chat,' says Mike.

'No such thing with you fuckers.'

The child beside her doesn't even wince.

'Well, is he?' Mike repeats.

'No,' she says, defiant.

'Any idea when you might expect him back?' I ask, taking a step closer.

'He's been doing a lot of shifts lately, security on a building site in town.'

'Where exactly?'

'I don't remember.'

'Temporary amnesia, is it?' Mike asks.

'I'm his sister, not his wife.' She goes to take a step forward.

'Not so fast,' I say, getting out of the car and blocking her. Mike does the same thing. 'We've a few more questions.' I take out the photograph of Becca Campbell. 'Do you know this girl?'

'Nope.'

'Take another look. It might jog your memory.'

She doesn't even attempt to glance at it a second time. 'I don't know her, okay?'

I look down at the little girl wearing a My Little Pony sweatshirt, her blue eyes wide open, like two deep oceans. She doesn't say a word, but she clutches her mother's hand, and for an instant, I think about myself, as a child, when the police called to our front door, and I was told by my father to go into another room. I'd already sensed something was wrong. The house felt darker, emptier. Later, when my father explained everything, I wasn't even surprised. I knew from the first sound of the police ringing the doorbell that nothing would ever be the same again. In a way, I'm glad we never discovered the names of the suspects, because if we had, I'm not sure what my father would have done, or what, even now, I would do. All I know is, in the end the police didn't have enough to pin the crime on anyone, but the person who killed my mother knows who he is, and nearly twenty years on, he still knows that, instead of doing the right thing, he ran away.

'Your brother doesn't have a great relationship with the law, does he?' I say, keeping my eyes firmly locked on Natasha.

'That's because you're always fucking him around.'

'Feeling victimised, is he?' Mike jokes.

'Maybe he is, and he doesn't much like that other cop either.'

'Which one is that?' I ask.

'That Fitzmaurice pig.'

'Gavin Fitzmaurice?'

'Yeah, he was around here the other day asking lots of stupid questions.'

Mike gives me a look, warning me: if Gavin's been playing pretend cop, he's up to no good.

'What did he want to know?' Mike asks.

'I dunno. Ben was working, so he was wasting his time.'

'It seems your brother is very dedicated to his profession,' Mike adds, not bothering to hide his sarcasm.

She doesn't rise to the bait. Instead she snaps, 'I told him exactly what I told you, but like you, the bastard wouldn't leave.'

'No?' I push her, sensing there could be more.

'He stood over there for nearly an hour, watching the house.' She points to the other side of the street.

I think about the prowler Aria Jackson saw.

Natasha steps forward, deciding she's had enough. 'Get out of my way. I need to bring Jenna to the dentist.'

I clear the way for her to pass, then watch mother and daughter, holding hands, reach the top of the road before disappearing out of view.

In the car, Mike doesn't say anything about Gavin. He doesn't have to. We both know that if Gavin is playing pretend cop there's a reason for it. Gavin wouldn't be the first ex-detective to use his previous career to open doors, but as I look back at number thirty-two, two questions loom large in my mind. Why is he hanging around Ben Donnelly's place, and what else is he hiding?

41
WREN

AFTER MY SHIFT IS OVER, driving home, I finally give in and call Meg.

'What's up?' she asks.

'Oh, you know, the usual stuff, life.'

'One of those conversations.' She laughs. 'Do you want me to call over?'

'I can offer you dinner, if it helps.'

'No need, I've already eaten, but I can see you at eight.'

When I hang up, my mind goes back to all those unanswered questions rolling around in my head. What is Gavin up to with Ben Donnelly? Could he be the prowler Aria saw at Nadine's place, and if he is, why? Nor do I understand why my father has Gavin's name in his notes, or what the hell it has to do with Evie Hunt. Perhaps Mike is right, and Patrick Mescal, the Hunts' family liaison officer, will have answers, but Cian Campbell is in my sights too. Like Becca, he seems to have fallen off the radar. Then there's the small matter of the unidentified limb found in the Dodder and, based on that anonymous tip-off, if Ben Donnelly is at the centre of all this, the sooner I get answers, the better.

At home, I heat a frozen pizza, as the light from outside creates an orange glow in the kitchen. For some reason, I think about snow, an old memory immediately taking hold. In it, my hands are bitter cold, but I don't care about that because I'm outside in the front garden making a snowman with my mother. It takes me ages to create his face, but finally he's finished. I remember what she said to me afterwards, when I asked her what would happen to the snowman when the snow melted. She said he'd be part of my memory, and once I kept him there, he would always exist. I was so worried about losing that snowman, I never thought about losing her.

I hear Meg's familiar ring and knock at the door.

As I let her in, she says. 'You look terrible, what's wrong?'

'I was just thinking about my mother.'

'Come here,' she says, wrapping her arms around me. 'You may be this super-efficient detective at work, but to me, you'll always be a big softy.'

'My superintendent might not agree on the efficiency bit.'

'He doesn't know you like I do.'

She kicks her shoes off and settles into the armchair. 'Why were you thinking about your mother?'

'I'm not sure.' I put my face in my hands.

'Wren, what is it?'

'Oh, God,' I say, 'bloody everything. Work, my father, Gavin, but mainly, I guess, me.'

'I don't understand.'

'Don't jump down my throat when I say this.'

'I promise you, I won't.'

'I still feel like an idiot when I think about how easily I was sucked in by Gavin, getting involved with someone who would do the dirt on me like that.'

'That wasn't your fault.'

'No?'

'No.'

'Look, Meg, I value you seeing the good in me, but lately, I've realised something else.'

'What?'

'Since my father became unwell ...' I pause, needing to get the words right in my head.

She waits.

I take my face out of my hands, letting out a long breath. 'The truth is, since then, I've desperately needed someone else in my life, a proper relationship, the his-and-her kind, and I think it made me jump in far too fast. I made myself believe it was something it wasn't.'

'Don't be so hard on yourself. There's nothing wrong with wanting someone in your life, and sometimes we all get it wrong.'

'I still miss her,' I say, 'my mother.'

'I know you do.'

'I miss my father too. I mean, he's still here, but it's not the same.'

'For Christ's sake, Wren, you're only human. It's okay to want the things you talked about, along with trying to get the bad guys, but somehow, you also thought you could make Gavin okay, only there are times in life you can't make things right – sometimes life has other ideas – so stop beating yourself up.'

'So, why do I feel so shit?'

'Do you want me to be completely honest?'

'Yeah.'

'I've known you a long time, so I also know, Wren, you still think you *can* fix everything. You set yourself a way higher bar than you would expect of anyone else.'

'I don't,' I say, but secretly I'm wondering if she's right. I look away, thinking about my mother again, and how, after she died, I tried to fix that too. I tried to make everything all right, only things were never all right, not like they were before.

'There's something else I haven't told you, Meg.'

'What?'

'I found some clippings about Evie Hunt in my father's stuff at the nursing home.'

'The girl who disappeared?'

'Yep.'

'Did he know her?'

'I'm trying to find out.'

'Have you spoken to Gavin?'

'No, but ...'

'What?'

'Do you remember me talking about Nadine Fitzmaurice, his sister, and how I saw her in the car park in Rathfarnham?'

'Yeah.'

'Her daughter's done a disappearing act.'

'Missing?'

'It might be nothing. I mean, people go AWOL all the time, and then turn up with a perfectly reasonable explanation.'

'So, what's worrying you?'

'Because, Meg, the opposite can also be true.'

42

NADINE

I COUNT DOWN THE HOURS UNTIL morning. I plan on being at my desk before any of the others arrive, conscious that I'm running out of time. There is no margin for error, not if I want to ensure Becca's safety, and today I face the trickiest task of all: corrupting the video footage in the master files.

In work, I do a quick review of the adjustments I've already made before printing hard copies. I'll have to rescan them into the system as if they're originals, and once that's done, I can adjust the final report for the underwriters. Thankfully, they're all based off site in the UK, meaning the documents will be reviewed online, and if I'm careful, and optimise the brightest levels, I can reduce the visibility of any overlap lines with the false information superimposed on the originals.

I put my name into the system as the main point of contact, pushing others further down the line. If I keep my nerve, I can do this.

I greet each of my colleagues as they arrive in to work. No one looks at me with suspicion. Why would they? I don't look like a criminal. I look like one of them.

I've decided lunchtime is the best opportunity to gain access to the master files because there'll be only one security officer on duty. He won't question my clearance. Like everyone else, he'll see me as a dedicated member of the managerial team, putting in extra hours, safe, no-life, boring Nadine, but lunchtime sneaks up on me far too fast. I don't feel ready. Even the sound of my breathing seems too loud. My physicality is awkward too. I keep hitting my knee off the desk. I have to calm down. I'm terrified someone is going to guess what I'm up to and start asking awkward questions. At any moment, one of them could discover something and call the police, telling them I'm a criminal, a bad person, someone who should be locked up.

It's now five past one. I can't delay any longer. I pick up my files and the laptop. This is it. There's no going back now. The data centre isn't far. I can do this. I have to do this.

When I spot the security guard, my nervousness increases. My knees are trembling, and I fear my voice will sound odd, scared. 'I may be a while,' I say to him.

He barely looks at me. He's downloaded a soccer match onto his phone, taking advantage of people being at lunch, and once inside the data centre, I'm on my own.

I flip open my laptop, noting the serial numbers of the files I need to pull. The information is spread over a series of folders and sub-folders. I work quickly, purposely leaving the surveillance tapes to last. Finally, I rewind the master file to a date before the last office virus attack, then reload a document carrying the lethal bug, which, after it infiltrated the main computer system, left hundreds of files damaged.

I check my watch. Soon everyone will return to their desks. I can't waste any time. I start reviewing the files, including the surveillance footage. Most of them, as expected, refuse to load, which is exactly what I want, and those that do open are so severely damaged they're unreadable.

I've done it.

Back at the desk, I submit the various files to Underwriting. It's nearly four o'clock, when an email pops into my inbox. I open it. They're having a problem accessing some of the footage. I tell them about the virus scare from a few weeks back. I agree to check the back-up files.

I wait another fifteen minutes before I send an updated email apologising for the delay, but also letting them know that the back-up files, especially the video footage, are also corrupted. As their main point of contact, I offer to answer any questions they might have on the readable data. Five minutes later, they ring me. The whole interaction lasts about an hour until, finally, the phone call ends.

I want to know if they've reached a decision on the claim, but I can't risk asking them directly. I would only arouse suspicion.

The desk telephone rings. I jump, because all phone calls fill me with terror now. Picking up, I tentatively say, 'Hello.'

'Nadine, it's Olivia at the front desk. There's a package here for you.'

I tell her I'll be right there. I don't normally get deliveries to the office, so I'm already on high alert as I make my way to pick it up.

'Here you go,' she says, handing me the small package with my name and place of work in bold print on the front. 'Personal' is written in red in the top right-hand corner. I recall the writing on the bathroom mirror. Is it the same? I can't be sure.

Back at my desk, everyone is preoccupied with other things. Some don't bother even looking up at me, while others glance in my direction, then away again. My fingers struggle with the Sellotape on the reverse side of the package. I can't rip it off. Giving up in frustration, I tear at the paper instead. I sense there isn't going to be anything good inside, and then I see it, the glint of a gold band, shiny under the fluorescent light. I recognise the tiny lines engraved at the edges too, along with 'C & N', for Cian and Nadine, on the inside. I let out a low gasp.

When I left Cian for dead I pulled the ring off his finger: if anyone found the body, the fewer personal effects on him, the better, especially if I needed to make a run for it. Afterwards, I put the ring, with his credit cards, in an old shoebox. If someone has them now, it means they were in my house. I should have checked that box after the break-ins, but now, I'm realising something else. This nightmare, if it involves Cian, may be only just beginning.

I shut down my laptop and put the ring into my handbag, then walk out of the office, knowing it's unlikely I'll ever return.

I don't know when Ben will phone. The control is in someone else's hands, but driving home, every kilometre feels longer than it should.

243

Opening the front door, I get a text from Gavin. He's on his way back to Dublin. He'll call to see me tomorrow. I wonder if Aria has told him about my movements, but a part of me doesn't care any more.

I check the shoebox in the bedroom. As I expected, the ring and the credit cards are missing. One side of my brain is telling me none of this is happening, but the other side is warning me it can only mean one thing: Cian is still alive, and if he wanted to, he could kill me, and finish off the task he started so many times before.

I remove the ring from my handbag. It shines back at me in warning. I think about the body in the garden again, the one no longer there. I feel disoriented. Perhaps it's a side-effect of stopping the medication too fast. I reach out to touch the wall, attempting to get my bearings, but it's already too late, because I hear that nursery rhyme again, 'Three blind mice, see how they run,' as I collapse to the floor.

43
WREN

THE FOLLOWING MORNING, I GET an early phone call from Adam of Berkley Shipping, Cian Campbell's last known place of work. It doesn't take me long to get into the city, and walking up the quays, the river Liffey slugs back and forth, green and murky. Birds swoop down for the meagre pickings from the night before, discarded chipper bags, half-eaten burgers and dozens of beer cans littering the pathway along the river wall. Soon, it will be cleared away by city council workers, but right now, the birds are partying.

I spoke with Meg for hours last night, mainly about my mother, as if years of grief forced their way forward, and how more than anything, I wanted to turn back time, change things, and for my mother not to be dead. I think about the other stuff Meg said to me too, about how I can't fix everything, no one can. I know she's right, but a part of me will damn well keep trying.

There's a bitter chill in the air, but I don't mind it. I like Dublin at this hour: too early for the city to be engulfed by shoppers and tourists, and long after its night life has subsided. This section of the quays, approaching Smithfield, has the appearance of a place left behind, with buildings in need of refurbishment, shop fronts with chipped and faded paint, and the scattering of businesses, legal, import and export, alongside discount furniture stores.

Berkley Shipping is located within the Smithfield Plaza, renamed after its facelift in the nineties, with four hundred thousand cobble-stones, laid 150 years before, lifted, cleaned and relaid. What was once the inner sanctum of animal trading, complete with 'farmyards' housing livestock, and horses as the main means of transport, today has a totally different vibe, including modern apartment blocks and offices, one of which, on the north section, is my destination.

I'm greeted at Reception by a guy who can't be any more than eighteen. He tells me Adam will be with me shortly. I take a seat and do a visual check of the offices, designed in a slick, no-nonsense grey against a pure white palette. I'm reminded of the deep colours in the oil paintings created by my mother, which my father put away in the attic because he couldn't bear to see them any more. Would she sit here and wonder at the lack of drama in the design, the blandness of the canvas, the unwillingness to take risks?

'Wren,' a male voice calls from the side.

I stand up. 'Adam, I assume.'

He shakes my hand. His grip is firm. 'I'm only one flight up,' he says.

Unlike the rest of the upstairs space, which is open-plan, his office is private, although styled in a similar fashion, with an abstract mural in striking red and black on the wall behind his desk.

'Who's the artist?' I ask, pointing to it.

'No idea. Nor do I have any idea what it means.'

'I see angry undertones.'

'Do you think?'

Once seated, I get down to business. 'I understand you knew Cian Campbell.'

'Yeah, that's right. We worked together for a couple of years.'

'What was his role exactly?'

'Mainly distribution, making sure product got from A to B.'

'Was he good at his job?'

'I'd say so, but the work can be stressful, irate customers, products with a short shelf life blocked at Customs. The bloody red tape would drive you mad.'

'Did the strain show in his work?'

'He had a temper, if that's what you're getting at.'

'What was he like when he lost it?'

'If he got rattled, the best thing you could do was leave him alone. Mostly, it would blow over.'

'And other times?'

'He'd rant, threatening to leave, sometimes not coming in for days.'

'I assume management had an issue with that?'

'They didn't like it, but it can be hard to get someone who knows how to work the field. I was a junior at the time, but I knew that if Cian Campbell wanted something done, it would happen.'

'And then he left?'

'Well, not quite. It wasn't totally his decision. There were complaints from staff and customers. He'd hit the bottle every now and then, and when he did, that temper of his would fire up. It ended with a formal warning just before he left.'

'Any idea where he went?'

'No, but he never asked for a reference. Probably too damn stubborn.'

'What about notice?'

'He didn't give any. He simply took the hump one day and went off like the world owed him a favour.'

'Did anyone try to make contact?'

'Sure. In fact, I was asked to track him down, but he'd done a runner, not just from here but from home as well. His wife, Nadine, was really upset. I felt sorry for her. They say it's hard, don't they, for women to leave men like him?'

'What do you mean?'

'Ah, fellas talk, and Cian could get mouthy with drink on him, acting like the big man, talking about not taking any shit from his wife, giving her what-for if he had to.'

'It sounds as if you're glad he never got in touch.'

'Most people were relieved not to have a loose cannon around the place.'

'Anything else?'

'Yeah, there was this guy he used to hang out with.'

'Oh?'

'Robin Kinsella. He works for another shipping company now, one of our competitors. That's how I remember the name.'

'Could you get me a number?'

'No problem.'

After I leave Berkley Shipping, I call Robin Kinsella's mobile phone number. He reluctantly agrees to meet me later in the afternoon. It's not much, but it's a start.

44

NADINE

WHEN I FINALLY COME TO, hours must have passed because the sunlight shooting in the window tells me it's already morning. I'm no longer in the bedroom. I'm lying on the floor in the kitchen, but I can't remember anything from when I blacked out to now. My mouth and throat are dry. I get up and pour myself a glass of water.

Gavin is due to call today. He'll want to know how I'm doing, and then what? Do I tell him about the insurance fraud? Will he even believe me?

I attempt to piece together all the bits I remember from the day before, up to the point when I blacked out. I remember the package with Cian's ring being delivered to the office. I did more work on the Prendergast file before I spoke to the underwriters. Once everything was in place, I left the office. I took Cian's wedding ring with me, placing it in my handbag. When I got home, I checked the shoebox: sure enough, the ring and the credit cards were missing. This means Cian could be alive, and if he wanted to, he could kill me. Only, that would be too easy. First, he would need to make me suffer. I walk back upstairs, but I refuse to open the door of the ensuite bathroom. I can't look at those words again. 'YOU LEFT ME TO DIE.'

I spot Cian's wedding ring on the floor. I must have dropped it. I pick it up, and as I do, I hear a phone ringing. It's my mobile, which is still in my handbag by the bed. I stare at the shattered glass, and just like before, the caller ID is unknown.

'Hello,' I say.

'You did well, Nadine. That Prendergast case seems to be sorted, and those involved are very pleased.'

'Ben,' I say, convinced now it's him, 'I want my daughter back.'

'Not just yet.'

'But you promised. You said if I did this last thing, if I sorted out the Prendergast case, you'd let Becca come home. She needs to be with ...' My words trail off.

'Her mother? Is that what you're trying to say, Nadine?'

'Stop it. I won't play this game any more.'

'Someone wants to meet you.'

'Who?'

'If I told you that, you might chicken out.'

'Tell me.'

'What – and ruin the surprise?'

'You said I'd get Becca back.'

'And you will.'

'How do I know you're not lying again? How do I know she's even alive?'

'You'll see Becca.'

'When?'

'Soon. Now, write this down.'

I do exactly as he instructs, scribbling the details of a fresh location, along with the time, tonight at eleven o'clock. I could be walking into a trap, but I don't have a choice, not until I find another way out of this mess.

I stare downwards at my feet. Somehow, the past flows into the present. I see the younger me in my old bedroom, the one where I grew up. My feet are wet after having a bath. The towel, given to me by my mother, is damp. It feels too small for my body. I'm shivering. It's then I see Gavin standing in the doorway. The light is fading. He asks me what's wrong, and I say, 'Nothing,' not wanting to cry. I can't tell him how sad I feel, or how, if I could, I'd run away and find a different family. If I told him that, he'd only think I was weak.

Finally, he turns and walks away, and I understand why. He doesn't know what to do, or say, so instead, he does nothing.

And now, my mind skips forward. This time my mother is dressing me. Her hands smell of Nivea Creme. I wanted those hands to make me feel safe but they can't, no more than Gavin could help that day he stood in the doorway. We were all broken things, trapped under the guise of family, incapable of helping one another. Instead, that day, my mother busied herself tidying the bedroom, switching on lights, pulling the curtains – *swish, swish, swish*. I guess there was some comfort in that, the ordinary, the mundane, the knowing what will happen next, but as I'm thinking this, I'm also thinking of how when my parents fell out of love, as many people do, my mother should have chiselled out a new life for herself, because staying, as I discovered with Cian, poisons you from the inside out. Eventually, all that's left is the damage that no amount of time can absolve.

I hear someone turn the key in the lock. I don't move, but soon he calls out my name. 'Nadine.'

I wait.

'It's me, Gavin.'

'I'm here in the bedroom.'

Then, just like when we were younger, he stands in the doorway.

'There's been another break-in,' I say.

He doesn't react, not even a flicker. I can tell he thinks I'm making things up again, looking for more attention.

'I've something to show you.'

'What?'

'Proof that someone was in the house.' I walk towards the en-suite bathroom, the one I haven't been able to enter until now.

Soon, Gavin is standing behind me.

I switch on the light, but the words are gone.

'Someone must have wiped them,' I say, shocked, unsure.

'Wiped what?' he asks, angry now.

'The words on the mirror. They were written in red. The person used my lipstick.'

'Nadine, stop it. Stop lying.'

'I'm not. They were there. I saw them.' I stare back at him. 'They scared me to death.'

'You must have imagined it.'

'I didn't.'

'You've been wrong about so many things lately. Your mind gets mixed up. You think things are a certain way, but then they're not.'

'No.' I shake my head.

'You were the same as a bloody child, with your overactive imagination, only now, it's worse. Don't you realise, Nadine, you need proper help?'

What's he talking about?

'Dr Ward was fine for a time, but with your condition deteriorating, I think you need a higher level of psychiatric support.'

'No, you're wrong. You don't understand. Cian is back. He wrote terrible words on the mirror.'

'What words?'

'YOU LEFT ME TO DIE.'

'Stop it, Nadine. You're wrong, the same way you're wrong about Evie coming back, and all that other stupid stuff about Ben.'

'Gavin, I swear, Cian wrote it. He must have.'

'What makes you so sure?'

'Because nothing else makes any sense.'

45
WREN

MIKE OPENS THE OFFICE DOOR looking pleased with himself. 'I got the contact details for the liaison officer, Patrick Mescal, on the old Evie Hunt case.'

'Thanks, Sherlock, that's exactly the news I wanted to hear.'

He hands me a note with Patrick Mescal's address in Templeogue and his landline number.

'Any word on Ben Donnelly?'

'Not yet. I've sent two separate squad cars around to his house, and there's still no sign of him.'

'Has anyone heard anything on the street?'

'There's nothing from the rumour mill.'

'I don't like it, and the longer Ben is in the shadows, the more I want to talk to him.'

'We may have a witness to that ATM attempt, too, a Thomas Dowling.'

'My day just keeps getting better.'

'I'll do the prelims with him, and if anything of value turns up, I'll let you know.'

'Great.'

'By the way, Patrick Mescal is already expecting you.'

'Thanks, Mike. I owe you.'

Ten minutes later, I'm driving around a suburban estate in Templeogue. Most of the houses are identical, three- or four-bedroom units surrounding a green area in front of a line of local shops. Patrick Mescal's house is further back, behind the national school and the Scouts' Den, but it doesn't take me long to find it.

When I ring the doorbell, he answers straight away with the efficiency of an older person who has hours to fill. His eyes look kind, and immediately I like him. He reminds me of my father, the grey hair, neat dress, and a lifetime of experience in his face.

'Wren,' he says.

'That's me.'

'Come into the living room. It'll be quieter there.'

I hear someone moving about in the kitchen, more than likely his wife. In the front living room, the walls are filled with photographs of communions, confirmations and graduations. It seems the Mescals have three children and, judging by how faded some of the images are, they've probably long since left the nest.

When we sit down, I spot an old notebook by his side. It intrigues me.

'You're here about the Evie Hunt missing-person case?'

'I am.'

'That one has niggled me for years.'

'Because she never turned up.'

'Yes, that, but also, I always felt her friends had something to hide.'

'Like what?'

'That's the thing, I could never quite figure it out, but something smelt rotten.'

'You were the liaison officer for the family.'

'Yes.'

'What can you tell me about them?'

'The mother was beside herself with worry, but there were other family stresses. The father, Nigel, was a bit of a bastard. You know the kind, constantly trying to appear like the main man, his opinions deserving to be heard above everyone else's. It might be a generational thing from back then, some guys behaving that way, but it wasn't just that.'

'Oh?'

'It was the way he took his daughter's disappearance as a personal affront. A few years later, after I left the force, I heard one of his nieces accused him of interfering with her, and I thought about Evie Hunt again.'

'Did the charges stick?'

'No, but even if the evidence was light on the ground, you get a nose for these things.'

I think again about Nadine's interview, telling me Evie's father abused the girl. If Nadine was telling the truth about that, what else might she be telling the truth about?

'There was a Truth or Dare game,' I say, 'that the group used to play.'

He opens his notebook, flipping through the pages. 'No one said anything about that to me.'

'Evie got the Dare card,' I add, 'just before she disappeared. It said, *Do something you will always be remembered for*, almost as if someone wanted her to try something risky, something out of the ordinary.'

'It could tie into her disappearance.'

'Maybe, but I'm interested in the group too. They seem to have got your attention. You said you thought they were hiding something.'

'They were an odd bunch. Ben Donnelly, one of them, was already into petty theft, trying to prove himself as the smart guy, but there were a couple of others I was suspicious of too.'

'Who?'

'Cian Campbell and Gavin Fitzmaurice, although I heard Gavin later joined the force. Makes you wonder, doesn't it?'

'The force can be a bit of a mixed bag,' I say. 'I believe Cian Campbell had a temper.'

'He had a chip on his shoulder. He thought the world owed him something. The atmosphere in a room would get uneasy the minute the likes of him entered it. But he was clever with it. Never gave too much away, although you always knew there was a lot going on in that brain of his.'

'What was his relationship with Evie like?'

'He claimed he didn't have one, but she was a looker, so I'd say he wouldn't have turned the other way if he'd got encouragement.'

'He went AWOL a while back, leaving his job, his wife and daughter, the whole works. So far, I can't find much on him.'

'He could have changed his identity. He'd be capable of pulling off something like that.'

'What can you tell me about Gavin Fitzmaurice?'

'At the time, he was already a person of interest.'

'Because of his relationship with Evie?'

'That wasn't the only reason.'

'What other reason was there?'

'A hit-and-run about a year before Evie's disappearance. The victim was a woman in her mid-thirties. There wasn't anything solid found against Gavin Fitzmaurice, other than third-party bravado, but he'd come to the attention of the law, and you know what that's like.'

'What can you tell me about the hit-and-run?'

'It was thought that Gavin and another teenager, Martin Prendergast, liked to play car-racing, boasting about being able to hijack any car they wanted.'

I suck in air, hearing the third name on my father's list being said aloud. Was my father doing some kind of miniature investigation?

Patrick looks at his notes again, then at me, his face appearing unsure.

'Did she survive,' I ask, 'the female victim of the hit-and-run?'

'No,' he says, 'she didn't.'

His expression tells me everything I need to know.

'You know the name of the victim, Patrick, don't you?'

'Yes.'

'It was my mother, wasn't it?'

He places the notebook aside. 'I didn't make the connection, DS Moore, until now.'

I hear more sounds coming from the kitchen, the dishwasher being emptied, plates clattering, cutlery clinking, as the sympathy on his face grows.

'Did you ever meet my father, Patrick?'

He stalls.

'Did you?'

'Only the once.'

'When?'

'About a year ago. Like you, he came to see me. I'm not even sure how he got my details, but one day, he stood at my front door, and wanted to know everything I could tell him about Gavin Fitzmaurice.'

'Did he tell you why?' The floor below me feels as if it's falling away.

'He knew Gavin was the main suspect in the hit-and-run, the suspected driver.'

For a second, I close my eyes, trying to take it all in. 'What did you tell him?'

'To be honest, I didn't have much, other than scant details. We talked a little about Gavin's family too, his sister, parents, that kind of thing.'

'I found newspaper clippings on the Evie Hunt case in my father's belongings. Why would he have been interested in those?'

'I'm not sure, but I know your father came across Gavin's media statement about Evie's disappearance. It is what led him to me, in the hope that I could help him track Gavin down.'

'Did you help?'

'Your father was very persuasive. He told me he needed to understand what had happened and why.'

'Why did you talk to him? I mean, he wasn't even in the force.'

At first, Patrick doesn't answer, but then he says, 'Your father already knew his mind was failing. He felt he was running out of time.'

'Go on.'

'Despite the intervening years, he was driven to find answers. My wife has the same horrible disease. That's why I talked to him.'

More plates clatter in the kitchen.

'Your father said he should have looked for answers a long time ago, but when he lost his wife, your mother, he was in too much pain.'

'Did he tell you anything else?'

He nods. 'Somehow your father got his hands on the eyewitness statements, and according to him, something didn't add up.'

'What?'

'I don't know. He kept that to himself.'

'And did he ever meet Gavin?'

'All I know is I gave him the only address I had, the one for the Fitzmaurices' old family home.'

Memories of that fatal day come flooding back, the police calling to the door, the sadness in the house, the knowledge that I would never see my mother again. The utter sense of loss, of things being outside my control, the inability to make things right. One moment we were a family, my father, my mother and I, and the next, it was only my father and me, two human beings hurting, one an adult and the other a child.

'It's hard, Wren,' Patrick says, 'losing someone close to you.'

I bite my bottom lip.

He walks to a graduation photograph of his son. 'David took a year out to go to Australia after he graduated. One night, a crowd of them left a bar in Melbourne. The driver of the car was inexperienced, so when another vehicle turned a corner on the wrong side of the road, he panicked and swerved towards it, instead of away. The oncoming car tore the passenger side of the vehicle apart. They all survived, except our son. He could have been sitting in the back seat, but instead, he sat upfront, wanting to help the driver with directions.'

'I'm so sorry,' I say, the tables suddenly reversed.

'Loss is a great leveller, Wren. It changes how you view the world.'

'I never knew who drove the car,' I say, 'or the identity of the other guy. I'm sure, if I wanted to, I could have found out, being in the force, but right up until this moment, I wasn't sure I wanted to know.'

'And now?'

'Now there's no way of not knowing.' My head is in a tailspin, almost as if a film is being rewound at speed. 'Do you remember Nadine Fitzmaurice?' I ask. 'Gavin's younger sister.'

'Oh, yes, I remember her. A quiet, shy little thing. She stuck to Gavin like glue, but harmless. She never said a word without looking to her brother first, almost as if she was seeking his permission to exist.'

'Her daughter went missing recently. She's eighteen, the same age Evie Hunt was when she disappeared.'

'That's strange.'

'Isn't it?'

Suddenly he takes my hand in his but, unlike when Aria Jackson touched me, I don't mind, shared grief forming an intimacy that few other things can.

'At times, Patrick, I still see my mother's face just before I closed the car door. It was the last time I saw her. It plays over and over in my mind, and each time it does, I feel scared again, realising at any moment everything can change.'

'You survived, Wren.' He squeezes my hand tighter. 'You were the lucky one. Don't waste that.'

As I walk back towards the squad car, more questions jump into my head. Did Gavin know who I was when we got together? That I was the child he left without a mother? Might he even have taken pleasure in it?

Patrick Mescal said they hadn't enough evidence to pin anything on the driver or his passenger, but that doesn't change a thing. The perpetrator always knows the truth. If it was Gavin driving that car, he knows exactly what he did, and if he did seek me out, his long-lost victim, right now, that's too weird to even contemplate.

And what about my father? Even if he discovered that Gavin, and perhaps Martin Prendergast, were in the car that day, why did he look into Evie Hunt's disappearance? He told Patrick that something about the witness statements didn't add up. Is that why Evie became the focus of his attention, or am I looking at this all wrong? My father's words from my last visit jump into my mind. He said, *Sometimes when you look hard enough, what seems like one thing can become something else entirely.*

At this moment, there's only one thing I'm sure of. I'm more determined than ever to find out what happened to Evie Hunt, including why she disappeared, and if there's any possibility, that Nadine Fitzmaurice, for all her faults, might be telling us the truth.

46
WREN

THE CAFÉ AT POWERSCOURT TOWN CENTRE is buzzing with shoppers and workers. I'm due to meet Robin Kinsella, Cian Campbell's old buddy, in about five minutes. Part of me is glad about the loud noises, as they shut out all the questions about Gavin and my father.

Soon, I spot Robin walking through the archway directly above the café area. I know it's him because he's already told me what he'll be wearing: a sky-blue suit, cream shirt, and a gold tie.

'Wren.' He smiles, shaking my hand, then sits down opposite. He stretches out his legs, confident, taking up more space than the tight café area should allow. A waitress walks past. He reaches out and catches her elbow. 'A double espresso with a side order of brown sugar,' he says, not wasting any time. I'm already sensing he's a bit of a player.

I wrap my hands around my cold latte. 'I believe you used to hang out with Cian Campbell.'

'We were buddies for a while, sure, before he did his vanishing act.'

'It was a bit sudden, wasn't it?'

'Yeah, but totally bloody Cian, always looking for the high drama.'

'It didn't surprise you, then?'

'Nothing surprised me with him. He liked to do his own thing, and brag about it too.'

'What about family and friends?'

'What about them?'

'Surely someone must have wondered where he went.'

'I was probably the closest friend he had, and I wasn't going to be running after him. If he wanted to be somewhere else, that was his business.'

'And family?'

'He became estranged from them years ago. There was a big argument when he got married. Cian didn't like being told what to do so he cut all ties.'

'What happened to them?'

'Last I heard his parents went to Boston to live near his older sister.'

'So, when he left Berkley Shipping, and his wife and child, there was no one to ask any questions?'

'Which was exactly the way Cian would have wanted it.'

The waitress drops off his coffee. He stirs in the sugar. 'Don't get me wrong,' he says. 'I knew Cian was a tosser, but in this industry you need all the friends you can get, and he was partly why I got the chance to work in shipping in the first place.'

'So, you owed him?'

'You could say that.'

'And you two went out socially?'

'We'd have a few scoops during the week, and sometimes, we'd go for dinner with the other halves.'

'Wives?'

'Yes and no. I wasn't married at the time.' He raises his left hand. 'Even if I'm locked in now.' He laughs.

'So, you knew Nadine?'

'Yep, and I know what a screwball she was too.'

'What makes you say that?'

He moves in closer, intimate, as if he's about to share an important secret, one that he wants only me to hear.

'We went to dinner in a gorgeous place in Rathgar once, the four of us.'

'Go on.'

'When my girlfriend left for the Ladies, Cian had to take a phone call outside, and I tried, wanting to be friendly, to strike up a conversation with Nadine. She wasn't usually one for small talk.'

'Okay.'

'At first, it was grand, but then she did something that really freaked me out.'

'What?'

'She put a steak knife in her bag.'

'Did you ask her about it?'

'Fucking sure I did.'

'And?'

'She joked she might use it on Cian. Slice him up.'

'She used those exact words, slice him?'

'Yeah, and not only that. She said she was only waiting for the chance to kill him.'

'And you believed her?'

'It's not the kind of thing you'd joke about.'

'Why do you think she told *you*?'

'I don't know. I mean, as I said, she had a screw loose.'

'What happened when Cian came back?'

'Nadine asked for another steak knife, as if the restaurant had forgotten to give her one.'

'Did you tell Cian?'

'Sure, I did. He just said she was mental, and not to pay her any heed.'

Was Nadine planning ahead? Was it a cry for help, telling a near stranger she wanted to kill her husband?

'Did you meet up again after that, as a foursome?'

'Not for a while.'

'How come?'

He shrugs his shoulders. 'Cian said Nadine wasn't well.'

'Did he say why?'

'Nope, but I assumed it was head stuff, you know, depression, that kind of thing.'

'Anything else?'

'You want to know if he messed her about?'

'Well, did he?'

'I saw the bruises, everyone did, but it can be hard to interfere.'

'I guess,' I say, 'but then again, at times, someone has to.'

If he takes my last comment as a criticism, he doesn't show any signs of it. I ask a few more questions before wrapping the conversation up. I doubt I'll get much more out of him, other than confirming what I already know, that Cian Campbell was physically abusive to his wife, and probably a whole lot more, and if he isn't six feet under, he's a very dangerous man indeed.

My mobile phone rings. It's Mike.

'Our ATM witness will be here at three o'clock. You'll want to talk to him.'

'Okay.'

'And Larry may have stumbled across something interesting too.'

'What?'

'A possible lead on our unidentified John Doe.'

'I'm on my way.'

Heading back to the station, a fresh thought is forming in my mind. Wherever Cian Campbell is, one thing is for certain: Nadine verbalised her intent to cause harm to her husband, and although it may have been little more than the ramblings of a woman on the edge, it may also be enough to convince the super to authorise a search of Becca Campbell's phone and bank records. As yet, I don't know what's happened to either Cian or Becca, but Nadine Fitzmaurice is the link. There is nothing surer.

∞

Twenty minutes later, Mike, Larry and I are seated in the incident room.

'Right, Larry, what have you got on our mystery man?'

'I had a phone call from some buddies of mine in Wicklow, after they pulled in a local group.'

'You're from there, aren't you?'

'Yep, and I know some of the geezers involved.'

'What went down?'

'A large seizure of coke.'

'Whereabouts?'

'Near Magheramore beach, only I doubt any of the guys involved were planning on going for a swim.'

'Street value?'

'Twenty big ones. A patrol car stopped them. They were caught red-handed with the first bag of stash. The rest of the stuff was nabbed when they raided the flat the guys were staying in.'

'So, how does this tie in with our mystery man?'

'Dylan Lynch's name came up in conversation.'

'Why does that sound familiar?' I ask.

'He's Joe Regan's nephew,' Mike replies.

'Joe Regan and Ben Donnelly used to work together.'

'By work, Wren,' Mike adds, raising his eyebrows, 'you're referring to them breaking the law on a regular basis?'

'Yeah, and for some reason, Ben Donnelly's name keeps popping up.'

I turn back to Larry. 'You were telling us about Dylan Lynch.'

'He's considered the top man in the group in Wicklow, but he was missing in action when the raid went down.'

'He might have been lying low, happy to let others take the rap.'

'I don't think so, Wren. It's not his MO. Also, he's been out of the picture for a while.'

'Tell me more about him.'

'He's a young pup whose name has moved up the ranks fast.'

Larry could win *Mastermind* if he were tested on his knowledge of Irish crime gangs. I don't bother commenting on Dylan, the young pup, being the same age as Larry. Instead, I let Larry talk, keen to hear everything he has on Dylan Lynch, and if he could possibly be our John Doe.

'I went to school with him. He's a sweet talker, only trouble with it, if you get on the wrong side of him.'

'Go on.'

'The word on the street from Wicklow is he did a vanishing act to

Dublin a couple of weeks back. There was some talk of him skipping across to Alicante for a while, but that was only talk.'

'Why the trip to Dublin?'

'A new girlfriend.'

'The point is,' Mike says, 'Dylan's been a no-show from around the time our unidentified limb turned up in the Dodder, so the timing fits. He matches the gender and age profile too.'

'I'm assuming his DNA record isn't on PULSE?'

'No,' replies Mike. 'As Larry said, he's been moving up the ranks fast.'

'What about the girl? Do we have any idea who she is?'

Larry shakes his head. 'Other than she lives in Dublin, no.'

I pace the room. 'Dylan is a long shot for our unidentified victim, but it wouldn't be the first time a long shot came up trumps.'

'That long shot may become more focused very soon,' adds Mike.

'How come?'

'Thomas Dowling, the ATM witness, is already set up in Interview Room Six.'

'And?'

'Joe Regan's name, Ben's old partner in crime, came up with him too.'

'Okay, then. Let's get talking to him.'

∞

Opening the door of Interview Room 6, I see Thomas Dowling sitting rigid in the chair, almost as if he's prepping himself for the witness stand. He's in his early seventies, wears bifocal lenses, and has a hearing aid. Mike might be convinced he's witness gold, but I'm not so sure.

'Thanks for coming down, Thomas,' I say, trying to sound cheery.

'Just doing my civic duty.'

'My colleague tells me you may have seen some of the guys who tried to pull that ATM from the wall in Rathfarnham shopping centre.'

'I saw them hanging around the place the night before.'

'What time was that?'

'About ten o'clock. I was out walking the dog, but right away, I knew they were up to no good, so I held back a little, but not so far I couldn't hear one of them say, "We'll need some heavy duty to pull that thing out."'

'Did you report this? The conversation and your suspicions?'

'No. I didn't know what they were talking about, but then yesterday, one of my neighbours told me about the ATM attempt, and I put the thing together. My reckoning is, they hit it the following night.'

'Can you describe any of the guys you saw?'

'I recognised one of them, the oldest one.'

'Who?'

'Joe Regan. He used to live around these parts.'

'It would have been dark, Thomas. How can you be so sure?'

'Don't let these glasses fool you. I've perfect vision once I'm wearing them.'

'Joe has a nephew, a Dylan Lynch.'

He shrugs his shoulders.

'He seems to be lying low right now. Could he be one of the others?'

'I don't know. All those young fellas look the same to me.'

Ten minutes later we wrap up the interview. Thomas looks relieved to be on his way.

'Short and sweet,' says Mike.

'Yeah, and in normal circumstances, it wouldn't be enough to pull Joe Regan in. Any lawyer worth his or her pay grade would have a field day with someone like Thomas as a witness, but still, let's put out feelers for his whereabouts. If we meet a brick wall, we may have to change tack, and fast.

47
NADINE

AT 10.45 P.M., I ARRIVE AT THE LOCATION. It's bitterly cold. As I wait, my eyes are drawn upwards to the sky. A full moon is partially hidden by heavy cloud, as stars appear, willing me to find them. I'm terrified about what's going to happen next: there are so many things I still don't know, including the identity of the person I'll soon meet.

The arranged meeting point is on the outskirts of Saggart. The area is deserted, and the site, surrounded by railings and wooden placards, has a planning notice telling everyone that permission has been granted for forty-five new homes on the field. Soon, it will look completely different. The hawthorn hedge will be uprooted, and the wildflowers, dandelions, primroses and thistles will be replaced by concrete floors, parking spots and street lighting, almost as if the field never existed.

I feel really scared now. I sense things are reaching a crescendo, but I don't know what other twists may lie ahead, or even if I'll survive them.

Normally I wouldn't consider entering this site in daylight, never mind late at night, but now I'm a different Nadine. Normal rules no longer apply. If I've learned nothing else since Becca's first phone call, telling me she killed someone, it's that I'm not prepared to run away any more. I won't hide behind others either, Gavin, Dr Ward, or anyone else.

On the metal gates, there's a large rusty padlock. I already know the key has been slipped behind the smaller planning notice to the side, tucked into a crack only found if you know what you're looking for.

I remove the key. It turns easily in the lock, as if it's well oiled. I glance frantically behind me to see if anyone is close by, but for now, I'm alone.

There's a large yellow digger at the rear of the site. It reminds me of the one I once thought buried Cian. The light from a nearby Chinese takeaway illuminates it like a child's toy, all bright and shiny under a Christmas tree. The ground underneath my feet is rough in parts, and the grasses are damp from the last fall of rain. The smell of earth rises in my nostrils. I've no idea what will happen next, but deep in my gut, I know everything that's happened since Becca's first phone call has been leading up to this point.

I reach the area beside the bags of cement and sand, and then I wait for the person who has gone to all this effort to ensure I'm both alone and defenceless.

A few minutes later, I hear movement behind me. I turn.

'It's been a long time,' the voice says, emerging from the shadows.

I note the chilled tone.

'A lifetime,' I reply.

'And now we're here, together again, you and me, Nadine, against the world.'

'We were never together, not in the proper sense.'

'Perhaps you're right.'

I stay silent. I don't have to wait long.

'I used to think I had you all figured out, but I was mistaken.'

'You thought the same as everyone else, that I was stupid.'

'But you proved us all wrong, didn't you?'

Again, I don't reply.

'That tiny room near Magheramore beach became my whole world for a time, and in it, before you found me, Nadine, I had felt so frightened and lost. You feel that now, don't you?'

'Yes.'

She moves closer, her face becoming clearer, like a ghost from another time. I note her high cheekbones, piercing eyes, and those lips, which always reminded me of ripe cherries.

'The teenage girl I used to be, Nadine, is long since gone.'

'We've all changed.'

'Yes, we have.' She lights a cigarette. 'Do you remember my small backpack, the one with all my worldly possessions, and that hairbrush I sent you?'

'Yes.'

'It even had my favourite perfume. I bet you still remember the name.'

'Fantasy.'

'Bravo.' She smirks.

'And the money,' I say, a new-found bitterness bursting to the surface, 'the money Ben gave you. Don't forget about that.'

'They say it makes the world go round.'

I sense she's enjoying my fear. 'I want Becca back,' I cry, determined, earnest.

'You took her from *me*, Nadine, remember?'

'You didn't want her. You abandoned Becca because you didn't want anything to do with her.'

'You're wrong, Nadine. I loved her, which was why I had to let her go ... only you didn't play by the rules, did you?'

'I couldn't give her away, Evie. I couldn't put her up for adoption.'

'But we agreed, a friend's word. You were to pretend she was yours, then say that you couldn't look after her.'

I shake my head.

'We both wanted Becca to have a better life.'

'She had a good life, with me.'

'I'm not so sure about that.'

'I love her. I raised her. I was there for her when you weren't. You've no right.'

'I have a biological right.'

'You had, once, but not now. You left everything and everyone behind, including your daughter.'

She looks away.

'There are times,' I say, feeling braver now, 'when I can still hear your screams before she was born. Then there was all that blood. It was terrifying, overwhelming. I've relived it so many times in my head, I've nearly convinced myself it was me, and not you, screaming.'

'But it was me.'

This time, I'm the one who looks away.

'I decided a long time ago, Nadine, not to have any more children.'

Is she looking for my pity?

'You used me, Evie, the same way you used everyone else. You only pretended to be my friend because you didn't want the world to know how Becca came to be. But it didn't matter to me how Becca was created because all I saw was a little girl in need of a mother's love. I wanted to be that mother, even if you wanted to run away from her.'

She flinches, but regains composure fast. 'And now that little girl is eighteen, only she didn't turn out as you hoped, did she?'

'I still love her.'

'But I was the one who had to save her.'

'What are you talking about?'

She lights another cigarette, the fresh smell of nicotine immediate, strong. We used to share cigarettes, huddled together in that tiny flat, stupidly feeling all grown-up.

'When I came back, Nadine, after my father died, I sought you out because I was curious. I didn't plan on rekindling old friendships, but I wanted to know what had happened to you. It wasn't long before I saw you with Becca, and I knew straight away who she was.'

'Is that why you took her? Wanting to reclaim the child you abandoned?'

'No.' She shakes her head. 'That's not why I intervened.'

'You're lying. You and Ben have been behind this all along.'

'Wrong again, Nadine. We saved her.'

'How?'

'When she got into too much shit to survive on her own, that's how.'

'I don't want to hear any more.'

271

'You already know she killed someone. She told you that on the phone.'

'She must have had her reasons.'

'As it happens, she did, but there was still a price to pay, and you, as it turns out, had to pay that for her. It was only fair, don't you think, after you fucked up as her *pretend* mother?'

'I cared for her more than you can ever know.'

'Is that why she ended up doped out of her head, hanging out with a loser like Dylan Lynch, needing to fight to defend herself?'

'Is that who she …' I can't finish the sentence. Instead, I repeat the name Dylan Lynch in my mind. It's the first time I've a name for the man Becca killed.

Evie is still talking. 'The only way we could save Becca was to take her against her will. So, you see, it was me, not you, who got her cleaned up, but, of course, on its own that wasn't enough. Someone still had to pay back the debt.'

'I don't understand.'

'They wanted to take Becca out for killing one of their own. Luckily, Ben and Dylan's uncle, Joe Regan, go back a long way, so it gave us a pathway to smooth things over.'

'Becca was scared of you,' I say. 'You told her lies about me. You locked her in a room.'

'A detox room in a secure unit to protect her until her brain could function properly, and when it comes to lies, Nadine, you have to admit, you're way ahead of me on that score.'

'What do you really want?'

'At first I thought I wanted revenge, that you needed to pay for what you did, but then I realised, when it came to messing up my daughter's life, I had to carry a certain amount of that burden, no matter how much I believed back then I was doing the right thing.'

'You never wanted her.'

'I had my reason. You know that.'

'Your father?'

'Yes, and Gavin too.'

'But he loved you.'

'I don't think Gavin really knows how to love someone.'

'You're wrong.'

'He's as messed up as you are, perhaps worse, because he pretends to himself he's doing okay.'

'No.' I shake my head again.

'Before I disappeared, Nadine, he went to a very dark place, as if he hated life nearly as much as he hated himself.'

'You don't know what you're talking about.'

'Something happened to him.'

'Stop it.' I put my hands over my ears, needing to block out her words.

'Don't you remember the Truth or Dare game? It was all Gavin's idea, wasn't it?' She takes a step closer. 'He liked to push people's buttons, play psychological games with them, see how far they'd go.'

I can't take it any longer. 'It was only a bloody game.'

'Not to Gavin it wasn't. He could be cruel if he wanted to, which is partly why he got on so well with Cian. He saw something worse in him than he saw in himself.'

'You're wrong. You don't know him the way I do. He loved you.'

'Do you know what he asked me once?'

'No.'

'He asked if I'd ever thought about killing someone.' She stubs out her cigarette. 'And do you know what the scariest thing was?'

'What?'

'I had.'

'Who?'

'My father.'

'I don't blame you for that,' I say, remembering what I did to Cian.

'When I got that Dare card, asking me to do something I would always be remembered for, I thought long and hard about it. I played the scene so many times in my mind, I was almost convinced I'd done it. So, perhaps I was a coward, abandoning Becca instead of standing up to my father, but believe me, the last thing I wanted was for her to suffer because of his badness. Only, that wasn't the only reason I ran away.'

'No?'

'I could never risk Gavin finding out, because if he did, there wasn't a doubt in my mind that he would have killed my father, even if I couldn't.'

'I never told him your secret. I never told anyone, not until I was put under pressure by the police, when I was out of my mind with worry over Becca.'

'Eighteen years is a long time to keep a secret.'

'I want her to come home.'

'Not yet, Nadine, not until it's safe.'

'She's nothing to fear from me.'

'Maybe not, but I've been watching your house.'

'Why?'

'At first, I wanted to know what you were up to.'

'So, what did you discover?'

'That some things aren't right.'

'It's Cian, isn't it? He's come back, hasn't he?' My words are pouring out fast. 'Someone's been in my house, searching for things. He's even written horrible messages, saying terrible things, things only he would know.'

She stares at me, the same way she did that first day in Magheramore, as if destiny had forced the two of us together, two girls equally untrusting of the other. Back then, the child growing inside her, Becca, was far more important than either of us. In a way, it's the same now. Eighteen years on, very little has changed.

'When I came back to Dublin, Nadine, I felt like a ghost returning home, picking up the embers of an old life. It made sense to me to watch everyone, including you, while also keeping my distance. In fact, that was how I found out about Becca, and the trouble she'd got herself into.'

'What do you mean?'

'If it weren't for Ben's help she'd be dead by now because of what she did. I didn't like how heavy-handed he was with you. He can be harsh, I know that, but as I said, someone had to pay for what Becca had done, and it seemed fitting, in the beginning, that it would be you. Which is why, after I knew Becca was getting the help she needed, I kept on watching you. I'd stand across the street, sometimes at night, and stare up at the bedroom window, increasingly curious about how you lived your life. That was when I realised there were times when you'd left the house, and it should have been empty, but soon someone else would be there.'

'Who?'

'I don't know.'

'You're making all this up.'

'Why would I do that?'

I shrug my shoulders.

'Despite everything, Nadine, I don't hate you.'

'No?'

'I want to help.'

'I don't believe you.'

'Your choice.'

'Tell me why I should trust you.'

'Because, right now, you don't have anyone else. I saw them again, a few days ago, after you left for work. I watched you leave, and I was about to do the same thing, when I spotted someone moving from one room to another upstairs.'

I think about the house being trashed for a second time.

'They were there for over an hour.'

'It's Cian,' I say. 'It has to be.'

'You need to be careful, Nadine, very careful.' She turns to walk away.

'Wait,' I shout after her.

'What?'

'I need to see Becca.'

'You will, but not until you make sure she doesn't come to any more harm.'

'How can I do that?'

'By becoming the mother you always wanted to be.'

I watch her walk away, her footsteps stamping on the wildflowers that will soon become concrete.

48
WREN

WITH FEELERS OUT FOR JOE REGAN and Ben Donnelly, top of my agenda this morning is getting the super to reconsider authorisation to search Becca Campbell's phone and bank records, especially after my recent conversation with Robin Kinsella. I'm not sure I've enough to push the super on it, but at the very least, I'm going to try.

I knock on his door, aware he's already expecting me, but that doesn't mean I'll get a warm welcome.

'Come in,' I hear him say.

Entering his office, I see him standing at the window with his back to me.

'Sit down,' he instructs, still not turning.

His stance slightly unnerves me, but I do as I'm told.

'The other day,' he says, 'I might have been a bit hard on you.'

'Police resources are limited.'

Finally, he turns. I wait for him to sit down. It feels somewhat less intimidating when both of us are at eye level. 'You're a good cop, Wren, which is partly why I have such high expectations, perhaps higher, of you than some of the others.'

'I do my best.'

'You're an achiever. I like that about you.'

'Thank you.' I'm not sure where this is going, but I'm figuring, either way, it will help my chances of getting those phone and bank records.

'Did you always want to be a cop?' he asks, leaning back in the chair.

'From the moment I got a fingerprint kit.' I laugh.

'When was that?'

'The Christmas after my mother died.'

'What age were you?'

'Eleven. I drove everyone crazy with it, friends, my father. I guess, even back then, I had a passion for solving things.'

'And you still do.'

'Yep.'

'It's what makes you different, Wren.'

'What do you mean?'

'It's been in your DNA from early on, and it's never left you. I know you'll move further up the force, and there will be more opportunities for sure, but you can also be over-zealous. Don't get me wrong. Passion, drive, determination are all required in this job, but sometimes you have to rein it in, because if you don't, you can jump into things too soon.'

'Are we talking about Nadine Fitzmaurice again, and digging up her back garden?'

'We are. If you had given it another couple of hours, we could have used geophysics and quantitative means to examine that soil before the guys dug down any further, saving us a huge amount of police resources, not to mention that disturbance of a potential crime scene should always be kept at a minimum.'

'The soil was already disturbed.'

'It was partially disturbed, and much and all as you may think you're an expert in everything, the professionals, not you, should have made that call.'

My earlier confidence about getting authorisation for the phone and bank records is waning by the second, but then again, when shit is going down, sometimes it pays to go for the jugular. It's not that I don't agree with the super, but right now, everything in my gut is telling me those records are important.

'Okay,' I say, 'you're right. I should have waited.'

'Good,' he replies, as if that settles everything.

'There's something else.'

'What?'

'We've got fresh evidence on the Becca Campbell missing-person case.'

'Okay,' he says, 'spit it out.'

'I spoke to an old acquaintance of Cian Campbell, Nadine's ex-husband.'

'This is the same woman who claims to have killed her husband and buried him in the garden. Only you didn't find a body, did you?'

'Robin Kinsella used to work with Cian.'

'And?'

'He says before Cian went AWOL, Nadine threatened to kill her husband with a knife.'

'I told you she was a nutjob, didn't I?'

'Only I haven't been able to find any trace of Cian Campbell, not in Ireland or the UK.'

'So?'

'What if Nadine is telling the truth, or even a version of it? Robin Kinsella can corroborate intent. Also, from what I've found out about Cian Campbell, disappearing isn't his style. He liked to throw his weight around, causing trouble wherever he can. And with Becca missing, I'm sure there's a tie-in.'

He gives me his you're-fucking-up-my-day face. 'What do you need?'

'Authorisation for bank and phone records of Becca Campbell.'

'And if I say yes, will you leave me in peace?'

'Absolutely.'

∞

Two hours later, I have both sets of records on my desk. Becca's bank card hasn't been used since several days before Gavin reported her missing. That on its own is worrying, but something else is bothering me. A refund on a purchase from a chain store has been sitting in the account, and with Becca not holding down a steady job, even without her drug dependency, leaving money in her account isn't a luxury she can afford, unless she can't access it. The phone records tell the same story, with no transactions on her account since she disappeared. I consider pinging the last time the phone was used, but as I scroll through the list of telephone numbers, prior to the line going quiet, one number keeps repeating itself, and several phone calls later, I've a name attached to it: Dylan Lynch.

I put a call through to Mike. 'Any luck on locating Joe Regan, or his nephew?'

'We have an address for Joe, but so far nothing on Dylan.'

'I've just gone through Becca Campbell's phone records.'

'And?'

'We may have hit the jackpot.'

49
WREN

HALF AN HOUR LATER, THE TEAM is gathered in the incident room, and the buzz is already building within the group. Everything has that electrifying feel about it, the place hinged with the intensity of an investigation that's about to turn. I wait until Mike arrives before I begin.

'Right, here's what we have,' I say, stepping up from the large table. 'Dylan Lynch, Joe Regan's nephew, is missing in action, and it's possible, based on timing, gender and age profile, that he could be our unidentified John Doe. We're pulling in his uncle, Joe Regan, so the next step is to get sample DNA from him. That should tell us what we need to know. If there's a family link to the victim, it will turn up there, and if Joe doesn't want to play ball, we'll look for approval under the Forensic Evidence Act and, if necessary, apply reasonable force. A point of note here: we're also looking at Joe Regan as part of the gang who tried unsuccessfully to extract that ATM from the wall in Rathfarnham.

'So, here's what else we know. We have an anonymous tip-off, via *Crimecall*, identifying Ben Donnelly as the guy in the CCTV footage potentially disposing of the limb in the river Dodder. History tells us Ben Donnelly and Joe Regan often work as a team. There's no record of any animosity between the men or, for that matter, Joe Regan's nephew, Dylan Lynch. That means there has to be more to this story than we're initially seeing. So, what else is at play?

'The pathology findings confirm our John Doe had some form of altercation before death. Based on the tears found on the surface area of the skin, this involved a female. So now our case opens up.' I circle Dylan Lynch's name with a question mark on the board. Out of it, I write Joe Regan, and then Ben Donnelly, followed by 'unknown female'.

I knock on the board. 'This female could be Becca Campbell. According to Larry, Dylan Lynch was moving up in the ranks. We know he came to Dublin because of a female acquaintance. Although we couldn't get confirmation on the name, what we do know is that he was with someone he was also supplying.

'This is where it gets interesting, because Becca Campbell, coincidentally, went missing at the same time Dylan went quiet.' I point to 'unknown female'. 'A trace was authorised this morning on Becca Campbell's phone and bank records. Within the phone records, there's a direct link to Dylan. They knew each other, and both are missing in action. So if Joe Regan's DNA confirms a family link to our unidentified limb, the next question is, how does Becca fit in?'

'And how does the mother, Nadine Fitzmaurice, tie in too?' says Mike.

'Exactly. Right now, we need to view Nadine's version of events with a health warning. Some or all of what she claims could be true. According to Nadine, her daughter was abducted. If so, then why? She also links Ben Donnelly to the abduction.' I write Nadine's name on the board alongside Ben and Joe. 'We have a statement from Aria Jackson, Nadine's neighbour, stating she heard screams coming from the house. Along with this, we have a possible prowler spotted by Aria Jackson. We know Gavin Fitzmaurice, Nadine's brother, was playing pretend cop at Ben Donnelly's place – so, another question: could he be the prowler? And if so, again why?

'To complicate matters,' I continue, 'some of this investigation could tie back to a series of historical crimes. First, Cian Campbell, Nadine's estranged husband, who walked out on his wife never to return. As of yet, we haven't been able to locate Cian, so at this point we're treating him as a missing person. Alongside this, we have the disappearance of Evie Hunt, a member of the gang Nadine, Gavin, Cian and Ben were all part of as teenagers. Evie Hunt vanished, *circa* eighteen years ago.'

Mike raises his hand.

'Go ahead.'

The others look towards him.

'We could have a third historical connection. There was a hit-and-run incident about a year before Evie Hunt's disappearance, in which Gavin Fitzmaurice and Martin Prendergast were key suspects. A lot of you may not be familiar with Martin Prendergast, but that doesn't mean he doesn't have a chequered past. He mainly operates in west Dublin, and DI O'Keeffe from Lucan has painted a very detailed picture. Let's just say he won't be joining the priesthood any time soon.'

'Thanks, Mike. I'll take it from here.'

Standing in front of the large board at the top of the room, I say, 'If Dylan Lynch is our John Doe, then my take on it is this. Assuming he was romantically involved with Becca Campbell, she could have got in over her head, and we may be looking at a classic case of a relatively law-abiding citizen, Becca, getting into a physical fight with Dylan, and him ending up dead. Based on Dylan's MO, it could have been a simple case of self-defence, but it isn't likely that Becca carried out the full extent of the crime on her own.'

I point to Ben's name on the board. 'The anonymous tip-off puts Ben Donnelly right in the fray. Why did he get involved? Perhaps to ease tensions within Dylan's crime group. After all, there would have been the need for payback for Dylan's death, assuming he's our victim. So far, there are no indicators of any retaliation on the streets, bringing us back, yet again, to Nadine Fitzmaurice and her claim that Ben abducted her daughter. As I said earlier, we need to be careful with her version of events, but either way, if we get the DNA result from Joe Regan, and it's a genetic match for our John Doe, this, with Becca's phone records and her connection to Dylan Lynch, means her disappearance is part of all this, and perhaps our resourceful Ben had some other ideas of his own about payback for Dylan's death.'

Mike raises his hand again. 'It's possible,' he says, 'that Ben Donnelly decided to use Becca as some form of bargaining chip, only we don't know for what.'

'And Nadine Fitzmaurice, her mother,' I say, 'claims whoever is holding Becca forced Nadine to carry out a series of illegal pickups.'

'It seems too small a payback,' Larry says, 'for a key gang member like Dylan.'

'You're probably right, but we have only bits of the story. We don't know what else is out there, and even if part of Nadine's story is true, all fingers point to her being the principal target.'

Another member of the team raises their hand. 'So, where do Evie Hunt and Cian Campbell fit in?'

'According to Nadine,' I say, 'Evie's in cahoots with Ben Donnelly, but Cian Campbell is perhaps the biggest unknown in all of this. What we do know is that he's a wife-beater, a loudmouth and a troublemaker.'

'And Evie Hunt?' asks Larry.

'We know her father recently passed away. She wasn't seen at the funeral, but that doesn't mean she wasn't there. His death could have precipitated her return, but getting back to Becca's supposed abduction, and the reason Nadine came to our attention in the first place, I've always felt Nadine Fitzmaurice, even within her wild accusations, was holding something else back.'

'What's your theory?' asks Mike.

'I'm not sure. We know Nadine left Dublin to go to a place near Magheramore beach shortly after Evie disappeared eighteen years ago. We also know Nadine was pregnant with Becca at this point, so perhaps she went there to hide her pregnancy. Dylan Lynch is part of a crime gang in Wicklow, and several of its members were arrested recently near Magheramore after a large coke seizure. The location is another coincidence too many. Dylan, Joe and Ben all have links to the area. When Nadine left Dublin to go to Magheramore eighteen years ago, was it coincidence or is there something more? Did Ben, because of his known links to the area, help her find a place to stay? We don't know, but what we're sure of is this: Nadine was in Magheramore for a period of time. We also know, based on her statements, that outside her teenage acquaintance with Evie Hunt, there's other history there too. At some point, the girls shared secrets. Something bonded them. My hunch is, it all goes back to the summer Evie went missing.'

'What about that hit-and-run you mentioned earlier,' Larry asks, 'the one involving Gavin Fitzmaurice and Martin Prendergast?'

'What about it?'

'How does it tie in?'

'It could be connected,' I say, 'or it may not, but it's in the loop so we shouldn't disregard it.'

Mike steps in again, aware of the tentative connection to my father. 'For now,' he says, 'we're going with it being on the outskirts of things, but you might as well all know, the victim of the hit-and-run, the woman who died, was Wren's mother.'

Every face in the room looks towards me.

'It's simple,' I say. 'If at any point a concrete link is found, I'll be taken off the case, so let's start tying up all these loose ends, beginning with getting DNA from our buddy Joe Regan, and locating Ben Donnelly.'

50
NADINE

I USE THE NOTEBOOK to write down everything Evie said to me last night, including all those terrible things she said about Gavin. But she was right about him changing. He did change, and it happened long before she went missing.

That name from the insurance fraud keeps circling in my head too. Is it possible it's the same Martin Prendergast who years ago hung out with Gavin? Ever since that question raised its head, I keep going back to the argument Gavin had with him. I never found out what it was about, but I do remember being really upset. I also remember Gavin roaring at me, telling me I was being stupid. I can't be sure, but now I'm wondering if it was then I first heard that nursery rhyme that keeps repeating in my head.

Could that be when Gavin changed too? But how would an argument with Martin Prendergast be the cause of anything, especially considering how much he suffered at the hands of our father? And then there's the other question Gavin asked of Evie – if she ever thought about killing someone. Why would you ask that? Unless, of course, it was something he'd already thought about.

Which is why I text him, asking him to call me. When he doesn't answer my first message, I send him another. Suddenly, it feels as if our roles are reversed, and instead of Gavin hunting me down, I'm the one with him in my sights.

I'm fed up trying to second-guess the truth. The time has come for answers, especially if Becca's safe return depends on it.

What I am sure of is that Gavin always knows more than he tells you, and somehow I have to get the truth out of him, no matter how dangerous that might be.

51
WREN

WHEN THE OTHERS LEAVE, Mike hangs back.

'When Joe Regan arrives,' I say, 'make sure I'm kept in the loop. Things are shifting, and my guess is, they're going to shift a hell of a lot faster if we get a concrete ID on our John Doe.'

'Agreed.'

'I'm also thinking it wouldn't do any harm to pull Nadine Fitzmaurice's phone records. Let's see if there's anything suspicious going back and forth.'

'You believe her, don't you?'

'I don't know what to believe, which is why everything's up for grabs.'

'The super will have to approve it.'

'If we get a genetic DNA match between Joe Regan and our severed limb, there won't be a problem, especially with Becca's phone links to Dylan.'

'Ben Donnelly is still a no-show. His sister claims he's away working.'

'I assume she doesn't know where.'

'Exactly, and if she does know, she's not telling us.'

'Okay. If we get Joe in here, let's hope things start rippling down, and fast.'

After he leaves, I scroll through the images of Evie Hunt on my mobile phone, the ones taken from the file at the Santry depot.

How the hell is this old missing-person case connected?

I study the photograph of Evie wearing that yellow party dress, pouting at the camera, and then the second one with Evie standing in woodland. There are tall spruce trees in the distance, tipped above the mountain peak in the upper frame, all set against a grey-blue sky.

I'd wager it's one of those forest walks in the Dublin Mountains, Massy's Wood or Cruagh Wood, or even the Hell Fire Club. The image is cropped from the waist down. She's gazing back at the camera over her shoulder, wearing a white denim jacket that looks far too big for her, her hair tied in two narrow plaits. Her eyes look as if they're trying to tell me something, willing me to search deeper, to go back to the beginning, to before she went missing, and find the answers there.

52
NADINE

I'VE HAD A COUPLE OF VOICE MESSAGES from work, asking if I'm okay, but there'll be time enough to answer those. Right now, I need to concentrate on Gavin. He's due to arrive in less than ten minutes, and he's seldom late. I could put any number of questions to him. I could mention meeting Evie last night, or question him about Martin Prendergast, and even ask what secrets he's hiding from all those years before. Instead I decide to concentrate on Cian. Evie said the two of them got on well together, and now I want to know why. I would never have imagined them as friends, but perhaps in the early days, or even later, they were.

In the darkness of the living room, I hear the key turn in the lock. He's bang on time.

'Nadine,' he calls out.

'I'm in here.'

'What are you doing with the curtains closed? It's the middle of the day.'

'I like the dark. It helps me to think.'

'Suit yourself.' He sits down in the corner armchair. 'So, what's the emergency this time?'

'You always try to belittle me, don't you?'

'No, I don't.'

'You've done it for years, and I'm so used to being the butt of your jokes, I barely notice it.'

'I don't mean to.'

'It doesn't matter what you mean. It's what you do. You've been that way ever since I started having panic attacks, as if my weakness is a source of annoyance for you.'

He doesn't answer. It's an affirmation of sorts. When Gavin agrees with you, a silence often follows.

'We used to get on well together, didn't we, Gavin?'

'I guess.'

'I remember us playing as kids, having fun. It felt as if we had a pact, a form of protection, looking out for one another.'

'That was a long time ago.'

'I used to warn you,' I say, 'whenever our father was on the prowl, so that you could keep out of his way. And sometimes, when I'd look for our mother, and she was depressed again, in bed, unwilling or unable to be there for us, unhappy with every aspect of her life, including me, you'd say, deep down, she loved me, and even if you were her favourite, that didn't mean she didn't care.'

'It was hard for her, Nadine,' he says, 'being married to a bastard.'

'I understand that. I also understand how a person can lose their sense of self, become lost.'

'You're talking about Cian now, aren't you?'

'Yes.'

'Do you still believe,' he asks, his eyes mocking, 'he wrote those words on the mirror upstairs?'

'Yes.'

'You imagined it, Nadine.'

'I didn't. I saw them.'

'Suit yourself,' he repeats.

'Gavin, I need to ask something.'

'What?'

'What makes you so damn sure Cian didn't write those words?'

'Because he couldn't have.'

'You can't know that for definite.'

He doesn't answer.

He's hiding something.

'What are you not telling me?'

'You don't need to know.'

'Stop treating me like a fool.'

'I'm not.'

'Then tell me.'

Still, he keeps his silence.

'When we spoke the other day,' I say, 'when you dismissed it out of hand, it wasn't just because you thought I was making stuff up again, there was something else, wasn't there?'

'Maybe.'

'What?'

'Nadine, stop this.'

'I won't. Tell me.'

'He's dead,' he says, his voice so deadpan, it scares me.

'You can't know that.' I shake my head, refusing to believe him.

'Don't you remember, Nadine, how you buried him in the garden?'

Why is he being like this?

He walks over to the window.

'But, Gavin, the police didn't find him.'

'Just because something isn't there doesn't mean it wasn't there before.'

'What are you talking about?'

'You said it yourself, Nadine. We used to protect each other, and now, it seems, for me, it's turned into a lifetime role.'

'What?'

'Did you really think I didn't notice your bruises? That I believed the excuses you made when your arm or leg was injured? Did you take me for a complete idiot?'

'But, at times, you and Cian were friendly.'

'We may have been friendly once, when I was young and bitter, but later, any friendliness I displayed was only to keep him onside.'

'Why?'

'So I could stay close.'

'Because you knew what he was doing to me?'

292

'Yes.'

'But how can you be so sure he's dead?'

Again, he stalls.

'How, Gavin? Tell me.'

'Because I called to the house that night.'

'What night?'

'The night you and Cian were having that almighty argument, before he ...'

'Before he what?'

'Fell down the stairs.'

My mind flips back to the moments before Cian went tumbling down, the anger rising inside me, telling me I needed to do something because if I didn't, I'd end up dead, and how somehow, when I pushed back at him, he lost his grip on me, and he fell, his head bouncing off the wall, the banisters on the stairs giving way, and all that blood spurting out, dark red, like the shade of lipstick used to write those words on the mirror. And then, he hit the bottom, and everything went quiet.

'Don't you remember, Nadine, I called to the door that night.'

'But that was before things got out of hand. I sent you away.'

'I came back. I stayed outside for a while, and soon after that, I heard the argument getting worse. Then I heard the sound of the staircase breaking, followed by that loud thump. For a moment, I thought it was you instead of him, but then you screamed and I knew.'

None of this is making sense. If he knew I was telling the truth when I told the police what I'd done to Cian, why did he question me? Does he want me to think I'm going mad?

'At first,' he says, 'I didn't know what to do, so I waited, and later I watched as you dragged Cian's body out the back, attempting to cover him up with soil, hoping the builder would do the rest of the work for you.'

'All this time you knew I killed Cian and you never said a word.'

'Leaving the body there like that was stupid, Nadine. The builder could easily have noticed it. I had to get rid of it. It was the smartest thing to do. So, again, Nadine, I covered up your bloody mess.'

'Where? Where did you bury him?'

'Somewhere in the Dublin Mountains, a place no one will ever find him.'

I think about the miniature Christmas tree, the one I saw the day I picked up that second package. For all I know, Cian's body could have been close by.

I had wanted to ask Gavin about that question he asked Evie, about killing people, but I already know the answer. If he had to, Gavin would destroy anyone who got in his way, perhaps even me.

'After a while, Nadine, it gets wearing having to clean up all your mistakes, fix things for you.'

'I never asked you to do any of it.'

'Didn't you?'

'I wanted you to love me and for you to want to help.'

'Well, you got lucky, Nadine, because for a while there, I thought big brothers were supposed to protect, but now I'm sick of it.'

He walks towards the living-room door, getting ready to leave, as if he's had enough of me, dismissive, angry.

'What about Martin Prendergast?' I ask.

'What about him?'

'Years ago, you two had this huge argument.'

'So?'

'There are things about it I don't remember, chunks of time missing from my memory, and in the gaps I keep hearing that old nursery rhyme.'

He stares at me in disbelief.

I begin to sing 'Three Blind Mice' as if perhaps, this one last time, it might jog those lost memories.

'Stop it, Nadine,' he shouts, but I keep on singing, and then, without expecting it, I start to cry, and everything that's happened seems so overwhelming, I'm not sure I'll survive any of it.

'They say the weak shall inherit the earth,' I mock, 'don't they?'

'I wouldn't lay money on it,' he replies, still trapped in his rage.

I want him to hold me, to tell me everything will be okay, but he can't. Evie was right: he has his own demons, deep, dark, scary memories that frame him too. And then I say something I already know I'll regret. 'You're getting more like him by the day.'

'Who?'

'Our father.'

'Fuck you, Nadine.'

Soon I hear the front door slam, leaving me behind, like he did that day when I was wrapped in a damp towel far too small for me, when he didn't know what else he could do.

Alone, I walk upstairs and stare at the blank mirror. I touch the surface, telling myself that I saw those words: 'YOU LEFT ME TO DIE.' I didn't make them up, and if I believe that, there's another truth I must face. If Cian is dead, only two people could have written them. And, if what Gavin says is true, about him burying Cian, the only other person who knows what happened that night is my brother. Did he write those words on the mirror? Or, did I?

It's only then I remember the small burned piece of paper I took from the grate, the fragment of a page from the notebook. Frantic, I pull the box from the secret compartment at the back of the wardrobe, searching for the envelope with the tiny piece of paper, half expecting it, too, to have disappeared, but it's still there.

The nursery rhyme repeats in my head. Dr Ward always said it was important, that somehow it was linked to my panic attacks and blackouts. Once more, the argument Gavin had with Martin Prendergast replays in my mind. I remember again how angry Gavin became, and afterwards, I did something I shouldn't. I ran to our uncle's house, the one who kept the pigeons in the loft, and I let them free. My uncle was furious, but again, Gavin took the blame for it.

I unlocked the loft because of my argument with Gavin, when he told me to go upstairs, and he called me stupid, but it wasn't only that. It was because after he had the fight with Martin Prendergast, he told me I didn't hear what I thought I had, that I was just being silly Nadine, always making up crazy stuff that no one else will ever believe.

53
WREN

MIKE AND LARRY HAVE JOE REGAN in Interview Room 3, and so far, he's been peddling the same story: that he knows nothing about any ATM attempt, or the whereabouts of his nephew, and that he hasn't seen Ben Donnelly in weeks.

I tap on the door. Larry opens it, and Mike immediately suspends the recording.

In the corridor, I ask, 'What's the latest?'

'Regan's still saying the same thing, although he let slip that Ben's been working on something off his own bat.'

'Does he know what?'

'Says not.'

'Let's get that DNA sample now. The only reason I've been holding off was to see if we might get more out of him the friendly way.'

'He won't give a sample willingly.'

'Then we'll do it the hard way.'

'Did you get approval?'

'The super's just authorised it. The doctor's on his way now. And, Mike, if necessary, use force.'

He nods.

'How long have we held him?'

'We're getting close to the three-hour mark.'

'Let's go for a Section 30 and hope the twenty-four hours will be enough. We need to push things up a notch. We have an eyewitness, and we have priors, not to mention his possible entanglement in the Becca Campbell missing-person case.'

'But we don't have anything solid to tie him to that.'

'Not yet, but Ben's name has been linked via Nadine, and Joe Regan is a known associate of his. If the DNA matches our victim, and it is his nephew, whether he's directly involved with Ben or not, he'll soon realise we're getting closer to what went down, and self-preservation will kick in. We already know Dylan is connected to Becca, and Joe won't want accessory to murder or a teenage abduction pinned on him, no matter how close he is with Ben Donnelly. Right now, we may only have the ATM attempt to hold him on, but if we get lucky, other doors will open.'

'Do you want to take over the interviewing?'

'Not yet. Let's get those DNA results in, and then I'll apply the pressure.'

Back at the office, I press the return key on the computer keyboard. Becca's bank statements are still on the screen. After Nadine's first interview, it was Gavin, not Nadine, who supplied us with her account details. He said he often made lodgements to her account, but as I scroll down the dates, going back over months, I notice something else. Each time Gavin paid funds into Becca's bank account, it was a couple of weeks after she'd withdrawn the same amount in cash. Could I have been looking at this all wrong? Was Becca, even in a small way, helping Gavin with money, and not the other way around?

I keep staring at the computer screen, asking myself yet again why Gavin, if he knew I was the girl he left without a mother, didn't run in the opposite direction. Why did he seek me out? Why was he so inquisitive about my mother's death, and always asking after my father? It was almost as if he wanted to keep me in plain sight, and as if there was more to the hit-and-run than anyone had realised.

I think again about that first day I saw him with Nadine, the sister he rarely spoke about. I sensed the sibling tension between them, and later, when I studied how he spoke to her, at times condescending, constantly doubting her and, in part, ashamed, it was almost as if he considered his life might be a whole lot better without her in it.

54
NADINE

AFTER GAVIN LEAVES, I FEEL bereft: if he wrote those words on the mirror, any love between us, past or present, is already gone. Now, I'm wondering what else he's hiding. Evie said he was partly the reason she left. She also said she'd been watching my house, which was why she could tell me someone had been inside. With Cian no longer a possibility, could it have been Gavin? And, if so, what was he searching for?

I put my face in my hands, rubbing it hard, as if trying to clear the fog in my brain. Gavin believes I need more psychiatric help, someone other than Dr Ward. Is he trying to convince me I'm going mad?

Evie said I needed to become the mother I'd always wanted to be, and she was right. I need to protect my daughter. Becca can't return here while there's still a threat, which means I have to find out what that threat is and who is behind it, even if it turns out to be my brother.

I know Gavin is capable of lying. He's capable of lots of things, and he can keep a secret for as long as it takes.

The burned piece of paper is back inside the box here in my room, hidden in the secret compartment. I've never told Gavin about the existence of my hiding place, and perhaps that's a good thing. I think about Cian's wedding ring. Whoever was in the house must have taken it, but afterwards, they came back, meaning they didn't get what they wanted the first time.

I'm about to go downstairs when I decide to take out the box one more time. Whatever they were searching for may be inside.

Becca's old passport photographs are still on the top. I rummage through, aware that most of the items are of sentimental value, but there are important documents too, like Becca's birth certificate, claiming me as her mother and Cian as her father. On my hunkers, I open the small black jewellery box with the gold locket belonging to my mother. It contains a photograph of me and, opposite, one of Gavin. The images were taken shortly after we both made our holy communion.

It couldn't be the locket, could it?

I stare at the images, brother and sister caught in time. I want to go back and tell my little-girl self, and Gavin, as a young boy, that it wasn't our fault. Life got complicated, our family broken, having a father filled with rage, and a mother who slowly gave up on life, and within all this unhappiness, Gavin and I turned from children to adults, only we became adults who were equally broken, with no way to undo the damage done. For some reason, perhaps to hold the photographs closer, I peel back the images, mine first, then Gavin's.

At the back of each, there's an identical message in my mother's handwriting. Reading her words, my eyes find it hard to focus, as if I can't quite believe what I see, as if the words refuse to settle. It takes a while for my mind and heart to align, as I read aloud: 'I love you both the same.' The sentence hangs in the air, as if searching for a home, until eventually, it sinks in. I feel something I only got a hint of in her final days: regret. I always thought she preferred Gavin to me, but maybe I was wrong about that too. Perhaps it was the guilt for all the beatings my father dished out to my brother, especially, because Gavin stood up to him when others didn't, including my mother.

I reread her message from the grave. I cling to it.

Finally I place the photographs back inside the locket, and for the first time, in a very long time, I think I understand her a little more.

Which is why this time when I open her last will and testament, the one in which she left everything equally between myself and Gavin, the one she wrote after she found out her cancer was terminal, superseding an older version with Gavin as the only beneficiary, I realise it was still possible for her, even close to the end, to do the right thing.

55
WREN

MIKE OPENS THE OFFICE DOOR. 'The blood sample from Joe Regan is a genetic match.'

'Bingo,' I say, pacing the room. 'With Dylan as the victim, this opens everything up, and as well as getting Ben Donnelly's arse in here, pronto, let's pull Nadine's phone records ASAP.'

'What's your theory, Wren? I know you have one.'

'As I said at the incident-room briefing, if Becca is tied to Dylan's death, and Ben Donnelly started playing mediator, including cutting up and disposing of body parts, he did so for a reason, and I doubt it was for Becca's sake. With him knowing Nadine, he would have seen her as a soft target, and if Nadine's version is true, Evie Hunt is also somehow involved.'

'Do you think she came back after her father's death?'

'Patrick Mescal, the family liaison officer attached to her disappearance, cited her father as a potential sex abuser. It makes sense she would have stayed away from him, but maybe she got homesick, especially with him out of the way. I still don't know exactly what links her to all this, but as I said, my gut tells me it ties into that summer she went missing and potentially Nadine Fitzmaurice.'

'And Gavin Fitzmaurice?'

'We've had question marks over Nadine's version of events from day one, but I'm starting to think Gavin might be a bigger player in all of this.'

'Why?'

'There was something dodgy in Becca's bank account.'

'What?'

'She may have been giving her uncle money, instead of the other way around.'

'You're thinking gambling debts, or something like that?'

'Possibly. It would fit with his life being a total fuck-up.'

'We don't have enough to pull his financial records.'

'No, but we've both seen what he's like with Nadine.'

'You mean, constantly trying to diminish everything she says.'

'It could be a form of coercive control.'

'To what end?'

'That's what I intend to find out.'

'So, what next?'

'Leave Joe Regan sitting for a while until we get Nadine's phone records. The more concrete evidence we have before we apply the final pressure, the better. I'll set up the authorisation with the super now, but in the meantime, I want you to ring Nadine's place of work. Find out the last time she was there, and what, if anything, she was working on. We're missing something and I want to know what.'

'And Gavin Fitzmaurice?'

'Leave him to me but keep searching for Ben Donnelly. If so much as a hair on his head appears, I want to know about it.'

56
NADINE

IT'S AFTER NINE O'CLOCK AT NIGHT when I decide the only way to find out the identity of the intruder is to set a trap for them. Each time they broke into the house, the place was empty. Which also means Evie wasn't the only one watching my movements. It's a long shot, and I've no guarantee they're going to bite first time, but it's worth a try.

After I leave the house, I stop to fill the car at a twenty-four-hour garage nearby. At this time of night, there's only one assistant at the pay desk. Inside, I glance at the newspapers on the counter, seeing a headline about drug gangs. 'Magheramore' catches my eye. I grab the newspaper and pay for it along with the fuel.

In the car, with only the overhead light on, I scan the news article. It's about a gang arrested near Magheramore beach. Those involved are currently being held in custody. I wonder if Ben is connected. Back when Evie was in hiding, he would visit her sometimes, saying he had to meet people close by. He never said who, but the implication was that they were involved in something shady.

When another car pulls into the garage, I fire the newspaper onto the passenger seat and drive out onto the main road. The article will have to wait. First, I need to trap an intruder, the person who not only broke into my home and ransacked the place but also wrote those horrible words on the mirror. They are likely to be the same person who sent Cian's wedding ring to my office too. They did all of it with one aim: finding something in the house they desperately need while convincing me I'm going mad.

Arriving back, at first I don't think my plan has worked because the house is still in darkness, but instead of going inside, I park in a laneway close by. The view isn't great from here, but if someone is watching me, they won't be able to see my car.

I start to dwell on how I haven't heard from Becca in days, and whether or not I can really trust Evie. Even now there's a chance she and Ben are planning something awful, and everything she said about wanting to help Becca is nothing more than a lie.

I wipe away the steam from the windscreen. The house looks exactly the same, and I'm about to abandon the plan for the night, when my thoughts shift back to Gavin and all the horrible things he said before storming out of the house. I always hated it when we argued. He never answered me properly about that argument he had with that boy called Prendergast either, the one with the same name as the person involved in the false insurance claim. The two may be the same person. I try hard to think back. I was fifteen, possibly sixteen, when the argument happened, Gavin a year older. I can still hear their raised voices, remembering again how afterwards Gavin tried to convince me I was mistaken about what I'd heard, but those words are still etched across my mind, just like the words scrawled in red on the bathroom mirror. Gavin had said, 'She's fucking dead.' And when I repeated the words to him, and he told me I was being stupid, I thought he was right. I didn't want to argue with him. I wanted Gavin to keep being my big brother and tell me everything would be okay.

My mobile phone rings. It's him. I don't answer it. I can't talk to him, not now.

After a few more minutes, I'm about to switch on the engine to go home, giving up on the idea of catching the intruder for the night, when a car speeds past. The roar of the engine forces me to take in my surroundings all over again, and it's only then I see that the house is no longer empty: upstairs, in my bedroom, someone has turned on the small bedside light.

57
WREN

THE AUTHORISATION FOR NADINE Fitzmaurice's phone records arrives a little before 10 p.m., while Joe Regan is still stewing in custody. There hasn't been a sign of Ben Donnelly, which heightens my suspicions. I ring through to Mike.

'What's the story with Nadine's place of work?'

'I was about to call you. It took a while to track someone down, being outside office hours, but it seems Nadine returned to work with a letter from Dr Ward. She stayed for a couple of days, and then became a no-show.'

'Did they contact her?'

'Yep, but she hasn't returned their calls.'

'She could be going through another bad patch.'

'Do you want me to send a squad car around?'

'Not yet. I don't want to spook her.'

'Okay.'

'What was she working on?'

'That's the odd bit.'

'Why?'

'She took over a big claim, one she wasn't directly involved with.'

'It wasn't assigned to her?'

'No.'

'I want details of that claim. If Nadine took it over, she had her reasons.'

'Agreed.'

'It may well be the real payback, Mike, for Dylan Lynch.'

'I'm already on it. Larry will be visiting them first thing in the morning.'

'Good.'

'Did you get the authorisation for Nadine's phone records?'

'Yes, and it looks as if they're coming through right now.'

'I'll be right there.'

It doesn't take Mike long to arrive. 'What have you got?' he asks.

'Several phone calls from pay-as-you-go mobiles.'

'Oh?'

'Each of them used just the once.'

'You think someone was trying to hide their ID and avoid being traced?'

'Maybe. We could ping the lines, and if any of them come within an inch of Ben Donnelly's place in Harold's Cross, it would be a concrete connection.'

'He's hiding low somewhere, Wren, but he can't hide for ever.'

As we scan through the balance of the phone records, most are easily identified, Nadine's place of work, Gavin, Dr Ward's office, calls to the dry cleaner and other retail outlets, along with a single call to a Sophie Fahy.

'Does the name mean anything to you?' Mike asks.

'Yeah, it does. I saw it in a news article under an old photograph of that teenage group.'

'Bringing us back to that old case.'

'It keeps coming up, doesn't it?'

Mike's phone rings. He answers it, and I can tell even before he hangs up that something has shifted.

'What is it?'

'The tech guys had a look at Becca's social media apps.'

'And?'

'Her Facebook account sent several private messages to Nadine a few days back.'

'What did they say?'

'*Await further instructions, Truth or Dare.*

'*Did you get the package?*

'*I sent you a few presents.*'

'Shit,' I say, my mind immediately going into overdrive.

'Do you think it could be Becca?'

'I doubt she would have known about the Truth or Dare game.'

'So it's someone from the old group?'

'Perhaps more than one.'

'Ben and Evie?'

'Yeah, and those items supposedly sent to Nadine, the hairbrush, the photograph and that rusty key, all tie in.'

'It looks, Wren, as if someone is trying very hard to mess with Nadine Fitzmaurice's head.'

'And Evie is part of all this.'

'Where do we start?'

'Her father's funeral.'

'No one saw her there.'

'I know, but even if there wasn't any love lost between her and her father, someone paid the funeral director, and whoever footed that bill is as good a place as any to start.'

58
NADINE

I LEAVE THE CAR PARKED IN THE laneway, my heart thumping fast in my chest. A lone cat wails in the distance, like the call of a banshee, as if warning of oncoming danger. As I get closer to the house, I'm mindful to keep out of sight, avoiding any streetlights or the houses with their lights still on. I can't risk alerting the intruder. I avoid the external light too, keeping to the left of the front door with the key clutched in my hand. I hesitate before putting it into the lock. If they hear me, they might make a run for it, and then I might never find out who they are.

Instead I check each of the downstairs windows. None looks tampered with. What if whoever is inside has a key? It could be Gavin. I know he has one, but if it is him, then why? What is he searching for?

It could be connected to the box, the one hidden in the secret compartment upstairs. That's the only thing that makes sense, because otherwise they would have found what they're looking for by now.

Another thought hits me. Could Gavin be searching for the new will?

That doesn't make any sense, because he already has a copy. But what if he wants to destroy mine, and present the old will and testament as the most up to date, with him as the beneficiary. Our mother didn't have time to file the updated one before she died. That's why she gave us both a copy, witnessed by two of the hospital staff.

It couldn't be that, could it? Money can't be what all this madness is about. But then I remember Evie's words about money making the world go round – a cliché, but one with more than an element of truth.

Still in the garden, I listen hard for any sounds. It takes a while to adjust my hearing, blocking out other street noises, but then I hear someone opening and closing drawers upstairs. I consider entering the house through the back door, but if I did that, the security light would come on. My only option is to go in through the front. I have to take that chance.

Finally, I put the key into the lock, with my mobile phone held tight in my other hand, ready to send a 999 text message if I have to.

Turning the key, I pray the door doesn't squeak as I push it open. Soon, I'm inside. I leave the door off the latch, ready to make a quick exit if I'm attacked.

Someone is definitely upstairs. They're hardly making a noise now, but I can see the light coming from under the bedroom door, and every now and then, a shadow wafts across it.

I move towards the kitchen as quietly as I can. The kitchen knives are on the wall opposite. I grab a long fillet blade, which I sharpened a couple of weeks back. I'll use it if I have to.

Seconds later, I'm at the foot of the stairs. I take them one at a time, quietly, as if I'm the intruder, not the other way around. My heart beats ever faster in my chest. My palms are sweaty. I move closer to the bedroom. I fear another panic attack, unsure what I'll do when I come face to face with this person inside my home.

Reaching the top step, a phone rings. At first, I panic, thinking it could be mine, but then I realise it's coming from my bedroom. I'm near the door as they answer it.

'Yes,' the voice says, 'I'm here now.'

There's a pause, as if someone is talking at the end of the line.

'Everything is fine,' the intruder says. 'Don't worry.'

I don't know what to do next, but doing nothing is no longer an option.

59
WREN

LUCKILY FOR US, FUNERAL DIRECTORS work twenty-four/seven, death waiting for no man. Once I put the phone call through, the undertakers who looked after Nigel Hunt's funeral were initially reluctant to reveal the source of payment, but a missing teenager, a murder victim and a potential fraud have a way of opening doors. Purchasing a bank draft with cash is unusual enough these days, but more important is the name of the person who wanted the draft, a woman without an Irish bank account, from whom the bank required both ID and proof of address as protection against money laundering. That person, as I suspected, was Evie Hunt, who recently opened a mobile phone account, and used the first utility bill, along with her UK passport, to satisfy the bank's identification process. More importantly, we have an address, not far from Ben Donnelly's place, located in a housing estate in Crumlin.

Mike and I head there in an unmarked car, knowing it's a long shot that she's at the address: it wouldn't have been difficult for her to give false information to the mobile phone company, but I'm hoping we'll get lucky.

It's nearing 10.30 p.m. by the time we reach our destination. The street, consisting of two lines of sixties corporation houses facing one another, is reasonably quiet. We manoeuvre our way past a series of parked cars, some on the kerb, others squashed into short driveways, the development designed for a time when having a phone, let alone a car, was unheard of.

I tell Mike to cruise by a couple of times for us to get our bearings. We've already run a search on the location, which, according to the last census, is divided into two flats and owned by a landlord living in the UK.

'Let's go for it,' I finally say. 'If Evie Hunt is at this address, eighteen years is long enough to wait.'

I take the lead, and a few seconds later, I'm ringing the doorbell of the downstairs flat at 13A Bangor Street. The hall lights up, as a door at the back of the flat opens. I see the shape of a woman through the glass panels in the front door. Is this Evie Hunt, the girl who accepted a dare all those years before and vanished? Instinctively, I hold my breath.

The door opens. Standing before me is an older version of the teenager in the photographs. She doesn't seem surprised to see us.

'Hello, Evie.' I flash my ID. 'We need to talk.'

She nods in agreement.

'The station might be best,' I say.

She turns and reaches for a cream trench coat hanging in the hall.

As we walk towards the squad car, I introduce myself and Mike. She appears only mildly interested. I sense she's been waiting for us and, perhaps, for her chance to set the record straight.

60
NADINE

I SHOULD CALL OUT, ALERT OTHERS, or press the emergency number on my phone, but I do none of these things. Instead I stand still, as if I'm watching everything happen in slow motion. All these weeks, ever since that first break-in, and later, when Becca was taken from me and I was forced to do things I never thought possible, I've doubted myself, questioning everything within this twisted and tangled web of lies.

The intruder hasn't yet noticed me, being so intent on their task, almost as if I don't exist, as if I never existed, unimportant, quiet, stupid Nadine. I watch them walk into the en-suite bathroom. Are they thinking about writing another message on the mirror, threatening me with the terrible things I did in the past, the terrible things I was forced to do? And if they are, why?

For so long, I've been jumping from one conclusion to another, blaming Evie, questioning Gavin, living in fear that Cian might have come back, but I was wrong, because it was none of those people. It was the person standing in plain sight all this time.

I twist the fillet knife in my hand.

The blade nips my skin.

I see blood, my blood, and there's relief in that, in the knowledge that this is real and, if so, then I can do what I need to.

I walk further into the bedroom, a stronger Nadine, a woman who has been through so much to save her daughter, who has been disbelieved at every step along the way, until finally I say aloud: 'I should have always known it was you.'

61
WREN

Driving back to the station, Evie keeps her silence. I don't push her, because when we talk, I want to be looking her straight in the eye. Apart from Nadine's earlier accusations, there's no concrete reason to be dragging her into a police station, but she's part of all this, even if I haven't been able to figure out exactly how.

At the front desk, Larry greets us.

'Which rooms are free?' I ask.

'All except Interview Room 3.'

'I'll take 6.'

I want to keep Evie Hunt as far away from Joe Regan as possible, certainly until I work out what, if anything, connects them.

After the preliminaries, explaining to Evie that she isn't under arrest, merely someone who might be able to help us with our enquiries, I begin by asking her something I've been trying to figure out, probably since I started my relationship with Gavin.

'Let's begin,' I say, 'with an easy one. Where have you been for the last eighteen years?'

'The UK, mostly.'

'Mostly?'

'I spent some time in Spain and Portugal in the early years, doing hotel work.'

'What brought you there?'

'The weather,' she shrugs, 'and it was a long way from here.'

'You disappeared. Why?'

'I didn't like being here any more.'

'Your parents reported you missing. They were distraught with worry.'

'I regret doing that to my mother.'

'And your father?'

'He was different.'

'How?'

'Being a bastard.'

'Is that why you left? Problems at home?'

'You could say that.'

She's hedging, being deliberately vague. 'Allegations were brought against your father a few years back for sexual abuse. They didn't stick, but still.'

'As I said,' a fresh harshness in her voice, 'he was a bastard.'

'We spoke to Nadine Fitzmaurice recently.'

She doesn't respond.

'She maintains you were abused.'

'Nadine says a lot of things.'

'Well, were you?'

'I don't want to talk about it.'

The lack of denial tells me everything I need to know. I change tack. 'Before you went missing, you played a Truth or Dare game, didn't you?'

'Yes.'

'The card you picked said you should do something you would always be remembered for.'

'And I did.'

'Was that another reason why you vanished, a kind of attention stunt?'

'I didn't want attention. I wanted the opposite.'

'At that time, you didn't seem the type to walk out on your life. You had friends, you'd just finished school, with a possibility of a college place and a bright life in front of you.'

'I didn't know there was a type,' she snaps.

'You said you were in the UK mostly, but spent some time in Spain and Portugal.'

'That's right.'

'Where did you go to after you left Dublin? The UK or Europe?'

'Neither.'

'Where, then?'

'Magheramore.'

My mind does a quick retake. Apart from the recent drug seizure, it was in Magheramore that Gavin found Nadine after Becca was born. Could the girls have met up there?

'What brought you to Magheramore?'

'I had an aunt who lived there. We would visit in the summer. I always liked it.'

'Did you stay with her?'

'No. She died the year before.'

'Where, then?'

'A house near the beach.'

'Were you on your own?'

'For a time.'

'And after that?'

She shifts in the chair. I've the same sense I had when we first called to the flat in Crumlin, that Evie's been waiting a long time to have her say.

'Nadine found me,' she says.

'Really?'

'She's a good listener. You get that way when you prefer to live in the shadows. No one notices you, so you have plenty of time to take in all the information you need.'

'Why didn't she tell anyone?'

'She is good with secrets.'

'You were in a relationship with her brother, Gavin?'

'For a time.'

'He was devastated when you went missing.'

'Was he?'

'It seems a lot of people were, but that didn't matter to you, did it, walking out on your life without giving anyone an explanation?'

'It mattered.'

'When Nadine found you, what happened then?'

'She stayed with me for a while.'

'And she didn't tell anyone where you were?'

'No. As I said, she could keep a secret. I think she liked that part of it, the mystery, the intrigue. It appealed to her dramatic side. Besides ...'

'What?'

'She desperately needed a friend.'

'Nadine was lonely?'

'Back then, everyone she knew was part of Gavin's circle, not hers.'

'Did you get on?'

'For a time, but soon I realised she became obsessed with me.'

'Obsessed?'

'I guess I was everything she wasn't. I was sociable, popular, cool, if you like, everything Nadine thought she wanted to be.'

'So popular and cool you had to disappear?'

Again, she doesn't reply.

'It takes money,' I say, 'to vanish like that, to pay for a place to stay, feed yourself.'

'I guess.'

'Where did you get the money?'

'Ben.'

'Ben Donnelly?'

'Yes.'

'Why was he so keen to help?'

She shrugs her shoulders again. 'He liked me. We had a thing for a while, before Gavin. Nothing serious, a teenage crush.'

'It must have been more than that for Ben to stick his neck out for you, not telling the police where you went, giving you money.'

'I suppose.'

'Did Ben get you the place too?'

'Yes.'

'Was it owned by the Regans?'

'The name sounds familiar.'

'Still, it couldn't have been easy for Ben to get money at that age.'

'He knew people, and he wanted to help.'

'Just like Nadine?'

'Not quite.'

'You seem to have a way with people, Evie, don't you, getting them to do things for you?'

'The circumstances were complicated.'

'How?'

She flinches. 'I don't have to tell you anything. I'm not under arrest.'

'No, you don't, but maybe you can tell me why Nadine Fitzmaurice claims you and Ben abducted her daughter.'

'As I said earlier, Nadine says a lot of things.'

'It doesn't mean she's lying.' My eyes lock with hers.

'My father,' she finally says, 'wasn't the only reason I left.'

I lean forward. 'Be more specific.'

'I was pregnant.'

Mike and I share quick glances.

'I was too far gone,' she continues, 'to do anything about it, but I had to make sure no one found out.'

I think about that photograph taken a couple of weeks before she went missing, where she is walking in the woods, and she is looking back at the camera over her shoulder, wearing a light white denim jacket that looks far too big for her.

'What happened to the baby?'

'Nadine took her.'

'What do you mean, "took her"? Are you saying, she *stole* your child?'

'It wasn't quite like that.'

'Well, what are you saying?'

'We had an agreement.'

'What kind?'

'She was supposed to say Becca was hers so that she could give her up for adoption.'

'Why?'

'Because if anyone found out she was mine, I would have been put under pressure to say who the father was, and that wasn't something I wanted to share. It would have ruined Becca's chances of a normal life.'

'You believed Becca was your father's child?'

'I knew she was.'

'How can you be so sure?'

'He was the only one.'

'So, you and Gavin never ...'

'No. He wanted to, of course, but for all my bravado, I was scared back then, and ashamed too, knowing what my father had done to me.'

'You could have lied.'

'I did lie. I told the biggest lie of all.'

She swallows hard, as if the next bit is going to be difficult to say.

'I hated my pregnant body, because it was a constant reminder of him, and the awful things he did to me. Even when I carried Becca to term, I felt more like a vessel than a mother, detached from the life growing inside me. And after she was born, I convinced myself I felt nothing.'

'You felt disconnected?'

'Yes, but I realise now I was wrong. I did care for her, and that awful shame wasn't Becca's or mine, it was all his.'

'And yet you paid for his funeral.'

'There's satisfaction in knowing he's six feet under.'

'So, before you disappeared, when you found out you were pregnant, you didn't tell anyone other than Ben, and then later, Nadine?'

'I couldn't.'

'At what point did you discover Nadine didn't follow through with her side of the bargain?'

'After I came home.'

'Did you approach Becca?'

'No, not at first.'

'When, then?'

'When I found out she'd got herself into some deep shit.'

Mike gives me a look that says, *Keep her talking*.

'It must have been hard for you,' I say, 'coming back after all this time. The death of your father would have opened up old wounds.'

'It did.'

'And then,' I continue, 'seeing Becca.'

'Initially, I was shocked.' She stalls, as if trying to revisit exactly how she had felt the first time she had seen her daughter after so long. 'I mean, in one way, it was so great to see her, but in another it was also terribly sad.'

'How?'

'To see your own flesh and blood, all grown-up, knowing ...'

'Knowing what?'

'You had no hand or part in how she became the young person standing in front of you.'

'What did you do?'

'I did the same thing I did to Nadine. I watched her. I watched her all the time. I saw who she was hanging out with. I knew she was doing drugs. I talked to Ben, and he told me Dylan Lynch was bad news.'

'So, what did you do then?'

'I decided to confront her. I was worried her drug dependency was getting out of control. I wanted to intervene, to do something, anything, to help her.'

'And then?'

She looks away.

'What about you and Ben?'

'What about us?'

'Did you rekindle your old friendship?'

'You could say that.'

'He seems to be your go-to guy.'

She makes eye contact with me again. 'He was there for me when no one else was.'

'Let's get back to Dylan Lynch and Becca.'

'I don't have to talk to you.'

'No, you don't, but then there's the small matter of a limb found in the Dodder.'

'So?'

'It belongs to Dylan, your daughter's boyfriend – or should I say ex-boyfriend?'

'You need to talk to Ben about that.'

'But Ben isn't here. You are.'

She flinches, and I sense she's on the cusp of hanging Ben out to dry, if it means saving her own skin.

'Let's go back to the beginning, Evie, when you came back to Dublin and found Becca hanging out with the wrong sort, doing drugs.'

'What about it?'

'It must have disappointed you that your daughter hadn't turned out the way you'd hoped.'

'It did.'

'Who did you blame?'

'At first Nadine, but I've changed my mind of late.'

'Oh?'

'I was at fault too, at least partially.'

'And now Becca is missing, and Dylan Lynch is dead, and I think you know exactly what happened to them both.'

Her eyes tell me she's weighing up what to do and say next.

'What do you want to know?'

'Did you and Ben abduct Becca Campbell?'

She laughs.

'Well, did you?'

'We didn't abduct her, we saved her.'

'How?'

'The night Dylan died,' she says, hesitating, 'I'd been watching the two of them for hours. I'd already decided it was time to tell Becca the truth.'

'Go on.'

'I heard the beginning of their argument from down below on the street.'

'And what then?'

'I waited. Then, everything went quiet, and I decided to approach Becca.'

'Go on.'

'But as I got closer, the argument started up again. I banged on the flat door. I heard Becca scream, but I was already too late.'

'Why?'

'Because she'd killed him.'

I shoot Mike a look.

'I mean,' Evie says, frantic now, 'she didn't mean to. It was self-defence.'

'Becca told you this?'

'Yes. During their first argument, she became really scared.'

'And then?'

'When it went quiet, after he'd crashed out from the booze and drugs, she tried to get away, only he heard her, and when he came to, he was even more enraged, the drugs fuelling his temper. She said he was completely out of his head, like a madman. They got into another struggle, and that's when he grabbed a knife, but somehow Becca got hold of it, and while they fought, he fell down, and it was only then she realised she'd stabbed him.'

'You didn't witness any of it?'

'No, but as I said, that was the night I decided to approach her, tell her the truth about me, but when I banged on the door, and she didn't answer, I got scared so I called Ben. When he got there, he broke the door down.'

'Go on.'

'We found Becca traumatised in the corner, covered in blood, sobbing.'

'And Dylan?'

'He was dead.'

'If it was self-defence, why didn't anyone call the police?'

'The law was the least of Becca's problems. Taking someone like Dylan down had bigger consequences.'

'Payback?'

'Yeah.'

'And how did Ben feature in all this?'

'He came up with a plan to smooth things over.'

'With Dylan's gang?'

She nods.

'And Joe Regan?'

'Him and Ben went back a long way, and Joe, being Dylan's uncle, carried a lot of weight.'

'What was the deal?'

'To sort out an insurance claim, one Nadine could help them with. But first, Ben said, we had to test her, make sure she would play her part.'

'So, you and Ben got her to run a few errands?'

'That was more Ben than me, but yes.'

'And what happened to Becca while all this was going on?'

'After a couple of days, we got her out of Dublin and, with some pressure from Ben, we were able to get her into rehab in a private clinic in Drogheda.'

'Who cleaned up the mess in the flat?'

'I did.'

'And the phone calls to Nadine, they were all made by Ben?'

'Yes. Once we convinced Becca to make that first phone call, telling Nadine what she'd done, the plan was set in motion.'

'Becca set up her own mother.'

'Nadine isn't her mother,' she fires back at me.

I want to say she was more of a mother to her than Evie ever was but, for now, I hold my tongue.

'Becca's head was all over the place. She knew there would be repercussions for what she did to Dylan, and she also knew his sort weren't going to let her away with it, not without paying a price.'

'Did you tell her who *you* were? After all, that was why you went there.'

'Not at first. As I said, Becca wasn't in a good place. Initially she didn't know who Ben or I were. It was easier that way, to get her to do what we needed her to do, in order to save her skin.'

'You said you were watching Becca for some time, and Nadine.'

'Yes.'

'Aria Jackson, Nadine's neighbour, said she noticed someone watching Nadine's house, a prowler.'

'So?'

'Was that you?'

She doesn't answer.

'There was also a break-in at that house, reported by Nadine weeks before Becca went AWOL.'

'I'm not responsible for that.'

'But you were watching her, weren't you?'

'It's not what you think.'

'Enlighten me.'

'When I came back to Dublin, it was only natural to seek out old acquaintances, especially Nadine. It was how I found out about Becca.'

'But you kept on watching her?'

'I've been watching her every step of the way.'

'Did you break into her house?'

'No.'

'If not you, then who?'

'I don't know.'

'You're aware Nadine's husband, Cian Campbell, left her a few years back?'

'Yes.'

'Do you think he's involved with the break-in?'

'I wouldn't put it past him.'

'It seems like lots of people want to mess up Nadine's life.'

'Some people get very unlucky.'

'Where's Becca now?'

'I can't tell you that.'

'Why not?'

'I need to look out for her. I don't want Becca caught in the crossfire. I didn't protect her in the past, so I'm sure as hell not going to put her in danger now.'

62
NADINE

THE INTRUDER DOESN'T ANSWER ME and, for a split second, I doubt myself again, thinking, if I take a step closer to the bathroom, a step closer to this person, they too might disappear, like the words on the mirror, and I'd be convinced all over again that I'm going crazy.

I can't move.

'Don't worry, Nadine,' she says, pretending to care. 'You know I'm always here for you.'

She steps out from the bathroom, this woman claiming she's somehow here to help, but I know she's lying. Her words sicken me. I twist the knife in my hand and, for a second, I see all the people, including Cian, who tried to control me, put me down, make me feel less worthy, and the anger rising inside me is like nothing I've ever felt before, as I leap towards her, not even thinking about the knife.

I hear a low scream. A trickle of blood drips down her neck. I stand back, suddenly terrified.

'Give me the knife, Nadine.'

'No.' I shake my head.

'You don't want to do anything stupid.'

The word 'stupid' pounds at my brain.

I clutch the knife in my hand. 'Why?'

A smirk rises either side of her lips. She tries to suppress it, but it's clearly there.

Again, I consider pressing the emergency number on my phone, calling the police, looking for help. Only, I'm already too late, because now I hear sounds coming from below. Someone is running upstairs, frantic, urgent. I realise I'm in more danger than I first thought, because now I know, she isn't working alone.

63
WREN

'YOU'RE TELLING ME YOU DON'T WANT to say where Becca is because you don't want to place her in danger?'

'Yes.'

'Are you still worried about retaliation for Dylan's death?'

'No.'

'What, then?'

'I'm worried about the intruder, and whoever else is out to get Nadine.'

'You think it's connected to whoever broke into Nadine's place?'

'All I know is someone's been sneaking around the house.'

'But you don't know who?'

'No.'

I shift tack. 'Let's get back to the insurance fraud, the one you and Ben embroiled Nadine in.'

'What about it?'

'Who were the beneficiaries?'

'I've already told you. People connected to Dylan.'

'Any names?'

'If I tell you, will it help Becca?'

'I can't make any promises, but I'll do what I can, for Becca's sake.'

'I only ever heard one name.'

'Which was?'

'Prendergast. Martin Prendergast. He has links to Dylan's gang, the Dublin side of things.'

I don't reply. Instead, I let the silence take hold, as I realise everything has come full circle, the crimes of the past and present colliding, connecting me, the child survivor, to all of it.

I stare at Evie. I wonder if she knows that a year before she became pregnant with Becca, and disappeared, Martin Prendergast and Gavin Fitzmaurice decided to steal a car and play speed driving, turning a corner near the junction where my mother, moments earlier, had dropped me off to school. They killed her. They took her away from me and my father, who never fully recovered, because the tragedy of that day set in motion a lifetime for both of us, a different life from the one we could have lived, the one we so desperately wanted.

'Martin Prendergast and Gavin were friends once, weren't they?'

'That was a long time ago,' she replies, dismissive.

All of a sudden, I see the younger Evie, the one who looked back at me from the photographs, a girl with dark secrets, and I think how, for a time, I wanted to find out what happened to her and, in my own way, attempt to make things okay. And even though terrible things were done to Evie Hunt by her father, the man who should have protected her, part of me wonders still if Nadine is right, telling me that Evie, for all her popularity, could be selfish too. And it's this more than anything that convinces me: if she needs to, she will hang Ben out to dry.

'Evie,' I say, 'I want you to think long and hard before you answer my next question, because I will know if you're lying.'

'What?'

'Who cut up the body?'

64
NADINE

'CHRIST, NADINE,' GAVIN ROARS, 'what the hell are you doing?'

'She broke into my house,' I roar back at him, my words spilling out at speed. 'It's been her all along. She's the one responsible for both break-ins, and for all I know, the writing on the mirror too.'

'You're not talking sense, Nadine.'

'You two are in this together. Aren't you?'

'Stop it.'

'Someone wrote those words on the mirror.'

'You're unwell, Nadine. You need help.'

As he takes a couple of steps towards me, so many things are jumping around in my brain, it takes me a while to remember that the only person, other than myself, who knew what happened to Cian that night was Gavin. He's the only person who could have written those words on the mirror, unless, of course, he betrayed me to her. I think of Judas betraying Jesus for thirty pieces of silver, and as I do, I remember something else too, my mother's previous will and testament, the one held by her solicitor, and the other one, witnessed in the hospital only hours before her death, leaving everything equally between me and Gavin.

He's standing right beside me now, taking the knife out of my hand. I don't put up a fight. I can't, because if Gavin is really behind all this, the brother I once thought protected me, loved me, when no one else did, then maybe, with Becca safe, I should stop fighting.

'Nadine,' he says, his voice lower, calmer, 'you need to stop this.'

His hands rest on my shoulders. They feel like heavy weights, crushing, destroying anything good we ever had between us.

I need to say something, part of me still unwilling to give up completely. 'Gavin, Evie's been watching the house.'

'What are you talking about?'

'She saw the intruder. She told me someone was inside the house when I wasn't here, not just the break-ins but other times too.'

'Listen to me,' he snarls, grabbing my arms, 'you're close to breaking point, and if you fuck up any more, you're going to be put away for good.'

'No,' I plead, 'you don't understand. It's her. She's the one who's been trying to mess with my head. You have to believe me.'

He turns away.

I stare at Aria. The same smirk is still hovering behind that pretend-shocked face of hers.

'She's always been horrible to me,' I say, 'bringing up Cian, then Becca, when she knew I was vulnerable, all the while pretending to care, when all she ever cared about was herself. She doesn't fool me.'

'Stop it!' Gavin yells, anger pushing him to near breaking point.

Aria moves her attention from me to him. 'She tried to kill me, Gavin. Thank God you arrived when you did.'

'It's okay,' he says, still seething. 'I'll handle it.' And then I see something I'd never noticed before, a certain intimate familiarity between them, and my heart wants to break even more.

'It was me, Nadine,' he says, 'who asked Aria to keep an eye on you.'

'But this is my house. She has no right to be here.'

'I couldn't get through to you on the phone, so I rang Aria. I asked her to check if everything was okay. I thought you might have done something stupid.'

'Like what?'

'Who the hell knows?'

It's only then I notice the shiny silver thing in Aria's hand. Some-one has given her a front-door key, and I already know that someone is Gavin.

'Here,' he insists, handing me some tablets. 'Take these. You'll feel better.'

I want to say, 'I know Aria was in this house long before that phone call.' Only now I doubt he'll believe anything I tell him.

'I won't take them,' I say, defiant. 'You can't make me.'

'If you don't, I'll call Dr Ward and tell her you attacked someone at knife-point.'

Reluctantly, I swallow the tablets.

Soon, Gavin is instructing me to lie down and get some rest, but as he leaves, he doesn't close the bedroom door completely. He thinks I'm already asleep, but even though the sedatives are taking hold, my eyelids remain partly open.

I see him reach out and touch Aria's arm, caring, sensitive. Then he removes something from the inside pocket of his jacket. At first, I can't quite make out what it is, but when she takes it from him, I have a much clearer view.

Aria looks down at the syringe.

'In case you need it,' he says, before leaving her alone with me.

65
WREN

I REPEAT THE QUESTION. 'Evie, who cut up the body?'

She stares at me as if she's already rehearsing what she might add to the mix and, most importantly, which words will reflect her in the best light, probably the same way, years before, when she disappeared, she weighed up all the odds. If everything she has said about Becca is true, she also knows her daughter will probably face a charge of manslaughter, and she, the mother who only returned after the death of her father, has aided and abetted a crime, implicating not just Becca but herself. The one thing I'm sure of is, no matter how long she takes to reply, despite everything Ben has done for her, she will put herself and her daughter first.

'It was Ben,' she finally says. 'Cutting up the body was his idea, not mine.'

'So, where is he?'

'The apartment upstairs in Crumlin.'

'The flat above yours?'

'Yes.'

Shit, he was right under our noses, and we didn't realise. I shut down the recording. Mike follows me out of the interview room.

'What next, Wren?'

'I want Ben Donnelly in here, and fast.'

'And Martin Prendergast?'

'Him too. Both are linked to the potential fraud, and if what Evie says is true, Becca's actions, killing Dylan, whether in self-defence or not, have set a series of events in motion, and Martin Prendergast is part of the chain, tying right back to Nadine, and perhaps even Gavin.'

'You're talking about the hit-and-run?'

'There isn't a concrete link, at least not yet.'

'Your call.'

'Mike, there's one more thing.'

'What?'

'I need you to wake up someone from that damn insurance company where Nadine works. Even if the fraud has already gone down, large sums of money like that are not paid over too fast.'

As Mike deploys the squad cars to pick up Ben Donnelly and Martin Prendergast, I make my way to Joe Regan's holding cell. When I arrive, he's lying on the bed facing the wall with his back to me.

'Joe, I want to ask you something.'

He doesn't reply.

'I'm sorry about Dylan,' I say.

Still he says nothing.

'We've identified him, or at least one of his limbs found in the Dodder.'

'Shit happens,' he grunts.

'We know what went down.'

'Do you now?' He turns to face me for the first time.

'But Ben cutting up the body ... That was harsh.'

'He did what he had to do.'

'And between you, you smoothed things over, didn't you, working out a way for the debt to be paid?'

'I wasn't part of any payback.'

'I believe you, but I also know you and Ben go back a long way.'

'What's that got to do with anything?'

'You know his history.'

'So?'

'Did Ben ever talk about a group he was part of in his teens, one involving Evie Hunt and Gavin Fitzmaurice?'

'Sure.'

'What can you tell me about them?'

'I can tell you Gavin Fitzmaurice isn't as squeaky clean as he likes people to think.'

'What do you mean?'

He sits up in the bed. 'You two were an item once, weren't you?'

'Ancient history.'

'Well, you're better off without the likes of him.'

'Why is that?'

'I know a bent fucker when I see one.'

'Go on.'

'He wasn't beyond taking the odd backhander when he was still in the force, turning a blind eye, if you get my meaning. Besides, I hear a gambling addiction requires an awful lot of money.'

I already know Joe's taking pleasure in this, in what he sees as him setting me straight, but I doubt he cares very much about my well-being.

'Cops,' he sneers, 'when they turn rotten are the worst kind.'

'Anything else you'd like to share with me?'

'Not at the moment, no.'

'I'll miss our tête-à-têtes, Joe, when you get out of here, although something tells me our paths will cross again real soon.'

I walk away, a series of future conversations with Ben Donnelly, Martin Prendergast and Gavin Fitzmaurice looming large in my mind. Ben and Martin will fill in some of the missing details, but Gavin has always known more than he is willing to say, and a part of me knows it goes way beyond taking the odd crooked backhander.

66
NADINE

THE MEDICATION MUST HAVE KNOCKED me out, because when I come to, the bedroom door is firmly closed. I remember the syringe, and shiver, but it's not only that. It's also the sense that I'm not alone. I can't hear any sounds, only that doesn't mean Aria isn't still here. I toss in the bed, groggy.

I hear a noise coming from the bedroom window, the sound of a bird pecking at the glass. My mind goes back to the day I set the pigeons free, hearing the clatter of their wings, almost as if I'm back there, struggling to turn the key in the lock. The birds were so close to the wire, their beaks pecked at my hand, their eyes, wide open, looking unguarded, as if they knew what I was going to do next. Our uncle warned us the birds' freedom had to be controlled. I didn't understand what he meant. It seemed wrong to me that they were locked up for so long when all they wanted to do was fly.

My mind skips again, and I'm back in our childhood home. The radio is on in the living room. I don't know where Mum and Dad are, but I know Gavin is here. 'Three Blind Mice' is playing. I hear raised voices coming from the kitchen. Gavin is shouting at someone. I'm curious, so I leave the living room and press my ear tight to the kitchen door. Gavin doesn't know I'm there. He's saying such awful things. I don't want to believe any of them are true.

Seconds later, Martin Prendergast storms out. Gavin is furious when he sees me, but somehow I build up the courage to ask, 'Who was killed?' He tells me I don't know what I'm talking about, that I've got everything mixed up. He warns me I'll only get into trouble if I keep making things up, and if I don't stop doing it, soon, no one will believe a word out of my mouth. So, I didn't say anything, not then, not ever, only it didn't make any difference, because now, no one believes me. Everyone has doubted me, including myself.

I hear footsteps move across the room. The bedside light is switched on.

'Wakey, wakey, Nadine,' she says. 'It's time we had a long chat, woman to woman.'

67
WREN

BEN DONNELLY IS HANDCUFFED as the uniformed police officers accompany him to Interview Room 4. He probably knows we have Evie in custody, but he doesn't know as yet that the woman he did so much to protect has just ratted him out, and that is exactly where I begin.

'Hello, Ben.'

He grunts, slumped in the chair, his legs spread apart.

'I hear you like to cut up dead bodies.'

'No comment.'

'We have CCTV footage of you firing Dylan Lynch's severed arm into the Dodder.'

'You mean that shit you put out on *Crimecall*?' He smirks. 'Do me a favour and stop clutching at straws, you can't prove anything with that.'

'No, we can't, but we don't need to any more.'

'Why is that?'

'Because your girlfriend has just snitched on you.'

Doubt flickers in his eyes.

'Evie says you were very helpful to her, Ben, when Becca found herself in over her head.'

'No comment.'

'And before that, too, all those years ago, when she first discovered she was pregnant.'

'She disappeared.'

'But you knew where she went, didn't you?'

He gives me another look that says, *Prove it*.

'She got under your skin, didn't she?'

'Who?'

'Evie.'

'No comment.'

'You wanted to be some kind of hero, didn't you? Love can be a dangerous game, Ben, especially if it's one-sided.'

'You're just fishing.'

'You chose the wrong woman to help. You wouldn't believe how eager she was to save her own skin. She told us all about Becca and Dylan, your ingenious plan to get rid of the body, not to mention your involvement with blackmail and fraud, and now, with things unravelling fast, I've a feeling you'll soon want to tell us your side of the story.'

He shrugs.

'Where's the rest of the body, Ben?'

'I want a fucking lawyer.'

'Did you enjoy pushing Nadine Fitzmaurice to the edge?'

'Nadine is nearly as fucked up as her brother.'

'You don't like him, do you?'

'Nope.'

'Because he used to be a cop?'

'I never liked the fucker.'

'I hear he's got gambling issues.'

'He owes money all right.'

'Yeah?'

'Liked to tamper with evidence too.'

'It's quite refreshing, Ben, how suddenly you want to talk.'

'I've got your attention now, though, haven't I?'

'Why don't you enlighten me further, Ben, about this tampering with evidence, seeing as how suddenly you've become so chatty.'

He sits up taller, enjoying the tables being temporarily turned. 'It was a hit-and-run from years back that no one gave a damn about except him.'

Mike shoots me a look.

'Which hit-and-run?'

'All I know is Gavin was caught removing witness statements, and he went to an awful lot of trouble to cover it up.'

'Go on.' My heart is racing, aware Mike's eyes are firmly on me.

'He paid people to look the other way, and that was when the gambling really messed him over.'

'Why should I believe you?'

'Believe what you want, but I hear his financial status is due to improve very soon.'

'How?'

'His mummy died, didn't she?'

I suspend the interview, needing to think this through. Out in the corridor, I breathe in deep, pacing up and down, attempting to connect all the various strands, before Mike joins me.

'Jesus, Wren,' he says, 'if you're connected to this, it's now personal. You'll have to step back.'

'I hear you, but this damn thing became personal a long time ago.' I scroll down the numbers in my phone, then press the dial button.

'Who are you calling?'

'Gavin Fitzmaurice. We're well overdue a talk.'

'Wren?'

'I know – I'll be careful.'

68
NADINE

I CAN NO LONGER FEEL MY LEGS or arms. The only part of my body capable of moving is my head, but even that is difficult.

'Feeling better?' Aria asks.

I see the near-empty syringe on the locker, remembering how Gavin gave it to her, and how they looked so intimate, like a couple, and he told her to use it on me if she needed to. Then he left me alone with her.

'What have you given me?'

'Something to knock you out, with a little extra for good measure.'

'You're crazy.'

'Don't you remember, Nadine? You're the one who is sick in the head, not me.'

'Why are you doing this?'

'Because you've always been a burden to Gavin, ever since he was a child.'

I see the long fillet knife, the one I brought upstairs, in her hand.

'It's always Nadine this, Nadine that, poor Nadine,' she chants, 'poor sick-in-the-head Nadine.'

'You hate me, don't you?'

'Hate is such a strong word.'

'Why else would you be doing this?'

'Don't you think,' she muses, as if all of a sudden she's in some kind of a weird trance, 'that the word love is far stronger.'

'What are you talking about.'

'Tut-tut, Nadine. Perhaps you are as stupid as everyone else thinks.'

'Then why don't you enlighten me?'

'If you must know, I've witnessed how stressed you've made Gavin over the years, getting him to come here at all hours of the night just to check that you're okay. He's tired of it. You don't blame him for that, do you?'

'No, I don't.' My tongue feels large and dry in my mouth.

'He has money worries too. It's put such a huge strain on him.'

'I ...' The words refuse to come out. I feel a tingling and numbness in my lower face.

'And then your mother died, and everything, the house, the entire estate, was supposed to go to him, only you had to interfere all over again, getting Mummy dearest to change her last will and testament right before she died.'

I want to tell her it was my mother's choice, and Gavin knows that too, but even if I could reply, I doubt it would make any difference.

She continues talking, almost as if confessing to me is giving her extra pleasure. 'I gave your brother a shoulder to cry on. I was there every time you fucked up. I was even there the night he took Cian's body away. While you were sobbing upstairs, feeling sorry for yourself, I watched your brother hide your dirty work.'

Somehow, despite my words being slurred, I manage to say. 'It – was – you – wasn't – it? You – wrote – those – words – on – the – mirror.'

'A bit too late to be clever, don't you think?'

I nod.

'And the ring, Nadine, that was me too. I found it, and I thought I'd play a few games with you.' She stares at me like she's examining a caged animal in the zoo. 'I also found your silly notes, your ridiculous attempts at being some kind of detective. It was fun messing with your head. You did that to Gavin for years. Emotional strain does take its toll, don't you think? That's why I like to meditate, because it grounds me, giving me a much clearer view of the world. Anyhow, finally I realised, for Gavin's sake, I needed to get rid of you.'

I stare back at her, my eyes the only part of me still able to move.

'Try moving your legs, Nadine,' she chides, 'or any other part of your body.'

I know she is planning to kill me.

'You're probably wondering how Gavin is connected to all this.' A fresh grin forms on her face. 'I waited such a long time, you see, but in the end I knew one day, Gavin would need me, and after your mother died, I had my chance. I listened to him as he cried, mourning her loss, and then later, when he talked about your father's cruelty, and all the burdens he had to endure, including dealing with his precious sister. He was like a broken thing, and bit by bit, I put him back together.'

I want to tell her she's wrong, only I can't. My eyes move to the knife, shiny in her hand, as I try to raise my arm, but it's as if it doesn't belong to my body. No matter how hard I try, I can't lift it.

'When I explained to Gavin how I watched him the night he took Cian's body away, at first he was shocked, but then he realised I hadn't told another soul, that I'd protected him. So, I gained his trust, and trust is important, Nadine, don't you think?'

I feel a tingling in my fingertips.

'One of the nights, shortly after your mother died, when he came to me for comfort, he happened to mention the second will and testament. I told him it was wrong of your mother to change it, especially considering how close they were, and that it must have been *you* who convinced her to do it. After all, he was the one who'd suffered the most over the years. He deserved everything.'

I can move my fingers. I pray she doesn't notice. She keeps on talking.

'Naturally Gavin was somewhat reluctant, but he didn't go to the solicitor straight away, did he? And that was when I knew I had to help him a little more. All I needed to do was find your copy. If we had that, then his and yours could be destroyed, and everything would be as it was supposed to be. Nobody would ever look for a couple of strangers in a hospital, the so-called witnesses, because no one would know they existed, except for you and Gavin, and who would ever believe crazy Nadine?'

I raise a finger, just a little. She doesn't notice it, and I cling to the hope that, just maybe, my body is coming back around.

'At first, Nadine, I thought it would be enough to push you over the edge, and Becca disappearing certainly helped, but I can see now I was wrong about that. You were never going to leave Gavin in peace. You would be constantly there, messing things up for us. Which is why, Nadine, you've left me with no other choice. I have to kill you. And when you're gone, Gavin will finally realise how much better his life is without you in it.'

69
WREN

MARTIN PRENDERGAST IS BROUGHT IN ten minutes after Ben Donnelly's interview is temporarily suspended.

'Do you want Larry and me to question him?' Mike asks, aware Gavin will arrive soon.

'I'm not sure. What's the latest from the insurance company?'

'Prendergast's name is all over the claim.'

'And the funds?'

'Frozen, pending more information from us.'

'Okay, good.'

'What exactly do you think has played out here?'

'Well, we know Evie and Ben go back a long way. In her own words, he helped her when no one else did. It's also pretty obvious that both Nadine and Ben knew exactly where Evie went eighteen years ago.'

'And both had their reasons for keeping it secret.'

'Especially Nadine, if what Evie says about Becca is true.'

'A simple DNA test will answer that.'

'I always knew she was holding something back, but I never would have guessed that.'

'She loves the girl, though.'

'Yep, and she was willing to do anything to save her, which brings us nicely to Dylan Lynch.'

'This story isn't new, Wren. We've heard it all before. Becca, young and stupid, gets in over her head, falls for the wrong prick, and once she's sufficiently hooked, he turns her into another punchbag to soothe his fucked-up feelings.'

'Sort of strange, though, isn't it, Mike, that Cian Campbell beat Nadine up too?'

'Domestic violence has a habit of slipping down the generations.'

'Only Becca fought back, and Dylan ended up dead.'

'If Evie hadn't returned, Wren, chances are we'd have found Becca curled up in a corner, terrified, unsure what to do next.'

'Only she did come back, her father's death opening that particular Pandora's box, and with Ben at her side, everything took a different turn.'

'And it seems it wasn't only Dylan Lynch's old gang and the Prendergast cell in Dublin that wanted payback. Evie wanted it too.'

'I agree, but at some point, with Ben putting pressure on Nadine, I think Evie had a change of heart.'

'She spilled the beans on Ben very fast.'

'Evie is a survivor. She's had to be.'

'What about Nadine Fitzmaurice?'

'A lot of what she told us is proving to be true.'

'And the rest? Claiming she killed her husband?'

'The missing body from the garden?'

'Yeah.'

'All I know, Mike, is that right now, Cian Campbell is suspiciously quiet.'

'Dead quiet?'

'Perhaps.'

'Either way, Wren, Nadine's implicated in that fraud, not to mention the earlier pick-ups.'

'All done under duress, fearing for her daughter's life.'

'And now Evie won't tell us where Becca is.'

'Because she's worried, and if she's worried, I'm worried too. There's something else in the mix. Something we're not seeing.'

'It could be tied to your mother's death, the hit-and-run?'

'Maybe, but if Gavin tampered with evidence, I also want to know why.'

'Probably to save his own skin.'

'Those witness statements are important. My father was interested in them. Patrick Mescal said my father thought something about them didn't add up.'

'What are you thinking?'

'Before my father became unwell, he was an extremely logical man, and a man who liked to solve puzzles.'

'Like you.'

'Only, that last puzzle eluded him, which might explain why he began to look at Evie's disappearance, knowing, somehow, the truth was tied up in that old group of friends, the ones who kept more secrets than most.'

'Every one of them lied in some shape or form – Evie, Nadine, Ben.'

'And what about Gavin? How many lies has he told?'

'What do you want to do about Martin Prendergast?'

'Let him stew for a while. I've a feeling, right now, getting information out of him about that fraudulent claim will be like communicating with a brick wall.'

'He's tied into the hit-and-run too.'

'I know, which is why I want to talk to Gavin first. There are too many questions he still needs to answer. If we get lucky, it might widen things out, and once Martin Prendergast gets a whiff that we have him nailed, with Ben and Evie implicating him, I've a feeling he'll develop the attributes of a canary, both about the fraud and the hit-and-run. Something about it stinks, and even if my father wasn't able to get to the bottom of it, I'm sure as hell going to try.'

The double doors to the corridor open. Gavin strolls in.

'Wren,' Mike warns, 'if you're going to question him, you shouldn't do it alone.'

'Give me an *unofficial* ten minutes.'

'But ...' he protests, concerned I could still fuck things up.

'I swear, Mike, after that, we'll go in together.'

70
NADINE

THE TINGLING IN MY FINGERS has moved further up my arm. The medication must be wearing off. I need to cling to that possibility.

'Nadine,' Aria says, 'it's nearing time.'

What does she mean?

'Very soon, if not already, you'll be able to feel some movement coming back into your body, and soon after that, you'll be able to speak again. You won't be capable of lifting yourself unaided from the bed, but you don't need to worry about that because like so many times in the past, I'm going to help you.'

I try to move my lips. They part ever so slightly. I whisper, 'My brother doesn't love you. He only ever loved Evie.'

'You mean the prowler, the person who liked to watch the house?'

'She warned me about you.'

'Only she didn't know who I was, did she?'

I don't answer.

'I see everything, Nadine, which is why I'm always one step ahead.'

I try to clench my fist. The medication is definitely wearing off. I need to buy myself some time.

'My brother finds it hard to commit,' I say, 'to fall in love. We both do.'

'Unfortunately, Nadine, that's what happens when parents mess up. They destroy a person from the inside out. Another reason I'll never have children.'

'Gavin doesn't think he deserves love. He never forgave Evie for reminding him of that.'

'She was cruel,' a fresh chill in her words, 'disappearing like that.'

It almost feels as if we're co-conspirators, and I wonder if, somehow, I can gain her trust.

'After she disappeared, Aria,' I whisper, with as much false empathy as I can muster, 'he stopped trusting people.'

'Is that what happened to you, Nadine? Did you stop trusting?'

'Yes.'

She tilts her head to the side. 'Poor Nadine. Over the years, I've watched you make one bad decision after another, up to and including the night you dragged your husband's body into the garden. You couldn't even do that right.'

'Why didn't you go to the police?'

'Because, as I already told you, I was biding my time, knowing one day I would get what I wanted.'

'Gavin?'

'Yes.'

I move my right leg ever so slightly. At first, I panic – she might have noticed it – but she's so engrossed in her thoughts that, for now, she's barely looking in my direction. I can tell she's enjoying this, as I also wonder how long she has waited for this pleasure.

She stares at me again. 'You know you're going to die, Nadine, don't you?'

'Yes.'

'Very soon, you won't exist. And when you're gone, you don't have to worry about Gavin because I'll take care of him.'

I swallow the bile built up in my throat.

She continues talking: 'Initially, after your death, he'll shed some tears, upset that life finally got too much for his little sister, forcing her to end it all.'

I try to lift my arm again. It barely moves. She smirks at my attempt.

'Will I tell you, Nadine, what I'm going to do next?'

'Okay.'

'I'm going to take you into the bathroom and place you in the bath. Then I will use this knife, the one you took from the kitchen, to slit your wrists. After all, Nadine, considering everything you've endured, I want to make things easy for you. I'm going to give you what you always wanted, true and permanent peace.'

71
WREN

'GAVIN,' I SAY, AS HE GETS CLOSER to myself and Mike.

'I came as soon as I could.' His words are fast, earnest.

'We need to talk.'

'Okay.'

'Ten minutes,' Mike warns, tapping his watch.

'What's going down?' Gavin asks, suddenly suspicious, as I open the door to one of the empty interview rooms.

'That's what I'm hoping you'll tell me.'

I wait until we're both seated before I say, 'I've a few questions.'

'What do you want to know?'

'Why you hooked up with me, and this time, Gavin, I want the truth, not some distilled version putting you in a good light.'

'I've already answered that.'

'I'm going to cut to the chase, because we don't have a lot of time here. I know you were involved in the hit-and-run that killed my mother.'

His face turns a shade paler.

'I also know, later on, when you entered the force, you tampered with evidence connected to it.'

'Who told you that?'

'Ben Donnelly.'

'He's scum, not worth your time.'

'Joe Regan tells me you have money worries too.'

'Is that who you're talking to now, criminals who would lie to their bloody mother?'

'Then, why don't *you* tell me the truth?'

'I've already told you.'

'Evie Hunt says you changed before she disappeared. Was it because of guilt – because you killed my mother?'

He looks at me, stunned. 'Evie?'

'Oh, didn't you know? She came back. Nadine was right about that.'

'I don't understand.'

'Then let me fill you in on a few home truths.'

He slouches in the chair.

'Evie came back to Dublin following her father's death. She kept her presence secret, but she did her fair share of snooping, initially tracking down Nadine.'

'Why?'

'She was curious about her, especially after Nadine helped her keep a very important secret.'

'What secret?'

'Not yet, Gavin. I'm the one asking the questions.'

He's still reeling about Evie's return, which is exactly how I want him to be.

'Not so long ago,' I say, 'I found some newspaper clippings in my father's possession, and some notes too, referring to witness statements.'

'So?'

'It's a funny thing, Gavin, but when so many people are saying similar things, you tend to believe them. Ben, Joe and, indirectly, my father, along with Patrick Mescal, the Hunt family liaison officer, all of them, in one way or another, are pointing the finger at you. So, tell me, is that why you were interested in me, to find out what my father knew? Were you worried he might have told me something, something you needed to know about so you could cover it up?'

'Believe what you want.'

'All that time, when I thought you cared for me, when you got me to talk about my mother's death, reliving the trauma, questioning me about her, and then about my father, the only person you were

351

concerned about was yourself, making sure all your dirty lies and wrongdoings were kept well hidden.'

'I cared for you.'

'Stop lying.'

'I'm not.'

'Answer this, then. Why were you hanging around Ben's place?'

No response.

'Nadine admitted, the night we brought her in for questioning, that Ben was harassing her.'

'You know my sister. She—'

I don't let him finish. 'Contrary to your high and mighty beliefs, it seems an awful lot of what Nadine said is true.'

'Like?'

'Evie did come back. She's also involved with Becca's disappearance, her and Ben Donnelly.'

He leaps from the chair. 'Where's Becca?'

'I don't know, not yet. So far, Evie refuses to tell us, but it wasn't only Evie that Nadine was right about. Ben was certainly harassing her, applying pressure, getting her to do things against her will, all in your sister's desperate efforts to get Becca back, so again, I'm going to ask you the same question: why were you hanging around Ben's place?'

'If you must know, when Nadine brought up his name, even though I thought it was more of her ramblings, I got worried. Ben Donnelly is bad news. I needed to make sure he wasn't causing any trouble, but I never got to talk to him.'

'Where's Nadine now?'

'At home. She's taken another turn.'

'Oh?'

'Don't worry, I haven't left her alone. Aria is with her. I had people to see earlier on, but when you called, I came straight here.'

'The people you had to see, did you owe them money?'

'That's none of your business.'

'I'm making it my business. I know about the gambling. I probably should have guessed it a long time ago, the way for no obvious reason, your moods would turn dark.'

I've struck a chord.

He sits back down, as if contemplating his next move. 'Wren,' he finally says, 'that question you asked earlier, about why I hooked up with you.'

'What about it?'

'Tell me, why were you interested in me?'

'At the start, I thought there was something good inside you, something worth saving.'

'And now?'

'Now I think I made a very big mistake.'

'I guess I deserve that.' He stalls. 'You're telling the truth, aren't you, Wren, about Evie being back?'

'Yes.'

'And about her and Ben putting pressure on Nadine?'

I nod in agreement. I'm not going to tell him we have Evie and Ben in custody.

'You know why Evie disappeared, Wren, don't you?'

'I've already told you, I'm the one asking the questions.'

'Please, Wren, I need to know.'

I shouldn't say anything, but I also know his not-knowing over the years has partly destroyed him.

'She was pregnant.'

'She couldn't have been. I never ...' He doesn't finish his sentence, the significance of my previous words sinking in.

'A few years back,' I say, 'Nigel Hunt, Evie's father, had allegations of child sex abuse brought against him.'

Gavin stiffens, the anger that's been tethering below the surface flaring. 'If I'd known, Wren, I would have bloody killed him.'

'Maybe that's another reason Evie followed through on that dare, doing something she would always be remembered for.'

'What happened the baby?'

'She survived.'

'She?'

'Becca.'

'No, no, you're wrong,' he says, leaping out of the chair again. 'You don't know what you're talking about.'

'I know exactly what I'm talking about.'

'But, then, why—'

'Why did Nadine lie to you? Tell you Becca was hers?'

'Yeah.'

'I could be wrong, but I think she saw it as an opportunity. She wanted someone to love, although there may have been another reason.'

'What?'

'Perhaps she wanted to rewrite history. You told me yourself your mother found it hard to show Nadine affection, so maybe your sister wanted to somehow reverse the mistakes of the past.'

'And I ... forced her to marry Cian.' He folds his arms tight across his chest.

'It was your parents too,' I say, 'and for what it's worth, Nadine probably hoped things would work out, making it easier for her to keep Becca.'

'You can't know that for sure.'

'No, I can't, but soon, Gavin, Mike will be back, and before that happens, you need to tell me about the hit-and-run.'

'Why?'

'Because, somehow, it's part of all this. Call it a gut feeling, but right now, my gut is telling me that what happened to my mother, directly or indirectly, set a series of events in motion.'

He stares back at me, silent.

'You were the driver of the car, weren't you? Admit it.'

'No comment.'

'I deserve the truth.'

'Truth is a funny thing, Wren. Everyone thinks they want it, but it's not always worth having.'

'What kind of sicko are you,' my voice louder, angry, 'getting

354

involved with the daughter of the woman you killed, the little girl you left without a mother?'

'Wren, I'm not going there.'

'We have Martin Prendergast in custody. He was your passenger, wasn't he?'

'You need to let it go.'

'You don't like to talk about the past, do you?'

'What's the point?'

'The point is that the past matters.' Even though I swore to Mike I'd keep it cool, the rage inside me is impossible to rein in. 'And while we're on the subject, you treat your sister pretty shit too.'

'What do you mean?'

'Since the get-go, you've undermined her, constantly doing and saying things that would cause us to doubt her every word.'

'My sister isn't well.'

'She wasn't wrong about Evie and Ben, or Becca being taken. All this time, Nadine was telling us the truth. They did have Becca. They took her for her own protection.'

'Why?'

'Because Becca killed someone, a person others wanted payback for.'

'I don't understand.'

'It's not that complicated, Gavin. Evie and Ben put pressure on Nadine, blackmailing her, telling her she wouldn't get Becca back unless she did exactly what they asked, up to and including major fraud.'

'Who did Becca kill?'

'A gang member called Dylan Lynch.'

'Joe Regan's nephew?'

'Yep.'

He puts his face in his hands. 'I didn't know, Wren, I swear to you. I thought Nadine was making it all up.'

'Peddling the mad-sister defence again, are you?'

'No, I'm not. Only ...' He pauses.

'What?'

'If the things Nadine said were true, about Evie and Ben, then ...'

'Then what, Gavin?'

'Who wrote the words on the mirror?'

'Now, you're not talking sense.'

'Nadine said someone broke into the house and tossed the place.'

'They did.'

'Yeah, I know, but it happened a second time. I didn't believe her. I thought she was pulling another stunt, just looking for attention.'

'I don't think she was.'

'What makes you so sure?'

'Evie gave a statement earlier on. She told us she saw someone in your sister's house. It happened more than once, and each time, Nadine wasn't there. Right now, Evie's refusing to tell us where Becca is, until she's sure her daughter is safe, and I think you know who that someone is.'

'Who?'

'You.'

'*What?* You can't be serious.'

'I couldn't be more so. You wanted to get Nadine out of the way, make her think she was going crazy, so perhaps she'd do something silly, like end it all.'

'Why would I do that?'

'Money.'

'What money?'

'The proceeds from your mother's estate. That house in Rathfarnham is valuable, not to mention the other assets potentially involved, savings, stocks and shares. Your family wasn't exactly poor, but now, because of your gambling, you are.'

'This is ridiculous.'

'Is it? Or is it because you need to dismiss anyone who doesn't agree with you, the way you dismissed Nadine?'

Mike opens the door. 'Wren, it's time we did this the proper way.'

'You're right, Mike, because I'm about to charge Gavin Fitzmaurice with breaking and entering, harassment, and anything else we can throw at him.'

'Wren,' Gavin protests, 'you're wrong. You have to listen to me.'

'I've done enough listening.'

'But you don't understand. Nadine's in danger.'

'What do you mean?'

'I've only just figured it out,' he says, walking up and down fast. 'I can't believe I couldn't see it until now.'

'See what, Gavin? And this better be good.'

'Aria.'

'What about her?'

'I've been so stupid. Shit, shit, shit ...'

'Gavin, what about Aria?'

'Don't you see?' he says, his hands waving frantically. 'It's been her all along.'

'What has?'

Something in his face changes. There's a look, something other than panic, one I haven't seen before. It takes me a couple of seconds to recognise it – shame.

'We had a thing together,' he says.

'By "thing" you mean you screwed her?'

'It was stupid, I know, but I needed to keep her sweet.'

'Why?'

'Because if I didn't, she could ruin Nadine's life, only ...'

'What?'

'I didn't put all of it together until now, but when you told me about Ben and Evie, and what they did to Nadine, and then afterwards, what Evie said about someone being in Nadine's house, other things didn't make sense.'

'What things?'

'The writing on the mirror. Nadine said whoever broke into her house wrote something on the mirror in the en-suite bathroom.'

'What were the words, Gavin?'

He hesitates for a split second, before saying. '*You left me to die.*'

The desperation in his voice makes me believe him. 'Who did Nadine leave to die, Gavin?'

'Cian,' he blurts. 'When I realised what she'd done,' his words coming out fast, 'I tried to cover it up for her. I know she didn't mean it. She was only trying to protect herself.'

'Like mother, like daughter,' I whisper.

'Afterwards I buried him myself.'

'Where?'

'A place he'd never be found.'

'Where, Gavin?' I repeat.

'In a ditch off Military Road in the Dublin Mountains – but don't you see, Wren? That doesn't matter now. What matters is my sister's life's in danger.'

'Why?'

'Because, other than Nadine and me, the only other person who knows about Cian is Aria.'

'You think *she* wrote the words on the mirror?'

'It can't have been anyone else, which also means she's more than likely responsible for the break-ins too, and probably a whole lot more, only I was too damn stupid to see it.'

Gavin's words sink fast into my brain. 'Mike,' I roar, 'call the Armed Response Unit. We need to get to Nadine's place *now*.'

72
NADINE

SECONDS LATER, ARIA IS DRAGGING me out of bed. My body feels so heavy, I'm surprised she can even pull me across the room, but somehow she does.

In the bathroom, she leaves me lying on the floor, discarded. I know I'm going to die. I think about Becca again, wondering if somehow, through my thoughts, I can tell her how much I love her.

I watch Aria put on a pair of yellow kitchen gloves, before cleaning the knife with hot water from the bathroom tap.

Soon I feel her arms beneath me, dragging me forward.

'We don't want to get blood everywhere, Nadine, do we?'

She heaves my body towards the bathtub, until finally, it slumps into it. On the way down, my head hits the taps, but Aria doesn't stop. She's too busy with the task in hand, repositioning my fully clothed body to look as if I placed it there.

'I doubt we'll need a note, Nadine, everyone knows you've been finding life too difficult of late.' She takes the near empty syringe and injects the last of its contents into my arm, before turning the bath taps on full throttle. 'Do you know what they'll say, Nadine, when they find you?'

My eyes are closing.

'They'll talk about what a terrible mother you are, leaving Becca, taking the coward's way out.'

I'm finding it increasingly hard to concentrate, but then, some- where in the distance, I hear voices. I feel a breeze whip up the stairs, as if the front door has been opened. The voices drift in and out, only they're so faint, I wonder if I'm already dying. I need to let go, but I can't. I have to fight back. It's then I hear a loud bang, as if something has fallen to the floor. People are running through the house. Someone calls my name. 'Nadine!' the woman shouts again. I recognise that female detective's voice. Somehow, I open my eyes.

Aria is staring at the bathroom door, just as Gavin pushes it open, a terrified look on his face. He grabs the knife out of her hand. Soon, a uniformed police officer is standing behind her, putting handcuffs on her wrists. Gavin is pulling me out of the bath, telling me how sorry he is, that all this time, he should have believed me.

'Everything's going to be okay,' he says. 'I'm here, and soon we'll get Becca home too.'

His words feel soothing. I so much want to believe him. I want him to keep telling me everything is okay, the way he used to when we were children.

There are more police officers in the bathroom. Aria is escorted out, and then, just like before, snippets of memory return in fragments, disjointed. I hear Gavin and me arguing. I'm angry at him. That's why I let the pigeons free from our uncle's loft, but there's something else too. What is it?

Suddenly, I see my younger self. I'm trying to appear all grown-up, as Martin Prendergast teases me about getting into a stolen car, calling me chicken. I want to prove him wrong, so I get behind the wheel. Soon after that, the car goes out of control, and the world is tumbling and tumbling, over and over, before everything goes quiet. At first, I think it must be a bad dream, but then I see the woman's body slide off the front bumper, blood streaming from her head. Martin tells me to make a run for it, to get the hell out of there. After I reach home, everything goes dark. It's probably my first blackout, and when I come to, 'Three Blind Mice' is playing on the radio. I hear Gavin arguing with Martin, talking about the woman being dead, and now, as my sedated body is held up by my brother, I realise, after all this time, they were fighting over what I'd done.

I try to tell Gavin I'm the one who should be sorry, because it wasn't only my father's cruelty that changed him. It was me. I was stupid and weak. I should never have driven that stolen car, because afterwards, in Gavin's efforts to protect me, he partly destroyed himself, and later, when Evie disappeared, everything he cared about was shrouded in secrets and lies.

73
WREN

AFTER NADINE IS ADMITTED TO HOSPITAL, and Aria Jackson is taken into custody, Mike and I resume the interview with Gavin Fitzmaurice. The time, date, location and the names of all present are recorded before the interview commences.

'Gavin,' I begin, 'I have a series of questions to ask you, and for your sake, it's probably best if you answer them as comprehensively as you can. Do you understand?'

'Yes.'

'For now, let's start at the beginning.'

'Okay.'

Mike shoots me a look that says, *This is going to be okay*, before Gavin starts talking.

'I've had a very chequered history, starting with physical abuse from my father, who I believe saw me as some kind of threat. I neither sought nor encouraged the abuse. My mother was a complicated woman who found life difficult, particularly parenting. She made the classic mistake of deciding one child was good, while the other was bad. I think this partly came from her desire to have someone else in her life when her relationship with my father was failing. I became the good child, the one who experienced the favouritism, but I also understood that when your sibling doesn't receive the same love, it's wrong. Despite the beatings frequently applied by my father, when it came to Nadine and myself, I felt like the lucky one.' He swallows hard.

'When Nadine got into that car with Martin Prendergast, as you said, Wren, a series of events was set in motion. First, in an effort to protect my sister, after she had her first blackout, I decided no one ever had to know the truth about what had happened. This plan worked for a time. But later, when I joined the force, I got curious about what the police knew or didn't know. That was when I realised a statement existed from a woman who witnessed the accident, stating she thought the driver could have been female. I decided it was best to get rid of it, or at least tamper with it.'

'How?'

'Simple. I spilled coffee over the hard copy, ensuring the writing was no longer legible.'

'And someone found out, didn't they?'

'Yes, which was when my gambling got more out of control, although I've been on a dark path for a very long time. It probably began with my parents, then later because of Nadine, and finally, the year I turned eighteen, after Evie went missing.'

'Go on.'

'When your mother was killed, I couldn't get my head around what my sister had done. I found it too hard to process. I think Evie suffered because of this too, as I became more and more withdrawn, darker, angrier, and every relationship I've had ever since your mother's death probably suffered because of it too. Then, when Evie went away, I felt lost, withdrawing further into myself, shutting people out, including Nadine. This was probably when she began looking to others for support, and perhaps, for a time, she found it that summer with Evie, and subsequently in her love for Becca. I was stupid to believe the lies she told me, but believe them I did. What followed was a terrible marriage between her and Cian, culminating in the night she killed him. Whether she purposely pushed him down the stairs, after years of abuse, is immaterial to me. For me, history was simply repeating itself. My sister was in trouble again. I needed to protect her, which was why I took his body from her back garden and disposed of it elsewhere.'

'Aria saw you.'

'Yes, but I didn't know that until years later.'

'After your mother died?'

He looks downwards, ashamed. 'After her death, things were really hard. I had all these unspoken issues, and Nadine was having a hard time with Becca too. It seems the happy-ever-after life she wanted for her wasn't turning out the way she expected. I did my best, but it was never enough.'

'So you turned to Aria?'

'Yes. It felt good to have someone in my life willing to listen and not judge me. We became close, very close, and soon after that, she told me she'd witnessed what I'd done all those years before with Cian's body. Initially, when she admitted how much she cared for me, her secrecy, protecting me, felt like an act of kindness, support, but as Nadine got increasingly agitated over the last few weeks, Aria kept going on about how much of a burden Nadine was, and how she had always been the same.' He pauses. 'In a way, she was right. Then, I stupidly told her about my mother's latest will and testament. She told me it was wrong of my mother to change it, especially because she and Nadine had had such a fractured relationship, while I'd been loyal to my mother, her favourite child.'

'So, you agreed with Aria?'

'For a while, I was angry, yes, which was why I delayed lodging the will with my mother's solicitor. For what it's worth, I believe I would have done the honourable thing in the end.'

'Your indecision encouraged Aria.'

'It would seem so, and the sister I'd tried for so long to protect became the target.'

'Ben and Evie had her in their sights too.'

'I know.'

'How does my father tie into all this?'

'Some of it you already know. Your father, probably through a friend in the force, got access to the witness statements surrounding your mother's hit-and-run. He was unsure about the statement I'd tampered with, which was why he decided to talk to the witness himself. Despite the intervening years, she had a very clear memory from that day. She told him exactly what had been in her statement, that the driver could have been female. This was probably when your father tracked down Patrick Mescal in relation to Evie's disappearance. Although the hit-and-run, and Evie leaving, are totally unrelated, it led your father to me.'

'You spoke to my father?'

'Yes, and it became obvious to me, quite soon, that something wasn't right with him. He kept mixing things up, saying things wrong, or losing track of why he came to see me.'

'What did you tell him?'

'I told him I didn't know anything. I said it was dead history.'

'And what did he say?'

'He said ...' He stalls.

'What?'

'He told me he knew he'd left it too late, but that if I could tell him the truth, he would at least know who killed his wife, and that would be something. Only, Wren, I couldn't.' Again, he lowers his head in shame.

'So, Gavin, back to my earlier question. Why me?'

'To protect Nadine. I had to find out if your father shared any information with you.'

'And when you discovered he hadn't, what then?'

'Then,' he scoffs, 'I thought we might work out, but damaged goods don't usually have good outcomes. By the time we split, when I cheated on you, my head was a complete mess. I was in huge financial debt. I had a sister who was going off the rails, and a niece I suspected to be involved in drugs, but that wasn't all of it.'

'No?'

'I think part of me has always wanted to press the self-destruct button. It was easy blaming Nadine for things, constantly reminding her of her issues, when all the time the person I was really criticising was myself. I guess I didn't feel I deserved to be loved, which was why it was never going to work out between you and me.'

This time, I look away. I've heard enough.

We conclude the interview at ten minutes past midnight. At this point, Gavin has given us the whereabouts of Cian's body, and Ben, in another interview room, has finally done the same regarding the multiple body parts of Dylan Lynch. Two dead men. Two domestic abusers. Two women, one eighteen years junior, responsible for the killings. Both seem to have acted in self-defence, but that will be for the courts to decide.

After Gavin is taken away, charged with obstruction of justice, tampering with evidence, and disposal of Cian Campbell's body, Mike hangs back in the interview room.

'A sorry tale, Wren, isn't it?'

'They're all sorry tales, Mike.'

'Strange, though, how we spend so much time fighting the crime gangs, the drugs on the street, the fallouts, both financial and human, and yet more people are killed in Ireland as a result of domestic violence than ever on the streets.'

'Behind closed doors, Mike, there's usually a story, and it isn't always a good one.'

74
NADINE

I WAKE IN A HOSPITAL BED. I hear the clatter of trolleys bringing early-morning tea and coffee. A nurse enters the room and checks my chart. When she opens the door to leave, I spot the uniformed police officer sitting outside.

The next time the door opens, it's the female detective called Wren.

I know I'll have to face charges for what I did to Cian, and potentially the fallout from the blackmail, but I also know I was the person who, nearly two decades earlier, as a teenage girl, got into that stolen car, and the woman I killed was Wren's mother.

Wren explains that Gavin, and some of the others, including Aria, have been charged.

'What's going to happen to me?'

'A file will be sent to the DPP, the director of public prosecutions. After that, she will decide if there's enough evidence to charge you for your husband's death.'

'And what about the death of your mother?'

'When it happened, you were a minor with no previous offences, so I'm not sure. Either way, it's not going to bring her back.'

'I spoke to Dr Ward,' I say, 'by telephone.'

'And?'

'I wanted to ask her why, for so long, I couldn't remember.'

'What did she say?'

'She said the mind is extremely efficient at forgetting troubling parts of our lives, and that, with a little encouragement from Gavin, it

367

easily became hidden. He offered me a lie, an alternative explanation, saying I was wrong, not only about what I heard but about a lot of other things too.'

'But it was a lie that kept on giving.'

'What do you mean?'

'Hiding from the truth, pretending things are something they're not, has a habit of repeating itself. I think, Nadine, that's ultimately what happened to you, and within everything that followed, it became harder for you to tell the difference between what is true and what is fantasy.'

'When I thought I'd lose Becca, it brought out something different in me.'

'What?'

'An inner resilience I didn't even know I had. For so long I'd felt weaker than others, but when you're tested, really tested, the real you comes out, no matter how good a job you've done at hiding it.'

'Dr Ward said that about you. She said you had more resilience than you, or others, knew, and she was right. All this time, when you believed your daughter was in danger, when other people didn't believe you, including me, doubting your sanity, some of them plotting to destroy you, you kept going. You never gave up, even though, at times, you must have been terrified.'

'It still doesn't take away the fact that I caused your mother's death.'

'For what it's worth, Nadine, I'm glad I now know it was you.'

'Why? So you can hate me?'

'I don't hate you.'

'You should,' I say, ashamed.

'Nadine, listen to me. For all these years, since my mother's death, I told myself I didn't want or need to know who did it. That there was no point. I suspect my father felt the same way for a very long time, until finally, when it was too late, he went looking for answers. And now, like my father, I realise it's important for me to know the truth, and it's the same reason I do this job, wanting to help teenagers out of their heads on drugs, kids looking to end it all, or a woman suffering years of domestic abuse. It's because when you understand the human being behind each of these tragedies, even if you're not able to forgive, you can at least accept.'

'Have you accepted it?'

'Yes, and I think, in time, I can forgive too, because now I know the young girl behind the wheel, and all the things she had to endure before and afterwards.'

'Wren, if I could talk to that young girl I used to be, I'd tell her to stop and think. I'd tell my younger self not to be so scared. I'd ask her to trust me when I say the world is made up of all kinds of people. Some can make you afraid or sad, but it shouldn't stop you doing the right thing, because if you don't, you end up living a half-life. For years I held myself back, terrified of Cian, and later, frightened I might lose Becca because I'd kept the truth from her. No one should live like that.'

'No, they shouldn't.'

'Dr Ward said something else.'

'What?'

'She said now that we know the origins of my panic attacks and blackouts, we can start to build our way back. I hope she's right, both for my sake and Becca's.'

'Becca is lucky,' Wren replies, 'to have a mother like you.'

'Why, after everything, do you say that?'

'Because at times in life, we all need someone to fight our corner, someone prepared to do whatever it takes.'

'I took your mother away.'

'I was luckier than most. Unlike you, I had a mother who loved me with all her heart, and nothing will ever change that.'

'Thank you.' I squeeze her hand.

'And now,' she smiles, 'you get to see your daughter.'

'I thought she'd be in custody.'

'She is, but after all this time, you deserve to be reunited, even if only for a short while.'

The door of the hospital room opens. I can't believe my eyes, because standing before me is the only person apart from Gavin I love with all my heart, my daughter, Becca.

SIX MONTHS LATER

75
WREN

THE TRIAL DATE HAS BEEN SET for Aria Jackson, charged with coercion, perverting the course of justice and, more importantly, attempting first-degree murder. Bail was refused by Justice Maria Keane, following a psychological evaluation, so Aria will spend another twelve months in prison awaiting her court appearance. Gavin has already begun his prison term, forty-eight months for perverting the course of justice, after admitting to burying Cian Fitzmaurice's remains in the Dublin Mountains, alongside an additional twelve months, running concurrently, for his admission of tampering with evidence. Because he was forthcoming with the details of his actions, including the location of Cian's remains, the four years will most likely be reduced to three, subject to good behaviour.

Ben Donnelly and Martin Prendergast are facing trial in the Central Criminal Court next week, each with similar charges – fraud, blackmail, extortion and perverting the course of justice – although Ben has the added bonus of accessory to manslaughter surrounding the death of Dylan Lynch, and the mutilation of his body. Based on their previous criminal records, if they're found guilty, little leniency will be shown.

Joe Regan is still pleading his innocence regarding the blackmail of Nadine, but he will soon be in court for his involvement in the failed ATM attempt. His prison term may be limited, but the likes of Joe will always raise his head again.

Evie Hunt's defence is already taking shape along the lines of mitigating circumstances due to the trauma of her father's death, based on his previous abuse, and her desire, having been separated from her daughter for over eighteen years, to protect her. Like Nadine and Becca, it's impossible to know what the DPP will ultimately decide, but with previous sexual abuse and trauma as mitigating factors in Evie's case, and domestic abuse in relation to Nadine and Becca, considering Becca's age, and Nadine's mental health history, each may do some time, but leniency will probably be shown.

Driving away from the station, after writing my final notes on each of the cases, it feels good to put it all behind me. Soon, I arrive at my father's nursing home. Out of necessity, like other times in the past, I flip my brain from being a detective to becoming a daughter. My father doesn't remember anything about the newspaper clippings, or his attempts at amateur detective work, but that doesn't matter.

As I enter the hallway, I realise the daily routine of the residents' evening meal is in full swing. I spot my father sitting at a table for four, the remains of roast chicken, potatoes and gravy on his plate.

'Oh, look, Christopher,' says one of the nurses, clearing the table, 'your daughter's here to see you.'

He looks up, slightly confused at first, but then he says, 'Wren, is that you?'

'It's me, Dad. Are you finished?'

'Yes.'

'Do you want to go upstairs?'

'Let's do that.'

I talk to him all the way to his room, and once he's settled in his chair by the window, I kneel beside him. A gleam appears in his eyes, the kind he gets when his mind is working full throttle. 'Your mother used to paint,' he says, almost surprised by this one simple truth.

'Yes, Dad, she did.'

'I always loved the ones she painted of the dandelions.'

'Me too,' I say, holding back happy tears.

'Sometimes, Wren, I can't work out what's true and what isn't.'

'What do you mean?'

'I forget bits, and all the missing parts can make things very confusing.'

'Don't worry. I'll do the working out for you.'

He nods. 'Can you bring me one of her paintings?'

I think about my mother's pictures gathering dust in the attic of our old family home, the one lying empty because neither my father nor I could admit, when he first came to the nursing home, that he would never return. 'Of course, Dad, I will.'

I wait until he's sleeping before I leave. It doesn't matter that tomorrow, when I turn up with the painting, he might forget all over again, because for a brief moment he remembered her, and that is all that counts.

∞

It's dark by the time I reach our old house. I carry a torch in my hand, because the electricity was cut off months ago, no one needing it. I climb the wooden attic steps, creaking under my weight. It doesn't take me long to spot the canvases in the corner, stacked back-to-back behind old Christmas decorations and childhood games – snakes and ladders, draughts, chess and Monopoly.

The largest canvas is my favourite one of the dandelions, but I'm not ready to look at it yet. Instead, I dig deep into a wooden crate filled with photographs, images of summer holidays from years before, our pet dog Scruples, a collie cross, and one of me standing by a Christmas tree wearing my best new clothes, a red tartan dress and black tights, while a matching hairband with a large black bow keeps my wild hair in check. I stare at my little-girl eyes, before I lost my mother, happy, unaware of the tragedy that lay ahead. I hold the image tight to my chest.

Soon, I put the photographs aside and pull out the canvas. The image floods my senses with the brightness of a sunny day, yellow ochre with splashes of cadmium red. After a while, I turn the canvas over. On the back is an inscription from my mother, one I hadn't noticed before: 'Sometimes I see the world differently from others, finding beauty where others discard.'

Sitting in the dark with only my torch to illuminate the room, I think long and hard about so many things that have happened, both recently and in the distant past. I guess we all look at the world differently, and sometimes we can get things wrong.

My mobile phone lights up. It's a message from Meg, wondering about meeting for a drink. I message back, *Can't wait*.

Meg wasn't completely right about me. It's not that I want to fix everything, but like my mother, and the way she saw beauty in parts of life that others failed to see, I see things differently too. Every day, I see the beauty and fragility of humanity – whether it's a young guy struggling with addiction, a homeless beggar, or someone like Nadine, who gets lost for a while, human, but damaged. The past always lives in the present, and even if it doesn't excuse what we do, the cards we are dealt in life can frame us, and flaws are part of who we are.

Acknowledgements

WHEN CREATING A STORY, WRITERS are often influenced by life experience, either consciously or subconsciously. For me, the starting point for *They All Lied* came many years before a single word was written. Two events happened quite close to one another. The first was when a boy our son knew, who had a great sporting career ahead of him, had a family member who had built up a major debt with a crime gang. Instead of targeting the relative with the drug problem, the gang targeted the family, threatening to attack the young sports star, ensuring his sporting career would be over, unless the family cleared the debt and more. The second incident happened when someone we knew decided to set up his own business, opening a restaurant as part of a chain. Being astute, he looked into everything in its entirety, including having friends of his in the police force check out that everything was above board. What he didn't know was that certain information given to him was either omitted or incorrect. And, shortly after investing his life savings in the business and relocating himself and his family, he was contacted by members of a crime gang who were using the chain for illegal activity, demanding payback money. Several years later, the man returned to Dublin, damaged both emotionally and financially. The exact details of how each of these stories finished, I do not know, but what I know is this: organised crime is not limited to those who are part of it. It doesn't end with a gangland killing on the street, one gang member fighting with another. It involves ordinary people too, and sometimes, if you're unlucky enough, you can find yourself placed in an extraordinary situation that can test you to your limits and beyond.

While the kernel of this story was fermenting in my mind, like so many others, I watched as the entire #metoo movement gathered momentum. It was a positive beginning for change, but I was also very well aware that women, young or old, are often doubted in our society, especially if we have a reason to question what they say, or if we can label them as unreliable. I got to thinking about how I would feel if I wasn't believed about something important to me. I hope in writing this story, I've explored in some small way these sparks of inspiration.

However, the writing and publication of a novel needs the support of many people, so firstly, I would like to thank my wonderful agent Gráinne Fox, of Fletcher & Co., New York, for her passion and support to me every step of the way. Also, thanks to Ciara Doorley, Editorial Director of Hachette Ireland, who, like Gráinne, believed in this story from the very beginning. Thanks also to Hazel Orme, for her eagle eye when copyediting this manuscript, alongside the rest of the team at Hachette, for their work and enthusiasm in the publication of *They All Lied*.

In the area of research, I am again grateful to those within An Garda Síochána, including ex-detective Tom Doyle, who assisted me on all aspects of police procedure, and if an error exists, it is mine alone and is not connected to the wonderful experts who gave of their precious time and knowledge.

I will never be able to repay the wonderful writers who read this novel in advance of publication, giving of their time and expertise. A simple thanks is never enough, but it is heartfelt.

Thanks also to everyone who has enjoyed and supported my earlier novels, and who I hope will enjoy this one too.

Finally, I would like to sincerely thank my family, whose love and support have encouraged me from the early days of my writing journey, particularly my husband, Robert, our children, Jennifer, Lorraine and Graham, and our grandchildren, Caitríona, Carrig and James, to whom this novel is dedicated.